In the movies they would have gone from yelling at each other to making out in a matter of seconds. But she knew instinctively that wasn't how they rolled. Their feud was a large, long-standing, heavy thing. Slow to turn. Like a warship retreating.

"What are you doing?" she whispered, even though she knew exactly what he was doing.

He dipped his head so their faces were inches apart. "I'm going to kiss you."

"Why?"

"Because that's a thing we do now, I think?"

It was a question, and though he moved even closer—she could feel his breath against her lips—he was waiting for her to answer it.

"Yeah," she breathed. "I guess it is."

PRAISE FOR JENNY HOLIDAY'S NOVELS

MERMAID INN

"Bursting with humor, grand (and small!) gestures guaranteed to make you swoon, Holiday elevates the classic small-town rom-com."
—*Entertainment Weekly*

"Holiday enchants with the sunny second-chance love story that launches her Matchmaker Bay series.... This sweet contemporary romance is sure to win readers' hearts."
—*Publishers Weekly*

"A picturesque locale, delightful citizens and some smoking-hot love scenes give this book all the feel-good joys."
—*BookPage*

"Entertaining, wonderfully funny, romantic as all get-out."
—All About Romance

PARADISE COVE

"Holiday writes beautiful prose, with quirky secondary characters and generous helpings of humor. [This] love story will break your heart and put it back together again better than before, and you'll be grateful for having experienced it all."
—*BookPage*, Starred Review

"This richly satisfying romance is a heart-wrenching and emotional tour de force."
—*Kirkus*, Starred Review

"Holiday balances heart-tugging romance with low-stakes medical drama and breezy exchanges.... Perfect for fans of Debbie Macomber and *Doc Martin*."

—*Publishers Weekly*

ONE AND ONLY

"The perfect rom-com."

—Refinery29

"A satisfying iteration of the contemporary bridezilla subgenre."
—*New York Times Book Review*

"When it comes to creating unputdownable contemporary romances, Holiday is in it to win it."

—*Booklist*, Starred Review

"Delightfully sexy and sweet, Holiday knows how to deliver the perfect combination of sexual tension and happily-ever-after."
—Lauren Layne, *New York Times* bestselling author

"*One and Only* is fantastic! A great start to a new series. Compelling characters, tons of heat, loads of heart. I highly recommend!"
—M. O'Keefe, *USA Today* bestselling author

IT TAKES TWO

"Jenny Holiday turns up the heat and the charm for a summer read more satisfying than a poolside popsicle.... It's hard to imagine finding a more delightful summer escape."

—*Entertainment Weekly*

"This is romantic comedy at its best, complete with clever, sexy banter, a vibrant cast of characters, [and] a wedding that is a character in itself."
—*Washington Post*

"Holiday combines class and sass with a hefty dose of humor.... This winning hero and heroine will take up residence in readers' hearts."

—*Publishers Weekly*

"[An] irresistible mix of lively, piquantly witty writing; sharply etched, marvelously memorable characters; and some completely combustible love scenes that are guaranteed to leave burn marks on readers' fingers."

—*Booklist*, Starred Review

THREE LITTLE WORDS

"A perfectly plotted emotional journey.... Intense, heartfelt, mature and sexy as hell."

—NPR

"Holiday adroitly combines all the requisite elements of a great rom-com—scintillating, witty banter and incendiary sexual chemistry—and a pair of protagonists whose emotional complexity and realistic flaws lend a welcome measure of gravitas to this brilliantly executed romance."

—*Booklist*, Starred Review

"Combines pure fun with surprising depth...Leavened with witty banter, Holiday's sweet-hot tale captivates."

—*Publishers Weekly*

"[The] HEA is reached with warmth, humor, steamy interludes, excellent friendships and really delicious-sounding food."

—*BookPage*

Sandcastle Beach

ALSO BY JENNY HOLIDAY

THE MATCHMAKER BAY SERIES

Mermaid Inn

Paradise Cove

Sandcastle Beach

THE BRIDESMAIDS BEHAVING BADLY SERIES

One and Only

It Takes Two

Three Little Words

sandcastle beach

A MATCHMAKER BAY NOVEL

JENNY HOLIDAY

FOREVER
New York Boston

Forever
Hachette Book Group
1290 Avenue of the Americas, New York, NY 10104
read-forever.com
twitter.com/readforeverpub

First Edition: March 2021

Forever is an imprint of Grand Central Publishing. The Forever name and logo are trademarks of Hachette Book Group, Inc.

The publisher is not responsible for websites (or their content) that are not owned by the publisher.

The Hachette Speakers Bureau provides a wide range of authors for speaking events. To find out more, go to www.hachettespeakersbureau.com or call (866) 376-6591.

ISBN: 978-1-5387-1657-1 (mass market), 978-1-5387-1658-8 (ebook)

Printed in the United States of America

CW

10 9 8 7 6 5 4 3 2 1

To Courtney, with a raspberry cordial toast in a tiny chocolate cup

Acknowledgments

My thanks to Tara Vinodrai for helping me think through issues of representation in this book. (Who would have thought, back when we had askabi in our hearts, that you'd end up consulting on straight-people romance novels?!) Thank you to my British nephew, football fanatic Finn (and his family, but mostly him!), for helping me with some of the Premier League details.

As always, I'm indebted to my agent, Courtney Miller-Callihan, and my friend Sandra Owens for brainstorming and beta reading.

Mostly, though, a huge thank-you to my editor Junessa Viloria, who saw through the muddle of the first draft of this book (some first drafts are more muddled than others; this one was right up there!) and hacked a path through the brush so we could get where we were meant to be going. Thanks to Estelle Hallick as well for some early insight.

And to everyone at Forever: Junessa, Leah, Estelle, Mari, S. B.—thank you so much for your work on my books. I'm so lucky to have you.

Once Upon a Bride had a previous life as an independently published (with a big assist from Forever) novella, and I want to thank Lexi Smail and Sarah Pesce for their work on that version of it.

Finally, to my beloved readers: thank you!

Chapter One

❧

$\mathscr{M}$oonflower Bay, Ontario, was known to the legions of tourists who descended on it every summer for lots of things. Spectacular Lake Huron sunsets. The Raspberry Festival. A so-cute-it-made-your-teeth-hurt wishing tradition that involved throwing flowers into the lake under the light of a full moon. Really good pie.

But to its citizens, it was arguably more (in)famous for its band of meddling old people. They had their hands in everything. The town council. The chamber of commerce. The love lives of their neighbors—they weren't nicknamed "the matchmakers" for nothing.

So when they came bustling into the town's theater company one August afternoon to inform its artistic director, Maya Mehta, that she had been elected queen of next weekend's Mermaid Parade, Maya should not have been surprised. This happened every year, after all.

Usually she could manufacture some enthusiasm, but this year they were interrupting a long and painful accounting session in which she was trying to see a way forward through the forest of red ink she was lost in.

There was nothing like impending financial doom to put a damper on being crowned mermaid queen.

"Hi," she said warily as Pearl, Art, Eiko, and Karl came strolling into her office off the theater's lobby. She minimized QuickBooks on her computer like she'd been caught watching porn at work. As the old folks filed into the small space, she tried to casually gather up the papers scattered on her desk. It wasn't as if the invoices themselves telegraphed *I have no money to pay these!* but still. You could never be too careful with this group of meddlers.

"What's up?" she asked, as if she didn't already know. Benjamin Lawson had struck again. You couldn't even give him points for creativity. This was, what? The fourth year running she'd been elected mermaid queen thanks to his machinations?

"Congratulations!" Eiko trilled, waving a sparkly tiara.

"Ms. Maya Mehta," Karl said with great solemnity, "As the executive committee of the Moonflower Bay town council, it is our pleasure to coronate you this year's mermaid queen."

"Wow. What a shock."

"There actually was a little surge of support for another candidate this year," Pearl said.

Really? "Who?"

"I can't say," Pearl said. "Election integrity demands confidentiality."

"Of course it does." Maya refrained from rolling her eyes, but only just.

Eiko shook the tiara at Maya. Maya sighed and bowed her head, and in so doing noticed that although she'd scooped up most of the paperwork on her desk, yesterday's letter from the Canada Council for the Arts was still lying on the far edge. The one that said, "Dear Ms. Mehta, we regret to inform you..." The one that might as well have said, "Neener neener, no grant for you."

After Eiko crowned her, Maya tried to subtly grab the letter, but it was just out of her reach. And Art was standing right next to it. Shoot. She needed a distraction.

"You know what?" she exclaimed, successfully drawing everyone's attention. "I want the trident. Why does the king get the trident and the queen gets nothing of actual use? Like, he can raise the minions of the sea—or, I guess, the lake—with his mighty trident and she can do what? Wave and look pretty?"

That gave them pause. There was a literal pause, in fact, a long one, while they absorbed her complaint. Pearl rebounded first. "You know what? She makes a point."

"She *was* the one who got us to expand the bachelor auction to include bachelorettes, and that was a huge success," Eiko said.

"We'll get you the trident," Karl said.

Disarmed, Maya blinked rapidly. That was the thing about the old folks. You had to be careful when you were trying to stand up to them. Sometimes they would just *agree* with you, which would *seem* like a victory, but before you knew it, you'd find yourself the chairperson of the town bachelor/ette auction. Or they'd award you custody of the mer-king's trident. "Who's king this year?"

"Jordan Riley," Pearl said.

"Really?" *That* was a new twist. "He doesn't seem like the type." Either the type to be interested or the type people would think to nominate. The auto mechanic was nice enough but a bit mysterious.

"His sister is trying to get him to be more social, so she encouraged people to vote for him," Eiko said.

"So what you're saying is there was election interference on *both* sides of the ballot this year. I don't even know why you have me give the crown back every year. You should let me keep it."

"We have to let democracy take its course," Karl said.

"I'm not sure what part of Benjamin Lawson giving free drinks to people who vote for me sounds like democracy to you, but okay."

"Here's your tail, hon." Eiko handed over the green-and-blue-

sequined creation. "The nice thing about your dynasty is we haven't
had to get this altered for years."

Art, the least vocal of the quartet of town meddlers, patted her
sympathetically on the shoulder. "Long may you reign."

Maya walked them out and reminded herself that as annoying
as Moonflower Bay's meddling old folks could be, she loved them.
Her affection for her hometown and its quirky residents was the
reason she'd come back after college to start the theater company.
It wasn't their fault her dream was withering on the vine—or that
Benjamin Lawson, her nemesis, was so steadfastly committed to
throwing the mermaid election in her "favor." The old folks were
just keeping the town traditions alive, and its traditions were part of
what made this town great.

"What's going on here?" Karl pointed to a bucket in the lobby
she'd positioned under a persistent drip.

"One of the toilets in the ladies' room on the balcony level is
leaking."

Karl frowned. "Who are you getting out here to deal with it?
There's a new plumber up in Bayshore who came into the store
last week." Karl ran Lakeside Hardware. Some towns had beauty
parlor–based gossip networks. Moonflower Bay had the hardware
store. "He left a card. You want me to drop it by later?"

*Does he take Monopoly money? Will he plumb in exchange for
theater tickets?* "Sure," she said, leaving out the part where her plan
was actually to stick an "Out of Order" sign on the stall in question,
leave the bucket where it was, and hope for the best.

"He's just starting out, so he's probably cheaper than Marco
Garretson," Karl added, naming the plumber most people in
town used.

Hmm. Maya was pretty sure they hadn't seen that rejection
letter, but the budget plumber recommendation made her wonder if
the old folks knew about her financial problems anyway. But that
was impossible, because she hadn't told anyone. Not her parents,
not her friends Eve and Nora. *No one.*

"I'm sure he can fix you right up." Karl tilted his head back again to look at the water-stained ceiling, which caused Maya and everyone else to do the same.

"Great!" she said with manufactured enthusiasm. "Looking forward to being fixed right up!"

And with that, a chunk of plaster fell on her head, bounced off a prong of the tiara she was still wearing, and shattered into dust on the floor at her feet.

A week later

"Where the *hell* is Carter?" Law muttered. He'd intended it as a mutter, anyway. It came out more like a shout.

It was a rhetorical question. He had a pretty good idea where Carter, who'd been due in an hour ago, was. Sleeping it off. Carter had closed last night, and when Carter closed, he tended to be late the next day.

Law flashed his everybody-knows-your-name smile at the tourist seated at the bar in front of him, a thirtysomething woman he did not, in fact, know. He'd startled her when he yelled, and she'd sloshed some of her drink onto the bar. "Sorry about that. Let me make you a new one on the house. Vodka soda, extra lemon, right?"

He whipped up her drink and slid it across the bar, smiling absently at her thanks—she was trying to engage him in conversation and he was trying to avoid being engaged— no he angled himself to try to see out the bar's propped-open front door.

He couldn't see anything, but he could hear. The high school marching band, which always led the parade, was playing "Under the Sea." Which meant it was starting. Dammit.

The Mermaid Parade was one of the two big annual festivals that lured outsiders to town, and the weekend was a mainstay of the Moonflower Bay economy. The bar had been busy before the parade and would be slammed after it—so Law's desire to duck out and watch it aside, Carter needed to get his ass in here.

Law had two employees. Carter, who was full-time, and Shane Calloway, who manned the outdoor pizza oven when it was open, which was from five until eleven every night except in the winter. When the young Grizzly Adams type wasn't at the bar, he was out shooting deer or pulling fish out of the lake with his bare hands or figuring out ways to get the remote cabin he lived in even further off the grid than it already was. Shane was the opposite of Carter in that he was 100 percent reliable—he'd be in today at four thirty on the dot to get the fire started—but he lived so far away he couldn't be called to come in last minute. Normally Law's retired dad would help out in a pinch, but his parents were already at the parade and he could hardly ask his dad to switch places with him.

Law picked up his phone to text Carter for the third time this afternoon. Dude, where are you? The parade is underway and we're about to be overrun. We gotta set up the outdoor bar. He tried to tell himself that he wasn't missing anything. You've seen one Mermaid Parade—or thirty-three—you've seen them all.

As evidenced by the fact that he knew the *whoop-whoop* of the sirens on his buddy Sawyer's police cruiser marked the half-way point.

He tried to distract himself by chopping citrus for garnishes, but something was happening beneath his skin. It felt like that soda he'd just poured was fizzing through his veins.

"You okay?"

He glanced up.

"You're all jumpy," Ms. Extra Lemon said. "Like you're waiting for bad news or something."

"I'm fine. Just..." About to miss the king-and-queen float. It wasn't a triumph if he wasn't there to witness it.

"Oh, okay. I was going to sympathize. I mean, you don't sit in a bar by yourself on a beautiful summer day in a beach town unless you've got problems." She gave a self-deprecating snort.

This was the part where he was supposed to do his bartender

duty and ask about her troubles. It was the role people expected him to play, and usually he didn't mind it. Enjoyed it, even. He'd grown up in this bar, and when the time had come for him to take over its day-to-day operations so his dad could retire, he'd been happy to do so. But right now, he could hear the distant strains of the Gorgons, the town's women's choir. They usually walked in front of the king-and-queen float.

Which meant she was coming.

Law's customer performed an overly loud sigh that was meant to be another cue. Instead of asking her what was up, he wondered if another free drink could convince her to watch the bar in his absence.

But no. He couldn't. Lawson's Lager House had been founded by his grandfather in 1943 and had been a town institution ever since. It had almost closed in the recession of the early 1990s, but his parents had pulled it back from the brink. It was his family's legacy, in other words, and you didn't just leave your family legacy unattended so you could go watch a parade.

Anyway, it wasn't like he didn't know exactly how it would go. The Gorgons would be singing something from the Spice Girls, and the same old float would come rolling down Main Street hitched to Art Ramsey's pickup. Then the band, which would be waiting at the end of the route, would back up the Gorgons for "Kiss the Girl" from *The Little Mermaid*, which was the big finale.

There would be no actual kissing of the girl, though, because the king was usually Karl, who had four decades on his queen. But also because the queen would be scowling, lips pursed in displeasure. He grinned just thinking about it.

Although the king this year was Jordan Riley.

Did that mean there might actually *be* kissing? A ceremonial kiss? Law vaguely remembered one year, long before the Maya Dynasty, when Allison Andersen and Charles Braithwaite had been king and queen and had shocked everyone by laughingly kissing— but, like, a real, drawn-out kiss—at the end of the song. And hadn't they gone on to date for a while? Allison was married to someone else now, but Law kind of thought so.

The carbonation in his veins was becoming unendurable. He had to get out there. Ms. Extra Lemon it was. You tended bar enough years, you became a decent judge of character. He'd come back and listen to her talk about her problems for as long as she liked. "Listen. I'm wondering if you can do me a—"

The bells on the door jingled. Ah! Saved by the only townsperson who wouldn't be at the parade. "Jake!"

His friend paused in the doorway. Yeah, that greeting had probably sounded way too enthusiastic, given that they saw each other all the time.

He tried again without the exclamation mark. "Jake. What are you doing here?" The town curmudgeon usually spent festival days holed up in his cottage in Paradise Cove.

"I was helping the new doctor get set up for her vaccine campaign, and I stupidly left my truck on the other side of Main, so I'm stuck until after the parade." He pulled out a stool.

"Well, help yourself to whatever you want, but do me a favor and watch the place for a few minutes, will you?" Law came out from behind the bar. With anyone else, he would have expected an interrogation about his sudden need to bail on his place of business, but he was counting on—and got—merely a grunt of assent from Jake. That was the nice thing about Jake. He wasn't always jumping to conclusions where there were none to be made.

He'd made it almost all the way to the door when Jake's voice caught up with him. "You'd better hurry or you're going to miss her."

"What's with the Spice Girls thing?" Sawyer asked a few minutes later as he came to stand next to Law on the curb near the end of the parade route. Sawyer had finished his role in it, parked his cruiser, and shown up to watch the end.

The Gorgons were approaching, performing an enthusiastic

version of that "If you wanna be my lover" song. Several of them sported headpieces that made it look like they had snakes for hair.

"Why is it always the Spice Girls?" Sawyer went on. "I mean, songs from *The Little Mermaid* I get. But the Spice Girls?"

"Maya got her undies in a bunch years ago because I didn't have any Spice Girls on the jukebox at the bar. So I think she gets them to sing it to stick it to me. Also, you may remember that the Gorgons never marched in front of the royalty float back in the day. They were further up in the parade, and..."

He trailed off, registering Sawyer's puzzled look. Yeah, Sawyer didn't remember that. It was a weirdly specific detail that only someone obsessed with the parade would recall.

"So what you're saying," Sawyer said, "is that you get Maya elected mermaid queen every year, and she responds by surrounding herself with a choir named after figures from Greek mythology whose whole schtick was to turn men to stone and she has them sing the Spice Girls purely to irritate you."

Ah, yes. That was what Law was saying. But he did realize how ridiculous it sounded when put like that. Annoying Maya was his main hobby, which maybe didn't reflect well on him, but he didn't care. Given that he was cursed by being wildly attracted to a woman who hated him, and given that the feeling was mostly mutual—though he couldn't honestly say he *hated* her as much as he was endlessly annoyed by her—the Mermaid Parade was pretty much the highlight of his year. He got to see Maya in all her glory, and he got to bug the shit out of her. Win-win. But he didn't know how to answer Sawyer's question. Law had learned to live with the contradictions inherent in his relationship with Maya, but his friends did not need to know about them. They wouldn't understand.

Sawyer shrugged, returned his attention to the float, and said, "That sounds about right, actually."

The Gorgons wrapped up the song, and the band began playing a royal flourish, heavy on the horns.

Maya was wearing her signature Converse high-tops—a sky-blue pair. After the first year of her reign, she'd cut a hole in the bottom of the tail so her feet could peek through, saying she "refused to be jailed," which was a very Maya-esque turn of phrase. The green and blue sequins on the tail made it sparkle in the sun. She wore a hot-pink tube top and had painted her lips a matching color. Her long, so-brown-it-was-almost-black hair hung loose down her back, which was a rare occurrence, and it was windy enough that she kept having to push it out of her face.

As the float came to a halt, she made one last rotation perched on her throne, waving first to the people on the other side of the street. It wasn't a fakey beauty-queen wave, but it also wasn't the kind of wave she'd do in her real life. That kind would be fast and enthusiastic—Law aside, she was always happy to see people. No, it was merely a slow, unremarkable, almost disinterested wave. And as she turned to face forward, he could see that it matched her expression, which was blank. She wasn't smiling. She wasn't scowling like she sometimes was on that throne. She was bored. Unmoved.

Well, damn. Maybe it was time to retire this stunt. He'd had people in the bar this past spring asking him for ballots before he'd even bothered to put any out, though, so he wasn't sure he *could* retire it.

She kept up the blasé waving as she rotated to face his side of the street, her arm moving mechanically in between brushing hair off her face—clouds were moving in, and the wind off the lake was picking up.

Something happened as their gazes met and she registered his presence. She rolled her eyes. Not a lot. Just a little. Enough to communicate, though, when you were capable of communicating in subtle gestures like they were, resigned disgust.

Ha! There it was. He choked back a grin and raised his eyebrows at her. Not a lot. Just a little. Enough to communicate, when you were capable of communicating in subtle gestures like they were, triumph.

As the Gorgons finished their song, a huge gust of wind tore across the beach from the lake. It was so strong and sudden that some people gasped. Maya had been about to climb down from the float, so she was standing. She grabbed a corner of her throne with one hand and flung the other out to balance herself. The wind caught her hair and blew it up and out behind her, so she looked like a Gorgon, too. Like the queen of the Gorgons, commanding the vengeful musical army at her feet.

But she also looked like the queen of the mermaids. The hand she'd flung out to balance herself was holding the trident, and with the drama of the gesture, you could almost believe she was *creating* the wind, like she was about to call forth the lake itself, to summon a tidal wave that would subsume them all.

She was stunning.

Chapter Two

❧

$\mathscr{B}$ack at the bar, Law had words with Carter, who'd shown up while he was out. "You can't just show up two hours late on one of the busiest days of the year." He hated to sound like a nag, but honestly, this was a place of business, not a frat house. "It's not like I have backup. It's me and you here, bud."

Though maybe that needed to change. Even if Carter were more reliable, running this place with only two bartenders was a stretch. Law used to have a third person, but Amber Grant quit when she graduated from nursing school, and now she worked for Nora Walsh, the new town doctor. Law had always known that his time with Amber, who'd been a stellar employee, was limited. He'd held off on replacing her, though, because of *his* plans. He didn't mind working a ton of hours himself right now if it meant saving money.

"Sorry, man. I'll do better," Carter said, and Law moved on to serve Nora, poacher of Amber, who was just pulling out a stool.

"Hey, Doc. I heard you were running a vaccine drive. How did it go?" There'd been a measles outbreak in the region, and Nora was determined to beat it back.

"Okay, I think. It was just an information table—I wasn't actually giving shots." She shook her head. "I'm still a bit gobsmacked by that parade."

"It's something, isn't it? You get so used to the craziness around here, you sometimes forget—"

She was here.

The door opening, which was what had drawn Law's attention, was not unusual. He was in the habit of quickly looking over when he heard the bells on the door. You tended bar enough years, you learned to keep an eye on the crowd.

When Maya came into the bar, which she did more days than not, it always felt like he'd been teleported into a cheesy Western where an outlaw cowboy type slammed open the saloon doors and the whole place fell silent, waiting for him to say something like, *This town ain't big enough for the both of us* as he challenged his nemesis to a shoot-out.

Maya never said that—though the sentiment was probably pretty representative of her opinion about him. And the whole place didn't pause when she came in. It just felt like it. Because the normal functioning of Law's brain *did* pause whenever she walked through his door. Not long enough that anyone ever noticed, thankfully, and usually muscle memory kept him from spilling anything if he was in the middle of pouring a drink. But her appearance always caused his brain to peace out of its surroundings for a second and run a little movie in his head—a movie called *Maya's Nineteenth Birthday*.

He'd been behind the bar, chatting idly with her brother, Rohan, who'd been home for the holidays. Law was six years older than Maya, so they hadn't overlapped in high school, but he was only three years older than Rohan, and they'd been on the track-and-field team together. Rohan had gone on to become a big-shot business exec in the US, but at that point he'd only recently graduated university and moved to Chicago, and they were chatting about how he was finding it.

The funny part was, if you had asked Law then if Rohan Mehta had a sibling, he'd have had to think about it. He knew Rohan, and he knew Rohan's dad, who owned A Rose by Any Other Name. Law's dad and Mr. Mehta had been active in the chamber of commerce when Law was a kid. And yes, he vaguely knew there was a little sister, the gangly theater girl who staged plays on the town green. He had never been to one at that point, though. He was already putting in a ton of hours at the bar helping his dad, and between that, school, and track, he didn't have time for much else. He wasn't even sure he'd known Maya's name at that point. She just hadn't registered in his brain.

But that day, she *did* register in his brain. Oh boy, did she ever.

It had been a quiet December afternoon. Law was working alone, his dad having moved into semiretirement, and there were only a handful of customers in the bar. When she arrived, both Law and Rohan turned to look at her, and Rohan grinned and got up. "Happy birthday, kid!"

"Hi, hi!" she exclaimed as she hugged him. "And thanks!"

"You been to the store yet?"

"Yeah, I dropped off my bag there. I told Dad we'd meet him there at six. We're going to the White Rhino in Bayshore."

"What a shock," Rohan deadpanned.

"Shut up. It's my birthday. I'm the boss. And I love that place." She shrugged off her coat. She was wearing skinny jeans and a fitted T-shirt that read "Drama Queen." Nothing about the outfit was revealing per se, but it did make Law wonder how he had ever thought of her as gangly. She had her hair in this big messy bun almost but not quite on the top of her head. It made him want to know how long her hair would be when it was down.

There was just something about her, though it was hard to say what. She wore no makeup, and that, together with her casual clothes and almost-messy hair, should not be having this effect on him—"this effect" being that he couldn't stop looking at her. Her light-brown skin was all glowy, and the smile she gave her brother was almost blinding even from Law's vantage point to the side. "It's your birthday?" Law said.

She swung around to look at him for the first time, and her eyes were the *exact* same color as the honey cream ale from Bayside Brewing they had on one of their permanent taps.

He wasn't sure why he was noticing all this stuff about her. Comparing her eyes to beer? Come on. She was pretty, for sure. But he was a bartender. Every subcategory of humanity had been through Lawson's Lager House, including "pretty," and he was generally indifferent. He would provide a friendly ear if one was wanted, but he didn't hit on customers. Especially the little sisters of old acquaintances—the key word there being *little*.

How little, though? He hoped not *too* little, because he could not deny that he was, suddenly, perving on Maya Mehta.

Until she started talking.

"Nineteen today," she said in answer to his question, and he breathed a sigh of relief. Nineteen was the drinking age, so he felt less gross for admiring her than he would have if she'd been younger. Not that he was going to do anything about it, but still.

"Hey, congrats. Nineteenth-birthday drinks are on the house. What can I get you?"

She kept staring at him, and if he wasn't mistaken, she didn't like what she was seeing. After an uncomfortably long time, she said, "I can pay for my own drink, thanks."

"You sure? Because—"

"I'll have a white wine, please."

"Any preference?" He'd recently talked his dad into expanding the wine list. It used to have two items: red and white. Now it contained six offerings, vintages he had researched and selected. He slid her one of the small laminated menus.

"What do you recommend?" she asked.

"The Tawse Chardonnay is nice."

"I'll have the Riesling, thanks."

Okay, then. Rohan's little sister was a sourpuss. Noted. Law turned to pour the wine, and by the time he set it in front of her, she was getting out her wallet.

"Take the free drink," Rohan said. "You were *just* complaining about the cost of living in Toronto." He turned to Law. "Maya's at Sheridan College studying theater. She just finished her first semester." He raised his glass to toast her, his pride apparent.

"I can pay for my own drink," she said again.

"By all means, don't let me stop you," Law said. "I'll happily take your money." He was teasing. Mostly. He didn't understand why she would turn her nose up at a free drink, or why her refusal was so snooty, but whatever.

"I would never let *you* stop me," she said.

Huh? But before he could even try to start parsing what she'd said, she'd pressed a ten-dollar bill into his hand, and it felt like she was electrocuting him.

And that was the story of how Law came to be wildly attracted to someone he didn't even like. If he were a superhero, that day would have gone down in the lore as the day Maya came into his bar, her bright, bitter beauty an injection of life on a slow, snowy afternoon, and stung him.

She had come into his bar *a lot* in the years after the sting. Not so much when she was in college, though there had been a few visits. But once she came home for good, she was in the bar all the damn time. And every single time she walked through his door, his brain stuttered for a second. It was irritating. It was *embarrassing*.

"Hey," Nora said as Maya plopped down next to her. Maya was still wearing the pink tube top from the parade—God help him— but the tail and tiara were gone. The top was now paired with her standard jeans and Cons, though she'd changed the Cons from her blue mermaid pair to a baby-pink pair. "That was really something. This whole town is really something."

"You'll get used to us." Maya smiled at Nora. Maya had a big, easy smile, but Law had still never seen it straight-on.

"So what's with the mermaid queen thing?" Nora asked, looking between him and Maya. "I hear you're behind her election every year?"

Sort of. He had been the first time. After that, it had taken on a life of its own. But he would take the credit. "I am."

"*Benjamin*," Maya said, finally deigning to greet him. Everyone in town called him Law except Maya and his mother. Maya had a certain way of saying his name, emphasizing it like it was heavy in her mouth, like it pained her to say it.

He set a wineglass down in front of her and poured her wine—that was his version of greeting her. It was still a Riesling, though a different one from that first time. After he'd taken over the bar full-time, he'd done even more tinkering with the wine list—although this one wasn't on the menu.

"Benjamin lives to antagonize me," Maya explained to Nora.

"You started it," he retorted.

"Untrue," Maya said, but, having dismissed him, she was talking to Nora. She was also wrong. She had been distinctly frosty since Sting Day.

Most people liked Law. He had always thought of himself as inherently likeable. Until she came along. It was kind of interesting to be the object of someone's disdain. No, not interesting. Exhilarating. Sparring with Maya was the highlight of his day—which he realized sounded crazy, but it was true. As downtown business owners whose jobs had them keeping late hours, they saw a lot of each other, and the odd day he *didn't* see her felt strangely off, like he'd gone around all day with his shirt inside out or something.

"But how did you even come up with the mermaid queen prank?" Nora asked Law. She turned to Maya. "And why do you hate it so much? I would think, with the whole theater thing, that it would be up your alley."

Maya picked up her wine. "We were all here one night during

the Raspberry Festival, so the place was crawling with tourists. There was a bachelorette party happening, and the bride had one of those beauty-queen sashes on, you know? Like, it said, 'The future Mrs. Brad McBoring' or whatever?" Nora nodded. "We somehow started talking about pageants, and we were laughing about what our talents would be if we were in one."

"You would do a dramatic monologue," Nora said.

"Yes, the one from Ibsen's *A Doll's House* where Nora—hey, her name is Nora, too!—is talking about how she subsumed her tastes into her husband's so much that she's effectively his doll." She struck a purposefully melodramatic pose and cried, "'You and Papa have committed a great sin against me! It is your fault that I have made nothing of my life!'" She made a silly face and broke character. "And then I made some big pronouncement about how I would die before I'd ever be a beauty queen, and..." She performed a big shrug. "Here I am."

Nora laughed. "And what was your talent going to be?" she asked Law.

"I'd make the perfect martini."

"Oh, Maya would definitely beat you," Nora said dismissively. "She's prettier, too."

He could not argue with that.

"Yeah," Nora said to Maya after Benjamin wandered away to serve someone else, "but *why* do you guys dislike each other so much? It feels like a long-standing grudge. Did he stand you up at the prom or something?" She laughed like the idea was ridiculous.

"Benjamin is six years older than I am, so no, no one was jilted at the prom," Maya said, fake-laughing along with Nora, but the truth wasn't that far off. She wasn't sure how—or how much— to explain. She liked Nora. They were fast becoming friends, and she didn't want to run her off by sounding like a lunatic with a gold medal in grudge holding. "We never really knew each other as kids," she added.

Well, he didn't know her. She knew him. Or knew of him. She'd always thought he was cute, running around at track meets in his little shorts, his muscles rippling as he hurled his body over the bar in pole vault. He and Rohan both competed in the eight-hundred-meter run, and Benjamin always won, which Ro always put down to the fact that he was older. The two boys had a friendly rivalry that was heavy on the friendliness, and indeed, Benjamin had always seemed like a nice guy. Everyone liked Benjamin, including Maya.

Until he ruined her first play. *Romeo and Juliet*. She was fifteen, and she'd had big dreams even then. She'd worked *so* hard to get that first play off the ground. Law had been dating her Juliet, and he'd talked her into impulsively skipping town the day of the show, forcing Maya to cancel it. She still remembered the anger and shame. All that work down the drain.

But she didn't want to get into it. It sounded so stupid from this vantage point. She'd just been so *mad* at him, and by the time the anger had faded, they were settled so far into their groove of bickering and feuding that there was no climbing out of it.

So she went for the rest of the story, which was all true. "We just don't like each other. When I opened the theater, we started having all these conflicts. Parking, noise from the bands he has in here on weekends, you name it. And the new pizza oven out back belches smoke. My patrons used to like to go out behind the theater during intermission, but they can't anymore." She shrugged. "We just sort of got into the habit of being at odds. Oil and water, you know?"

"But doesn't it get tiring?"

Not at all. If anything, it was the reverse. Fighting with Benjamin made Maya feel alive in a way that nothing else did—which was annoying, but it was what it was. She picked up her drink. "Everyone needs hobbies."

An hour later, Maya was still sitting at the bar, though Nora had left. She should just leave, too. But as in the aftermath of a play, the mermaid queen gig had her hyped up. It was a common phenomenon among actors. The energy you needed to put on a show couldn't be turned off with the flip of a switch. She needed a step-down of sorts before she went back to her quiet apartment. If she was doing a play, she usually wasn't out of the theater until well after eleven, and Lawson's Lager House was the only thing open. Plus, its proprietor aside, she loved this place. It was familiar and cozy and she could always find someone to talk to if she was in the mood. If she wasn't, she could sit at the bar and read or work on memorizing lines. She almost thought of it as an extension of her living space, which was a crappy studio. A communal living room of sorts.

She took a tiny sip of her wine. She always ordered a glass because she wasn't about to sit in Benjamin's bar without ordering anything. He wasn't going to be able to accuse her of freeloading. But she never drank very fast, as she was aware that her almost daily presence in the bar would make it easy to start drinking too much.

Also there was the part where she had no money.

"So tomorrow is your last show, right?" Benjamin asked.

"Yes," she said warily. Her summer play always coincided with Mermaid Parade weekend—there was a preparade matinee on the Saturday and an evening show on the Sunday. This year was *Grease*. She'd thought it would be a crowd-pleaser, but she'd sold only a third of the seats today, which made her panic when she thought about it too hard. She shoved aside thoughts of impending financial ruin. She was pretty sure Benjamin was about to start something, so she needed to be on her toes.

"I want half the parking spots tomorrow night," he said. "I have Final Vinyl in for their last show of the summer, and it's going to be packed."

"Okay."

He reared back a little, and she laughed. She'd shocked him with her easy acquiescence. They were forever battling over parking. The bar and the theater were separated only by the *Moonflower Bay*

Monitor building, and the reserved parking spots right out front were in demand in the evenings.

"On one condition," she added.

"Ah," he said, "that's more like it."

"I'm thinking of adding wine to the concessions at the theater." She was thinking of a lot of things, actually, probably none of which would be enough to make up for the blow of not getting the grant she'd been counting on, but this was one he could help with. Booze, according to her research, had high margins, and if she could get a deal on the supply end, she could turn an even bigger profit. "I'm not totally sold, as I'll need cups and corkscrews and all that, and I'm not sure about the legality of my concessions guy, who's a high schooler, serving."

"Your high schooler has to be eighteen. And there's actually some decent wine in cans these days. You could serve it straight out of the can with a straw—no cups or corkscrews needed. Act like you're doing it on purpose—pretend you're being trendy."

That was a great idea. But no need to get overtly excited. "I don't have to *pretend* to be trendy, Benjamin." She narrowed her eyes.

"Says the woman wearing a tube top. Nineteen eighty-three called, and they want their outfit back." He leaned closer over the bar and held her gaze. They did this. Staring contests. Glaring contests. She wasn't sure when it had started, only that when you were in one, the goal was to not look away first.

She usually won, if only because he had actual work to do. As was the case now, when Carter came up to ask him a question. She smirked.

"So how do I get these cans of wine?" she asked after he was done with Carter. "Advise me and you can have the parking spots tomorrow. Do I just buy them in bulk from the liquor store?"

"No. You tell me what you want, and I add it to my wholesale order. Your per-unit price will be better that way. I'll invoice you."

That was unexpectedly generous of him. But that was the strange thing about Benjamin. Though they battled pretty much constantly, he would sometimes surprise her by doing something decent.

He left to serve other customers, leaving her to ponder the mess she was in. She had opened the theater with a start-up economic development grant and a big investment from her parents. She had kept it operating the past five years through a combination of arts grants and the money she made from ticket sales and the summer arts camps she ran for kids.

On paper, she should have been profitable by now—certainly past the point where losing out on one grant was enough to do her in. The problem was the building. It had started its life as a theater in the late nineteenth century and had been converted to a movie house in the 1970s. But that had been shuttered fifteen years ago, and the building had sat vacant until she bought it for a song. She'd known it was going to need work but had underestimated just how much. The leak in the lobby ceiling was only the latest in a series of problems—electrical fires causing her to have to rewire, pipes freezing—that had demanded influxes of cash that was supposed to be going to operating and payroll.

What was she going to *do*? She was already running as lean an operation as she could. She had only two full-time employees—Marjorie Nicolson, who did box office and admin, and Richard Lanister, who was her tech guru and jack-of-all-trades, overseeing set building and running the light board during shows. Everyone else was part-time—the concessions kid, for example, who wasn't eighteen, which was a new little problem to deal with. The cast and crew she hired on contract for each show. The ushers worked for free in exchange for getting to see the show. Everything else she did herself, meaning not only was she the Moonflower Bay Theater Company's artistic director, she was also its janitor.

So she needed to think of something, and she needed to think of it quick. Something more than wine in a can.

She was starting to get kind of panicky, so she pulled out her phone. There had been a football match today, and though she'd checked the final score, she hadn't had time to do anything beyond that. Even though her beloved Crystal Palace had lost, watching the match highlights would soothe her.

Except...Ugh. She'd forgotten that as part of her attempt to cut her personal expenses because she'd started paying herself less, she'd dumped the app that was the only way to watch English Premier League football in Canada. It had gone in a moment of resolve, along with Netflix and even the Wi-Fi in her apartment—she had Wi-Fi at the theater and that was enough, she'd reasoned. "Ugh." She said it out loud this time.

"Everything okay here?" Benjamin was back.

"Yep, I just forgot I'm out of data this month," she lied. She didn't like anyone knowing about her money troubles, but she *especially* didn't want him knowing. Showing weakness in front of Benjamin Lawson was *not* in her playbook. "And since you're a troglodyte with no Wi-Fi, I can't check how the football match went earlier."

"Who needs Wi-Fi at a bar?" he said. "You come to a bar to forget your troubles, not surf the internet."

She rolled her eyes. She'd have to go back to the theater and pull up some of her UK sites to get a recap. Damn, she was going to miss watching matches this season. But when it came down to it, what was more important, football or the theater? No question. She slung her purse over her shoulder and hopped off her stool.

"Hang on, though, I think I get English Premier League soccer." Benjamin picked up a remote and aimed it at one of the TVs mounted above the bar. "I get my NFL from this app that I think now has English Premier League, too."

"Are you kidding me?" she practically shouted, not sure if she was happy he had the app or mad that he'd never mentioned it.

He shot her a look. "Calm yourself." He futzed with the TV, and there it was. He pulled up the menu and handed her the remote. "Knock yourself out."

"Hang on a sec," she called after him. He'd been on his way down the bar but he came back, eyebrows raised impatiently. "If you don't have Wi-Fi in this bar, how do you run the app?" His face froze. Ha. Busted. "You *do* have Wi-Fi!"

"Keep your voice down," he whisper-yelled, looking around and leaning in like they were preparing to do a drug deal. "Yes, I have Wi-Fi—in the whole building. I need it for some of the streaming services and apps I need to show the sports people want." He gestured at the TV above them. "Like your precious soccer."

"And no one has put two and two together before?" She'd seen people ask him for the Wi-Fi password before and him answer that there wasn't one.

"Look, I just want this to be a certain kind of place—a place where people can hang out and not be slaves to their phones." He rolled his eyes. "Not that it really matters. They already are. I just figure I don't have to help them along with Wi-Fi."

She actually understood that. How many times had she had some idiot ignore the turn-your-devices-off announcement before a show and then been interrupted by a phone ringing? And the living room feeling she liked about the bar came from its communal vibe. Not its everyone-staring-at-their-own-phone vibe.

Most importantly, she wasn't in a position to complain if she wanted to watch football here. So she just said, "Okay."

"Okay? That's it? You're not going to expose me as a fraud?"

"Not today." She shot him a saccharine smile. "Maybe later." But actually . . . "What's the password for the Wi-Fi?" If she could get Wi-Fi in her living room away from home, that would be awesome.

"Why?"

So I can mooch off your Wi-Fi. "I really, really need to check something." She shook her phone at him, and he raised an eyebrow. "It's an emergency. Tell it to me, and I promise I won't tell anyone."

He shook his head, but he leaned farther in—he smelled good—and whispered "LLH1943."

"How original."

"Well, we can't all be creative geniuses."

She typed it in, connected to his network, and shot him another fake smile. "That's true."

Chapter Three

Four months later

Law looked up from garnishing an old-fashioned when the bells on the door jingled.

It was Maya.

Which was a surprise. She generally didn't come in on nights he had bands in.

As if on cue, she paused in the doorway, glanced at the band, and rolled her eyes.

She pulled up a stool next to Eve and Sawyer, who were oblivious to her arrival because they were half making out, half whispering to each other. Maya rolled her eyes again, but this time it was an inclusive eye roll, like she expected Law to share her view on how annoying the lovebirds were. He had the sudden urge to wink in solidarity with her, but he held back. They didn't do solidarity.

"How come you have a band here tonight?" she asked him. "I would have thought that'd be *tomorrow* night."

Tomorrow was New Year's Eve, and she was right; he did usually have a band on New Year's Eve, and since he didn't usually do bands more than once a week, her surprise at finding one here tonight was logical. "I'm trying a DJ for New Year's this year."

"Well, I was hoping to watch football, but now it's going to be impossible to hear it." She sighed, but not in her usual theatrical way. Something was off. She seemed almost...sad?

He handed her the remote for her preferred TV. "My sincerest apologies that the normal operation of my business is getting in the way of your recreation," he said in a way that was neither apologetic nor sincere. Thrown a little by how out of sorts she seemed, he was trying to goad her back to her usual self, but she didn't take the bait. So he set a wineglass in front of her, filled it, and left her to her sulking.

A while later, when the band was on a break between sets and Eve and Sawyer were settling their tab, he was drawn into a conversation between them that Maya was tangentially part of as she half listened, half watched her match.

"It's December thirtieth," Eve said, leaning over to speak to both Law and Sawyer. "You think Jake is okay?"

"Yeah," Law said.

"Well, as okay as he ever is," Maya said.

"You and I should probably go check on him tomorrow, though?" Sawyer asked Law.

Law nodded his agreement. Jake's son, Jude, who had died of the flu several years ago, just shy of his first birthday, had been born on December thirtieth. Jake always marked the day in self-imposed solitary confinement in his cottage, and he also never appeared for any New Year's Eve happenings. Law and Sawyer had tried, that first year, to be there for him on and around significant days, like Jude's birthday and the anniversary of his death, but Jake had made it abundantly clear that he wanted to be left alone. That wouldn't stop them from checking in on him, though.

"Has anyone heard from Nora?" Law asked, since they were taking stock of absent friends. Nora had left town abruptly a little before Christmas because her grandmother was dying.

"Yes," Maya said. "Her grandma died on the twenty-sixth."

They were all silent for a moment. "Any idea when she's coming back?" Law asked.

"Nope. I'll ask her next time I talk to her, though," Maya said.

Eve and Sawyer made their farewells, and Maya picked up the remote and turned the volume up on her match. "Sheesh. I could hardly breathe through all the pheromones there." Law chuckled. Eve and Sawyer were definitely still in their honeymoon phase. The band started making tuning rumblings.

"Are they playing *another* set?" Maya asked.

"Yeah, one more short one before closing."

She sighed—once again, she seemed sad, which wasn't usual for her—and handed him the remote. "Well, this is pointless."

She moved for her coat, and he said, "Actually..." But wait. Was he insane?

"What?" she said impatiently.

"I have the app on my TV upstairs, too, if you want to go watch up there." Yes, he was insane. "It'll be quiet." Like, very, very insane.

"Really?"

"Yeah, the app allows more than one log-in, so I have it in my apartment, though I don't think I've ever used it up there." He realized that didn't address her shock, and honestly, since his subscription came with three log-ins and he only had two in use, what he really should do was give her the third. But he liked having her watch soccer at his bar. Since she'd found out he had the app, she'd taken to coming in at night, parking herself in front of the TV he now thought of as hers, and cueing up the day's league highlights. He'd even gotten a little into it himself.

Weirdly, she hadn't even given him crap—well, not much— about his secret Wi-Fi. Probably because it benefited her.

"You're inviting me up to your apartment to watch football," she said, clearly still not quite believing him.

"Well, I'm not *inviting* you up. *I'm* not going to be there." He gestured at the still-buzzing bar. "I'm just saying you can go up there if you want." He fished his keys out of his pocket and held them out. Her mouth fell open. She was agog. Fair enough. He was kind of agog himself. He didn't know what had possessed him, except he was pretty sure he hadn't imagined those flashes of sadness in her eyes earlier. And her soccer team made her so happy.

He also hadn't truly expected her to take him up on the offer, so he was *extra* agog when she grabbed the keys out of his hand and hopped off the stool.

Well, damn. "Will you be able to figure out the TV?"

"Yes, *Benjamin*. I can run a light board. I aced video editing in college. I can figure out a TV."

Ah, that was more like it.

And she must have figured it out, because after she left, he didn't see her again. Knowing she was upstairs, in his personal space, while he carried on like normal down here was strange. There was an intimacy to it, which should have been the wrong descriptor, because she was there and he was here. After closing up, he rushed through only the most pressing cleaning tasks, telling himself he'd come down early and finish in the morning.

Upstairs, he pushed open the unlocked door to his apartment, his heart beating faster than he could explain away as a result of having run up the stairs. The place was dark, but he could hear the TV.

"Hey," he called as he made his way through the dining room that connected the kitchen and living room, announcing his presence so as not to startle her.

"Hey," she said back, and there she was, cozied up on his sofa. He sat on the other end and looked at the screen.

"Benjamin," she said, without emphasizing his name in that annoyed-schoolmarm way she usually did, "this"—she waved her arms around—"is awesome."

"What? The apartment?"

"Yes, the apartment. But also your giant TV. Watching a match on your giant TV. All of the above. What's *with* this place? Why is it so huge and nice? Who even are you?"

He shrugged, trying not to show how pleased he was by her approval. "I grew up in this apartment."

"You *did*?"

"Yeah. Well, my parents had a house when I was born, but they moved up here—they owned the building—when I was little, so this has always been home." When they retired, they'd bought a little house up the lake a way, and Law had done a remodel on the apartment to make it less of a family place and more of a swish bachelor pad—hence the giant TV. "What are you watching?"

"Just an old archived match. Sorry, I should have left when I finished today's. This setup is just so amazing."

She started to get up, but he motioned for her to stay. "You don't have to go. It takes me a while to wind down after closing the bar."

"Theater is the same. It's hard to switch off right away."

"I usually watch mindless TV for a while when I get home. This is as good as any. So don't leave on my account."

"Are you calling Crystal Palace versus Man City mindless?"

He quirked a smile. "I would never do that."

They watched in silence for a few minutes until she said, "Benjamin?"

"Mmm?" He was getting sleepy.

"Are we having a truce?"

"It would appear so."

"Don't get used to it."

"I wouldn't dream of it."

Bang, bang, bang.

Maya jolted awake in her bed, startled by a sudden pounding on her door.

"What the hell?" came a voice from nearby—a rough, gravelly, *masculine* voice. And it was *very* nearby.

Oh. My.

The pounding wasn't on her door, and she wasn't in her bed. She was on Benjamin's couch, and someone was at *his* door.

She'd fallen asleep, and so had he, judging from the wild look in his eyes—his eyes that were inches from her own. He had the prettiest green eyes. They were the exact color of the moss that grew on the town gazebo, and they were bracketed by laugh lines of the sort that a person got when he was funny and friendly—to other people—and expressive.

It was annoying.

Bang, bang, bang.

Right. This was not the time to be admiring Benjamin's eyes. "Get up," she whisper-yelled. Somehow, though they had been sitting on opposite ends of the couch last night, now they were tangled up together, sort of half sitting, half lying on the sofa.

"I can't until you get off me," he "yelled" back, tapping her calves. Mortifyingly, her legs were stretched out on his lap.

His hands resting on her bare ankles suddenly felt like brands. She snatched her legs back. "What time is it?"

He glanced at his watch. "Ten thirty."

Holy crap. "No one can know I'm here," she said urgently.

"No shit."

"Thanks a lot." All she'd meant was that the old folks couldn't catch wind of this. They would not accept the entirely innocent and entirely true we-fell-asleep-watching-football excuse, and she would have to spend the next year dodging their matchmaking attempts.

He placed his finger against his lips to signal for quiet as he smoothed his hair, which was sticking out at all angles in a way that was difficult not to find adorable. He disappeared through the dining room, and she could hear him sliding the dead bolt on the door. She went to the kitchen and pressed her ear to the door to eavesdrop.

"How'd you get in?" she heard him say.

"You gave me a key when I was building your pizza oven." It was Jake. Strange. She hoped he was okay. As they'd been discussing last night, this time of year was hard for him.

"Right," Benjamin said. "What can I do for you?"

"I know this is going to sound weird, but can you make me a pizza? Like, an uncooked one that I can finish at home?"

"Let's go downstairs," Benjamin said.

Why did Jake want a pizza at ten thirty in the morning on New Year's Eve? They had just been talking about how Jake didn't do New Year's.

The more immediate question, though, was, Should she try to make a getaway while they were downstairs? In the winter, Benjamin's pizza making moved into a small, conventional indoor oven in a tiny kitchen he had carved out of the back of the bar.

In the end she decided an escape attempt was too risky, so she went back to the living room to wait—and to ask herself what the hell had happened to her judgment. Why had she allowed herself to fall asleep here? Why had she come up here to begin with? Had she lost her mind? She and Benjamin argued. That was how they interacted. She was comfortable with that. She *wasn't* comfortable cozying up on the couch with him in his apartment. Well, she was comfortable in a literal sense, because the dude really did have the best couch, the nicest apartment. She had pared her own life so close to the bone that being in a warm, cozy, welcoming place like this was so soothing. But she was *existentially* uncomfortable.

Benjamin was only gone a few minutes. When she heard him come in, she gathered her stuff and met him in the kitchen.

"That was Jake," he said. "He wanted a pizza."

"I heard."

"And he wanted pineapple on it."

"That's Nora's topping." Curious.

"I know. But Nora's in Toronto, right?"

"As far as I know. They have been getting kind of chummy

lately, though, don't you think?" Maya had assumed it was platonic, as Nora, who had recently been dumped in spectacular fashion, had been adamant she was done with men for a long while.

"I do think." His brow knit. "Hmm."

Maya didn't have time to stand here gossiping about her friends. She had several decades left before she became one of those types. It was almost a new year, and she had a list of resolutions a mile long. She had a theater to save. "Thanks for . . ." She gestured back toward the living room.

"Anytime," he said.

"Really?"

He didn't answer, just opened the door. "Come on. I'll make sure the coast is clear."

It was, and as she was leaving, he said, "You coming in for New Year's Eve tonight?"

She usually did, but she wasn't in the mood this year. "So I can stand there and be the only one without someone to kiss at the end of the countdown? No thanks."

Something flared in his stupid green eyes. He was probably about to say something mean, so she turned to go before he could. As she made her way down the stairs, the most absurd image popped into her mind: kissing *him* at the stroke of midnight tonight. She shook the ridiculous idea out of her head. Her brain was on the fritz. She needed to get more sleep—at her own apartment.

Chapter Four

❦

Six months later

Law was accustomed to Maya staggering into his bar all bloody and dirty, but the tourists weren't.

You could use the approach of Maya as a catalogue of who in Lawson's Lager House was local and who wasn't. For example, the old folks sitting at a table near the front door merely waved as she passed, unmoved by the poufy, baby-blue formal gown she wore and by the dramatic trail of blood down its front.

But when she pulled out a stool at the bar next to a woman nursing a White Claw, the woman screamed bloody murder. "Oh my stars!" She shot off her stool. "What happened? Someone call 911!"

Law chuckled. If the woman's reaction to Maya hadn't given her away as an outsider, her American southern drawl would have.

Maya held up her hands like there was a gun and Miss I Have Bad Taste in Booze was holding it. "It's fake! It's a costume!"

"Oh my stars!" the woman said again, pressing a hand to her chest.

"Sorry to alarm you."

Law bent down to grab Maya's Riesling from a fridge under the bar, set a wineglass in front of her, and started pouring.

"We're in the middle of a run of a murder mystery play," Maya explained to the woman, "and I'm the victim. Also the director. Also the playwright."

The tourist was delighted. "I have to say, your dress reminds me of the formal I wore when I was crowned Miss Louisiana Teen USA in 1989."

"Louisiana!" Maya exclaimed. "You're far from home!"

"It's a long story."

Law could practically see the pleasure centers in Maya's brain firing. Maya loved stories, the longer and more riddled with twists and turns the better.

Someone farther down the bar hailed him, and after he'd served that customer and ambled back over, Maya was deep into telling the tourist about her current production.

"The show is called *Dancing in the Dark*—and it's set during a prom in 1985, so you were right on track with your Miss Louisiana Teen USA 1989 observation. It's about a girl named Heather who goes to the prom, and during the first song the lights go out. When they come back on..." She crossed her palms over her throat and made a melodramatic choking sound as she collapsed on the bar. But then she reversed course and popped back up, her wide smile at odds with her "murder." Law twisted his torso a little, trying to put himself into the line of that smile—he still had never seen one full-on—but he wasn't successful.

The tourist laughed, and when she spotted him, said, "May I have another White Claw, please?"

"I'm all out."

"No he's not." Maya snapped her fingers at him. *Snapped her fingers at him.* He enjoyed sparring with Maya, but it genuinely riled him when she did that. "Give the lady another White Claw."

Law tried not to be a booze snob, he really did, but White Claw was a bridge too far. Maya knew how he felt about the alcoholic seltzer. He'd decided to stock it because people kept asking for it, but White Claw did not belong on his menu next to the carefully sourced local craft beers and the cocktails he made from the best spirits he could get his hands on.

She glared at him. He knew how she felt about him being "snobby," which was pretty rich coming from her. He wasn't the one staging Greek tragedy, experimental theater, and "the classics, except gender swapped."

She leaned forward over the bar, closer to him, her stare unwavering. He bent down and rummaged in the fridge for another White Claw, but he held her gaze the whole time, as awkward as it was. Despite the fact that he could identify the White Claw by feel, he couldn't tell which flavor he'd retrieved.

"That's a lovely corsage you have there." The woman pointed to Maya's wrist.

Maya had to look away or risk coming off like a weirdo in front of her new friend. So she did, but she gave Law one of her little eye rolls as a parting gift. Quick, subtle, almost undetectable.

But detectable by him.

Ha! He smirked, triumphant, as he held up the canned abomination. "Thought you might want to try black cherry this time." He said it with the merest hint of snark in his tone, enough that Maya would hear it but the tourist wouldn't.

The woman made a happy noise, and Law cracked open the new can for her before turning his attention to Maya. She was extra bloody today, and she had a "wound" on her forehead—that hadn't been there last night.

It was interesting how she looked "bad"—she was a murder victim, after all—yet simultaneously amazing. It was confusing. But not any more confusing than being attracted to someone you didn't like, and he was accustomed to living with that contradiction. So he turned his attention to playing his role. "I don't understand why you don't change at the theater before you come in here and scare my customers. Or, hell, even just wash your face."

"You know there's no shower in the theater. Anyway, I wasn't at the theater. It was Murder at the Mermaid tonight." She pointed in the direction of the Mermaid Inn, the site of her annual murder mystery play.

"Yeah, but you live right across the street. Why don't you go home and change before you come here?"

She pressed her palms on the bar and leaned forward. "*Benjamin.* Has it ever occurred to you that maybe I come here dressed like this because I'm *trying* to scare your customers?"

That had actually *not* occurred to him. Even though their ongoing battle of wits raged as strongly as ever—they had experienced a détente of sorts last winter, but it had not lasted beyond the end of the soccer season—he didn't think they truly wished each other ill on the business front. Hell, he was passing his wholesale discount on wine along to her.

"Eve and Nora are meeting me in a bit," she said, "but I need to talk to you about the parking situation first."

"I thought we came to a compromise on the parking situation."

"We did. So why are there cars in my spots?"

"Murder mystery is at the Mermaid," he said. "There's nothing happening at the actual theater tonight." Which was why he'd gone out and covered her signs, as he always did on nights when there were no plays. As per the agreement they had finally come to a couple months ago. Which one would think was a case in point on not truly wishing each other's business ill.

"Those are my spots."

"In front of your empty theater."

"*Benjamin.* I told *Holden Hampshire* he could park there, and when he arrived, the spots were full. So he was late to the show, and he missed the big dramatic lights-out moment."

The lights-out moments of Maya's murder plays *were* pretty dramatic. The story would reach a fever pitch, and suddenly the whole place would go dark—which was when the "murder" happened. The audience always loved it, gasping in a mixture of fear and delight. "Who is Holden Hampshire?"

"Two Squared? *Babble Town*?"

"I have no idea what those words mean."

She sighed, like he was an ancient fuddy-duddy ignorant of the ways of the modern world. "Holden Hampshire is a Toronto-based actor who used to be in a boy band called Two Squared. They sang that song 'Petal Power,' you remember? It was supposed to be about flowers, but the video was them goofing around on tandem bikes? Get it? Flower petal, bike pedal? I'm sure you've seen it."

"Nope."

"He was the token Canadian in the band, so everyone was obsessed with him? Then he was on *Babble Town*? That talk show on MuchMusic? He would interview musicians? Anything ringing a bell here?"

"Still nope."

Cue the eye roll. "Probably due to your advanced age."

The six years between them probably *was* enough of a gap to explain differing teen pop culture touchstones. Or would have been if he'd ever been the kind of person who cared about boy bands.

"I know who Holden Hampshire is, and I'm much older than you are," Miss White Claw said to Law. She had been watching their conversation like she was a spectator at a Ping-Pong match.

"*Thank you*," Maya said to the woman before turning back to Law. "He's been sort of low-level famous since the band broke up," she went on, "but his star is rising as an actor. He had a small part in that submarine movie, *Submergence*. I heard from a friend of a friend in the Toronto film scene that he was looking to try some theater and he has an open summer, so I hunted down the contact info for his agent, and I'm trying to lure him out to star in *Much Ado about Nothing*."

She did that sometimes. Though her theater was mostly a community theater, which meant she cast actors from around the region, she sometimes brought in a big name from Toronto or the nearby

Stratford Festival to headline a show. But they'd never had a legit celebrity in town before.

"So the point is"—she leaned forward over the bar—"Holden Hampshire was going to come check out a show, and *I told him to park in one of the reserved spots*."

The tourist whistled. "Ooh, you're in trouble now!"

Well, crap. But he couldn't feel too bad about it on account of his *not being a mind reader*. "*Much Ado about Nothing*, though? I thought the summer play was always a musical. I thought you were doing *My Fair Lady*."

"I was, until my source told me that Holden was looking to try some Shakespeare. Apparently he wants to acquire some serious acting cred."

"A boy-band dude is going to star in a Shakespeare play?" It was hard to imagine.

"Well, I don't know, *Benjamin*. I wanted him to. I was intending to show him my directing prowess, but he *missed* the dramatic lights-out moment on account of the *parking situation*." She deflated a little.

Aww, crap. He pulled out her wine and topped up her drink.

Maya's friends arrived and pulled out stools. "Hey!" Eve said. "That went well!"

Nora climbed onto a stool with a little more difficulty than usual. She was pregnant and starting to show. It still blew his mind that Nora had managed to penetrate the fortress Jake had erected around himself.

"Did Holden leave already?" Nora asked.

"He sure did. I invited him for a drink, but he said he had to run and he'd call me." Maya took a gulp of her wine without acknowledging the top-up—not that she ever did. "Well, actually, he said he'd have 'his people' call me." Another gulp. "I don't know what I was thinking. He's way out of my league."

Law topped up her glass some more.

"Also, he missed the dramatic lights-out moment because he

had nowhere to park." Maya was talking to her friends but looking at him.

He ignored her. He didn't do glaring contests when they had an audience. He capped her wine bottle and stowed it in a fridge under the bar. "What can I get you ladies?"

As he was setting up Eve with a beer and Nora with a virgin mojito, Maya introduced them to the tourist.

"So what's this I hear about y'all throwing flowers in the lake?" Miss Louisiana Teen USA asked, leaning over to direct the question to all three women.

"It's a town tradition," Maya said. "When the moon is full, you throw a flower into the lake and make a wish, and legend has it your wish will come true."

"Does it work?"

"It kind of does," Eve said at the same time Maya said, "Not at all."

The women all cracked up. The tourist turned to Nora. "What do you think? It would seem you're the deciding vote."

Nora made an apologetic face at Maya. "I have to say I've had a lot of good luck since I moved here, but the scientist in me has to point out that correlation is not causation."

"Damn. I could use some good luck right about now."

"Let's go, then!" Maya said.

"Is there a full moon tonight, though?" the tourist asked.

Maya shrugged. "Close enough."

"You're always saying that!" Eve said. "Maybe that's why your wishes don't work."

Maya shook her head affectionately at Eve. "Well, you don't have to come." She turned to Nora. "You, either. You already have your perfect lives."

It was true. Jake and Nora were newlyweds with a baby on the way, and Eve and Sawyer were all loved up at the Mermaid Inn. Things had changed a lot around here. But there had been a hint of wistfulness in Maya's tone just then, which mystified Law. He hadn't thought she wanted any of that domestic stuff. She'd never had a boyfriend in all the time he'd known her, and while she was always swiping through Tinder while she sat at his bar, it never seemed to manifest any real-life men.

"Hang on." Nora threw her head back and chugged her drink. "I'm coming."

"Me, too," Eve said.

"But where will we get flowers this late at night?" the tourist asked.

"Don't you worry about that," Maya said. "I have an in with the town florist." She tilted her head and furrowed her brow—that was her thinking face. She pointed at Law. "Actually, you should sell wishing flowers here."

"What?"

"You could get a mini-fridge and set it on the bar so everyone can see it. My dad stays open late on actual full-moon nights to sell flowers, but you know how you sometimes see people chucking flowers in the lake on random dates? You're open late every night. I bet lots of drunk people would buy them." She chuckled, staring into space like she was seeing a scene that was invisible to the rest of them—she did that. "You could totally price gouge them. If I didn't have a key to my dad's shop, you'd have made four sales right now."

"That—" Was actually a really good idea. He couldn't quite make himself say it, though

And she didn't seem to be waiting for any sort of response— not that she ever did. She hopped off her stool and looked down at herself. "Should I change first?"

"Nah," Eve said. "I feel like you are totally rocking the murderous 1980s prom queen thing."

Maya and her friends—old and new—started gathering their things when Maya's phone chimed. "Hang on a sec." She picked it up, and after a beat she winced and hung her head.

When she looked back up, she was back to normal. Well, she

was back to being pissed, which was pretty much the same thing. She leaned over the bar, resuming the position she'd been in earlier when she'd been glaring at him.

He raised his eyebrows. She didn't speak. Just did her laser-death-beams stare thing. "What?" he said snappishly.

"Have you ever heard the term *patron of the arts*, Benjamin?"

"Yeah."

"Well." She leaned closer. "You're whatever the opposite of that is. What's the opposite of patron?"

"Antipatron of the arts?" Eve suggested cheerfully.

"No," Maya said.

"Enemy of the arts?" Nora said.

"No." Maya put both hands on the bar and leaned even closer, stopping about six inches from his face. "Destroyer. You, Benjamin, are a destroyer of the arts." She lifted her hands suddenly, like the bar was a hot stove, and started walking backward. "But don't worry. I will have my revenge."

It was a relief when Jake and Sawyer arrived a little later. Law had been watching for them. They had a tradition of hanging out at the bar on Friday nights, and he could use their advice this particular Friday.

He started pulling their preferred pints as they approached.

"Hey," Sawyer said. "The girls are down at the lake. We thought we'd join them." Law set a beer in front of him. "But I guess we're having a drink instead."

Law motioned for them to huddle in. The bar wasn't crowded, but you could never be too careful in this town. If Karl and Pearl and company got wind of his plans, they'd be all up in his face with recipes and contractors and oversight he did *not* need.

"I got approved for the business loan," he whispered.

"Whoa!" Sawyer said, and, realizing he was being too loud, he grimaced and lowered his voice. "That's great, man, congrats."

"Yeah, thanks."

"What's the matter?" Sawyer asked, probably picking up on the lack of enthusiasm in Law's tone. "This is good news, isn't it?"

"It is." It was. Everything was going according to plan. "I'm just...I guess it's sinking in that it's real now." He was going to have to tell people besides Sawyer and Jake. But you couldn't open a restaurant without telling people. So he didn't know why he felt so unsettled.

"You're not getting cold feet, are you?" Sawyer asked. "It's going to be great. You have a business plan and a loan—and great instincts for food and booze. The pizza here is a huge hit."

It was. The pizza was what had started this all. When Law had first started thinking about adding a limited menu to the taproom—which had been literally that, a taproom, in all the time his father and grandfather had run it—he'd done a ton of research and had decided to focus on one thing and to do it well. He'd settled on wood-fired Neapolitan-style pizza and built the oven out back. His father had been skeptical, but it had taken off dramatically, spreading through word of mouth and earning a spot in a recent *Globe and Mail* article on Ontario's hidden culinary gems. Hence all the random Miss Louisiana Teen USA 1989 tourists.

So after the pizza, he'd started noodling. Before he knew it, he was researching how to write a business plan and enrolling in an online college course. As he learned the business side of things, his idea started taking more concrete shape. A restaurant with a stream-lined menu. The pizza he was already known for, and a couple pastas. One featured meaty dish and one vegetarian, changing depending on what was in season. Farm-to-table, but without using the phrase *farm-to-table*, because that was obnoxious. He even had a name: Lawson's Lunch.

But..."Maybe I should just expand the food offerings at the bar. I could easily start serving sandwiches here," he said, aware that he was talking to himself as much as to his friends. He did sandwiches outside on a press during the town's festivals, and they were always popular. Adding sandwiches to the bar permanently would be a logical next step.

"Nah," said Sawyer. "We've been over this. You don't have the space to do sandwiches here unless you rip out a chunk of this beauty to expand the kitchen." He stroked the polished cherrywood bar that had been Law's grandpa's pride and joy. "And that would be a crime."

It was true. Aside from the fact that there was *no way* Law was hacking into this bar, there was only so much he could do incrementally here. He'd thought about doing a more dramatic reno. He didn't mind closing for a week or two, but for what he wanted to do, he'd have to shutter for a season. Lawson's Lager House was a community institution that had provided an unbroken line of service spanning three generations. Closed only one day a year— Christmas Day. This was where people had gathered on September 11. Hell, his grandfather had held a V-Day celebration at Lawson's Lager House. Law had been over this all. Why was he mentally rehashing it now?

"And you got the loan," Sawyer said. "Doesn't that mean the bank thinks the idea is solid?"

"I guess, though I'm not sure *I* would loan me money."

He'd been joking, but Jake scowled. "If you don't want to do the restaurant, don't do it. But don't sell yourself short like that, man."

Jake's calling him out was sobering. In addition to being the strong, silent type, Jake didn't have a high threshold for bullshit.

All right. Law huffed out a breath. Apparently he was doing this. "The next big thing is location. I'm going to ask Eiko about the newspaper building." His business plan had factored in the cost of renting and renovating the ground floor of one of the buildings on Main Street, and the *Moonflower Bay Monitor* building next door would be ideal. "She keeps talking about retiring, and even if the paper carries on beyond her, I don't think they need that much space anymore. I was thinking maybe I could get her to move the newsroom upstairs, and I could take over the main floor." The building had housed the town newspaper since the late nineteenth century, when it had been typeset and printed on-site. Today, Eiko *was* the newspaper, along with a part-time reporter, and the *Monitor* was designed digitally and printed off-site. "The pizza oven out back could do double duty."

"Oh no, no, no. Do *not* tell Eiko," Sawyer said. Jake conveyed the same sentiment by shaking his head vigorously. "Not if you want the plan to stay under wraps."

Law did want to keep things quiet as long as possible. Not that any of the old folks in town were going to be anything less than delighted with the new place, but they also wouldn't be able to resist sticking their noses in everything. He'd thought, though, that maybe there was a way to approach Eiko alone. "I was thinking about how Eiko's a journalist, right? Doesn't she have to follow a code of ethics about protecting sources?"

"Sources who are breaking news stories," Sawyer said. "Not 'sources' who want to open new restaurants in town. You tell her, and that's it: the whole town will know. Anyway, I think her journalistic ethics are probably more situational than fixed."

"Yeah, you're right." He'd been foolish to consider it. "I'll have to find someplace else. Anyway, I don't need the hassle of being next door to the theater." Maya already gave him enough trouble with a building between them as a buffer.

"What about that vacant place out on Oak Road?" Jake asked. "The old laundromat that went out?"

"In the strip mall with Sadie's?"

"Yeah."

"No way. Sadie's is fantastic. I don't want to compete that directly with her."

"Yeah, don't do that," Sawyer said. "You set up shop there, and before you know it you'll be in a rom-com directed by the old folks, and you and Sadie will have pancake wars, but then you'll end up married."

Jake snort-laughed, but that was exactly what Law had meant about the old folks getting up in everyone's business.

"Not that there's anything wrong with Sadie," Sawyer added. "You could do a hell of a lot worse."

"Except he's already at war with Maya," Jake said. "And really, how many wars that might end in marriage can one man have going at a time?"

"It's not a *war*." *War* implied a massive marshaling of resources, required a near obsession with one's enemy. "She's just always on my case about parking and the smoke from the oven and, you know, the fact that I exist in this world." But his bickering with Maya wasn't a *war*. It was more like... a hobby.

His friends looked at him like they were trying not to laugh.

"And even if it *was* a war," he went on, "which it's *not*, it would *never* be the kind of war that would end in marriage."

Sawyer smirked. "You know what they say."

"No, I do not know what they say. Please enlighten me."

"All's fair in love and war."

He wasn't in a damn war. But if he protested too much, they would interpret it as evidence in support of their take on things. So he went with evasive maneuvers. "I actually dated Sadie briefly."

"You *did*?" Sawyer's jaw literally dropped.

Law chuckled. Evasive technique: successful. "For less than a month, maybe twelve years ago. If you blinked, you missed it."

Law was a bit older than Jake and Sawyer, and though they'd always known each other, it had only been in passing until they'd gotten older and evolved into their Friday-night hangouts. Jake and Sawyer would have been teenagers during his brief flirtation with Sadie.

"Well, I'll be damned," Sawyer said. "What happened?"

"Nothing. We had some fun." He smiled, thinking back to that weekend in Toronto.

"How come you never told us?"

Law shrugged. "It was years ago. Nothing came of it."

"That's your answer every time you've hooked up with anyone in the time I've known you," Sawyer said.

"Oh, so since you two are all settled and besotted now, I have to be, too?" Law was happy for his buddies, he really was, but he sometimes missed the days when they were all contentedly single.

"No," Sawyer said. "I just wonder why nothing ever sticks. What happened to that woman who was here last summer?"

Sawyer was talking about a tourist who'd been in town for a month. She'd hung out at the bar a lot and eventually asked him to go on a hike. She'd been friendly and pretty and smart, so he'd made himself accept her invitation. They'd had some fun. But when she left pledging to keep in touch, he'd known he wouldn't keep up his end of the bargain.

Dating had always felt like a diversion to Law. A pleasant enough way to pass the time when presented with the opportunity, but not important enough to keep him from other stuff. And since he'd gotten going on restaurant planning, "other stuff" was expanding to fill all the time he had. He shrugged and answered Sawyer's question. "Nothing came of it."

"I rest my case," Sawyer said.

"I don't have time for women right now. I work here way more than full-time, and if all goes well, I'm about to open a second place. The only woman I care about at the moment is Shirley Kenner, who's supposed to be delivering a cord of firewood for the oven." He wanted to see if, hypothetically, he could double his order. If he wasn't getting the building next door for the restaurant, he'd need a second oven at the new site.

"I actually have an idea for you for a location," Jake said.

"Yeah?"

Jake looked around, his gaze settling on Carter. "Can you take off for a bit?"

"Sure." Law wiped his hands on a bar towel. "Give me five minutes."

* * *

"I gotta talk to you guys," Maya said after the girls had thrown their flowers into the lake—she had wished for a financial miracle—and said goodbye to their southern friend.

"Ooh, this sounds serious," Eve joked as they started walking back downtown.

"It is." Maya knew they weren't used to this from her—she was the fun-loving, lighthearted friend. But she'd decided she needed some moral support. She'd been carrying this burden around for the better part of a year, and she just couldn't do it on her own anymore.

"Okay." Eve dropped the joking tone. "You want to go back to the inn?"

"No, I don't want to risk anyone overhearing." Maya pointed to the gazebo in the town square. "Let's hide in there." But what was she afraid of? That her best friends would think she was a bad businesswoman? Maybe. Ha. It was just she *hated* coming off as weak.

"What's up?" Nora asked when they were all seated on the benches that lined the perimeter of the gazebo.

"I think I'm going to have to close the theater," Maya said, and promptly burst into tears, shocking herself as much as her friends.

They showered her with hugs and expressions of surprise and sympathy. When she calmed down, she told them the story of the money trap of a building and the grant she hadn't gotten. "It's like a perfect storm, basically. An imperfect storm."

"And I get the feeling the nonprofit arts sector is hard at the best of times," Nora said sympathetically.

"I guess, but honestly, when I started this, I had visions of scaling *up* by now. Of making the theater a regional destination. But not only am I still small potatoes, I can only make payroll through the end of September."

"Are you paying yourself?" Eve asked gently.

"No." She swallowed her shame even as she told herself there wasn't any reason to feel shame. "About ten months ago, when I found out about the grant, I cut my own living expenses as much as

I could and reduced my salary. But I haven't paid myself anything since May."

"So that's a month with no income," Nora said. "What are you doing for money?"

She brushed her tears away and cleared her throat. "I still have enough to operate through the end of September, but only if I don't pay myself, so my own living expenses for the past month have gone on credit cards. I'm trying to avoid having to lay off Marjorie and Richard."

Both women were silent for a moment. She supposed it *was* a lot to take in. She had hidden her struggle well.

"So you need a loan," Nora finally said, shifting into brisk efficiency mode.

"But do I? How would that do anything other than postpone the inevitable?"

"You need a loan and a *plan*," Nora amended.

"Right. And I had one. Holden Hampshire."

"Oh, now I get it!" Eve said. "I wondered why you were so fixated on him."

"He was my Hail Mary. I've been doing all this stuff around the edges to try to increase revenue: selling wine at intermission, delaying repairs, reusing costumes. But I thought if I could get a big name in for the summer, I could sell out the run—and do a longer run, and shamelessly jack up ticket prices. I was planning to do that and then use some of the resulting cash to *finally* fix all the problems with the building. If the building isn't sucking up all my money, and if the next round of granting goes better, then maybe I could get back on an even footing."

"Maybe you'll still hear from him?" Nora asked gently.

"I did hear from him." Maya got out her phone and showed them the text where he said he was going to take a pass on the play.

"Dammit," Eve said.

Maya stretched her neck, which ached all the time now. "What's the matter with me? I gambled too much on the idea of him. I'm doing *Much Ado about Nothing* because I heard he wanted to do some Shakespeare and I thought the character of Benedick would be perfect for him. And now I'm stuck with a Shakespeare play instead of a musical."

"You love Shakespeare, though," Eve pointed out. "You always grumble about the summer musical."

"That's true. And hey, if I'm going to flame out, I might as well have my last show be one I like." She performed a fake laugh.

"There's got to be something we can do," Nora said.

"I'm starting to think I should just call it," Maya said. "A Rose by Any Other Name is mine for the taking. My brother doesn't want it."

"No, no," Eve said quickly.

"I mean, I'm lucky. I've had this built-in safety net this whole time. All I have to do is . . . fall."

"Okay, no," said Nora. "That is *not* happening. We're not letting that happen."

Maya started crying again, this time because she was so relieved to have told her friends. She wasn't sure why she hadn't done it earlier. She didn't think it would change anything, not elementally, but it felt good to have the burden not be hers alone anymore.

"Give us a day or two to put our thinking caps on," Eve said, "then we'll get together and make a plan."

"Okay," Maya said weakly. They weren't going to be able to think of anything she hadn't already, but it wasn't like she needed to decide anything right now. "But you guys won't tell anyone, will you? Not even Sawyer and Jake?"

"Cross my heart," Eve said.

"Same," said Nora. "And I think right now, we should go get you some pizza."

"Yes!" Nora was always Maya's cover in her secret pizza operations.

"But I'm getting Hawaiian," Nora added. "And you can only have half."

Maya smiled through her tears. She loved the way her friends had taken in her news but weren't treating her any differently than normal. "Deal."

They went back to Lawson's and Nora ordered "her" pizza. Carter had arrived since they'd left and was manning the bar, so possibly Maya could have ordered her own. She'd also been tempted, from time to time, to go around back and try to bribe Shane Calloway to sell her one directly from the oven. But she never felt like she could risk it.

As they waited, though, Maya wondered if she'd pushed the whole I-hate-your-pizza thing too far. If she didn't have to eat it in secret, she could have it here. Finishing out the football season parked in front of the TV here had made her feel even more like Lawson's Lager House was her living room away from home. But there was no changing course now.

"Does it really matter if Law finds out you're eating his pizza?" Nora asked once they were back outside and had said goodbye to Eve.

"Are you kidding me? I didn't testify at the town council against the zoning variance for that stupid oven to turn around and eat the pizza from it." She dug in her pocket, extracted a ten-dollar bill, and extended it to Nora. She felt like she was doing a drug deal.

Nora ignored the money. "But you *are* eating it."

"I made a PowerPoint that showed demonstrable damage to my business from all that smoke." She dropped the cash in Nora's purse.

"But you're eating it," Nora said again.

"Secretly. I am eating it secretly. I have my pride." Maya looked around to make sure no one was watching, opened the box—her mouth watered at the smell of the pancetta—and ninja-ed the pizza in half.

"You want me to come up to your place to do the transfer?" Nora seemed like she was trying not to laugh.

"Nope." Maya folded her half of the pizza over on itself. It was so hot she had to sort of bounce it around like a game of hot potato in order to avoid burning her hands. Nora seized the moment to fish the ten-dollar bill out of her purse and shove it in Maya's jeans pocket. Maya, her hands full, couldn't do anything about it. So she darted across the street, juggling her secret pizza.

"So glad to see you still have your pride!" Nora called after her.

"Oh, shut up." But she made kissy-lips at Nora and watched her head down the street. She was on her way home to Paradise Cove, where her hunky silent husband would be waiting for her. Which was fine. It wasn't like Maya was jealous or anything.

She sighed. Okay, so she was a teeny bit jealous. She didn't want a husband and kids at this point, but being perpetually single was lonely sometimes.

But it was what it was. At least she had her pizza.

"This is a fantastic idea," Sawyer said as Jake unlocked the door to the little house at the far end of Main Street.

"What is this place?" Law asked as Jake flipped on the lights. Main Street in Moonflower Bay was mostly lined with nineteenth-century redbrick buildings ranging from one to three stories, but a little ways out of downtown proper were some old bungalows from the 1940s he supposed used to be actual homes for people. These days they had dentists and chiropractors and insurance brokers in them.

"This used to be Jason Sims's place," Jake said.

Right. The town lawyer used to live in the house and have his legal practice in the front. "You're working on Jason Sims's house?" Something had gone down regarding Jason Sims when Jake and Nora were getting together. Law didn't know what, but it was safe to say Jake was not the president of the Jason Sims fan club.

Jake snorted derisively, but Sawyer said, "Jason asked us if we were free to do some work here, and as far as I can tell, Jake decided that taking the job was the surest way to get the dude out of town."

"Out of town?"

"He built a new house on the lake outside Bayshore and is moving his practice," Jake said with a smirk, unable to hide his satisfaction at the idea of Jason Sims moving away. "Says they're more litigious than we are."

"So he's putting this place on the market." Sawyer gestured toward a wall of rickety-looking built-in shelving. "He hired us to rip out these crappy 1970s built-ins and do something new." Sawyer and Jake ran a carpentry business together, though Jake did most of the actual work since Sawyer was otherwise employed as the chief of police. "He's getting it ready to list, but I bet he'd do a private sale."

"I can't buy anything," Law said, even as he looked around. The place was a little worse for wear—some 1970s crimes against good taste had indeed been committed—but it had good bones. Original wood trim, a brick fireplace in the living room, hardwood floors.

"You could keep the separate rooms up front here," Sawyer said, sticking his head into a small den off the living room. "It would create little nooks."

"Buying is not in the budget," Law said, though this could really work with the spirit of what he was imagining. A place that seemed unassuming but then surprised you with its great food. "And look at the kitchen." He led the guys to the tiny kitchen at the rear of the place. "It's too small to do restaurant-scale stuff." So, there, this place was a no-go.

"There's room to push out into the yard." Sawyer opened the sliding glass door from the dining room, and they all peered out into an overgrown but sizable yard.

Jake nodded his agreement. "We can push the existing kitchen into the yard. Then we get rid of this wall"—he crossed back to the dining room and patted a wall that looked pretty load-bearing to Law, but he trusted his friends—"and that will open up this space into the hallway. You could open the bedrooms, too, or keep them as separate rooms. I like Sawyer's idea of dining nooks."

They weren't listening to him. "I can't buy a place," he said again.

"Why not?" Sawyer asked. "You buy a place, you own it outright eventually. Isn't that better than paying rent forever?"

"I can't buy a place without getting a loan against the bar, and then I won't own the bar outright anymore."

"So?" Sawyer said.

"I've got the biggest personal loan I qualify for, and that to-gether with my savings is enough to float a reno of an existing commercial space and four months of the restaurant's operations," he said, reciting the gist of his business plan—which he was aware didn't answer Sawyer's question. "And my father..." He paused, not knowing how to explain his dilemma.

"But your dad passed the bar on to you, right?" Sawyer said. "He doesn't have a stake in it anymore."

"Right, but this isn't about him." Well, it was, in a way. It was about his dad and his grandfather. It was about the family legacy the bar represented. Law might own the bar, but he didn't own that legacy. He merely stewarded it. Hell, his dad jokingly referred to the bar as his second child. His parents had just about killed themselves keeping it open in the economic downturn of the 1990s. He remembered the day he and his mom had come down before opening to find his dad sitting at the bar *crying*. Dad hadn't heard them come in, and Mom had looked at Law with such sadness in her eyes, laid a finger against her lips to signal quiet, and led him back up to their apartment. Law had been too young to understand the wider economic context at that point, but he'd understood stress. He'd understood pain.

So he wasn't going to risk Lawson's Lager House on what was, ultimately, a whim. He had a sound business plan, and he believed in his idea, but restaurants failed all the time for lots of reasons. "I just can't have a mortgage."

"I don't understand what the problem is," Sawyer said. "Normal people have mortgages. It's not unusual."

"You don't," Law pointed out. "Eve doesn't." Eve had inherited the Mermaid Inn from her great-aunt, and Sawyer had sold his house in town when he'd moved into the inn.

"Yeah, but Sawyer's not normal," Jake pointed out, and Law had to laugh at that, not least because Jake so rarely made jokes.

"Your cottage is paid for!" Sawyer protested.

"Yeah," Jake said, "but we have payments on the loan we took out to buy Nora's practice, and the building itself has a mortgage on it." Nora had bought the medical practice from the previous town doctor, and the pair of them had recently decided to purchase the building that housed it, too. "The two are rolled into one pretty hefty payment."

"See?" Sawyer said. "Not that I'd ever call Jake normal, but you get the point." He turned to Law. "So what's the problem?"

"The newspaper building is a blank box. Once you get the desks out, it would be easy to drop in restaurant infrastructure. That's what I planned on. Reno and rent."

"This place would actually be a pretty easy reno," Jake said, looking around.

"Too bad you don't know any contractors who can fit you in," Sawyer said.

"You guys aren't contractors." They made it a point to limit their business to fine carpentry—custom shelves and furniture and canoes.

Sawyer shrugged. "I did the inn with Eve. And Jake did all that work on Nora's old house."

"Yeah, and you ended up married to those girls." Law snorted. "I somehow think they were the exception." He took their point, though. They were more than capable. But of course that wasn't what was holding him back.

"Sawyer's not married yet," Jake said drily. "So he could still throw Eve over and marry you, if that's what you want."

Sawyer rolled his eyes. "I told you, Eve and I are taking an if-it-ain't-broke-don't-fix-it attitude toward the whole marriage-and-kids thing right now."

"Yeah, not everyone is as much of an overachiever on that front as you, dude," Law said to Jake, whose romance with Nora and subsequent "shotgun marriage"—that was Nora's joking phrase—had been conducted with whirlwind speed.

"The point is," Sawyer said, "we'll help you if you want us to. With this place or any other. Just say the word."

Jake grunted in assent, and a rush of gratitude filled Law's chest. Sawyer's sister Clara was always teasing the three of them about having a "three-way bromance," but it was kind of true. He wasn't really sure how it had happened, but somehow, over the years, these two guys had become family. He would do anything for them.

So he wasn't sure why he was so surprised the sentiment ran in the other direction, too. He also wasn't sure why he was afraid to tell them the truth. It made him sound like a sentimental dork, but so what? He had been through a lot with these guys. They might give him shit, but they weren't *actually* going to judge him. He blew out a breath. "So here's the thing. I have this block about mortgaging the bar. My grandfather opened it in 1943. It's been through wars, recessions, you name it. My parents almost had to close it in the nineties. I grew up there. I just can't risk it. I *won't* risk it."

"Ah," Sawyer said.

"You think I'm being stupid." Maybe he was. Jason's house was pretty damn ideal.

"Not stupid," Jake said. "Realistic about your limits."

"We'll figure something else out," Sawyer said.

"Thanks." Law had to clear his throat. "I should get back. I don't like leaving Carter alone for too long."

As they walked back down Main, Law thought about how he had never actually left Carter alone in the building. There were times Carter worked the bar on his own, but Law was always upstairs. He had never come to trust Carter the way he had Amber. "I need to hire some people—for both places."

"You sure do," Sawyer agreed. "It's funny. When you think of the stereotype of a workaholic, it's usually an office type. Not a bar owner."

"I'm not a workaholic. I live upstairs, so it just seems like I'm there a lot." Law wasn't sure why he was disputing Sawyer's take. He would never ask anyone else to work as much as he did. But it wasn't really workaholism so much as a question of what else he was going to do. He wasn't handy like these guys, so no canoe making on the side for him. He didn't really follow any sports. Well...almost none.

"I'm not saying there's anything wrong with it," Sawyer said. "Just noting that you work a lot. And if you're going to be splitting your time between two places, you're going to have to be smart about it."

"I know. And not only will I need servers for the restaurant, I'll need a chef. That's not something just anyone can do." Law had all this factored into his plan, but like the loan, it was an example of the restaurant starting to feel unnervingly real.

"This is it for me," Sawyer said as they approached the Mermaid Inn. He was smiling at his phone, no doubt reading a text from Eve.

"It's not even eleven," Law said. Historically the three of them had spent Friday nights at the bar—Jake and Sawyer sitting at it and Law working behind it. They still observed the Friday-night tradition, but the other two were ducking out earlier these days.

"The girls are done at the lake." Sawyer glanced at Jake. "Nora said to tell you she went home."

One corner of Jake's mouth turned up, which for him was the equivalent of a swoon. "I'm out, then, too."

All right, so his friends were getting all domestic. It was what it was. The nice thing about being a "workaholic" was he had work to do.

Speaking of employees, when Law got back to the bar, Carter waved at him from across the room. "Hey."

The jukebox started playing the Spice Girls, startling Law. He thought Maya had left. He surveyed the room. She wasn't at her usual spot at the bar. She wasn't at the jukebox. A couple of thirty-something women he didn't know were bopping around next to it. Okay, false alarm.

Maya was always saying she wasn't the only person in town who liked the Spice Girls. He hated it when there was evidence that she was right. But he also sort of loved it. He smiled despite himself.

"What's up?" he said to Carter when he reached the bar.

"It's quieting down. Mind if I take off early?"

He started to agree but thought better of it. Carter was scheduled to close. This would be good practice for the new regime, when Law wouldn't be around to pick up the slack all the time. "Sorry, man. I have some stuff I have to do upstairs."

Carter looked surprised but didn't object. Law actually did have a lot to do. He was behind on ordering. And he needed to think about that hiring. He'd always relied on word of mouth, or placed ads in the *Moonflower Bay Monitor*, but maybe this time he should take a more methodical approach. What did that mean? LinkedIn?

He didn't turn on the lights as he walked through his apartment to his living room, moved the curtain aside, and looked out.

It was a habit that had begun when she'd come home from college five years ago and moved into an apartment across the street. He wasn't sure why he continued to do it.

Maya's light was on.

She never left her curtains open at night, so it wasn't like he could see in. It wasn't like he *wanted* to see in.

He just...wanted to know that she was there.

Chapter Five

❧

A few days later, Maya came in and plunked herself down at the bar. When Law set a wineglass in front of her, she shocked him by looking around furtively and whispering, "Truce?"

He wasn't prepared for a truce. The last time he'd seen her, she'd left literally vowing revenge, aka the opposite of a truce.

After that night last December, she had taken to watching matches in the bar. But they had also developed a habit whereby, every once in a while, when there was an extra-important match, she would discreetly whisper, "Truce?" He would agree, and they would meet back at the bar later and sneak up to his apartment to watch.

They hadn't done it a lot—seven times, to be exact. And curiously, it hadn't changed anything about their relationship outside of their truces.

But the Premier League season had ended in May, and with it their détente. And the next season didn't start until August. So he had no idea what she was doing now. He studied her. On the surface of things, she looked the same as ever. Well, it was Monday—no theater on Mondays—so she didn't look like an overdressed murder victim circa 1985, but her hair was piled on top of her head like it always was when she wasn't playing a character. She was wearing a green T-shirt with Shakespeare's face on it that said "Will Power." She was probably wearing her green Converse high-tops to match. He leaned forward to peek over the bar. Yep.

Everything was normal, was the point.

Except maybe her eyes were a little less bright than usual. Her eyes were usually glinting with . . . something. Her latest entrepreneurial impulse, general mischief, bloody revenge, whatever.

Today, though, they seemed less sparkly.

He hadn't responded to her inquiry about a truce. He nodded and pulled out her bottle of wine. He had no idea what they would watch. He didn't even know if the app archived matches once the season was over.

But a person didn't question a truce. That was the whole *point* of a truce. You suspended hostilities and truced.

She put her hand out to stop him from pouring her wine. "I can't. I have to be somewhere." She slid off her stool. "You closing tonight?"

She was asking what time the truce would commence. "Nope," he lied. Since she didn't have a show tonight, she didn't have to be up late, and it was usually two thirty before he made it upstairs after he closed. This would be some more practice for Carter.

And for him. He had to get used to letting other people take more responsibility at the bar.

"Off at nine," he said.

Maya should have had the wine at the bar. As she trudged up the path to her parents' house, she could have used the liquid courage.

But as much as she enjoyed sipping wine at Lawson's Lager House, alcohol wasn't going to solve her problems.

Money was going to solve her problems. She had talked to her friends some more, and they'd come up with a plan and a budget to tackle all the repairs needed at the theater. And given that, she'd let herself be talked into going after a loan.

She just wasn't going to get it from TD Bank. Or RBC. Or Scotiabank. All three—RBC just today—had turned her down for a small-business loan. Not that that was much of a surprise. On paper, the extremely not-for-profit Moonflower Bay Theater Company probably wasn't the greatest bet. But if they would come see a play, understand the potential. Experience it.

Which she'd asked the bank officers—fine, young, tie-wearing men all—to do.

"That's not really how we parse loan applications," the TD guy had said. And from Mr. Scotiabank: "I'm more of a TV person. Did you watch *Game of Thrones*? Epic. *Epic.*" RBC had merely said no thanks. She'd been like, *Really? That's it? Just "no"?*

The aroma of charcoal suggested her dad was out back grilling, so she let herself in the side gate and plastered a smile on her face. "Hi! What are you grilling? I thought we were doing takeout?" Not that she cared. She'd be happy with anything. Her own budget-constrained diet of late had been heavy on packaged ramen noodles, which Jenna had had on sale for fifty cents apiece recently. And since Maya's car was currently dead behind her building, making runs to a proper grocery store impossible, she'd stocked up.

"Hi," her dad said. "Your mom is bringing some takeout home, but I bought some fish from Jake Ramsey today. We thought we'd do a bit of a smorgasbord—eat the fish while it's fresh."

Jake, who was all but retired as a commercial fisherman, still went out occasionally and sold to the townspeople directly from the pier at the little beach. "You want to thread those onto skewers for me?" Her dad nodded toward a Ziploc in which chunks of fish were marinating in a mixture of yogurt and spices.

Her mother came through the gate, dressed in her work clothes. She was a nuclear engineer. Everyone's stereotype of a nuclear engineer was a dude in a hard hat and a hazmat suit, but her mom wore standard Hillary Clinton–style pantsuits to work. "Hi! Happy

Monday!" Maya usually had dinner with her parents on Mondays. Even if she was in the middle of a run of shows, Mondays were always free.

Her dad aimed a great big moony smile at her mom. Maya's parents had met as kids in Brampton when they were paired as science partners in eighth grade. "Only time I ever got an A in science," her artistically inclined dad always said. They had bonded over the sometimes stressful pressure of being kids of immigrants who had done their growing up—they had both arrived as toddlers—in suburban Canada. "You should have seen how mad I made Nani when I brought home a paisley minidress and announced I was going to wear it to prom," her mom would say. And Dad would grin and say, "Oh, but you should have seen the dress."

Dad had followed Mom across the country as she did university, grad school, and a postdoc and finally to Moonflower Bay, when she got a job at a power plant a ways up the lake.

It was gross. It was cute. Maya was jealous.

She was jealous of her *parents*. She was pathetic.

Her mom set a bag on the table on the deck. "I'll go inside and get dishes and drinks."

"You sit," Maya said. "Take a load off, and I'll get everything. I'm going to throw in a load of laundry anyway."

"Machine broken in your building again?" her dad asked.

"Yep."

Nope. But two bucks could buy a load of laundry or four packages of Jenna's sale ramen. Or one-third of a glass of Riesling at Lawson's.

Maya entered the kitchen through the back door, its cheerful, familiar yellow walls and cozy breakfast nook bringing her back to happy days. She and her brother used to let themselves in this door, once they were deemed old enough to come directly home from school rather than kill time at the store waiting for their mom to swing by on her way home from work. That table was where

Maya would set up with her homework or, later, with scripts to memorize.

She'd always imagined having a house like this someday. A smaller one, maybe, but in this neighborhood near the lake. Maybe eventually with a boyfriend as part of the package. On paper, it had sounded like a doable dream.

In reality, her friends were pairing off, she lived in a decaying apartment, and she wasn't going to be able to make the payments on her commercial mortgage beyond September. So yeah, she could sort of see why the fine young men of the Canadian banking sector were not falling over themselves to lend her money. Hopefully, the Bank of Mom and Dad had lower standards.

Her stomach did a little flip. Hooboy, was she nervous, even though she was pretty sure her parents would give her the money. Her parents were always in the front row at her plays, her dad in particular clapping louder than anyone. It was just more of that icky feeling of having to admit that she'd failed. She should have thought more about her approach tonight. Maybe she should have drawn up some papers? Shown that she had a specific plan for the money? Which she did—she had a list of repairs as long as her arm.

"You coming out?" Her mom popped her head in through the back door. "Everything okay?"

"Yes, yes! Just daydreaming."

She jogged down the stairs to the basement to empty her duffel bag into the washer and back up to grab dishes and utensils. Her stomach lurched as she went back outside. Having to ask her parents for money made her feel young. And not in a good way. It made her feel small. Five years ago, when she arrived home with a head full of plays and a heart full of hope and they'd offered her a chunk of cash, it had been different. She'd been so confident, so sure she would make it. This time, she was asking out of desperation.

Well. She should just come out with it. Or, no. Maybe she should wait until they'd started eating, because that way—

"We have news," her dad said.

Oh. Okay.

"We have to get Rohan on FaceTime first," her mom said to her dad.

"What's going on?" Maya asked, suddenly concerned. She talked to her brother, and her parents talked to her brother—she assumed—but they never had group confabs.

"Hang on and we'll tell you." Her mom poked at her phone.

"Oh my God, is someone sick? Is someone dying?" Here she was prepared to hit them up for money, and something was wrong. She ran through the mental list of their relatives in Brampton and Toronto and Vancouver. Last she'd heard, everyone was okay.

"Hey, what's up?" Her brother's face appeared on the small screen. He was all sweaty, and he had a towel around his neck.

"Are you at the *gym*?" Maya asked, temporarily distracted from the impending demise of her family.

"You say that like you're asking if I'm at a crack house."

"It's a gorgeous summer evening. You live on Lake Michigan. You should be outside doing your Rambo moves." Her brother was one of those CrossFit cultists, always leaping over things or randomly jumping up on park benches. Because it wasn't enough that he was rich and successful and lived in a glamorous high-rise condo in the Loop, he had to be ripped, too.

"It's AMRAP night at my box."

"I have no idea what those words mean." Heh. Benjamin had said that very sentence to her a few days ago when she'd been talking about Holden Hampshire.

"Children of my heart," her mother said. "Shut up."

Right. Someone was dying. "What's wrong?"

"Yeah, what's happening?" Rohan asked. "I admit I got a little nervous when you said you wanted to schedule a FaceTime for all of us."

Crap. If her devil-may-care brother was worried, someone was definitely dying.

"Well, let's just come out with it so we can get on with dinner," her mom said, turning to her dad.

Maya braced her hands on the table.

"We're going to retire," her dad said.

"Okay?" her brother said warily.

"I'm a little surprised," Maya said, understating it entirely. Her parents were in their early fifties. She turned to her dad. "What about the store?"

"I'm going to sell it."

"*What?*" Rohan said, the shock in his voice echoing Maya's feeling on the matter.

"Neither of you want it," her dad said. He looked between them. "You don't want it, do you?"

"No?" Maya said, aware that her answer came out sounding more like a question. She didn't want it, but the sudden prospect of the store being gone underscored just how much the idea of it as her backup plan was entrenched in her consciousness. The store had always been there. Had felt like it always *would* be.

"Let's back up a bit," her mom said. "We know this sounds out of the blue, but there's some logic here. Last winter, at a routine physical, your dad was diagnosed with type 2 diabetes and high blood pressure."

Oh my God.

"Thank God Nora Walsh came to town," her mom added. "I've been after him to get a checkup for years."

"It's not as bad as it sounds," her dad said quickly. "We made a plan, and it's working."

"Why didn't Nora *tell* me about this?" Maya exclaimed, but of course the answer was doctor–patient confidentiality.

"Yes, no need to worry about your dad," her mom said. "He's taking his meds and we're working on lifestyle changes, but for that we need time. Time for long walks and workouts at the community center. The point is, the health scare has made us reevaluate things. We've both worked so hard for so long—especially your dad."

It was true. Her dad staffed the store all the hours it was open, except on the weekends, when her mom rotated in, either to relieve him or to keep him company.

"We want to travel while we still can, too," her dad said. "Other than the handful of times I've been to India, I've never been outside of Canada."

This was also true. Maya's mom traveled for work sometimes, to conferences in the US mostly. And she took Maya's grandmother to visit relatives in India every other year—which struck Maya as kind of funny, because in Mom's stories about her youth, she always painted a picture of herself in constant rebellion against her parents. But because of the store, her dad rarely traveled.

"We ran the numbers," her dad said, "and while we're not going to be living in luxury, we can swing it. We just feel like we've worked hard and saved money, and now it's time for that investment to pay off." He smiled at Maya's mom. "Mostly, I just want to hang out with your mother."

Again: so gross. So cute.

"So that's it!" said her mom. "Sorry for the drama. It's all good, though."

"So you're really going to sell the shop," Rohan said.

"Yes," her dad said. "I've had a commercial agent in. She's going to give me her thoughts next week. The goal is to get it on the market in the fall, and your mom is going to retire at the end of the calendar year."

Well then. So much for Maya's safety net.

And so much for her loan. There was no way she was asking them for money now.

"So, change of subject," Rohan said weakly. He seemed thrown for a loop by this news, not that Maya could blame him. "Maya, can you send me the dates for your summer play?"

"Sure," she said. "But you don't have to come."

Her brother, like her parents, was a big supporter of the theater. He drove up from Chicago for every show. She always told him he didn't have to, but she secretly loved all the big-brother boosterism.

"No, I'm going to come. But I'm going to run the North Country Trail marathon in western Michigan—it's this trail run in a national forest there—so I gotta get organized with dates. I'm going to do a loop—hit Moonflower Bay before or after the race, depending on what the play dates are."

"You run marathons now?" Jeez. How was she related to this guy? And "trail" marathons? She didn't even know what those were, but they sounded a lot harder than, say, pavement marathons.

"Yeah. Kara got me into long-distance running." Kara was his latest girlfriend. "You remember how my event in track was always the long jump? But then I'd also run the eight-hundred-meter and Ben Lawson would kick my butt?"

"Not really," Maya lied, picturing teenage Benjamin all sweaty and panting in his little running outfit.

"Well, I could run circles around him now."

"Anyway," Maya said, changing the subject, "I'm excited to meet Kara."

"Oh, Kara's not coming home with me," Rohan said. "I'm not sure we're at the meet-the-family point yet."

"So, what? You're just going to leave her in the forest?" It boggled Maya's mind how her nice, sweet brother who made it a point to come to all her shows had turned into such a player when it came to his own dating life.

"Just send me the dates, and I'll let you know when I'm coming, okay?"

"Yeah, yeah."

After they hung up, they tucked into dinner. Maya noticed that her dad served himself only his grilled fish and rice, leaving the Chinese food for her and her mom—this must be the lifestyle changes in action. "In a way, it's too bad that you're doing such a great job with the theater," he said. "You have such a head for business."

"I do?" If he only knew.

"It was your idea for us to stay open until midnight on full-moon nights, and honestly, I'd never have believed the amount of traffic we'd get. And oh, I forgot to tell you—Ben Lawson stopped in the other day and told me about your idea to sell flowers in the bar."

"He *did*?"

"'She has such a head for business,' I told him, and he agreed. That says a lot. He's done a lot with that bar since he took over from his dad."

She stifled a sigh. She just wanted to be at Benjamin's apartment already. Which was a weird thing to think. It was weird all around, her asking for an off-season truce. But she'd been so nervous about today. The idea of kicking back on his big fluffy couch and watching some of her beloved Crystal Palace had felt like a sanctuary, a soothing, end-of-day respite.

Of course, if there were a way for her to watch her beloved Crystal Palace on Benjamin's big, cushy couch without Benjamin himself being involved, that would be even better. But as the universe had so recently and decidedly shown her, a girl could not always get what she wanted.

"Have a fortune cookie," her mom said, handing her the plastic takeout bag. "Take the rest home. Lisa Kim always gives me a bunch of them because she knows you like them so much."

Maya did like fortune cookies. Or she had when she was a kid. Back when the future had seemed limitless and she'd still believed in the power of wishes.

She broke open the cookie and pulled out the little strip of paper. YOUR HARD WORK IS ABOUT TO PAY OFF.

Yeah, right.

Chapter Six

❧

The knock on his door came too early.

Law had left the bar at seven thirty and, not expecting Maya until nine, was sitting on his couch watching *Much Ado about Nothing* while he paged through the loan paperwork for Lawson's Lunch and tried to get Jason Sims's house out of his mind.

He jumped about a foot when her knock came. He started toward the door, but no. He was watching a movie version of Maya's upcoming play, and he had to turn the TV off before he let her in. *Shit.*

The remote had disappeared somewhere in the couch, so he jogged to the TV and started feeling around for actual, physical buttons. TVs still had those, right?

She kept knocking.

"Hold your horses!" His fingers slid over a patch of the casing that was differently textured from the rest, and he pressed frantically, like he was trying to defuse a bomb.

Success! He raised his arms like he was some kind of tent

preacher at a revival. But then he got control of himself and went
to answer the door.

She handed him a bottle of sparkling water. "This is a fake
hospitality gesture since I sort of sprang this on you. I hope you
have some of my Riesling."

He did. "Her" Riesling was a limited edition from a Niagara
winery. He'd had it on the menu at the bar briefly three years ago.
When Maya had gone bananas over it, he'd pulled it from the list
and served it only to her because he only had a case of it left.
He'd gone on to order as much more as was out there, and the next
year the vineyard had produced a remarkably similar vintage, but a
smaller one. He would eventually run out, so he was rationing it.

He waved away the "fake hospitality" water and turned for the
kitchen, where he pulled the wine from the fridge. As he poured,
he studied her face. She still looked...not sparkly. He kind of
wanted to know what was wrong, but the thing about truces was
that they didn't involve talking. There might be some logistical
discussion regarding the menus in the app. But that was it. After
that, they watched in silence. It was an interesting contrast to their
usual, public mode of constant bickering. All in all, they probably
spoke less than a hundred words to each other during truces. Maya
might talk to the TV, of course, to her beloved Crystal Palace, but
to him? No.

He carried a couple glasses of wine over to the coffee table,
realizing that when he turned the TV on, *Much Ado about Nothing*
would still be on. "Do me a favor and grab me a glass of that
sparkling water while I futz with this? My Apple TV has been
acting up."

Miraculously, she got up and went to the kitchen. He found the
remote and did some speedy ninja moves to dispose of the *Much
Ado about Nothing* evidence.

By the time she was back—she'd gotten the water, but she set the
glass down on the coffee table with a much louder thump than was
necessary, as if it pained her to wait on him—he had their menu up.

"We can watch old matches or highlights reels." He scrolled back. "What's your pleasure?"

"Whatever," she said in a monotone. "You pick."

This was the part where if they were friends—or if he were the bartender and she were a generic customer—he would ask what was wrong. But neither of those things was the case, so he selected a match. "Versus Man United last March. That was a good one." Manchester United was one of the only Premier League clubs he'd heard of before Maya and her Crystal Palace obsession came into his life. They'd been favored in this match, but in the end Crystal Palace had eked out a win. Maybe revisiting it would help with whatever stick Maya had up her butt. "Okay?"

"Sure," she said with that same unnerving flatness.

He cued it up and sat next to her on the sofa, but as always, he left a couple feet between them.

She heaved a huge sigh as it started, which wasn't unusual, but normally it would be a happier sigh. Like she'd had a long day, was unwinding from a show, and was settling in to watch her team. This was more resigned sounding. Defeated, even? And here he'd begun to think, by the end of last season, that she considered his apartment a haven of sorts. Clearly he was delusional.

She was jumpy, too, which also wasn't normal. It wasn't that she couldn't be excitable. God help you if Maya had an idea and you stood in the path of it. The woman had willed her theater company into being. But excitable wasn't the same as jumpy. Normally she had good control of herself—he supposed that was the acting training—which was why it was so satisfying to watch her lose it when she got mad at him. He had seen her leading the theater camp kids she taught in the summer in meditation outside on the town green, and he swore she hadn't so much as twitched an eyelid for ten minutes.

But now her knee was bouncing up and down like she was on speed. His first impulse was to put his hand on it. To use the weight of his body to steady hers.

But that wasn't right.

So instead he pointed to the bouncing knee and said, "A little hyper, are we?"

"Oh, shut up." She kept jiggling, probably just to irritate him.

Law was an only child. He sometimes wondered if sitting watching soccer in silence with Maya while they suspended their hostilities was what having a sibling would be like. A little sister. Two people who annoyed each other but were frequently in proximity and had learned to make the best of it.

She took out the hair thing that had been holding up her topknot. She did that when she was here. He tried not to stare, but seeing her with her hair down was so novel. He was always amazed at how such a seemingly sturdy construction was held in place by a single ring of elastic. She ran her fingers through her hair and massaged her neck, like it hurt, and let her head fall back against the sofa. Her dark hair fanned out against the pale-blue upholstery and looked like a waterfall with the colors reversed, raven water against blue rock.

Yeah, this was not the way he would think about his sister.

But whatever. He was overanalyzing this.

She stopped jiggling, and he stopped comparing her hair to the wonders of nature. They settled into silence, the default mode for truces.

He could tell when she fell asleep, about an hour later. She'd left her head lolled back on the sofa while she watched, as if it were too heavy to keep holding up, but she'd angled it sideways so she could see the TV. Nothing about her body position changed as she fell asleep, but her breathing became audible and gradually slowed.

He took the opportunity to study her face. He'd thought of it, earlier, as "less sparkly" than usual, but he could see now, now that he had at-peace mode for contrast, that she'd been unsettled before, deeply unsettled.

Should he let her sleep? She was obviously stressed about something.

No. He was getting soft. The match was over, so there was no reason for her to stick around.

He reached his hand out, intending to … What? Intending to what? If they rarely spoke during truces, they never touched.

Forget truces, they never touched at all. They came close sometimes, usually when she was leaning forward at the bar and getting in his face about something. But it never actually happened. Not even the incidental contact he had with other customers. He always set Maya's glass on the bar before pouring wine into it, and she always left cash for her bill lying on the bar.

The only times he ever touched Maya were when they accidentally fell asleep in front of soccer. It didn't happen often, but occasionally, if they were having a truce in the wee hours, after bar closing, the soft couch and the lulling, white-noise effect of the TV would conk them out. When that happened, sometimes he'd wake up with her head on his shoulder, or her legs on his lap. In that case, shifting out from under her was enough to wake her. Or *he'd* awaken to *her* violently shoving him into consciousness.

So all right, maybe it was okay to touch her gently to wake her. There was precedent. It was kinder than her shoving method, anyway. Although "kind" wasn't usually an approach he felt the need to employ when it came to Maya, people were defenseless when they were asleep. Sparring with Maya would be jerky if she weren't so capable of dishing it back to him.

Okay, then. He was going to do it. His first premeditated touch.

But how? A hand on the cheek?

No. That was weird.

Her hair. He could sort of stroke her head. His hand floated out like it had its own agenda, but he put the brakes on. No. No stroking. *Pat* her head? He wouldn't mind touching her hair, actually. It was so rarely down. Other than in her mermaid queen persona, he'd never seen it down except here in his apartment. It was probably soft. But if he patted, as opposed to stroked, would he even be able to tell it was soft?

What was *wrong* with him? He wasn't going to *stroke* her hair. *God.*

She shifted in her sleep, and he caught a whiff of something woodsy. He leaned over her. She smelled like cedar but also like...sugar?

No. He sniffed again. Vanilla? Whatever it was, it was a more subtle note than the wood. This was harder than the wine-tasting courses he'd taken when he'd started to get serious about the wine list at the bar.

Her eyes slipped open. Shit. Busted. His hand with a mind of its own was still floating a few inches from her head, and his face was right in there, too. He braced himself for the flaying that was coming, but she surprised him by smiling. He had often watched her smile at other people and thought about how he'd never gotten one of his own. But here it was. It was different from the smile she gave other people, though, the one he'd thought he wanted. Those smiles were big and blinding. This was soft. Warm and sleepy. *Sexy.* Like waking up next to him was something she did on the regular—like being *happy* to wake up next to him was something she did on the regular.

He was frozen. He ordered himself to retract his ridiculous floating hand, at least, and just as he was about to, she tilted her head so it nestled in his palm, like a cat in search of a caress. Her hair *was* soft. It was—

Oh shit. She was kissing him. *She was kissing him.*

Well, sort of. It was more like she was touching her lips against his. There was barely any pressure at all, but it was such a goddamn jolt. It felt like his entire body had been plunged into the lake with no warning. It was—

Over.

"Oh my God!" She lurched away from him, doing a sort of roll under his still-hovering palm. "I...I thought you were someone else!"

She'd thought he was someone else? She definitely had a

Tinder-swiping habit, but damn, if she was actually hooking up with someone, she was being masterfully secretive about it. Who else was she waking up with? Who else was getting those intimate, sexy smiles?

But maybe the more relevant question was, What was he supposed to do now? How to explain why he'd been hovering over her like a creeper? *Hi, I was about to wake you up and I got distracted smelling you*?

Her phone rang, startling them both. Saved by the bell.

She frowned at it before answering. He wondered who was calling her at eleven on a weeknight. But he wondered from afar—he took himself and his nose and his sentient hand as far away as possible, getting up and taking their empty glasses into the kitchen and trying to shake off that intimate, charged moment.

"Hello?" Judging by Maya's wary tone as she answered the phone, she didn't know who was calling her at eleven on a weeknight, either. But then pure elation: "Oh my gosh, hi! I wasn't expecting to hear from you! No, I wasn't asleep!" Then some silence followed by, "Are you *kidding* me? Of course the offer still stands! I'm thrilled!"

He had never heard her use so many exclamation points in a row. Was it the boy-band douchebag? It must be. Who else would make her so happy?

Law made a mental note to check out this World War I movie Band Boy was supposedly so good in. He'd heard people talking about it since word had gotten out that Holden had been in town to attend a play.

She laughed uproariously at something Holden said.

I thought you were someone else.

But no. Maya had only met Band Boy that one time, when he'd come to her murder mystery play.

As far as Law knew. Which…wasn't maybe that far. He got up and went back into the living room, hovering in the archway that divided it from the dining room.

"But *Much Ado about Nothing* can definitely be serious," she was saying. "I'm planning to make an analogy between the accusation of Hero and modern-day social media bullying with my staging." She was silent for a while, listening. "No, not *a* hero. Hero is the name of one of the female leads in *Much Ado*." She rolled her eyes, and Law smirked. It sounded like Band Boy didn't know what the hell he was talking about. "Definitely! Have your manager send me your numbers, and I'll see what I can do." After some more silence, she started murmuring sympathetically. "That I can definitely help with. Of course it's included!" She nodded as she listened, and when she spoke again, her voice had taken on a more pragmatic tone. "Well, we *are* a nonprofit community theater, but let me see what I can do on that front."

She got up and started pacing. "Great!" She turned and threw one arm in the air in triumph. The sudden move made her hair, which she hadn't returned to its topknot after waking, fan out like she was in a shampoo commercial. "I'm so thrilled, Holden!" She nodded enthusiastically while she listened to him. "Okay! Yes! Great! I'll speak to you soon! Thank you so much!"

She turned as she disconnected the call, and she either didn't realize Law was back from the kitchen or she didn't care. She didn't make eye contact with him, just pressed one hand to her forehead like she was overwhelmed—with joy. Then, as if her legs could no longer hold her up, she collapsed into a smiling heap on his sofa.

"Good news?" he inquired mildly, drawing her attention. Hopefully, whatever it was, it had eclipsed the odd moment they'd shared earlier.

"Yes!" She shot up to a sitting position, her spine ramrod straight. With all the dramatic up-down-up, she was like a yo-yo in human form. "Except now I have to—" She stopped, became utterly still. She was staring at the coffee table.

"What?"

He realized with a thud in his gut what she was staring at. In his hurry to get the TV turned off, he'd forgotten his other piece of incriminating evidence—the restaurant loan paperwork. He lunged, but she got there first.

Her mouth fell as she read silently. "Lawson's Lunch!" she exclaimed. "Are you opening a *restaurant*?"

She started paging through the business plan that had been under the loan papers, so there was no hiding it. "Yeah. It's still in the early stages, but yeah."

Her lip curled as she let the papers flutter to the table like they were radioactive.

"I don't know why you care," he said. As much as he hadn't wanted her to see those papers, now that she had, he was annoyed by her disdain. "My entrepreneurial ambitions have no bearing on you or your life."

He expected her to say something like *Except when your entrepreneurial ambitions are belching smoke all over my theater.* But instead she merely said, "You're right. They don't." She stood. "I have to go."

He followed her to the door. "You want me to walk you home?" he asked, as he always did when she was leaving his place at night.

"No, I do not," she said, as she always did. "I live less than a hundred feet from here."

It was good to be back to "normal," going through the motions of their customary farewell, saying their lines like they were in a play.

His body didn't seem to be getting the back-to-normal message, though. He was jittery, and his hand, the one that had touched her face briefly, was tingling. "It's been nice doing business with you." That was always his final line. Delivered in a monotone that suggested that it had not, in fact, been nice. So he leaned into it.

"Yep." And that was her final line.

Except actually, this time, he needed to go off script. Say one more thing. "Hey, uh, I haven't told very many people about the restaurant. I don't want—" Ugh. He hated having to ask her for anything, the idea of being in her debt.

"You don't want Pearl and Karl and Eiko all up in your face second-guessing every move you make until you're driven to the brink of insanity before you even open?" she supplied cheerfully.

He swallowed a laugh. She was confusing. In the space of ten seconds, she had him whooshing from panic to laughter. "Yeah. That."

"When are you opening?" she asked.

"October, I hope. I want to get a winter under my belt before I get hit with tourist season."

"I will make you a deal, Benjamin Lawson." She poked his chest. She actually physically poked him. It took him aback. It also caused a little shock at the spot where she'd made contact. "You." She poked again. "Lay off your mermaid queen shenanigans this summer, and I will keep your little secret." A final poke, a harder one, like the period at the end of a sentence.

He considered her proposal. It seemed wrong to agree to it, because it seemed wrong to imagine anyone else as mermaid queen. But whatever. He was pretty sure she would end up elected regardless of what he did or didn't do, because anyone could see that Maya *was* the mermaid queen.

He opened his mouth to agree, but she cut him off. "In fact, no, that's probably not enough." The finger landed on his chest again, and with it came another zap of electricity. "You make sure *someone else* gets elected mermaid queen, and you got yourself a deal."

Carefully and deliberately, he took her finger between his thumb and forefinger and moved if off his chest. He was trying for as little skin-to-skin contact as possible, because touching Maya felt like sticking his finger in an electrical socket, and he'd had about as much electrocution as he could handle for one night. "All right. Deal." But then, if they were striking a deal, they should probably shake on it. So much for no skin-to-skin contact. He extended his hand.

She looked at her index finger, which was still suspended in the air, for a long moment before unfurling the rest of her fingers to join it. Slowly she lowered her hand and inserted it into his. She looked like a robot trying out this thing called a hand for the first time.

Her hand wasn't cold like a robot's would have been. It was warm. But it made him shiver. Which didn't make any sense. She was that Disney ice princess, shooting a bolt of frigid lightning up through his arm and down his spine. She had a good handshake, though. It was firm and confident. Like her. He was not surprised she had lured a celebrity to town.

He was also pretty sure he could trust her, which was another thing that didn't make sense, given that she lived to antagonize him. But the way she looked directly into his eyes, like she was trying to suck his soul out through them, made him feel that on this topic at least, he didn't have to worry about her betraying his confidence.

They were still shaking hands. Well, really, they had stopped shaking, so it was more like they were holding hands. Just standing there holding hands and staring at each other while little electrical charges zinged up his arm. But it wasn't their usual glaring-contest type of staring. And she seemed to realize it all of a sudden, because she looked away. Looked *down*, like she was hit with a bout of shyness, which was wildly, *wildly* out of character. So that couldn't be it.

Before he could puzzle it out, she said, curtly, "I have to go"— as if he were keeping her here—and turned away.

He stood at the door listening to her clomping down the stairs that led to the back door of the building. When the clomping stopped, he crossed to the living room window. There was a passageway between the bar and Pie with Pearl next door that functioned as a shortcut between the backs of the buildings on this side of Main, which were otherwise attached to each other, and the street itself. It wasn't as late as it usually was when Maya left his place, but sometimes people got up to no good in that passageway, so he drummed his fingers on the windowsill waiting for her to appear.

She emerged and crossed the street, digging in her pocket for her keys. She hopped onto the sidewalk on the far side and did another little skip for good measure. She was back to being happy. He somehow knew she was thinking about Holden Hampshire.

The door to her place was an unmarked one next to the entrance to Jenna's General, which Maya lived above. She spent a long time futzing with the lock, which always gave her trouble. That lock was probably as old as the 1880s building.

Finally she opened the door and disappeared behind it.

He waited until her light went on upstairs before turning away.

Chapter Seven

❧

*U*nable to get Jason's house out of his mind, Law went to the bank the next morning, where he had it confirmed that the only way to raise the cash he'd need to buy it was to mortgage the bar building. He hadn't expected a different outcome, but still, it put him in a bad mood—a mood that was only exacerbated by Eiko's showing up and insisting that he appear at a "mandatory town meeting" later that evening.

Which could only mean one thing. The old folks had plotted a scheme they couldn't implement by themselves. No thanks.

"I don't think there is such a thing as a 'mandatory' town meeting," he said as he dried glasses. "That's the nice thing about democracy. The government can't make you do things you don't want to do."

"Oh, come on. Where's your sense of civic responsibility?"

"Who's the mayor these days?" All the old folks were on the town council, and they seemed to pass the mayorship around—one of them was always running unopposed—and he'd lost track. They always operated as a bloc anyway. "Is it you?"

"Of course not. I can't be mayor. I'm the editor of the newspaper. That would be a massive conflict of interest. Karl's the mayor."

"Right." He barely refrained from rolling his eyes. Hadn't Sawyer just referenced Eiko's "situational" approach to journalistic ethics?

"Anyway," Eiko said, delivering her closing argument, "this isn't something I should have to guilt you into attending. You're going to want to hear the news. We have quite an exciting opportunity for some entrepreneurial young person or other looking to innovate." She winked.

Hold on. *Hold right on.*

Did Eiko know about his restaurant ambitions? How was that possible? He'd taken Sawyer's advice and *not* spoken to her about it. He hadn't spoken to anyone except…

God *damn* her.

And God damn *him.* He'd been sure he could trust her as she looked into his eyes and shook his hand, there in one of their truce bubbles where the usual rules did not apply.

He should have known better.

He should *also* know better than to feel hurt.

But this sense he had suddenly of not being able to get a full breath in, almost like someone had delivered a swift, sharp, invisible blow to his solar plexus, seemed an awful lot like hurt.

But that was dumb. He was being melodramatic. Not to mention illogical. *Hurt* implied a baseline of goodwill available to be breached. He and Maya did not have that. If he'd thought for a minute that last night had meant something, with her snuggling against his hand and kissing him, all he had to do to jolt himself back to reality was remember her saying, "I thought you were someone else." So yeah, *hurt* was the wrong reaction. He worked on summoning some anger instead, and oh, look, it turned out he had a well of that to draw on.

"Can you get Maya to come, too?" Eiko asked. "She'll want to be there."

"Why would you think I could get Maya to come?" he snapped. He winced. That had come out much more harshly than he'd intended. There was no call to be yelling at little old ladies, even maddeningly meddlesome ones.

Eiko narrowed her eyes. "Because she listens to you."

"Uh, no, she hates me."

And right now, it was pretty damn mutual.

Eiko shook her head. "Whatever. Just be there at six. I guarantee you won't regret it."

After a jam-packed day that included a lengthy phone call with Holden Hampshire's manager—Holden Hampshire's manager!— Maya kicked off her shoes, sprawled on her bed, and stared at her ceiling. Slowly but inexorably, a displacement started to happen. The amazed elation that had been crackling up and down her spine faded in favor of a creeping sense of dread.

This had been happening all day, this cycling of joy and panic. She was on a roller coaster of giddy highs followed by the reality check of free falls that might or might not herald her doom. Holden Hampshire was either going to make the Moonflower Bay Theater Company or he was going to break it.

She blew out a breath and examined her ceiling. It was an ugly, water-stained drop ceiling that was probably forty years old if it was a day. She wondered what was behind it. Ductwork? Asbestos that was slowly killing her? Perhaps a previously undiscovered Shakespeare manuscript worth millions?

She hadn't told Eve and Nora about Holden yet. She'd been waiting for the end of the day, because she wanted to toast her amazing news. She grabbed her phone. I need to transform my apartment into guest quarters fit for Hollywood royalty. Any ideas?

Well, okay, "royalty" might be a bit of a stretch, but he had some attention for his role in *Submergence*, and it was getting to the point where people were talking about him as an actor as much as they'd ever talked about him as a musician. Also, come over. It's

happy hour. And I'm happy. And about to cue up "Petal Power."
We have something to toast.

> *Eve:* Does this mean what I think it does?!
> *Nora:* OMG!
> *Eve:* I'll be right over.
> *Nora:* Same.

Maya rummaged in her purse, pulled out a fortune cookie from
the stash her mother had given her yesterday, and crunched it open.
A WISE MAN ONCE SAID DO NOT PUT ALL EGGS IN A SINGLE
BASKET.

Well, screw that. She had one giant egg named Holden
Hampshire, and into her last basket he was going.

Fifteen minutes later, with her friends installed on her sofa, Maya
poured tequila for Eve and made a sad face at pregnant Nora.

"Well?" Eve demanded. "Is he coming?"

"Yes, Holden Hampshire is coming!"

The girls reacted with glee, and soon they were dancing around
to "Petal Power."

"Man, I loved this song back in the day," Nora said, giving up
partway through the song and returning to the sofa and putting her
feet up—she'd been complaining about her feet hurting lately.

"Me, too," Eve said. "Two Squared was kind of known
for their whole boys-sing-vaguely-girl-power-esque-songs thing,
weren't they?"

"They were," Nora said. "But in retrospect, I wonder why we
didn't listen to *girl* bands singing about girl power."

"Hello, Spice Girls?" Maya said.

"Yeah, but they were a little before our time. I would think
especially yours, Maya."

It was true that Eve and Nora were older than Maya, but that was
no excuse. "So was Mozart. So was Shakespeare. You don't ignore

Shakespeare because he was"—she made quotation marks with her fingers—"'before our time.'"

"Did you just compare the Spice Girls to Shakespeare?" Nora asked.

"What if I did?" Maya winked. "I have highbrow taste *and* I have lowbrow taste, thank you very much."

"Maybe you have unibrow taste?" Eve joked.

"*Anyway*, the point is, Holden is coming and I've promised him a place to live. And since I will be paying him every cent I have left, I need to transform my apartment into a small-but-glamorous pied-à-terre suitable for a B-list ex-boy-band member slumming it in Moonflower Bay for the summer."

"But *do* you have any cents left?" Nora asked. "You already aren't paying yourself."

"I had enough to pay Richard and Marjorie and the mortgage on the theater through the end of September. The September money will now be the Holden money. If my Holden Hail Mary works, it works. If it doesn't, I figure it doesn't really matter if I default on the theater mortgage, or if I have to do layoffs a month earlier than I'd planned." She tried to keep her tone light. *Ha ha, failing a month earlier than planned, no biggie!* But the thought made her breathless.

"So you're giving Holden all your money *and* your apartment," Eve said. "Where are you going to live?"

"At my parents' house. Unless..." She made puppy-dog eyes at Eve. She loved her parents, but she did *not* want to move back in with them.

"You can stay in the pink room if you want," Eve said.

Yes! "I was hoping you'd say that."

The pink room was a tiny room at the top of the Mermaid that had not been included in Eve's recent renovation. It had been Eve's room as a girl, when she'd come to spend summers with her great-aunt. It had also briefly been home to Nora when she'd needed a place.

"Jamila can lend you furniture for this place, I'm sure," said Nora, whose stepmother-in-law was an avid antiques collector. "We could go full-on Victorian with the furniture and juxtapose that with your exposed brick and the loft-like atmosphere of the place."

"That would be awesome." Maya looked around at the dump she called home. "Though 'loft-like' is kind of a stretch." There was an exposed brick wall along one side of the main room, but it was less "industrial chic" exposed brick and more "the wall is crumbling" exposed brick.

Her no-good slumlord, a guy named Harold who had retired to Florida while he let his real estate holdings in Moonflower Bay go to pot, refused to turn the heat on until December first or to fix the stove when it crapped out. But he was *also* ignoring the fact that she was currently behind on her rent, so she wasn't exactly occupying the moral high ground with him.

Still, she was pretty good with a paintbrush. "I'm going to treat it like a stage set. Make it look good on the cheap, and it only has to be superficially good. It doesn't have to last. Richard is going to help." Her tech guy had embraced the challenge even though she hadn't told him how high the stakes were. Somehow she hadn't found a way to say, *Help me fix up this apartment or I'm going to have to lay you off.*

Ugh. And here came the panic part of the cycle again.

"Jake and Sawyer can help, too," Eve said.

"I'll get Jamila going on furniture," said Nora.

"We can store your stuff in the basement of the inn," Eve said.

Maya took a deep breath. It was going to be okay. It *had* to be. "Thank you. I don't know what I'd do without you guys."

"What did you say to me a few months ago?" Nora asked. "It takes a village, and we're your village?"

"Yeah, but I was talking about your bun in the oven." Maya pointed affectionately at Nora's baby bump. "It takes a village to raise a child."

"Yeah," Eve said, "but it also takes a village to attract and retain a B-list Hollywood ex-boy-band member, am I right?"

Maya was flooded with love for her friends. She might be poor when it came to money, but she was rich when it came to the things that mattered. "You guys are the best."

Nora preened. "We really are."

"How long do we have?" Eve asked.

"Three weeks. He's coming the last weekend of July. We'll do a month of rehearsals, which I sincerely hope and pray will be enough. I'm going to open the show a week earlier than usual and do two mini runs. I'll do the Saturday and Sunday of Mermaid Parade weekend like usual, but I'm also going to do Thursday through Sunday the week before."

"Six shows!" Eve exclaimed. "You're leveling up."

"I'm banking—*literally*—on Holden being a big draw. I figure if I do the right kind of advertising, I might even be able to attract people from Toronto."

"So this means Holden arrives Raspberry Festival weekend?" Nora asked. "That's kind of cute—his time here will be bookended by the two festivals. In with the raspberries, out with the mermaids."

"I guess he will arrive during the Raspberry Festival." Maya hadn't thought of that, but it was good. It would paint the town in a positive light—and not a light that included her being mermaid queen. She wanted to present herself as a serious theater person, not an aquatic beauty queen, which was why she'd struck that deal with Benjamin.

It was strange to think she wasn't going to be queen this year, though, to imagine someone else on that float, wearing her tiara.

No, not *her* tiara. *The* tiara. She was getting what she wanted here, so there was no need to feel wistful. "Speaking of the Raspberry Festival, I need to show you guys my plans for the sandcastle competition this year. Benjamin is going *down*." She hopped up. "Hang on, I'll get them."

"We'll have to look at them later." Eve looked at her watch. "I forgot to tell you. There's a town meeting tonight. Pearl accosted me on my way here. She said it was mandatory." She turned to Maya. "She made a big deal about you in particular needing to come, actually."

Maya groaned. "No way. I have way too much to do. I'm not going to a town meeting tonight."

She went to the town meeting.

After arguing with Pearl for a solid five minutes—Pearl had called four times in a row until Maya finally picked up—Maya decided that sitting through the meeting was the path of least resistance. She could cruise Pinterest for apartment-makeover inspiration while the old people talked about whatever was their latest thing.

"Hey, it's my king!" she said to Jordan as she and the girls squeezed by him along a row of folding chairs set up in the multi-purpose room at the community center. He nodded good-naturedly as they settled next to Jake and Sawyer.

And then Benjamin arrived on the other side of the guys.

Benjamin. She had been so busy—and gleeful—all day that she'd managed not to think about him. Well, that wasn't totally true. She'd *started* to think about him a lot. Specifically about how his hand had felt on her cheek, all callused and rough, but in a strangely nice way. But *then* she'd think about the reason she knew what his hand felt like: she had, in a moment of sleep-addled insanity, snuggled into that hand. *And then she had kissed him.* It was *mortifying.* So she'd shut down those thoughts.

In truth, her stated reason for not wanting to come here tonight—she had too much to do—had been an excuse. Really, she hadn't wanted to face Benjamin. What had *possessed* her? It had been so long since she'd truly relaxed, but there, on his sofa, she had conked out. Had been in the middle of a dream, in fact, that she was lost in a field of flowers. Which for most people would probably be a pleasant dream, but not for her, given that she was about to lose her flower-shop safety net. And then she'd woken...sort of. She'd jolted from dead asleep and dreaming into a moment of insanity when her defenses were down. He was just so *handsome*, and she'd been so *relieved* to have escaped the flowers.

She'd wondered suddenly what it would be like to kiss him, and then, to her horror, she hadn't been just wondering, she'd been *doing* it.

Ugh. Ugh. Ugh. She *really* didn't want things to be weird. What if he wanted to talk about it? She was a little surprised he'd let her go last night without making a federal case of it. What if he—

He glared at her—*glared*. Wow. This felt way more intense than their usual showdown-style staring.

Well, okay. At least he didn't want to talk? She glared back. Or tried to. It was a little unsettling how much animosity was radiating from him.

"Wow, huge turnout," Sawyer said, twisting around to look at the crowd.

"They said it was mandatory," Eve said.

"I don't think that's a legally compellable thing, is it, Sawyer?" Maya asked, trying to turn the conversation to something benign so as to get the Look of Death to stop.

"No," Sawyer said, "but it's easier to do what they want."

That was often the best strategy for dealing with the elderly meddlers of Moonflower Bay. Stand there and let them talk. Let it all flow in one ear and out the other like you were listening to the teacher talking in a Charlie Brown cartoon. A week ago, she would have said she was glad her own parents were a generation younger and still working and therefore not part of this crowd. Now? She fully expected her dad to join up.

Karl came to the podium, and Maya glanced at Benjamin. He was no longer looking at her. That was a relief.

Right?

Somehow, she didn't feel any less uncomfortable without his attention.

"As you all know," Karl said, "the Anti-Festival in the fall is so named because it's our annual festival just for us. We have fun and raise money for local town causes. The library and the food bank have been the traditional beneficiaries of our generosity, but this year we've decided to take a different approach."

Blah, blah, blah. She tilted her head back and stared at the ceiling. They were in the community center so it was just acoustic tiles, but she suddenly thought of the ceiling at Lawson's Lager House, which was an old-fashioned tin one. That would be a good idea for her apartment. There must be somewhere to get cheap fake tin ceiling tiles. She got out her phone.

"The town council has voted to fund a downtown economic development grant. At this year's Anti-Festival, we will be awarding one Moonflower Bay business owner a one-hundred-thousand-dollar grant."

Uh, *what now*? Maya's head shot up as an excited murmur rippled through the crowd. Eve slapped Maya's arm, but then, seeming to realize that no one was supposed to know about her financial trouble, turned it into a strange arm wiggle.

"The town is contributing thirty thousand off the bat, from our pot of money from past festivals," Karl said. "Provincial and federal matching programs take us to ninety thousand, and my Junior Achievement kids have committed to raising the final ten thousand through their summer businesses. The winning applicant will be a business owner who contributes significantly to the economy and culture of Moonflower Bay. Please raise your hand if you're interested in an application package."

Maya shot her hand in the air so hard something crunched in her elbow.

A hundred thousand dollars. That would be a game changer, even more than Holden. *Way* more than Holden. She'd run the numbers on the best-case scenario on the expanded run of *Much*

Ado. With the higher ticket prices she was planning to charge, she figured that after Holden's fee, she'd have enough to catch up on her mortgage payments, keep her employees, *and* make a few of the most critical repairs. But if she got this grant... Wow. She could do even more. One of the things she'd had on her to-do list forever was getting a fundraising program up and running. Letters and emails and a system that let people round up the price of their tickets to make a donation. With this kind of money, she could even hire a fundraising consultant.

The question was who else was going to be applying for this grant. Who would be her competition? Who else would... Oh. Oh *no*.

Lawson's Freaking Lunch.

She looked over to find Benjamin looking at her again. His arm was in the air, too. He didn't look as ragey as he had a moment ago. He looked determined.

She had been so shocked when she'd seen his plans yesterday. A bit taken aback, too. Here she was struggling to keep her first and only business afloat and he was just casually planning to open a second.

It was funny how many different ways there were to stare at someone. She and Benjamin had their usual showdown way of staring at each other. And as she'd so recently learned, there was also a death stare.

This was yet another type. It reminded her of last night, when they'd stared at each other as they shook hands. They'd both been oddly vulnerable at different points in the evening. Maya when she'd come to her senses after reflexively snuggling up to Benjamin and kissing him. But Benjamin, too, she thought, when she'd seen his loan paperwork. He so clearly hadn't wanted her to, yet he hadn't lashed out. He'd just held her hand and asked her to keep his secret.

It was all very confusing.

Animosity was easier.

So she narrowed her eyes at him, steering them back to the more familiar territory of plain old antagonism.

He did the same.

It was like looking in a mirror.

Except not, because when she looked in a mirror, she didn't see moss-green eyes topped by absurdly long lashes. It wasn't fair. Someone with such a sour personality shouldn't be allowed to be so good-looking.

Her face heated, and she wanted to look away. But she couldn't.

"You want one of these?" It was Pearl, trying to hand her an application packet. This was her out. It was okay to look away when she was being interrupted by someone else.

Listen to her: "It was okay"? Like there were defined rules of engagement? She needed to calm down. Interacting with the town bartender did not require her to adhere to the Geneva Conventions.

She flipped through the packet and tried to get her face to chill out. It looked like a standard grant application. No problem. She'd applied for a million grants in her life. Not successfully last time, but still. She could do this in her sleep.

You know who could *not* do this in his sleep? Who had zero experience applying for grants?

Ha. She flipped the page. She totally had this in the bag. Benjamin Lawson was going *down*.

Except, hang on.

She waved her hand in the air.

Karl called on her. "Maya? Yes?"

"What's this about decisions being made based on the application *and* on a 'demonstrated devotion to the well-being of the town of Moonflower Bay'?"

"We want to make sure the money goes to a person who really cares about this town."

Okay, then! She had this *even more* in the bag. Who cared more than the girl who had come back to her hometown with the express purpose of bringing drama and culture to it?

"How do you measure that?" Benjamin piped up.

Crap. Benjamin cared about this town, too. He might be a jerk, but he was a jerk who cared about this town. He was always looking in on Pearl, in her bakery next door to his bar. And you could hardly make your way through a Raspberry or Anti-Festival event without someone making a speech about "the generous support of Lawson's Lager House."

But it was important to remember that he would be using the grant to open a restaurant. A commercial establishment. She, on the other hand, would be using it for a nonprofit. For *the arts*.

"We'll be scoring each application based on the viability of your project and the financial and business data you provide—that's all set out in your packets," Karl said in answer to Benjamin's question. "We'll also be assigning a 'community-mindedness' score. We'll add the two up, and that will produce our winner."

"A community-mindedness score?" Maya asked, not waiting to be called on. "So that's like a loyalty test judged by you guys subjectively?"

Karl stared evenly at her. "Yes. It's a loyalty test judged by us subjectively."

"Oh, come on." Eiko edged Karl out of the way to speak into the microphone. "A community-mindedness score is a way to make sure the money benefits the town. For example, what if someone won a grant for a business located in town, but they didn't live in town themselves, and the profits got spent elsewhere? We just want to make sure the winning applicant benefits, but that the town does, too."

"And who is doing the judging?" Jenna asked. Uh-oh. Did Jenna have secret entrepreneurial ambitions, too?

"The executive committee of the town council."

Meaning the old folks. The meddlers.

But okay. That was fine. Maya was still the best candidate, and she could charm the pants off them. She was their mermaid queen, after all. Well, she *had* been, past tense. It was still a little disconcerting to think that her reign was over.

The point was, she had this grant in the bag. One hundred percent.

94 Jenny Holiday

She glanced at Benjamin, who was shuffling through his own package of papers and wearing a little smile.

Ninety percent.

He looked up suddenly, right at her, as if he could feel her attention. He quirked a little smile. An overconfident smile.

Seventy-five percent.

Well, whatever. She had this. Forget mermaid queen. Maya was about to become the community-mindedness queen.

Chapter Eight

❧

"Law, hon, can you do me a favor?"

It was Eiko, flashing him a merry smile. Law stifled a sigh. He had been doing her—and the other members of the town council—favors for the past three weeks. These favors had ranged from helping Pearl pass judgment on her Tinder matches—usually Maya's job, but she hadn't been around lately—to agreeing to be on a panel at Karl's Junior Achievement meeting later in the week.

Because that was what "community-minded" people did.

He was operating under the assumption that Eiko knew about Lawson's Lunch—and if she knew, so did her coconspirators. Of course, they'd all seen him take a grant application, so they knew he wanted the cash regardless, but Eiko had made a few cryptic comments that reinforced his sense that Maya had ratted him out.

Regardless, for a hundred thousand dollars he would happily become an errand boy. Yeah, he'd still need a mortgage against the bar, but a much smaller one. If he could get the grant, and fold in what he'd earmarked for the first few months' rent, he could buy Jason's place with a huge down payment. By his calculations, if the restaurant was even moderately successful, he'd have the mortgage cleared in six years. He could live with that in a way he couldn't the idea of the bar being on the line for twenty-plus years.

So he was getting that money, even if he had to kiss elderly ass all summer long. It did mean he had to put the restaurant plans on hold until he actually *got* the grant, but that was okay. He wanted to open in the off-season anyway. Waiting would just mean opening a little deeper into it.

He manufactured a smile. "What can I do for you?"

"I was poking around on the roof next door," Eiko said. "I'm thinking of converting it to a green roof, so I was doing some measuring, and I left my purse up there." She pulled out a bar stool. "I'm not as young as I used to be. All that squatting and standing. Honestly, as much as I hate to admit it, I..." She huffed a sad little sigh. "I really don't want to walk up all those stairs again."

Well, crap. He'd always thought of Eiko as invincible. Of all the "matchmakers," she seemed the most spry.

"I'll get it, no problem." He scanned the almost-empty bar. It was the Tuesday before Raspberry Festival weekend, and he was appreciating the calm before the storm. "Will you keep an eye on the bar? I won't be long."

"Sure thing, hon." She beamed at him. "Thanks. You're a lifesaver."

A few minutes later, he emerged onto the roof of the *Moonflower Bay Monitor* building. He spotted the purse on top of a raised exhaust vent, but he walked past it to take in the view.

The lake was serving up a truly stunning Huron sunset. He got so busy he sometimes forgot he lived on a Great Lake. He had a boat he kept up the river a ways in a marina, and he used to take his friends out semiregularly. But that had fallen by the wayside as he'd thrown himself into restaurant planning.

The sound of someone coming through the door drew his attention. He was dawdling. Crap, he'd made Eiko walk up all those stairs after all. "Your purse is here. Sorry, I—"

It was not Eiko. "Maya?" He'd thought maybe she was out of town. She hadn't been into the bar since the town meeting, and he hadn't seen the lights on in her apartment. He'd been wanting to confront her, to ask her if she'd told Eiko about his plans, but she'd disappeared. "Community-minded" tasks aside, it had been a disconcertingly quiet few weeks, actually.

"Benjamin?" She squinted at him. "What are you doing here?"

"What are *you* doing here?" he countered. He should confront her now.

"Pearl apparently left her gaming...thingy up here and she asked me to come get it."

"Nintendo Switch," he said. In addition to being an excellent baker, Pearl was a championship gamer.

Maya looked around. She walked toward the purse. "Is this hers? Maybe it's in here."

They were just going to have a normal conversation? Here on the roof after she'd blabbed his business around town? What was the matter with him? He was *mad* at her. He opened his mouth to say something to that effect, to let her have it, but what came out instead was, "Nope, that's Eiko's. She sent me up for it."

He was losing his momentum. Losing his anger. He'd been so *pissed* the night of the town meeting, and now he was...not that pissed.

"Hmm." She scanned the rooftop, and he scanned her. She was wearing her red *Hamilton* T-shirt, red Cons, and skinny jeans. Her hair was in its usual topknot. And she was gilded in the glowing orange light of the sunset. *Dammit.* "Ah," she said, pointing toward a ledge that, upon further inspection, was home to Pearl's Switch. "I wonder why Pearl is gaming up here."

He shook his head. He needed to start paying attention to what was actually happening—beyond the ridiculous sunset making

Maya even prettier than she usually was. "Maybe she was helping Eiko, who was up here doing some measuring because she's thinking of putting in a green roof. Seems oddly forward-thinking of her. I wonder how she got that idea into her head."

Maya shrugged. "The less known about what the old folks are up to, the better, don't you find?"

"I do find." It seemed odd that Eiko and Pearl—they were both old, but sharp—had left their things up here, but Maya was right. It was better not to ask why. He picked up the purse. "Shall we?"

"We shall."

He pulled on the door. Nothing happened.

He yanked again.

Nothing.

He pushed instead of pulled, in case he was being an idiot.

"Hooboy," Maya said from behind him.

Well, *shit*. He turned. "You have a phone, right?"

"Don't you?"

"No. It's behind the bar."

"What kind of person leaves their phone behind a bar?"

"The kind of person who *works* at a bar and is just running next door for a second. Where's *your* phone?"

She winced. "In my room at the Mermaid."

Huh? "Your room at the Mermaid?"

"I'm staying at the Mermaid until after *Much Ado about Nothing*."

"Why?" Although that explained why her place had been dark.

"Holden Hampshire is going to stay in my apartment while he's in town."

"Why?"

"Because I promised him housing as part of his contract, and if he stays at my place I don't have to pay for that housing."

"But he's not here yet."

"Right, but I'm doing a bunch of work on the place to class it up."

He found himself bristling at the idea. Surely Maya's apartment was good enough for this boy-band poseur.

She must have seen the disapproval in his expression. "Have you *seen* my place?"

"How would I have seen your place?" All those times she'd invited him over for tea parties?

"Well, it's a dump. You probably forget that Harold Burgess owns the building."

He had not forgotten that Harold Burgess owned the building. It was why Maya always had so much trouble with the lock. He had also not forgotten that another property owned by Harold Burgess, a house Nora had rented when she'd first come to town, had turned out to have black mold in it. He'd wondered about the building across the street but hadn't found a way to say, *Hey, I know you hate me, but I'm concerned about your long-term respiratory health*.

But none of this mattered. What mattered was... "We're stuck up here with no way to call for help."

"I wouldn't say that." She walked over to the front of the building, leaned over the ledge, and shouted, "Can anyone hear me?"

"Be careful!" He rushed over and physically grabbed the back of her T-shirt. The ledge came up to her waist, but still.

He nudged her back and took her place, scanning what he could see of the street—the building was so tall that he could only see the sidewalk on the other side, and it was devoid of pedestrian traffic at the moment. He was a fair bit taller than Maya, so he suspected she could see none of the street and had merely been shouting blindly over the edge.

"Help!" she bellowed, as if to prove his point.

He could feel her resisting his arm, trying to push her way back to the ledge. He turned around and stuck both arms out like he was guarding her in a basketball game. "If you insist on yelling, do it from there."

"If I 'insist on yelling'? How else are we going to get down from here? You're lucky I have theatrical training." She placed her hands on her upper belly and made a strange but silent sort of retching motion. "I can project from the diaphragm all day long."

"I can see the sidewalk on the other side of the street. I'm going to wait for someone to walk by, and then you can have at it."

"Can you see anyone?"

"Not yet. In the meantime, though"—he gestured at the horizon—"you can see this."

"Wow." She followed his arm with her gaze. "*Wow*."

"Yeah." The sky was even more stunning than it had been a few minutes ago, giant swaths of flaming orange and hot pink streaking up from the lake.

"I can't believe this has been here all along and I didn't notice." She blew out a breath, like she was disgusted with herself. "I need to get out more."

He had just been thinking the same thing about the boat. Maybe Sawyer was right—maybe he *was* working too much.

"You know what? Pearl can wait for her gaming thingy." She walked back to the bricked-in vestibule that housed the door from the stairway and slid down its wall until she was sitting on the ground. "I'm going to watch the sunset."

"Great idea." If Pearl could wait for her Switch, Eiko could wait for her purse.

Maya shot him a look, no doubt thrown off by his proclaiming an idea of hers "great." He shrugged and slid down next to her. He landed in such a way that their shoulders touched. His first instinct was to move over to create some space between them, but he checked it. Let her accommodate him for once.

She did not move.

They sat in silence while he racked his brain for something to say and tried not to obsess over the spot where his arm touched hers. "So. A boy-band dude does Shakespeare in Moonflower Bay. You don't see that every day."

It was a stupid thing to say, not least because what he *should* be saying was something more along the lines of *Why the hell would you tell Eiko about my plans?* But his upper arm was getting all warm and tingly, and it was getting harder and harder to hold on to the idea that he was mad at her.

"To be honest, I have no idea how it's going to go," she said thoughtfully. "It's a bit of a gamble. But I actually hate *My Fair Lady*, so at least in that sense it works out?"

He barked a laugh. That was not what he'd thought she'd been going to say. Not that he'd been expecting her to answer at all. If they were going to sit and watch the sunset, it was probably more natural for it to be like watching soccer, i.e., an activity conducted in silence. But he'd started this conversation, so he asked a follow-up question. "Then why were you planning to do *My Fair Lady* to begin with?"

"It's perennially popular. A crowd-pleaser. You know, 'The rain in Spain stays mainly in the plain'? Who doesn't love that?"

"Don't take this the wrong way, but it seems to me that crowd-pleasing has not generally been a huge priority for you." He thought back to her gender-swapped *Death of a Saleswoman*. And to that time she'd gotten Pearl and Eiko to do *Waiting for Godot-ette*, which had turned out to be a wee bit too experimental for the town of Moonflower Bay.

But that was Maya. She had visions, and she didn't rest until they were realized. There weren't a lot of people like that in the world.

"I know. I just…" She heaved a sigh and tilted her head back so it bonked against the wall. Then she did it again. That heaviness he'd been seeing in her eyes recently was back.

"What?" he asked quietly, wanting—needing—her to finish her thought. It was all he could do not to lift his arm and float it around her shoulders.

"I really need this play to do well." She sighed again, but it was a small, almost defeated one this time. "Like, financially."

"Ah." He wasn't sure what else to say. It seemed to him that her plays were popular. Pretty much everyone in town went to them, even the weird ones. But he supposed the town was not that big. They didn't fill all the seats in the theater.

She pulled her legs, which had been extended along the ground, up so her knees were bent and her feet were flat on the floor. He was in the same position, so now their upper thighs were touching, too. The entire left side of his body was tingling now. Maybe he was having a stroke?

They sat in silence for another minute until she said, "So, Lawson's Lunch, eh?"

"Yeah." Okay, here was his chance. That anger he'd been trying to rustle up earlier was completely gone, so he just asked her. "Did you tell Eiko about that?"

"No!" she exclaimed, whipping around to look at him, and her indignation seemed genuine. The move broke the contact between them, and he regretted the question.

Maybe Eiko *didn't* know. Maybe her *You'll want to come to this meeting* directive *hadn't* had any deeper meaning. "You really didn't tell anyone?"

"I promised you I wouldn't. So why would you think I would? I mean, I know you hate me, but I like to think you also know me. A little, anyway."

Aww, shit. He felt terrible. And she wasn't even yelling at him, like he would expect. She just sounded quietly hurt. Also, he didn't hate her. She annoyed the crap out of him a lot of the time, and he found his ever-simmering attraction to her wildly inconvenient, but he had never *hated* her.

"I'm sorry," he said. "I know you wouldn't do that. It's just that Eiko's been acting extra coy lately, and I thought..." What? What had he thought? He had jumped to the worst conclusion. It didn't make him proud. "I'm..." Why could he not finish a sentence?

"Currently being manipulated and gaslit by Pearl and Eiko and Karl and maybe even the usually lower-key Art as they ask you to perform increasingly absurd 'favors' to such an extent that you're questioning your very existence?" she suggested cheerfully.

He laughed. "Pretty much."

"I didn't tell them. I didn't tell anyone. Not even Nora or Eve. I promise."

She was still being uncharacteristically subdued, which made him feel like even more of a jerk. "Well, I told Sawyer and Jake, so I wouldn't be surprised if Eve and Nora know, and— Oh, hang on." He groaned.

"What?" she said.

"I just remembered I also told my firewood supplier. I wanted to find out if she could handle an order that was double the usual size on an ongoing basis." Shirley lived on a big parcel of forested land and he never saw her in town other than when she was doing wood deliveries, so he hadn't hesitated to tell her about his restaurant plans.

Maya made a theatrical noise of irritation. "So what you are saying is that a ton of other people know about your plans but you jumped to the conclusion that I'm the one who told on you. I mean, you irritate the hell out of me, Benjamin, but *I* would never carry out such a betrayal."

Her emphasis on the *I* there, intimating that he *would* carry out such a betrayal, gave him pause.

"Lawson's Lunch," he said, going back to her original question. "I have this vision for it." Why not tell her, since she already know about his plans in the broad sense? And she was creative and entrepreneurial. She might have some good thoughts.

Which she probably wouldn't deign to share with him, but whatever.

Mostly he felt like he should tell her something real. To make up for having assumed the worst about her.

"I want it to be a proper restaurant. More than pizza at the bar." He braced for her to yell at him about the pizza oven. When she didn't, he kept going. "I'm calling it Lawson's Lunch because of the *L* thing, obviously, but also because I want it to have a casual vibe. Like an old-school lunch counter. Except with better food."

"That's a great idea."

He blinked, surprised by her easy praise. "You think so?"

"Yeah, everyone loves your sandwiches at the festivals. And your stupid pizza, too. Not that I would know. I've never had it." She sniffed as she returned to her original position with her back to the wall. Except this time, no part of her was touching him.

"Do you have any advice for me?"

She swiveled her head to look at him. The fading orange light was now making her skin glow like copper. "Why would you want my advice? You have a loan already. You might have a town grant. It sounds like you have a great plan. Everyone in town is going to be thrilled."

He was kind of embarrassed. But why? Because everyone was going to be happy with his new venture? Why would that embarrass him? He was being stupid.

"This town is getting fancy!" she added.

"I do sort of worry about that," he admitted.

"What do you mean?"

"I don't know. Am I a gentrifying force for evil?"

"No! Why would you say that?"

"Well, the bar has been around a long time. I've made some changes, but I've tried to balance that with keeping the core of it the same. But sometimes I'll be pouring a summer cocktail for a tourist, and I'll think, *Why am I messing with what works? Am I getting too pretentious?*"

"Well, your fancy pizza aside, I don't think I'd call the bar pretentious."

"And probably no one has noticed, but even though I've futzed with the wine and beer lists, I've kept several taps the same, along with their accompanying prices. A pint of Labatt's has been five bucks for a decade. I do that on purpose. And I haven't changed anything about the decor. I want the bar to be a place where everyone is welcome." He needed to stop talking. He sounded like he was making a case in court, but no one had accused him of anything.

"Why do I feel like you're talking to me, but you're really talking to someone else?"

Yep. She'd hit the nail on the head, which shouldn't have been a surprise. Maya was as smart as they came. It stung a little that he was so transparent, but he huffed a sigh of acknowledgment.

"Who?" she asked. "Your dad?"

"It's more like the *idea* of my dad. And my grandfather."

"A legacy."

"Yes." It was the exact word he'd been using in his head. "The bar opened in 1943. It's been through some serious milestones with this town. And my parents almost lost it in the 1990s. I remember that a little bit. I was just a kid, but...I remember it." That day he'd seen his stoic father cry—something he'd never seen before or since. "They laid off the employees, and my parents started doing everything themselves."

"Is that why your family moved to the apartment?"

"Yes."

"I wonder if they ever thought of closing it. Just giving up and doing something else."

"I never asked them, but my dad wouldn't have. They'd have had to drag his cold, dead body out of there. He has this idea of Lawson's as a kind of community center. A place where anyone can come and sit for a while, even without having to order anything. You remember when we did frozen pizza in that toaster oven behind the bar? Before I put in the wood-burning oven?" He expected some sass from her about the oven, but she just nodded. "You might be too young to remember this, but Sawyer worked at the hardware store across the street when he was a teenager. He was still living at home with his dad, technically, but really, he and Clara were fending for themselves. On the days he was at the store, my dad used to heat up a pizza and run it across to the store, all low-key like. It wasn't a big deal, but Sawyer told me years later how much they relied on those pizzas."

"This is a good town," she said quietly.

"I feel the same way about the restaurant," he went on, because now that he had started running his mouth, he couldn't seem to stop. "I want it to have good food but not fancy food, you know? Tables but also counter seating, so it's less of a big deal for someone to pop in and eat on their own. I was even thinking . . ." He was getting carried away. He'd spouted off long enough about his anxieties. He didn't need to have a monologue about his business plan, too.

"What?" she prompted, with seemingly genuine interest.

"I read about this restaurant in Toronto called the Ladybug Café that does this thing with tokens. Anyone can buy a token, and it goes into a bin by the cash register. Then anyone who needs a token can take one and use it toward an order. That way, people—" He cut himself off. He sounded like Pollyanna.

"That's a really good idea. I could imagine someone like, say, Sawyer's dad taking advantage of that."

That's exactly who he'd been thinking of. Sawyer's dad had had a long battle with addiction and unemployment and had burned a lot of bridges in town. But he'd recently started trying to get his life back on track. "Thanks," Law said, relieved she wasn't mocking him but also a little embarrassed that he'd just laid his ambition out so plainly for her to see. There was no guaranteeing she wouldn't mock it later.

"Well, Benjamin, as much as it pains me to say this, I think your plan sounds excellent."

"I know it's a big leap," he went on. "I'll need a staff, a chef, and I've been thinking it's finally time to get a manager for the bar. I need to free up some time to work on the plans, and once the restaurant is open, I'll have to go back and forth between the two spots. I mean, I love the bar. I grew up there. In a lot of ways, it will always be home. But I don't want to stand behind it slinging drinks until I die. Not that there's anything wrong with that," he added quickly. "My grandpa and dad had good lives. It's just that . . ." Ugh, he was rambling again.

"You have ambition. That's allowed, you know."

Yes. That was well put. Not that he needed her blessing.

"It's hard to be the inheritor of a legacy," she added.

She knew. Well, of course she knew. "Does your dad want you to take over the flower shop?"

She was silent for a long time, her lips pressed together like she was angry. The rest of her body didn't telegraph "angry," though. The way she was slumped against the wall suggested defeat. When she finally spoke, her voice was quiet, quavery. "No. He's been remarkably supportive of both me and my brother. I think he'd be thrilled if one of us wanted the store, but he would never push it. I mean, all he ever wanted to do was flowers, and there was no precedent for that in his family. And let's face it, not a lot of little boys grow up wanting to become florists, so he had to work pretty hard to get what he wanted. So he respects that we have different dreams. I'm just—"

"What?"

"I'm starting to wonder if I *should* just hang it up and take over the store."

Everything started shifting in his mind. Her comment about needing *Much Ado about Nothing* to do well. How upset she'd been the other night at his place, before Holden called. Her competitiveness when it came to the grant.

"But my dad is selling and retiring," she went on, "so if I want to do that, I gotta make the call now."

Wait. What? He'd heard that Mr. Mehta was retiring, but it would never in a million years have occurred to him that Maya might want to run the store.

She turned her head away from him, but he didn't miss the hand that darted up and swiped at something on her face. Holy *crap*. Was that a *tear*? What was happening here?

He had no idea what to say. Maya was normally so fearless. His first impulse was to say, *No, no, you shouldn't take over the flower shop!* She was so clearly meant to be doing what she was doing—murder mysteries and Shakespeare and teaching

ten-year-old campers stage combat on the town green. But he
checked himself. He didn't know what kind of pressure she was
facing, and she didn't need empty platitudes. If she was seriously
thinking of taking over the store, she must have her reasons. "Well,
A Rose by Any Other Name. Who doesn't love roses?"

He had been trying to lighten the mood. It must have worked,
because she did one of her little eye rolls. And he must have imagined that tear before, because now she looked fine. "A wise man
once said every rose has its thorn," she said.

"I think that was Bret Michaels from Poison."

"Exactly."

He laughed. One of the best things about Maya was how funny
she was.

"The thing is," she said, turning thoughtful, "I do like flowers.
And I'm actually good at running the store."

He'd thought their jokey exchange would signal an end to the
conversation, but clearly she wanted to keep talking. That was a
little unprecedented, but he was here for it. "You say 'actually' like
the default position would be that you're *not* good at it. You're the
one who had the idea for me to start selling flowers at the bar. Your
dad and I worked out a deal on that, by the way." She hadn't been
around the past few weeks, so she hadn't seen the small fridge he
had sitting on one end of the bar.

She ignored the compliment. "It would be easier, in a sense, if I
hated the store. If the idea of spending my life there felt like a death
sentence."

"It doesn't?"

"Well, it's not like death by firing squad. It's an okay way to
pass the time."

"But maybe death by a thousand cuts? Death by a thousand
thorns?"

She nodded.

"You have ambition. That's allowed." He paused, unsure if he
should go further. "A wise person once told me that."

She smiled, a small one, but it felt like a triumph. "Benjamin, are we having a truce without football?"

"I think we might be."

"Well, don't get used to it." She stood up, and she was back to herself. He could tell from her posture. Her confidence had returned. "Now come over here and help me scream."

In the end, no one heard them scream. Ha. That sounded like a line that belonged in one of her Murder at the Mermaid shows. No one heard them scream because they didn't *have* to scream. As soon as Maya stood up and shook off her melancholy—she had spoken uncharacteristically openly to Benjamin and put herself into a little funk—Pearl and Eiko burst through the door.

"Oh my goodness!" Pearl said. "We wondered if you two had gotten locked up here!"

"I told you to prop the door open," Eiko said to Benjamin.

He looked confused. "No you didn't."

"All's well that ends well, right?" Pearl trilled. "I'm actually glad you're both here. I have something to ask you. I was at Whispering Pines the other day, and they want you to do a pretheater talk, Maya."

"Of course." She often visited the old folks' home to do an orientation for whatever play was coming up.

Pearl transferred her attention to Benjamin. "Also, a few of them were talking about how they miss getting out on the lake."

Benjamin chuckled. "I'm happy to offer a boat ride if that's what you're getting at. I've actually been thinking about how I so rarely get out on the lake these days."

That was true. But probably that was partly down to her. Maya was, historically, the one who organized boat rides among their friend group. And her friend group and Benjamin's friend group severely overlapped—that was the downside to life in a small town. She had gotten so busy and stressed lately she'd let that kind of stuff drop. But she'd missed the boat rides, missed the lake. Missed the company. Well, *some* of it—no need to get carried away.

"Great!" Pearl said. "Because I was thinking, what if the theater talk *happens on the boat*?" She waved her hands around in front of her excitedly.

"Oh my, what a wonderful idea!" Eiko said, and you didn't need to be a theater director to recognize how bad an actor she was.

"Sure," Benjamin said. "It'll have to be after the Raspberry Festival, though. I'm going to be busy at the bar this week getting ready. And Karl has me on a Junior Achievement panel later in the week."

Hmm. Karl had *her* on a Junior Achievement panel later in the week.

"Monday?" Pearl asked. "The day after the festival? Say yes because I kind of already told them."

Benjamin met Maya's gaze and raised his eyebrows. He was asking if she was okay with this plan so they could present a united front. She nodded. This was another of those scenarios in which it was easier to go along with what the old folks wanted. Still, it was nice to be in solidarity with Benjamin. Weird, but nice. She sent him a sympathetic eye roll as she said, "Yeah, Monday works for me."

"Monday's okay on my end, too, as long as we're done by five," he said. "So maybe we start at three? Can you get the Whispering Pines shuttle to drop them at the marina?" he asked Pearl. "I have life jackets for eight."

"You got it!" Pearl said. "Thanks, you two!"

They made their way down to the main level and said good-bye to Eiko, who was headed back to the newsroom. Maya was kind of glad Pearl was with them as they took off down the street. Things might have gotten awkward if she and Benjamin had been left alone. Because they had, like, bonded for a second there? And she'd shed an actual tear in front of him. Though she was pretty sure he hadn't noticed—thank goodness.

He had told her some stuff, too. He was stressed about the restaurant. She had always thought of him as a person who had it easy. Unlike her, he *wanted* his family business, so all he had to do was sit back and let it happen—or so she'd always thought. But he was constantly innovating, now that she thought about it, and apparently worried over whether it was the right kind, or amount, of innovating.

She shook her head. So weird.

"Well, that was a nice idea Law had," Pearl said after Benjamin peeled off at the lager house, but then she clapped her hand over her mouth.

"What was a nice idea?"

Pearl's eyes darted around, giving Maya the impression that she'd said something she regretted. "Nothing. Ignore me."

Yeah, not happening. "What are you talking about?"

"Well, if you must know, Law had already suggested taking the Whispering Pines group on a boat ride. It was his idea for you to join and do the theater talk." She shrugged, as if the ways of men were mysterious to her.

Huh? That was odd. "Why didn't he just ask me himself?" And why would *he* have the idea for a theater talk? Something was off here. A game of broken telephone. Pearl did not have her information right.

They'd arrived at the bakery. "I don't know!" Pearl said. "Maybe he was too nervous to ask you himself! You want to know my theory?" She lowered her voice and leaned in. "He fancies you!" She blew a kiss and disappeared inside the bakery.

Whaaat? Pearl *definitely* did not have her information right. Maya had done a little reevaluating of her opinion on Benjamin just now, but Pearl's theory was so absurd, she was left sputtering on the sidewalk.

But only for a moment. She shook her head and, with it, that ridiculous notion out of her consciousness.

Chapter Nine

❧

*L*aw had spent the time between the roof incident and Karl's Junior Achievement meeting thinking about Maya's dad. So it was funny that when he showed up at said Junior Achievement meeting, Mr. Mehta was there.

As was his daughter.

He didn't know how to act around her now. They'd spoken so openly on the roof. They'd *told* each other stuff. It felt awkward now, and he didn't know what to do.

So he fell back on the methodology employed by teenage boys since time immemorial: he ignored her. "Hi, Mr. Mehta." He knew Maya's dad. They were both members of the Moonflower Bay Chamber of Commerce and the Downtown Business Improvement Association.

"Law." Mr. Mehta stuck his hand out, and they shook.

"Hi, Mr. Lawson," Maya said, and Law did a double take. He was used to her calling him "Benjamin" when no one else did, but—

"Maya. Nice to see you. Looking forward to *Much Ado about*

Nothing. Turns out my wife is a big fan of this young man you've got coming to town."

Law turned. *His* dad was here, too?

"Hey, Son." His dad gave him a half hug, and Law tried not to panic. He'd been avoiding his parents. He knew he had to tell them about the restaurant sooner or later, but right now he was going for later. It wasn't that he thought they would disapprove. But that was part of the problem. His dad was always saying little things about how Grandpa would be proud of whatever Law's latest innovation was—the seasonal cocktail list, the pizza. Still, it was one thing to tell them he was opening a second place, another to tell them he was thinking of mortgaging the first to indulge himself with the second.

But he was getting ahead of himself. He was only going to do that if he won the grant.

Right?

"Good evening." Karl tapped the microphone. As the longtime proprietor of Lakeside Hardware and president of the chamber of commerce, Karl was committed to instilling entrepreneurial ambition in the younger generation. Hence his devotion to Junior Achievement—it was the economic development arm of his meddling nature. "Welcome to our special guests. As you know, our students are spending eighteen weeks planning and starting a small business. We're early in the process, and I thought they would benefit from hearing from a panel of local entrepreneurs." He turned to the kids. "As a special twist, I thought it would be fun for you to hear from families that each have two generations of entrepreneurs."

Well, that was a twist Law didn't need right now. From the look on Maya's face, she had not been aware that the program was going to take this format any more than Law had. She was probably here for the same reason he was: Karl had asked, and these kids were going to be the source of ten grand of the grant money that was up for grabs.

After telling everyone about Lawson's, A Rose by Any Other

Name, and the Moonflower Bay Theater Company, Karl asked the panelists to introduce themselves.

"It's actually three generations of entrepreneurship in our family," said Law's dad, who went first. "My father founded Lawson's Lager House in 1943. It's been a community treasure since the day it opened, bringing a sense of consistency and tradition through the decades. If there's one thing you can count on in this town, it's Lawson's Lager House."

Yep. Law had to look away from his dad, which meant he ended up looking at Maya. She did one of her tiny eye rolls, but it was a friendly one, like the one she'd shot him when Pearl and Eiko were entrapping them in the theater-talk-on-a-boat plan. Aimed so he alone could see it, it seemed intended to express solidarity. Which was unfamiliar coming from her. He didn't hate it.

After they were done and the floor opened to questions, a teenage girl came to the mic and said, "No offense to the rest of you, but as I see it, the only one who really started something from nothing, like, with no help, no family background, was you." She pointed at Maya.

Law chuckled. It was certainly true that he'd had the good fortune to be born into the family business. The same could be said for his dad.

Maya's dad had the mic, and instead of passing it to his daughter, he picked it up and said, "That's totally true. Obviously I'm biased, but my daughter is a marvel. Every time I walk by the Moonflower Bay Theater Company and think of how she created this living, thriving, beautiful resource for this town, my heart just about bursts with pride."

Wow. So clearly Maya's dad didn't know about her financial trouble. Was Law imagining things, or did she wince a little as her father passed the mic?

"I appreciate the sentiment," she said, "but it's not really true. I had a big investor early on who really believed in me." She winked at her dad, and he beamed at her. Turning back to the questioner, she said, "Actually, if anyone fits your description, it's my dad. He and my mom moved to this area for my mom's job, and they didn't know anyone. He'd worked in the floral industry, but he hadn't owned his own store before. My mom had been in grad school for a long time, and they didn't have much money. So the way I see it, deciding to open the store was a big risk." Her attention swung back to her dad, and she looked a little bit overcome. "I'm really proud of him."

She cleared her throat and turned back to the audience. "But heck, I will take a little bit of credit. It *is* hard to start something from nothing, as you said, especially trying to do the arts in a small town. The more normal career path for a theater director would have been going to a big city and putting on shows at fringe festivals or trying to get into established theaters." She sent one of her million-megawatt smiles at Karl. "But I was committed to bringing arts and culture to this town I so love, and to doing my part in contributing to its economy."

Oh, for God's sake. Now she was blatantly pandering on account of the whole "community-mindedness" thing. Law turned and aimed one of those miniature eye rolls back at her. She put her hand over her mouth to shield it from everyone else and stuck her tongue out at him. He had to cough so he didn't laugh.

"I have a follow-up question," said the girl from the audience, who was clearly the brains of the Junior Achievement operation. "Do you think you've faced extra barriers because you're a woman and/or because you're not white?"

"Of course," Maya said. "That doesn't surprise you, does it?"

The questioner, who looked like she was probably of East Asian descent, shook her head.

"Just last week," Maya said, "I struck up a conversation with someone in the grocery store in Grand View. First off, he assumed I was a summer person visiting from Toronto. I had to be like, 'Nope, born and raised in the next town down the lake.' Then when I told him I was a theater director, he asked me if I was doing

Bollywood shows. Like, *what*? I mean, nothing against Bollywood. Bollywood's great. But *no*, I'm not doing Bollywood shows."

Really? People were that ignorant?

"I mean, you know, right?" Maya said to the girl. "That kind of stuff happens all the time. As for sexism, I don't know about other industries, but I'm sorry to say it's alive and well in the theater world. There are lots of women actors, but the other side— directing and production—is still very much an old boys' club." She whistled. "I could tell you some stories. But they're not very family-friendly."

What the hell? Law kind of wanted to hear those stories so he could find the culprits and...well, end them, basically.

"So what do you do?" the girl asked. "How do you handle it?"

"Well, honestly, that's part of why I came home after college. It's not that this town is magically free of prejudice, but I feel like more people here know me than don't. They know my family. Here, when I get that crap, it's mostly—not exclusively but mostly—from tourists. But really, the answer is I keep telling myself that I belong as much as anyone." She shrugged. "It wears you down, but you just have to keep telling yourself that."

Well, shit. It wasn't like he didn't know, intellectually, that he didn't face the same barriers someone like Maya did. But to hear examples of it so casually brought up—*Oh, here's something that happened yesterday*—was sobering.

"My question is for Maya, too," said the next kid, another girl, this one younger than the first. "Is it true you got Holden Hampshire to come to town?"

"It's true!" Maya threw her arms in the air excitedly, and a cheer worked its way through the room, even though Law would have assumed this crowd was too young to care about Holden Hampshire.

Law was subdued through most of the rest of the panel, answering questions directed at him but keeping quiet otherwise. He wanted to talk to Maya. He wasn't sure about what, really, just that between this panel and their surprisingly open chat on the roof, he felt like they were starting to see each other—like really *see* each other. When she'd rolled her eyes at him when his dad got going on the history of Lawson's Lager House, it had felt, for a moment, like she was the only person in the world who understood. He wanted to return the favor. He wasn't sure how. Maybe bequeath her the contested parking spaces permanently?

After the panel was over, Law's dad cornered him. "It's been too long. Your mother misses you. Come for dinner soon."

"Your mother misses you" was Law's dad's way of saying that *he* missed his son. Too bad his dad wasn't a jerk. It would be easier to just throw the bar on the poker table and make his bets.

"Yeah, sorry, keeping the family legacy alive has kept me extra busy lately." He'd been going for a joking tone but had fallen short, judging by the way his dad's brow knit. Ah, shit. He really needed to talk to his parents. He just...didn't want to.

"Hey, Benjamin, you still free to discuss next week's theater talk? Oh, wait, I'm sorry. I'm interrupting." It was Maya. "Interrupting" on purpose, because she somehow knew he was freaking out. He could kiss her.

Well, no. But he was grateful, was the point.

"Yes, of course," he said. And to his dad: "Maya and I are running a boat ride/theater talk for a group from Whispering Pines on Monday. We were going to hammer out some of the details after this panel."

"Which reminds me," Maya said to her dad, "I'm going to have to bail on Monday dinner with you and Mom next week." She kissed him on the cheek. "But I'll see you at the Raspberry Festival?"

"Yes," Mr. Mehta said. "Good luck with the pop star."

Once they were outside the community center and walking up the sidewalk, Law said, "Thanks for the rescue."

"No problem. I gather you haven't told your parents about your restaurant ambitions."

"I gather you haven't told yours about your financial problems."

"Touché."

"Yeah, I haven't told anyone but Sawyer and Jake. And you."

She made a silly face at him. "Well, don't forget you told your wood supplier, but I take your point. I haven't told anyone but Eve and Nora. And you."

Well. They were suddenly confidants. It was strangely gratifying. "I have to be done by five on Monday, so you can still make dinner with your parents."

"I know, but I need a break from them. All the talk about selling the shop is stressing me out."

"It's actually kind of funny how in some ways, we have similar things going on," Law said. "Family businesses, legacy issues with fathers."

"Yeah, but you *want* your family business."

"Right. And what you said in there makes me realize how ..." She raised an eyebrow. "I don't know, I guess how easy I have had it, relatively speaking." So why couldn't he just sit back and *let* things be easy? Run the bar and be happy with his life the way it was?

"So what I hear you saying, Benjamin, is that you're withdrawing from the grant competition because I deserve it more." She side-eyed him, and just when he was starting to question if she was serious, she cracked up.

Good. Enough confiding in each other. It was confusing. "No. That is most decidedly *not* what I'm saying."

"Good," she said. "Because when I win, it's going to be all the sweeter knowing that I took you down."

He tamped down a smile. "Keep telling yourself that." They walked in silence until they got to the bar. "You want to come in for a glass of wine?"

"I can't."

He was more disappointed than he should have been.

She pointed to the *Moonflower Bay Monitor* building. "I told Eiko I'd help her with distribution of the Raspberry Festival special edition of the paper." She flashed him a fake-looking smile. "Because I am sooo community-minded. In fact, I sincerely hope you are making progress on your mission to find another mermaid queen, because you're looking at the queen of community-mindedness. You, Benjamin, are not going to be able to turn a corner in this town the rest of this summer without running into me doing someone a good turn."

Maya hadn't really considered, when she'd signed up to sit in the dunk tank on the Saturday of the Raspberry Festival, that Benjamin would be there, too. But of course he was. Whatever job there was to be done in service to the town or its geriatric bosses—beach cleanup, driving Pearl to one of her gaming competitions—the two of them were competing over it. If Maya was the queen of community-mindedness, Benjamin was the king. It was clear that a handful of other people were after the grant, too. But it was also clear that if you judged by who was falling over themselves to ingratiate themselves to the town council, the real contest was between her and Benjamin.

Maya had seen a lot of Benjamin in daylight in recent weeks. It was weird. Daylight Benjamin was softer than she was used to. More sympathetic. Though maybe that was because they were starting to realize they had some stuff in common.

It was also true that in the bright light of day, brown-haired Benjamin had little glints of auburn in his stubble, which she had never noticed before.

"Oh, shoot!" Pearl, standing in front of the tank, frowned down at her clipboard. "I think I double-scheduled this shift."

"I'll take the shift," Maya said. "I'm already changed."

"I am, too." Benjamin took his shirt off and dropped it on the ground like he had thrown the gauntlet, leaving him standing there wearing only swim trunks and flip-flops. Hooboy.

Usually Maya saw Benjamin without a shirt exactly once a year. That day this year would be tomorrow—the day of the sandcastle-building competition. She was ready for it. Meaning that she was prepared to beat him—they had a long-standing rivalry at the contest—but maybe also that if she was going to have to see him half-naked, she was prepared to do that *tomorrow*. Not today.

She sighed, and her mind came to the same conclusion it always did on the annual See Benjamin's Chest Day: the dude must be hauling a lot of kegs. He was surprisingly toned for someone who worked all the time. But hang on. Maybe she needed to get a little more serious about her recreational Tinder swiping if she was getting hot and bothered over *Benjamin*.

"I already got Carter to cover the bar," Benjamin said, "so I have nothing better to do."

A few seconds passed while he looked at her. Ugh, she had dropped the ball on their argument, struck dumb by his stupid chest. Just because he was annoying her slightly less than usual didn't mean she had to lose her head. "I *said* I can do it." There, that was back to normal.

"But it makes more sense for me to do it."

"I called it first."

"Because you're twelve?" he shot back.

Pearl rapped her pencil against the edge of her clipboard. "While it's lovely to see you both so enthusiastic, might I suggest you split the shift? And maybe save your trash talk for tomorrow?"

"I'll go first," Benjamin said, but Maya had already taken off jogging toward the tank.

He was hot on her heels. The frame of the tank was made of wood and had a little staircase in the back. She reached it before Benjamin and started to scramble up it, but she had so much momentum from the running that when she made the sharp turn to mount the stairs, her body kept moving in the original direction. Shrieking, she splayed her arms out to try to balance herself, but there was nothing to grab on to. She was going to fall and break her head. So much for back to normal with Benjamin. So much for the grant. So much for Holden Hampshire.

Well, at least she wouldn't have to live to see the demise of her theater. Her dad could make the floral arrangements for her funeral.

Hands materialized on her body, one large palm splayed over her midback and another, mortifyingly, wrapped around one hip so while Benjamin's thumb was pressed against her hip bone, he basically had a handful of butt cheek. The little staircase had no railings, so she wobbled back and forth, his hands still on her, while she regained her equilibrium. His hands were warm and strong. Which was exactly what she'd been thinking during their awkwardly long handshake at his place a few weeks ago. Except that had been one hand. This was two hands. And her butt.

"You're okay," he said in her ear.

That was the strange thing about Benjamin. He was her sworn enemy. But she knew somehow that he would never let her fall—physically, anyway. There was that movie *An Officer and a Gentleman*, but was there such a thing as a jerk and a gentleman?

Once she'd righted herself, he let her go, but for a moment his hands hovered an inch above her skin, as if he wanted to make sure she was okay before he fully retreated. She could have sworn she still felt them on her, though, still felt the heat of them.

"Actually," said Pearl, who had registered neither the butt grabbing nor Maya's near-death experience, "Jake Ramsey built that dunk tank for Joe Wilkerson, may he rest in peace, to sit in years ago, and if you recall, Joe was a larger gentleman. So if you squeeze in, I suspect there's room on that seat for both of you!" She sounded delighted with this plan. "I wonder if we can charge double if you're both sitting in there."

Could they share the seat? Maya eyed Benjamin. He raised his eyebrows. A challenge.

She sat.

He did, too, and hooboy. Maybe she should have given up and let him have this gig. The seat was technically big enough for both of them, but only when they were smushed together, her right side plastered to his left. Way more than the contact between them that had occurred on the roof of the newspaper building. She tried to do the thing you do on public transport next to a manspreader, to curl inward and make yourself as small as possible, but there simply was not enough room. This was going to be full-contact dunk-tank victimhood.

She steeled herself.

It took a while for Pearl to get the booth officially open—she had to hunt down Karl, who was the one scheduled to operate it, and find him some cash with which to make change. A line formed.

She and Benjamin didn't speak. It was a gorgeous day. Blue sky, warm sun, slight breeze off the lake, the scent of honeysuckle on the air.

Torture.

The line got longer.

The silence grew heavier.

Finally Karl appeared, rubbing his palms together as he conferred with Pearl. "All right!" he shouted to the crowd. "Here we go! Dunk Maya and Law! A buck a ball or five balls for three. Step right up!"

Their first would-be assailant was someone she didn't recognize. "Do you know who that is?" she asked Benjamin.

"Eric Handler. He's from south of town a ways. He's the—"

Splat.

She was plunged into freezing water.

And shrieking again. She needed to quit the shrieking. It was unbecoming. It did not communicate any of the things she wanted to communicate—to the town or to Benjamin.

She just hadn't expected the water to be so *cold*. It was colder than the lake in May.

"—captain of the Grand View softball team," Benjamin finished as he resurfaced.

"Clearly." Eric Handler had perfect aim.

When she stood, the water was only up to her boobs, but she'd fallen with such force that her head had briefly gone under. She wiped her eyes and pushed her hair out of her face. She'd twisted it up even higher on her head than usual to try to keep it dry, but it was coming loose.

"Jesus Christ, this is cold." Benjamin shook himself like a dog and got water all over her. She snarled at him and rewiped her face.

They scrambled back onto the seat and sat through a failed attempt by CJ from the hair salon.

While CJ dug in her purse for more money, Maya glanced around trying to suss out who else was coming for them. Certainly nobody was going to have the lethal aim the captain of the Grand View softball team had. There wasn't—

Oh. Oh no. "That's Holden Hampshire!"

Benjamin followed her gaze. "The guy in the sweater?"

"Yep. *Arg!*" She'd known he was arriving today, but they were supposed to meet later. *Much* later, at seven, after she'd had a chance to un-drowned-rat-ify herself. "Maybe he won't recognize me."

"You don't want him to recognize you?"

"Not like this."

"Why not?"

"Uh, let's see. The part where I look like a waterlogged rat? The part where my arm fat is showing? The part where I'm supposed to be his boss and therefore projecting authority and competence and not dishevelment and chaos? All of the above?"

He twisted his upper body so he was fully facing her and regarded her with a quizzical expression.

Splat.

They were plunged again into the freezing water.

Whereas she emerged coughing and sputtering, he stood from the dunk and calmly hopped back onto the platform. "You look fine."

"I do not look fine." She squirmed her way back up with considerably less grace and surveyed what she could see of the festival, trying to locate Holden again. Thankfully, he'd made a turn and was in line at the outdoor bar Benjamin had set up that was being manned by his dad.

"You do, though," Benjamin said peevishly, and how was it they were arguing about her appearance and *he* was the one taking the position that she looked good? "You're just wet. It's a thing that happens when you're in a dunk tank."

"I can feel my mascara running." She'd worn waterproof, but clearly it wasn't up to the task.

Splat.

Ugh! She struggled to her feet again and wiped her eyes. Jordan Riley, her mer-king from last year, had been the thrower of that direct hit. So much for royal solidarity.

"I'm not sure how smart it was to wear mascara for dunk-tank duty," Benjamin said mildly, unaffected by the fact that their conversation kept getting interrupted by their being plunged into icy water. He turned to Karl. "Give us a minute to get our bearings, will you?"

He didn't need to get his bearings. He was just standing there with his skin glistening in the sun, completely unruffled. Apparently Benjamin Lawson was effortlessly good at being dunked. Everything came easily to him. Blinding good looks and bank loans. He collected them like they were his right. It irritated her. But ... maybe that wasn't entirely fair. He had more going on than met the eye, she'd recently learned.

"Sure," Karl said. "Take five. I'm gonna go check on the pie walk." He turned to the line. "We're taking a little break. Back in a few."

Maya eyed the line—and beyond. Holden Hampshire was strolling in this direction. "Crap. He's coming over here." She grabbed Benjamin's arms and maneuvered him so he was in front of her. He was broad-chested enough to obscure her. Naturally.

"What are you doing?" he said peevishly, resisting her attempts to manipulate him.

She decided to go with the truth. "I'm hiding."

Law blinked. Maya's admission that she was hiding from Band Boy unnerved him.

It also annoyed him. He hadn't been lying before: she looked *fine*. Honestly, she looked more than fine. She was wearing a swimsuit that looked like it came from the pinup era. It was like a sailor's uniform in swimsuit format. The top was navy and white stripes, but under her breasts it changed to solid navy. There were two rows of red buttons—actual buttons—running up her middle. The physicality of those buttons on otherwise smooth swimsuit fabric was a little jarring. You had to hold yourself back from touching them. The overall effect was really . . . something.

He allowed himself to be used as a human shield, even though there was no reason she should be hiding. She was holding his arms out to the sides, her fingers wrapped around his biceps, like he really was a shield she was brandishing.

"What's Holden doing?" she whispered.

He searched the crowd for the overgrown emo boy they'd seen before. "I have to say, I expected him to look different."

"Different how?"

Ah crap. This was *not* the part where he would admit to having googled Holden Hampshire. He'd read the dude's Wikipedia entry but apparently hadn't paid attention to his photo. "I don't know. Older." Less like a thirty-five-year-old douchebag. It was hard to believe that Holden was a couple years *older* than Law was.

This guy was wearing jeans, which, fine. It was hot, though. Normal people came to the Raspberry Festival in shorts. But the kicker was that on top, he was wearing a sweater. A black one. In July. It wasn't a regular sweater, though. It was loosely woven, like a giant had knit a sweater out of rope using oversize needles.

So it wouldn't have worked as a sweater in *actual* sweater weather, either. It was a completely-inappropriate-for-any-season sweater.

"Don't let him see me!" Maya tightened her grip on him.

She looked *fine*. If you were partial to the sun glinting off wet skin and smudgy eye makeup that called to mind a night spent—

He shook his head. All this hiding was unnecessary, was the point.

But actually, when he thought of Holden seeing those red buttons, those tactile, shiny little discs running from beneath her breasts to the bones of her hips...

He puffed out his chest to try to make it bigger, more of a shield.

His attention was drawn by the approach of someone else. It was Maya's brother. He hadn't realized Rohan was in town. "Hey," he said.

"Get rid of him," Maya whisper-implored. Law tried to pull away, but she was still clinging to him, which caused a little tussle. Her breasts brushed his back. He sucked in a breath. It felt like she was sparking. Or he was. Someone was sparking.

"Nice to see you," he said to Rohan, pulling harder so as to make the sparks stop. Interestingly, they did not, even as he successfully broke contact. "I didn't know you were in town."

"Oh my God, no!" she whimpered, still under the impression that he was talking to Holden. It pained him that she thought he would sell her out like that. Yes, they disliked each other—sort of...not really—but he would never set her up for actual humiliation.

The fact that she could so easily think he would lit a spark of irritation in his chest.

Which was actually fine, because *that* kind of spark he was familiar with.

"It's your brother," he said, stepping aside and not even bothering to temper the annoyance in his tone. "Your precious pop star has gone into Pearl's."

"Wait. What?"

"Hey, kid," Rohan said to his sister.

"Rohan? Oh my God, Rohan!" Maya clapped her hands and jumped up and down, spraying Law in the process. He sputtered. She didn't notice. "What are you *doing* here?"

"I had a sudden yen for a vacation. Thought I'd hit the Raspberry Festival, stay on for your play."

"But that's in like a month!"

Ro just shrugged.

"What?" Maya exclaimed. "What about voluntarily running twenty-six miles through the forest? What about Kara? What about your *job*?"

Rohan shrugged. "Change of plans on the marathon, Kara and I broke up, and as for the job, I just ... felt like a break."

"Rohan!" Maya sloshed over to the edge of the tank. "You broke up with another one? I didn't even get to meet her!"

He shrugged. Maya shook her head and threw her arms around him, drenching him in the process.

Unbothered, he hugged her back. "Good to see you, kid."

Chapter Ten

❧

$\mathcal{M}$aya used Ro's appearance as an excuse to get out of the rest of her dunk-tank shift without making it look like she was shirking her community-mindedness duties—or letting Benjamin win something. She pulled on a cover-up, and they walked down to the lake.

"What's going on?" she asked when they reached the pier. When he shrugged, she slugged him in the arm. "What. Is. Going. On?" *Something* was. Rohan made plans and executed them. He didn't show up unannounced.

"Ow! Okay. If I tell you, you have to swear you won't tell Mom or Dad. Or anyone."

"All right." Crap. She was starting to get scared. Was he dying?

He turned to her. "I quit my job. And broke up with Kara, but I told you that part."

"*What?* Why?" Kara she wasn't surprised about. Rohan was a serial dater. But the job? She'd always wondered if part of the reason girlfriends never stuck was that he was married to his job.

"I think I'm having a third-life crisis. Is that a thing?"

She laughed, but only from relief—only because she was happy he wasn't dying. "I don't know. I've heard of midlife crises and quarter-life crises. So you're either ahead of the curve or behind?" She was teasing, or trying to. She didn't know what to say. Her brother was normally easygoing. This kind of drama was not his style.

"I just... I don't know." He rested his elbows on the railing and stared out at the lake. "I turn thirty in the fall and I started thinking, what am I doing? What have I done with my life?"

"Um, you have a BA from U of T and an MBA from Wharton and you're a VP at Boeing—or I guess you *were* a VP at Boeing—and you have an awesome condo in Chicago? And you serially date amazing ladies that you break up with after a few months?"

"Yeah, but what does all of that *mean*?" He was still resting on his elbows on the railing, but he turned to her with a strange, almost pained look on his face. "I have money. I have fancy degrees. But I work for a company that makes airplanes that are destroying the climate. And in my free time, I spend hours running, like, literally running. What's it all *for*?"

"Oh my God, you *are* having a third-life crisis!"

"Yeah." His straightforward agreement alarmed her.

She went in for a hug, forcing him to peel his arms off the railing. "Well, I'm glad you came home, then. How can I help?"

He gave her a short, hard squeeze before letting her go, and when he pulled away he looked more like his usual self. "Number one, by not telling Mom and Dad. I need to get my head on straight before I tell them I quit my job." She nodded. "When Dad said he was going to sell the store, it sort of tipped me over the edge."

"Oh my God! You want the store!"

"No. Maybe. I don't know."

"Holy shit, Rohan!"

"I just... When he said he was going to sell the store, it was a little bit..."

"I know." It was a little bit... fill in the blank. Shocking. Confusing. Sad. Scary—for her, anyway, because it made her realize how much she'd come to rely on the store as her backup career.

"It's not like I *want* it," he went on. "So I don't know why it threw me for such a loop."

"I know. It did me, too." He put his elbows back on the railing, but instead of looking out on the lake he dropped his head in his hands and started massaging his forehead. "I just need some space. A break from my life." He was silent for a long time, and she thought he was done talking, so she laid a hand on his back. He lifted his head and looked out over the lake. "I was running along the lake at home with Kara. We were toward the end of a long training session, and my building was in sight. I just suddenly didn't want any of it. Including Kara, which is *terrible*, I know. She was sweet and fun. What is *wrong* with me?"

"That part I can't help you with, because I ask myself that about you all the time."

"It was just that she was so agreeable."

"You dumped your girlfriend because she was too agreeable?"

He huffed a laugh. "I think I did. I meet these women that on paper I'm compatible with, and then it's so... boring. Kara was into the same stuff I was. She worked in the same industry. She was..."

"Perfect. Perfectly boring." Maya saw his point. It was hard to imagine getting excited about someone who always agreed with you.

"Yeah," he said. "So the day after this run, I was getting a massage. My usual therapist was on vacation, so I was seeing someone new. She wasn't using enough pressure. I could barely feel it. For a massage to work, you need some pressure, you know? Some friction." He shrugged. "I started to think maybe that's true in life, too?"

Maya could not help but laugh. "So you had a massage-as-metaphor epiphany and bailed on your whole life."

"Pretty much." The corners of his mouth turned up as he looked at her. But he grew serious again as he pushed off the railing. "But you can't tell Mom and Dad any of this. Not till I figure out what I'm going to do."

"Of course. What have you told them so far?"

"Just that I had a bunch of use-it-or-lose-it vacation so I'm here for a month. I couched it like I was going to help them get ready to sell."

"I'm glad you came home. You don't have to figure everything out immediately."

He smiled fondly at her. "I actually feel relieved having told you. But yeah, I thought I'd hang out, help Dad. Maybe you, too, if there's any theater stuff I can do."

"Yes! There is so much theater stuff you can do." She surprised herself by telling him everything. About how close to the edge the theater was, about her big gamble on Holden.

"I can help you with money," he said when she was done.

"I appreciate it, but I don't think that's the answer. I was going to ask Mom and Dad for a loan, but then they dropped their bomb and started talking about how retiring early was going to be tight financially but doable. It wasn't a great idea anyway. Turning to family to bail me out isn't a long-term strategy. If *Much Ado* does well, and I can get this grant, I think I'll be able to turn a corner. I want to use the grant money to set up a fund-raising program that will help the theater be more self-sustaining. I think." She was a little worried about how "community-minded" it was to use the grant money for fundraising. Maybe she should be expanding her camp and education offerings. She wasn't even running any camps this August, having decided to focus entirely on Holden and *Much Ado*. She winced, thinking back to that A WISE MAN ONCE SAID DO NOT PUT ALL EGGS IN A SINGLE BASKET fortune.

"Okay, so no cash," Rohan said. "But you'll accept contributions in the form of manual labor? Or brainpower? I have a friend in marketing at the Art Institute of Chicago. I could pick her brain on how best to publicize the show."

"That would be amazing. I think with Holden in the cast, I should be marketing further afield than I usually do. I just haven't had time to think about it."

"Luckily for you, I have nothing but time. Let's make a plan, and I'll get to work."

She pulled out her phone to check the time. "I hate to say it, but can we talk more later? I'm supposed to meet Holden for dinner."

Ro whistled. "Look at you. Lured a genuine celebrity to town."

She did a silly little victory dance to make him laugh.

"I gotta go, too. I told Mom and Dad I'd be home by six for dinner." He laughed. "I had this romantic idea of 'coming home' to clear my head, but I forgot how much they're all over me when I'm here. I hope I can deflect all their questions about work and not give off a weird vibe."

"Have you seen the accounting software Dad got last winter? Ask him about that. He can talk for days about it."

They started to part ways, but suddenly he was back, pulling her into a hug. She and her brother generally expressed affection by harassing each other. But she went with it. Hugged him back tightly and said, "I'm so glad you came home."

An hour later, showered and made up, she was unlocking the door to her apartment and ushering Holden freaking Hampshire in. "So here we are." She gestured at the space as if it were a room at the Ritz.

And honestly, it might as well have been, considering the transformation it had undergone.

Her crappy furniture had been moved out, replaced with a selection of antiques curated by Jake's stepmom. As Nora had envisioned, they'd juxtaposed the old-fashioned furniture with modern art, the pièce de résistance of which was a giant canvas she'd once used as a prop hanging on the apartment's exposed brick wall. It was a Banksy knockoff, a graffiti-style portrait of a little girl holding a bouquet of flowers, but in such a way that she looked like she was about to throw it like a grenade.

Maya had switched things around, making her old sleeping area, which was an alcove off the main room, into a sitting area with a TV. She'd signed up for free trials of all the streaming services. The main space she'd left to be dominated by an obnoxiously-over-the-top-but-in-a-good-way king-size bed—like a hotel room. She had chucked her old double and ordered one of those inexpensive mattress-in-a-box things, and Jake had built her a bed frame.

Even the kitchen had undergone a makeover thanks to Richard's set-design skills, boasting freshly painted cabinets and a new backsplash—and if the latter was peel-and-stick tile instead of the real thing, no one need know. And if Richard didn't realize that he was decorating an apartment to save his job, that was also fine.

She—and her community—had worked so hard. Her chest swelled with pride and gratitude. Which was a nice change from her chest sparking with annoyance or seizing with fear as it had done this afternoon at the dunk tank.

Holden barely seemed to look at anything as he dragged a suitcase into the space while looking at his phone. She followed with a duffel bag she'd offered to carry, and since he was absorbed in his phone, she took the opportunity to examine him.

He managed to look like his old Two Squared self yet entirely different. The sweet, boyish blue eyes and dimple were still there, but they were set in an older, more angular face, one with fine lines around the eyes—kind of like Benjamin's. It was like Holden had kept all the best parts of the boy face but added in all the best stuff that happened to men's faces as they aged.

He was so pretty. It wasn't fair.

Also: *Holden freaking Hampshire was here!*

But okay. She could be cool. It wasn't like a Spice Girl was here. She needed to stop thinking of him as Holden *freaking* Hampshire. He was just a person. She cleared her throat. He didn't look up from his phone. "Everything seem okay?"

He looked around absently, his eyes snagging on the bed. "Do you have a lighter duvet? I run hot."

"Sure. I'll—" What? What would she do? She would run across the street and raid the Mermaid Inn, that was what she would do. "I'll have one sent over. Anything else?"

"Wi-Fi password?"

"In here." She pointed at a cute little welcome binder she'd made and left on the kitchen counter.

"Great."

"So, in terms of dinner, there's a great little diner called Sadie's. Or...wood-fired pizza across the street at Lawson's Lager House." Surely she could be seen eating Benjamin's pizza with Holden Hampshire. "Or there's a fantastic place in the next town up the lake."

She would be thrilled with whatever he chose. It had been so long since she'd eaten out. She wouldn't splurge on a restaurant meal on her own, but if she was "forced" to take her star out for a welcome-to-town dinner, she was going to enjoy the heck out of it. She had even paid Jordan to bring her car back from the dead. "I was thinking we could chat a bit about the play. I'm doing a few things with the staging that may be a bit unexpected, though they apply more to the Hero-and-Claudio storyline than to ours." She was playing Beatrice to his Benedick rather than cast someone else. She'd never had the chance to play that role, and it was one of the greats. Also, she wasn't paying herself, so she was a bargain.

"I'd love to do dinner, but I'm beat," he said absently, finally actually looking at the apartment. "I think I'll call it a night. Rain check?"

"Oh, okay." That was disappointing. But whatever, the man didn't want to go to dinner. It wasn't the end of the world. "Jenna's downstairs is open until eight if you're in the market for any snacks or need any toiletries or anything."

So she found herself back out on the street unexpectedly early. Also hungry: she had skipped lunch in anticipation of a big dinner with Holden. She dug in her purse and extracted a fortune cookie and broke it open.

DON'T CONFUSE RECKLESSNESS WITH CONFIDENCE.

That was...not a great one. She popped the cookie in her mouth and texted her brother as her stomach growled. Are you guys still eating? I got jilted by the pop star, so I thought maybe I'd come by and join you.

> ***Rohan:*** Nope. En route to the store. Dad wants to show me the accounting software. Good call on that one!

She let herself into the closed store to wait for them. The shop was so familiar. Like her parents' house, it held a lot of good childhood memories. Helping her dad load the refrigerators when a delivery came. Pitching in on full-moon nights. That hilarious night Eve had gotten locked in the cooler and Sawyer had rescued her.

Just the smell, that wall of green that hit your nose the moment you walked in the door. That was the smell of the end of the school day, the smell of summer. The smell of family.

The bells on the door drew her from her memories. "How was Holden?" her mother, first through the door, asked.

Boring. "*Great!*"

"Did you eat?"

"He was tired, so no. But I'll get something on my way back to the inn." Or, more accurately, she'd have some granola bars in her room.

Soon she and her brother were manufacturing enthusiasm over the new software. Or at least she was. Ro's actually seemed genuine.

"This is a huge improvement, Dad," he said. "And if you have bigger orders where the payments are being spread out, you can set this up to automatically generate the invoices."

"Oh, I didn't realize that. I don't think I'm going to bother learning a new system at this point, though."

"Right. Of course."

"Hey, you said you had an agent coming in to look at the building," Maya said. "Will the new owner keep the store open?"

"I told the agent I'm happy to sell all the contents if by chance the buyer is interested in the store, too. But it's unlikely."

"But what about the wishing flowers?" Rohan said.

"I've thought of that," her dad said. "Maya's idea for Ben Lawson to start selling a few flowers at the bar actually made me think about why I personally was deriving all the profits from the wishing flowers. I definitely don't want the town to lose the tradition. What if all the businesses in town—or all who wanted to—sold flowers? I'm planning to talk to the town council about it."

"That's an interesting idea," Rohan said, and Maya could see his entrepreneurial brain firing up as he and their dad chatted. She listened to them for a while, letting the familiar strains of their voices wash over her. It was nice to all be together for a while.

But her happiness was tempered with uncertainty. Maybe she should just call it on the theater. What were the chances she was going to get that grant? What were the chances Holden was going to be the magic bullet she was hoping for?

Maybe she *was* confusing recklessness and confidence?

Worse, maybe she had been all along?

Maya was going to win the sandcastle competition this year. She was *ready*.

"Builders, you know the rules," Pearl, who was head judge this year, called out to the assembled throng. "You're allowed two buckets and two shovels, and you can use anything you find on the beach. You have two hours. You may begin."

A couple years ago, Benjamin had trounced her by interpreting "anything you find on the beach" to mean "anything you found on the beach at any time in the past" and had walked away with first place based on a castle decorated with a ton of sea glass he'd collected. Then last year he'd won with a creation that was more driftwood than sand.

No more. She was ready with a back-to-basics strategy that was going to blow whatever he had planned out of the water. Also: there wasn't a lot of stuff on the beaches of Huron. This wasn't an ocean beach. No cute starfish or shiny seashells here. Unless he was planning to redo sea glass or driftwood—and a rerun was as good as an admission of defeat—he was out of bells and whistles. And who was the one who had aced set design in school? She cracked her knuckles and unrolled her diagram.

"Is that a *blueprint*?"

Maya smiled at the approaching Eve. "You'd better believe it." No more freestyling for her.

"And," Pearl called, finishing her instructions to the builders, "You're allowed two helpers. Spectators are welcome but may not participate unless they are designated helpers."

"Where's my other helper?" Maya asked, looking around the crowded beach for Nora, but also for Benjamin. Why wasn't he here yet? Usually Maya and Benjamin were among the first arrivals, and they spent some time trash-talking each other.

"I'm here!" Nora came jogging up—she was pregnant enough now that she was almost at the waddling stage. Jake was with her, which was odd, because usually he helped Benjamin with his castle—which wasn't fair because Jake was a construction genius. But that was okay, because Maya was *ready* this year.

"Where's Benjamin?" she asked, trying to sound casual.

"He was doing sandwiches out front of the bar when we came out of the clinic," Nora said. "He seemed like he was by himself."

"Yeah, I hear he's having trouble with Carter not showing up. Maybe he's stuck." Eve elbowed Maya. "In which case, you totally have this in the bag."

"But…" Winning by default wouldn't be the same. Winning

the sandcastle competition was not the same as beating Benjamin at the sandcastle competition. But she wasn't going to say that. "Right."

Jake smirked. "He'll be here."

"Oh, are you working for the enemy?" Nora asked. This was her first Raspberry Festival, so she probably didn't know the extent of her husband's usual involvement.

"He always does," Maya said, motioning for Eve and Nora to scooch in. It was kind of funny how her two best friends had hooked up with Benjamin's two best friends. And not funny ha ha, funny irritating as heck. "Jake, I love you, but I can't trust you not to sell me out to Benjamin, so I'm gonna need you to skedaddle. No offense."

Jake chuckled. "None taken." He looked at Nora. "I'll catch you later." It still sort of amazed Maya that quiet, sad Jake was married to Nora. That they were going to have a baby.

Something twinged inside Maya. It was jealousy, but not in the specific sense. She didn't want a baby, but the way Jake looked at Nora. She just…wanted that, too. Someday.

But whatever. Rome wasn't built in a day. She had a theater to save first.

You know what was built in a day, though? A winning sandcastle. She could almost feel the heft of the trophy in her hand, returned to its rightful owner after two summers of injustice. She set the girls to doing their jobs—Nora on turrets and Eve on trenches.

When Benjamin finally showed up with Jake and Sawyer in tow—and carrying several buckets of something she couldn't see— he set up a perimeter around his work space with what looked like those road closure thingies the town used to block off Main Street for the Mermaid Parade.

She craned her neck to try to see what was going on. He must have felt her attention because he paused, standing, holding one of his mystery buckets. "What are you *doing*?" she yelled, then mouthed, "Sorry" at her neighbor, Dennis Bates, who had been working on a replica of the lift bridge he operated but was now holding his ears.

"I'm building a sandcastle. What are you doing?" Benjamin shouted back.

"Excuse me!" Maya swiveled her head around. "I need a judge here!"

Eiko, who had been huddled with Art and Pearl, came jogging over. "What's up, hon?"

"Is that legal?" She pointed to Benjamin's barricades.

"We were just talking about that. There's nothing in the rules that prohibits it."

Maya harrumphed. "It doesn't seem very in the spirit of a public competition."

"I don't disagree," Eiko said, "and you can expect to see an amendment to the rules for next year."

"I can just go over there and see what's happening," Eve said. "If you stand right next to the barriers, you can see down to what they're doing."

It was true. There was a stream of spectators doing just that, so clearly the barriers were meant to block her view specifically. "Nah, it's okay. It's not like it actually matters." She didn't need to see what Benjamin had up his sleeve. She just needed to keep her eyes on her own paper and crush him.

Two hours later, she was sweaty and had sand in places where sand did not belong. But she was also surveying a huge, precisely designed and constructed classic sandcastle. There was no way he could beat this. It was—

A collective "Ooh" from the crowd drew her attention. The guys were taking their barriers away.

"Uh-oh," Nora said.

"No way," Eve said.

Maya followed her friends over there and was struck dumb. He'd made a replica of the Palace of Versailles, which was amazing on its own, but the kicker was that he had used an astounding array of dried seaweed in different colors to create its formal gardens.

It looked amazing.

And there was her answer to what was left to collect on the beach. He had done sea glass and driftwood. Leave it to Benjamin to turn a gross nuisance—seaweed, for heaven's sake—into a thing of beauty.

He stood up all of a sudden from where he'd been squatting next to his stupid buckets—which had been full of seaweed, no doubt.

Welcome to National See Benjamin's Chest Day. Except this was the second day running this year.

He made eye contact with her right away and winked and did a stupid little finger-wagging "gotcha" kind of gesture.

He so clearly had, she couldn't even be mad. Pearl confirmed his victory a moment later, making an announcement and handing him the trophy.

"I gotta get one of those grilled-cheese sandwiches Law is doing," Eve said as they approached Lawson's Lager House a little later. The girls had gone for a swim after the competition to cool off, so Benjamin was already back at work behind the outdoor bar.

"Mmm," Nora said as they got in line.

"He's doing aged cheddar with raspberry-thyme jam and a drizzle of balsamic glaze this year," Karl said, turning to speak to them from his spot in line.

Hmm.

Lawson's Lunch sounded like the name of a place that would make good grilled-cheese sandwiches.

Grilled-cheese sandwiches that everyone apparently already loved.

Crap. Benjamin might actually win the grant.

Maya stood in line behind the girls while they ordered sandwiches and drinks—raspberry sangria for Eve and a sparkling raspberry mocktail for Nora—undecided about whether she could order a sandwich. Probably not. Probably the pizza logic applied.

"Next," Benjamin said, as Eve and Nora cleared out with their purchases. He'd been sliding a sandwich out of a press, but as he looked up and locked eyes with Maya, he burned himself. "Shit." The sandwich fell to the pavement as he shook out his hand, which caused more cursing.

He glared at her like it was her fault. As if. She glared back, because that was what she was supposed to do. They hadn't done this for a while, so it felt a little strange, like trying to put on an ill-fitting item of clothing.

Nora stepped in. "Let me see."

He let her take his hand but kept looking at Maya. "I don't have your wine out here. My dad's inside. Tell him your wine is in the small fridge with the Mill Street decal on it."

"Oh, I'm not—"

"You'd better go in with her," Nora said. "Put some cool water on this."

"It'll be fine," Benjamin said.

"Not cold water. *Cool*," Nora said, ignoring him. "And no ice. Get yourself a basin of cool water and sit down for a bit and immerse your hand in it."

"I got this covered." Eve stepped behind the bar. Benjamin rolled his eyes—he didn't like being fussed over—but he went, holding the door for Maya with his unburned hand.

She paused. She hadn't intended to hang around after the sandcastles. Rehearsals started tomorrow, and she'd been planning to hole up in her room at the Mermaid and work on her first-day-of-rehearsal, everything-is-normal-even-though-we-have-a-huge-celebrity-among-us speech.

Benjamin made an impatient are-you-or-aren't-you gesture as he held the door. Screw it. A glass of wine would be good. She missed the bar. She hadn't been able to stop in as much recently, given the work she'd been doing getting her apartment ready for Holden.

"Hi, Mr. Lawson," she said to Benjamin's dad, who was behind the bar. Benjamin himself headed back to the tiny kitchen.

"Hi, Maya. Lots of talk about your movie star."

"Ha ha, yes! His being here is very exciting!" Hopefully it would also be lucrative.

"What can I get you?"

"I'll have a glass of the Riesling."

She noticed as he uncorked it that it wasn't the same one she usually drank. "Oh, not that one, if you don't mind. The other one." Was this why Benjamin had been jawing about it being in some refrigerator or other?

Mr. Lawson peered at the bottle, which looked different from the kind Benjamin usually poured from. "I don't think there is another one." Well, she didn't want to be a jerk, so she said, "I must be confused. That one is great, thanks."

The living room effect of the bar, of feeling at home and like she belonged, was not as strong as it usually was. Probably because the bar wasn't very crowded. Everyone was outside for raspberry festivities and fancy sandwiches, so there was no one nearby she could chat with.

Benjamin reappeared with a bowl of water and came to sit next to her. She suddenly felt a little more comfortable. Probably because she was used to his being here. For better or worse, he was part of the background of her living room away from home.

"What happened?" his dad said.

"Burned my hand. Doc Walsh is out there and isn't going to let me come back out until I've soaked it for a while."

Mr. Lawson nodded and moved to the other end of the bar to serve a customer. Maya and Benjamin sat in silence for a long moment until he said, "FYI, I'm working on getting Sadie Saunders elected mermaid queen."

Sadie? That was not what Maya'd had in mind when she'd ordered him to cease and desist. "Have you...seen a lot of Sadie recently?" As far as she knew, Sadie and Benjamin had not been a thing since way back in the day. Since they had ruined her life. Temporarily.

Okay, that was a bit much, even for a championship grudge-holder such as herself. Really, she should thank them. They were responsible for her current work ethic. For the mental policies-and-procedures manual that had made it so she'd never had to cancel a play again. And never would.

"I haven't seen much of Sadie lately," Law said, "but I tried to think about who might make a good queen, and she came to mind."

Sadie did not have good tiara hair. With her short and curly hair, she was going to look like Little Orphan Annie playing dress-up. Also, her acting skills had never been that good—Maya wasn't sure what she'd been thinking with casting her that one time. But the point was, Sadie wasn't going to be able to *inhabit* the role of the mermaid queen the way that was required to really sell it.

Also, Maya had *just* gotten custody of the trident last parade. The old folks might try to give it back to the king. Benjamin made a face suddenly. He seemed to be looking at something behind her. She turned.

Holden pulled out the stool next to her. "Hey."

She was sitting next to Holden Hampshire at her local bar. Surreal. She shot him a smile. "I'm excited for tomorrow."

"What's tomorrow?" Benjamin asked.

"First day of rehearsals for *Much Ado*," she said.

"About that," Holden said. "Is there any way we could start a little later? I mean, eight a.m. . . . " He scrunched his nose.

"Oh! Ha! Well, our actors playing Hero and Claudio are in high school, right, because I'm using their storyline to make a point about online bullying? And Claudio is doing summer school this week, which is in the afternoons, so we need to be wrapped up by one, hence the early start." It was actually stressing her out. Her Hero was a star in the making, but the boy she'd cast as Claudio she was less sure about.

Maybe the whole high school angle had been a mistake. But she really had thought the social media theme was a good one.

Also, Holden had blown her budget, and high schoolers came cheap.

"High school." Holden's tone was blank, but somehow she detected a note of snobbery. Which was good! Very Benedick!

"Yes, well, we all started somewhere, right?" she said, taking a sip of the wrong Riesling.

"Maya was directing when *she* was in high school," said Benjamin, who she'd completely forgotten about. *Almost* forgotten about. To be fair, it was hard to really forget about Benjamin on account of his looming presence and his constant grumbling. Also maybe his moss-green eyes that saw everything.

"Were you an actor when you were in high school?" Benjamin asked Holden.

"No," Holden said. "I was a musician in high school. And then I quit a year early when my professional career took off."

"Did you do anything I'd know?" Benjamin inquired mildly.

"I was in Two Squared."

Benjamin scrunched his forehead. "Hmm. Don't know them. You, I guess. Don't know you." That was a lie. She herself had told Benjamin about Holden's past. Benjamin lifted his hand from the water bowl, shook it out, and extended it across Maya's space to Holden. "Ben Lawson. I own this place."

I own this place. He said it like he was talking about more than the bar. The territorialism in his tone made it sound like he was talking about the whole town.

"Holden Hampshire," came the reply after a beat, though Holden ignored the damp hand. He waited another beat, pushed back his chair, and said, "I gotta jet. See you tomorrow, Maya?"

"At eight," Benjamin said.

Ignoring Benjamin, Holden winked at her. "I'll do my best."

She smiled and waved, and when he was safely out of earshot, she turned to Benjamin, preparing to interrogate him about what that little pissing contest had been about, but he spoke first. "What a dick."

"Oh, come on."

"He has to rehearse for five hours a day in a beach town in the summer, and he can't be bothered to get out of bed in the mornings?"

"He's an artist. He's sensitive. He's probably an insomniac."

"You're an artist, and you work all the time."

"So do you."

She had no idea why they were arguing. Or even what they were arguing about. Who worked more? Who worked less? She wasn't even sure whether working more or working less represented the moral high ground here and therefore the winning argument.

"What happened to the Keith's tap?" Mr. Lawson asked Benjamin as he came back over.

"I swapped in KLB Raspberry Wheat for the festival," Benjamin said. "I'll bring it back when the KLB is gone."

"I'm surprised you chose the Keith's, though. I don't think we've ever not had Keith's on tap, even in your grandpa's time."

Hooboy. Maya didn't think Mr. Lawson meant anything by his comment, but she could see what Law meant about the whole legacy thing.

Mr. Lawson moved down the bar to serve a customer who had just arrived, and Maya noticed the new sandcastle trophy sitting behind the bar, next to the ones Benjamin had won in previous years. She pointed at it. "I guess congratulations are in order. Bitter congratulations. I have to say, you deserved to win this year."

He smiled. "Thanks."

"You're welcome," she said, and to her surprise she meant it.

Chapter Eleven

❧

The weather was perfect for a boat ride. Warm and clear and not too breezy. Law finished shuttling the life jackets off the boat and laid them on the hood of his car. Usually he had people put them on in the boat, but with the geriatric crowd, he planned to get them outfitted first.

His phone rang. Eiko.

"Law, hon, there's been a bit of a mix-up."

"What's up?"

"The Whispering Pines crew isn't coming."

"Oh. Okay." Truth be told, he was a little annoyed. Not only had he left Carter alone at the bar, he had really been looking forward to getting out on the lake.

And he wasn't even minding the prospect of listening to Maya give a lecture.

"The bus was double-booked. There was a long-scheduled trip to the casino in Rodham that no one told me about." Law had a view of the parking lot from his slip, and he turned when he heard a car pulling in. It was Maya's ancient rust bucket. "I was going to shuttle people over myself," Eiko said, "but it turns out everyone went to the casino. I guess gambling wins out over theater. Sorry!"

He watched Maya get out of the car. And then lean back in and rummage around in the back seat. The way she was leaning made it impossible not to, well, look at her ass. Which was encased in a pair of denim shorts. Short shorts. And instead of her usual sneakers, she was wearing flip-flops—a historic day. Well, at least he had nothing on hand with which to burn himself as he'd done last time he'd seen her.

"Well, okay," he said to Eiko. "I'll head back into town."

"Listen, I wasn't able to reach Maya, but I think the two of you should still go. I, well..." Eiko was acting oddly. She wasn't the type to hesitate over speaking her mind. "I'm not sure if I should..."

"What?"

Maya emerged from her car with a bag slung over her shoulder and started across the parking lot.

"I shouldn't say anything," Eiko said.

"Yes you should."

"Well, I ran into Maya this morning, and..." She lowered her voice. "She told me how much she was looking forward to seeing you."

"She did?" Maya spotted him and froze in place, halting her progress across the lot. She scowled. "You must have heard wrong."

"No, I don't think so! I think..."

"What?" He was starting to feel a little unnerved. Eiko was being vague, and Maya was looking at him like she wanted to murder him. "You think what?"

"Nope, I've said enough! You kids enjoy the lake—and each other's company. You're already out there! It would be a shame to waste such a beautiful day!" She hung up.

"Hi," he said warily as Maya resumed her approach. Her hair was in a long braid down her back. He'd never seen it like that before.

"Hi." She jammed a big, floppy sunhat on her head. That probably explained why she didn't have her hair in its usual topknot—it wouldn't fit under the hat.

"What's wrong?"

"What do you mean what's wrong?"

"You looked like you were sucking on a lemon just now."

"Well, *Benjamin*, maybe that's just my natural face."

Right. It was her natural face when she was looking at him, anyway. He just hadn't seen it for a while, had been lulled into complacency by the recent thaw between them. "I just got off the phone with Eiko," he said. "There was some kind of mix-up. The Whispering Pines people aren't coming."

"I heard."

"You did?" Eiko had said she couldn't reach Maya. But okay.

"I ran into Pearl on my way out of town."

Right. So she'd run into Pearl, but she'd come anyway. Was there any way to interpret that other than that it meant she still wanted to go out on the boat?

With him?

Dear God. Had Eiko been right? Was Maya here because she wanted to spend time with him? Just him? He started to sweat. "You, uh, want to go for a quick spin anyway? Since we're here?"

A pickup truck vroomed up, taking the turn into the lot too fast.

"I was hoping you'd say that, because I invited Holden Hampshire."

If there was anyone who didn't need a pickup, it was a city-dwelling actor. Honestly. Holden jumped out, and he was wearing the most obnoxious pair of board shorts. They were tight, white, and long—they came to below his knees. He was shirtless, and his feet were stuffed into a pair of slides that said "Givenchy." He looked like a North Toronto kid dressing up like a California surfer—which was actually exactly what he was. Or, no, a North Toronto kid dressing up like a California surfer playing at being a cowboy in that ridiculous truck.

"I'm trying, to, like, show him a good time," Maya whispered, leaning in so much that he caught a whiff of that botanical-sugar scent. "But I have to say, he is trying my patience."

"Okay," he said, though he was a little surprised at how much he did not want to take Holden Hampshire on a boat ride. But also, maybe Maya's murderous scowl of a moment ago hadn't been intended for him? That would be a twist.

Another car pulled up, and Rohan got out.

"Oh, and I invited my brother, too," she said. She shrugged. "I figured we had a lot of extra capacity."

Law didn't mind Rohan's joining them. And Rohan was dressed like a normal person in shorts, a plain T-shirt, and Birkenstocks.

But so much for Eiko's crackpot theory that Maya had been looking forward to seeing him. She'd brought an army of other men.

Well, just men. No *other*. *Other* implied...whatever was the opposite of *other*. *One, Singular, Exclusive.* None of those words applied. "No problem," he said.

Maya made introductions, and they were off, Maya and Holden talking about something up front while Law chatted with Rohan. As they approached the lift bridge, Maya twisted and said to Rohan, "There have been a few sightings of Pearl in there, even though she swears she has no interest in Dennis Bates." She turned to Holden. "Have you met Pearl from Pie with Pearl? She's an avid internet dater. But we all think she has a secret affair going on with the guy who runs the lift bridge, even though she swears she doesn't."

"Cute," Holden said noncommittally as he looked at his phone.

The bridge was up, so they cruised out into the lake, and Law could feel himself relaxing, and that, in turn, made him realize how not-relaxed he had been for so long. The stress of the restaurant situation had really been getting to him.

"Too bad I wasted my time preparing a theater talk for the old folks," Maya said.

"Hit us with it anyway," Law suggested. To his great surprise, he wanted to hear what she had to say.

"Yeah," said Rohan. "Let's hear it."

"Nah, you guys don't want to listen to me."

"I think it might be good for my characterization to hear your thoughts on Benedick," Holden said.

"But you heard my thoughts on Benedick all day," Maya said. "First day of rehearsal," she explained to Law and Rohan, "so I talked a lot. But okay." She launched into a very entertaining talk on the play, explaining what she thought some of the enduring themes were and how its message of bullying and cancel culture resonated today.

"And," she added when she was done, "it has a *great* song in it. Often the songs in Shakespearean plays get cut or glossed over." She turned to Holden. "But usually you don't have a musical genius in the cast."

Holden, without warning, broke into song. Something about sighing ladies? Holden was a good singer, but it turned out that having an ex-boy-band member sing you a song from *Much Ado about Nothing* acapella was a little awkward.

When he finished, they all clapped. Well, Maya and Rohan clapped. Law moved his hands back and forth like he was clapping, but he stopped short of letting them actually touch, because no way was he going to applaud this dude.

After an enjoyable couple hours touring around—well, Law had enjoyed himself, and it seemed the Mehta siblings had, too, but Holden had spent most of the time looking at his phone—they were back in the marina.

Rohan and Holden drove off, and Law waved off Maya's attempt to help him stow the life jackets under the boat's seats. "I can handle this."

"Nah, let me help. I appreciate your doing this even though we lost our audience."

"I'm sorry, what did you just say?"

She looked up, confused. "I don't know?"

"Did you say you appreciated something about me?"

She rolled her eyes. "One thing. I appreciated one thing about you. Don't let it go to your head."

He let her help him cover the boat and walked her to her car— which didn't start. He wasn't particularly surprised, given the way it had wheezed into the parking lot to begin with.

She made a little mew of dismay and let her head fall on the top of the steering wheel before straightening and trying again. No luck. Nothing but a not-promising clicking noise. "Noooo," she moaned. "I do *not* need this right now."

"I can drop you back in town."

She dragged herself to the passenger seat of his car like she was a teenager being marched to detention.

"You want me to take you to Jordan's?" he asked. "You can ride back out on the tow truck with him?"

"Nope."

"You're going to leave the car dead in the marina?"

"For now. It needs a new battery. It dies all the time. Last time Jordan looked at it, he told me I was living on borrowed time. In fact, no, he told me that the Pontiac Bonneville was such a terrible car that it helped kill Pontiac as a company." She laughed, but it turned into a mock sob. "I'm going to get Jake to come out and try to jump it." Law eyed her. Her dismay seemed over the top for a dead battery. "But that will have to be tomorrow," she added, "because he and Nora are at a midwife appointment in Grand View." She sighed in a way that seemed more wistful than her previous car-related sighs had been. "Just take me back to the Mermaid. I'm starving."

"What's for dinner?"

She snorted. "Packaged ramen. Dinner of champions."

The idea took hold on the drive back downtown. He was going up to Bayshore tonight to spy on the sous-chef at the White Rhino—his industry contacts reported that she ran the kitchen on Mondays. He figured even if Lawson's Lunch was mostly on hold until after the grant announcement, he could still get the ball rolling on some of the big stuff—and there was nothing bigger than who was going to be head chef.

He glanced at Maya. Why should she eat packaged ramen for dinner when he was going to literally have more food than he could stomach? "So, uh..." She turned. "I'm going to Bayshore for dinner tonight, and..."

"Spit it out, Benjamin. If you're gonna be late, you can drop me at Bluewater and Confederation and I'll walk the rest of the way."

"No," he said, probably a little too vehemently. But honestly, she thought he was just going to drop her at the side of the highway? "I'm going to check out the sous-chef at the White Rhino, but secretly."

"Ooh, you mean to see if you want to try to woo him away?"

"Her, and maybe. I'm going to sample a bunch of dishes."

"Mmm, must be hard to be you right now."

"Right, so there's going to be so much food that..." God, he felt like he was in junior high.

"Benjamin Lawson!" she exclaimed so loudly he flinched. "Are you asking me to go to dinner with you?"

"Well, not like a date."

"Ahh! Of *course* not. Why would you *say* that?" She made a noise like a cat coughing up a hairball.

"Well, I don't know. Asking someone to dinner usually implies—"

"Gah. *No.* But are you trying to say you want to suspend hostilities long enough for me to help you with the problem of a feast that's too big for you? That you need my particular expertise in hoovering an astonishing amount of food and passing judgment on it?"

He chuckled. "That is what I'm trying to say."

"Then hooboy, yes! Wait. You're paying for this nondate, right?"

"Right."

She did a little fist pump. "Do I have time to go back to the Mermaid and change?"

"Sure, but you don't have to. The food is great at the White Rhino, but it isn't fancy." Most places in these beach towns weren't. You couldn't really have a dress code without alienating the tourists. "You look fine."

"Oh, but I want to look more than fine."

Maya's hair was down, which was Law's catnip. He used to think he liked it that way because it was so rare—he only ever saw it down in the Mermaid Parade. But then they started doing late-night truces, and it became almost normal. Except not. Because it never ceased to bowl him over.

It came to well past her shoulders, and it was so . . . healthy-looking. That was probably a dumb observation. But he was a dumb guy when it came to hair knowledge. It was just that hers was so shiny and bouncy. And she made it worse—better?—when she opened the passenger-side window as they drove out of town. The wind made her look like a supermodel as she declared, "Hooboy! I am so excited!"

There was also the dress. Which he was reminded of anew when they got out of the car in Bayshore. He'd seen her in dresses before, but only onstage. She didn't wear dresses as herself.

Objectively speaking, there was nothing particularly exciting about this one. It was a solid, regular blue—the color of the blue crayon. It had a neckline shaped like a half circle, and it showed a little cleavage but not much. As she started off down the sidewalk, he could see that it had a ruffle at the bottom.

"What?" Her brow furrowed as she looked over her shoulder

at him. He was just standing there slightly slack-jawed. But only, he told himself, because seeing her in a dress was so novel. And she was wearing strappy sandals instead of her usual high-tops. She looked down at herself. "Is this too much? Was I supposed to come in disguise as a tourist? Should I be wearing a shirt that says, 'I heart Lake Huron'?"

"No, no. You look fine." Had he been saying that to her a lot lately? Like in the dunk tank? Maybe he should be a little more generous than "fine," a little more specific. "Nice dress," he tried.

"It has pockets!" she exclaimed with a grin, sticking her hands in said pockets to demonstrate.

"That's, uh, great." Maybe this had been a mistake. What were they going to talk about seated across from each other for who knew how long? They had no problem carrying on a conversation when that conversation largely amounted to picking at each other. And they had no problem sitting next to each other in silence and staring at a TV. And lately there had been a few instances, like on the roof at Eiko's, or walking back from the Junior Achievement panel, when they'd talked more deeply than usual, but those encounters had been brief, and they'd been walking or sitting side by side.

But sitting across a table from each other and carrying on a conversation for what could be a couple hours? Could they even do it?

It turned out they could. After they ordered a truly ridiculous amount of food, Maya picked up her water and said, "Here's to Lawson's Lunch."

He clinked his glass against hers.

"I haven't heard a word about it from anyone in town," she said. "So good job on that front. How are you keeping everything under wraps?"

"Well, there isn't really anything happening until late fall."

"I thought it was more imminent."

"Yeah, well." He shrugged. He didn't want to say that he was waiting for the grant results—that he was waiting until he beat her—because only then would he know what he was going to do locationwise. Mortgagewise.

"Don't sound too enthusiastic there. Wait. Are you getting cold feet?"

"No." Well, not cold feet exactly, but... "I do sometimes wonder, why do the restaurant at all? Why do more? Why can't I be happy with what I have?"

"Because you're ambitious. I said it before—that's allowed."

It sounded so simple when she said it. It sounded so *reasonable*.

It was a relief when the server arrived. Make that servers, plural—it took two people to carry their food. Maya looked like she was trying not to laugh, which caused a mirroring sort of bubble to make its way up Law's chest. To make it worse, the lead server was narrating as she and her helper set the dishes down.

"Baby back ribs and garlic frites. Bánh mì bowl. Beet and buffalo mozzarella salad. Jackfruit crab cakes. Brown butter pickerel. Side of buttermilk truffle mashed potatoes."

Maya's shoulders were shaking, and she had her lips pressed together. The bubble in his chest floated higher.

"Caesar salad. Lobster bisque. Carbonara. Fish tacos. Steak."

Maya glanced at him—just with her eyeballs, though. The rest of her face stayed perfectly still in a way that was inexplicably hilarious. He started coughing.

The server put her hands on her hips. "Is there anything else I can get you?"

"Yes. Could we please have some vinegar for our fries?" Maya said almost regally, still wearing her poker face.

"And ketchup," he choked out. He wasn't as good an actor as she was.

"Of course."

"And I believe we are going to need some butter, aren't we, Benjamin?"

He could not speak, but managed to nod even though he couldn't see anything in front of them that would require butter.

"And possibly some hot sauce?"

She was doing this on purpose, trying to get him to break and laugh. "Yes," he managed.

The server turned away—he caught her sharing a look with her colleague—and Maya called after her, "And some mayo, too, please!"

He held his breath until the servers were out of sight and, finally, let loose a great big belly laugh. Maya joined him, and it felt like they were allied somehow, the two of them against the world. Which was dumb. All they were doing was ordering too much food.

He eyed the still-laughing Maya, her grin lighting up her face and her honey-cream-ale eyes dancing.

Aww, he was so fucked.

She rearranged the dishes so the steak was in front of him. "This one's yours. No cows for me."

"That's Hinduism, right?"

"Yeah. It's a bit arbitrary, because we aren't observant, and my mother is actually kind of vehemently nonobservant, but..." She shrugged.

He wanted to ask more. He wanted to know everything about her, suddenly, about what she believed and why she loved theater and if she ever got scared about the future. It was a bit alarming, actually.

He was distracted from his unsettling line of thinking when she picked up a rib, dragged her teeth along it to get the meat off the bone, and moaned. "Benjamin."

He had to kind of squirm around in his chair to get comfortable. Watching someone eat should not be such a turn-on, but as was well established, nothing about his cursed attraction to her made sense. "I'm guessing you like the ribs?"

She moved on to a fry, which, hilariously, she dipped in mashed potatoes before putting in her mouth. She moaned again. "You must hire this woman." She flopped back against the booth, which was upholstered in a royal-blue velvet. Her hair snagged on the texture and fanned out. It was like at his place on their last truce night, when he'd thought her hair looked like a reverse waterfall. It was like...

He didn't even know. She was the one who was good with words.

"I am overcome, Benjamin," she proclaimed. "I am overcome."

He knew the feeling.

"Ugh, I don't know if I can walk." Maya's stomach hurt, but in a good way. "I might fall into a coma on the way home."

"Let's walk to the lake." Benjamin pointed at the walkway that ran from the main street in Bayshore to the beach. "See it from a new vantage point. I'll stick our leftovers in the car. Be right back."

Maya started to pivot. It was going to take a while for her over-stuffed body to change directions, but she wasn't going to argue with the guy who'd just picked up the five-hundred-dollar tab for the best food she'd had in ages, maybe ever.

The walk to the beach would be good for them. By the time he was back from the car, she'd gotten herself pointed in the right direction, and they walked past the marina. When they arrived at the beach, he plopped down unceremoniously in the sand.

"Hooboy. I may need a forklift." She started to sit, and he reached a hand up as if to steady her descent. She looked at it—for a moment too long, perhaps, because he retracted it before she could grab it. She did her best to lower herself gracefully. She wasn't used to wearing a dress.

"What are you going to do with the grant money in the extremely unlikely event you win it?" he said.

"Not close the theater," she said automatically. "Oh shit." She clapped a hand over her mouth. For a moment she'd thought she was talking to Nora or Eve. To someone who already knew she was that close to the edge with the theater. Damn him. He had seduced her into feeling all comfortable with him.

"*What?*" He turned to face her, and his arm shot out like his first reflex had been to touch her, but he pulled it back before he made contact.

"I mean, I'm going to use it to set up a fundraising program for the theater," she said quickly.

"No, hang on. You're thinking of closing the theater?" His brow knit. "But you love the theater."

As if that made any difference when it came to the bottom line. "Yes? And?"

"Why do you love the theater?" he asked, startling her a bit.

"That's a big question."

"Don't overthink it. Answer it in a couple sentences."

"Well, when you go to a play, there's this moment where the lights go down, just before anything starts, when it's silent and dark. It's only a few seconds, usually, but it's enough for you to think, *Wow, this is a total blank slate. Anything can happen.* And you buckle up and let it happen." She smiled. "That moment is the best feeling in the world."

He nodded as if he'd asked an exam question and she'd answered correctly. "Right. So you can't quit."

"Well, as much as I love the theater, I'm not sure it loves me back."

"Is it really that bad?" he asked quietly.

Yes, it was really that bad. But he didn't need to know that. She had said too much already. She must be drunk on mashed potatoes.

"You want me to take a look at your grant application?" he asked when she didn't answer his question.

Okay, whoa. She had been lulled by too much amazing food. She'd let her guard down and allowed herself to consider that maybe, just maybe, Benjamin wasn't a *total* jerk. But here he was, being all paternalistic and condescending. Still feeling decidedly blimp-like, she struggled to her feet. "I have written dozens of grants in my time. Why would I need help from you?" Her voice had gone a little shrill.

He blinked rapidly, tilting his head back to look up at her—he was still sitting on the sand.

"Also." She paused and ordered herself to speak in a lower register. She wanted to convey disgust, not hysteria. "*Dude,* I am your main competition. You think I'm going to let you see my application?" She scoffed. "Get up. Dinner's over."

Chapter Twelve

❧

*R*ehearsal was going...not super well. They were a week and a half in, and Maya was starting to wonder if they'd be ready for their late-August opening.

"Are you okay?" Maya called when Claudio tripped over his own feet and landed face-first in a box of plastic swords during what was supposed to be a serious funeral procession.

Claudio, who was turning out to be not a bad actor if not the sharpest sword in the arsenal—there was a reason he was doing summer school, she suspected—waved and said, "Yeah, sorry." But when he stood up, he had a cut on his face, causing Hero to gasp.

"Okay, you need to go clean that up. Everyone take thirty." She pointed at Holden. "Except you." He looked up from the phone he already had out. "Let's you and I work on Beatrice and Benedick's first scene." Holden was having trouble getting off book. She wasn't officially requiring it until next week, but most of the others were doing chunks of some scenes without the script. She was trying to cut Holden some slack. He was new to acting, and even newer to the language of Shakespeare.

They installed themselves in a corner backstage, and she said, "I think you should concentrate your energies right now on a couple pivotal scenes, and this is one of them. This is the first time we see Benedick and Beatrice sparring, and it will set the tone for the rest of their interactions, which are really the heart of the play. The comic relief, too. I'll start. You ready?" He nodded, and she took a quick, cleansing breath to shift into character. "'I wonder that you will still be talking, Signior Benedick: nobody marks you.'"

He delivered his next line from memory, so that was some progress, though he sounded rather mechanical reciting it.

On they went, wobbly but off book, until he said, "'It is certain I am loved of all ladies, only you...'"

"'Excepted...,'" she prompted.

"'Excepted,'" he echoed, and it took him a while, but he came up with the rest of the line. "'And I would I could find in my heart that I had not a hard heart: for truly, I love none.'" It started out with the same woodenness, but he got so excited when he realized he was going to make it to the end of the line that he started "acting." The problem was he was interpreting the line as an angry one. He was yelling at her, which wasn't right.

"Okay, pause. Think back to times in your life where you've been at odds with someone. Was there ever a time you were arguing, but you were drawing energy from that arguing?"

"Like you enjoyed the arguing?"

"Well, like, sparring, you know? Sparring can be invigorating, even if it's not strictly enjoyable."

"Right. I get it."

He didn't sound like he got it.

"Okay, let's take it from my next line." Soon they were going back and forth. But they were not doing anything close to sparring. She signaled for him to stop.

"Maybe the problem is that when you're a celebrity, no one really spars with you," he said. "People kind of do the opposite. They're all deferential."

That was a smart observation. Not that it helped her, but it was interesting.

"Well." She patted his arm. "I can always start yelling at you tomorrow." People were starting to make their way back in, so she raised her voice to reach everyone. "Let's run the final song and dance, and we'll wrap for the day." One of the directing tricks she'd picked up in school was to try to end each day of rehearsals on a positive note, and everyone loved this part. The reprise of the play's signature song let Holden shine. And when Holden sparkled, so did everyone else, because although he might be struggling with Benedick's lines, he exuded charm when he sang and danced.

The song originated earlier in the play and was sung by another character, but they were doing a reprise for the curtain call, in a pop-music format. She and Holden had choreographed the accompanying dance as a sort of pastoral romp with some steps lifted from Two Squared's videos. It was all meant as a kind of lighthearted wink to the audience in keeping with the play's upbeat ending.

"I'm going to watch today rather than participate," she said. A few people were struggling with the choreography, and she wanted to get a handle on where the weak spots were. She hit play on her phone and smiled as she sat back and watched...everyone except Holden dance?

"Cut! Holden, why aren't you dancing?"

"I know the steps already. I figure I'll let everyone catch up, then jump back in."

Arg. The other day, when Benjamin had accused her of looking like she was sucking a lemon, it had been day one of rehearsals. Now she feared her face was going to freeze in lemon-sucking mode.

Maya took a deep breath and forced herself to smile. "I need you in there, Holden. They're supposed to be dancing around us." *Also, don't be a dick.* "And right now I'm not there, so that means they're dancing around *you*." She and Holden were supposed to be doing the boy-band moves in the center of the "garden," and everyone else was sort of frolicking around them in a more traditional "Shakespearey" way. The juxtaposition was intended to be funny.

Holden did this thing with his face she was starting to become familiar with. It wasn't an eye roll, exactly. It was more subtle than that. More like a slight loosening of his face. It seemed like something a teenager would do if he knew he couldn't get away with a more strident display of displeasure.

It pissed her right off.

But what could she do? She needed Holden. She had bet the farm on Holden.

"You know what, folks? Let's call it. Work on your lines— remember we're off book on Monday—and I'll see you tomorrow."

Law hadn't seen Maya in the almost two weeks that had elapsed since their dinner in Bayshore. She hadn't come into the bar. He hadn't seen her on the street. He'd even gone down to the lake last night, a full-moon night, but though Eve and Nora had been there, there'd been no sign of Maya.

Her absence gave him occasion to ponder the fraught end of what had been a pleasant evening in Bayshore, and to conclude that he should not have offered to look at her grant application. He'd only meant it to be helpful—an extra set of eyes.

Because he'd been so gobsmacked over the notion that she might have to close the theater. *Close* the theater. It was impossible to imagine Moonflower Bay without the theater.

But why was he so surprised? She had *told* him, that night on the roof, how much she needed *Much Ado about Nothing* to succeed. And there had been all that talk about taking over her dad's store.

But of course his offer to look at her grant application had come off as condescending. She was right. He had never applied for a grant before. If anything, he should have asked *her* to look at *his* application.

He couldn't get their conversation—or her—out of his head.

The more time elapsed without her coming into the bar, the more
he thought about her. It was getting to the point where she was
crowding out other stuff, like remembering to pay Shane and Carter,
which he had done a day late this week.

"Ben Lawson?"

A woman on the other side of the bar drew him from his thoughts.
She was dressed up—for Lawson's Lager House, anyway. She was
wearing a silk top with a blazer over it, and her hair was in some
kind of elaborate updo. Like Maya's, but fancier.

"Yes. You must be Brie?" His leading candidate for the bar
manager position he'd posted last week. Even if he didn't get
started on the restaurant until after Labor Day, he'd decided to hire
someone to oversee the bar now. He'd decided that day on the boat,
in fact, with Maya and Rohan and Holden. He wanted more time to
do stuff like that.

He stuck his hand out. "Thanks for coming all this way." Brie
had responded to his ad, and after he'd looked at her résumé—
which was great—they'd done a phone interview. She was currently
managing an outpost of the Milestones chain in suburban Toronto,
which was probably a lot more complicated than his bar gig would
be. She'd told him she'd decided to flee the city and was looking
for a job in a place that would lower her cost of living but keep her
in reasonable proximity to family in Toronto.

She seemed great, on paper anyway, so he'd asked if she'd be
willing to make the trek out to meet in person and see the place.
They'd spoken so easily and she'd asked such good questions that
he'd ended up telling her about the new restaurant. And now that
she was here, he kind of felt like she was auditioning him as much
as the reverse.

"Hey, Carter, I'm going to take a break." Carter nodded, and
Law ushered Brie to the far end of the bar. "This place is probably
rougher than you're used to."

"Well, maybe," she said, taking the last stool while he leaned his
elbows on the bar from the inside, "but it's also got great wine and

beer lists. Milestones isn't serving Revel Cider or Bellwoods Jelly King—those are perfect summer taps."

"You must have looked at the website, which I have to admit is a little embarrassing. That's *definitely* rough."

"I could help with that. I know a little about web design. I actually studied graphic design in college."

"So how come you're managing restaurants?"

"I got a job as a designer out of college, but for a bank. I hated it. I'd worked in bars and restaurants since high school. I always thought of it as a way to pay for my studies, as a temporary phase. But at some point, sitting there in my lightless cubicle arguing with executives about which shade of green best conveyed fiscal responsibility, I thought, *Why am I doing this? This is making me unhappy.* I *like* the restaurant world."

"What do you like about it?"

"The buzz of a busy night. The feeling of a roomful of customers who start out happy and the challenge of keeping them that way. The camaraderie among the staff. The hours—I think all my formative years spent in the industry turned me into a permanent night owl."

"I agree. Don't you find—" The bells on the door, which he had trained himself to hear even over the din of a busy night, drew his attention.

It was Maya. With Holden.

Maybe he had thought about her so much that he'd finally manifested her.

Except manifesting someone with your thoughts was not a thing.

They approached the bar, and he watched Carter, who was in the middle of serving someone else, acknowledge them. He turned to Brie. "Will you excuse me for a moment? I'll be right back."

The director and her muse had their heads together and didn't hear his approach. "Hey," he said. "What can I get you?" The question was directed at the muse. He was already grabbing Maya's wine.

"White Claw?" Holden said.

For God's sake. He snorted.

"What?" Holden said.

Law just shook his head, and Maya rolled her eyes at him as he filled her glass.

"What are you guys up to?" he asked, glancing at a sheaf of paper on the bar.

"Running lines," Maya said. She seemed a little stressed.

He'd been wondering if she wanted to call a truce and watch the Crystal Palace first match of the season, which was coming up, but he wasn't about to ask her in front of Holden. In fact, he wasn't about to ask her at all. She was the one who initiated truces. Because truces were about *her* using *him* for his app and his big TV.

"I'll leave you to it." He made his way back to Brie. "Let me ask you a question. What are your thoughts on White Claw?"

She wrinkled her nose. "Yuck."

"Right, but people keep asking for it. Should I not stock it because I don't approve? Is that snobbery? I've always wanted this place to be good but not snooty, you know?"

"Well, I think what I would do in your place is stock it, but also make my own version. Infuse some vodkas yourself. You could do lemon, but make it really lemony. Maybe add something like basil. Then do a berry one. Don't you guys have a raspberry festival?"

Wow. That was a great idea. He leaned in.

"Make up batches of vodka," she went on, "in big mason jars you keep visible. You can label them with the number of days the vodka has been infusing and create an assembly line of batches. That will pique people's interest. You can get jars with spigots at the bottom, so to serve, you fill a glass with a shot, add soda, garnish, and voilà, homemade White Claw."

"That is genius," he said, delighted with this idea.

"You can't actually call it Homemade White Claw, though— that's copyright infringement. But you could call it something kind of funny that everyone will get. The town mascot is a mermaid, right?" Wow, she had really done her research. "Maybe White

Fin?" she mused. "White Tail? That needs work, but something along those lines. And it doesn't have to be expensive. No need to use top-shelf vodka for something like this, and that way you can keep the price down on the finished drink."

Well, this was a no-brainer. "Look, I'm going to level with you. I kind of think your talents will be wasted on this place, but if you want it, the job is yours."

"Who is that over there with Benjamin?" Maya asked Carter when he came to check on them. Carter looked over to where Benjamin was huddled with a woman Maya didn't know. He was leaning way over the bar, his attention riveted. Every once in a while he would smile and shake his head as she talked, like he couldn't quite believe the amazing and delightful things coming out of her mouth.

Sheesh, you disappear for a couple weeks and everything changes.

Maybe she shouldn't have stayed away. She just felt so weird after their dinner in Bayshore, like he felt sorry for her. She could handle pretty much anything from Benjamin except pity. So it had been easy to just "be too busy" to pop into the bar like usual. It wasn't even that much of a lie. She was busy willing Holden into remembering his lines.

"No idea," Carter said.

If the woman was a customer Benjamin had been casually chatting with, why had he gone directly back to her after he'd come over and served them?

And one more question: Why was she so pretty? Her blond hair was twisted into a perfect chignon, and her delicate features were lightly made up—that was the kind of makeup men always thought was "natural" but actually took an hour.

She looked like a Banana Republic model, basically.

"How's the play coming?" Pearl appeared on her other side, pulling out a stool.

"Do you know who that is over there with Benjamin?" If anyone would know, it would be Pearl.

She followed Maya's gaze. "Nope." She turned her attention to Maya. "Why?"

"Just wondering."

Pearl got out her phone. "We haven't done Tinder for a while." Maya and Pearl, who were both all talk and no action on Tinder, occasionally swapped phones and swiped for each other. It always made for some interesting DMs after Pearl had had possession of her phone.

Maya started to say she couldn't right now, as she was working on lines with Holden, but what the heck. Maybe there was a boy Banana Republic model just waiting for her to swipe right.

"You're on Tinder?" Holden asked.

Maya initially thought he was asking Pearl, as everyone always thought it was funny that such an old woman was on Tinder— everyone was ageist, basically. But he seemed to be directing the question to her.

"Yeah," she said as Carter appeared to take Pearl's order, which was, as always, a White Russian.

"Can we get another round, too?" Maya asked as she got out her phone, opened Tinder, and slid it toward Pearl. And heck, she was going to tell Pearl the secret Wi-Fi password.

She leaned over to whisper in her ear, but suddenly Benjamin was there, pushing Carter out of the way. "I have this." He re-filled Maya's wineglass. He looked at Pearl. "White Russian?" And Holden. "And another White Claw?"

She wanted so badly to ask him who the mystery woman was, but she reminded herself that she didn't care and picked up Pearl's phone.

"You want to order a pizza?" Holden asked when Benjamin was back with the drinks.

"No," Maya said, answering Holden but making eye contact with Benjamin. "I don't eat the pizza here."

Chapter Thirteen

⟡

The next Friday, Rohan appeared at the bar just after Jake and Sawyer arrived for their Friday-night hangout. Everyone greeted each other, and when Law asked, "What can I get you?" Rohan sighed and said, "I don't know, something wet and alcoholic."

"Tough day?" Sawyer asked.

"I've been helping my dad at the store, and I meant to order a hundred gardenias to arrive today. Turns out I ordered a thousand."

Nora and Eve arrived at the bar. "Hey," Eve said, "we're not crashing bromance night. We've got a table. We're just grabbing drinks."

Law was about to take their order when he was distracted by a Spice Girl asking him what he really wanted. He whipped his head up. The familiar opening strains of that stupid song blasting from the jukebox had a Pavlovian effect on him.

It was Maya.

With Holden.

Law had a band playing tonight but they were on a break, and Maya and Holden were bent over the jukebox, perusing the offerings.

Which was fine.

That's what it was there for.

All of a sudden, she looked up and right at him, almost like she'd felt his attention.

And then came the glare.

Okay, they were back to the glaring. Which was…strangely disappointing.

"Wow," Rohan said, "you guys still hate each other, eh? You seemed cool on the boat the other day."

It felt wrong to agree: *Yes, I hate your sister.* But it also felt too exposing to tell the truth: *It's more like a complex mixture of attraction and annoyance.*

"Yeah, I still don't get that." Nora turned to Law. "I know you say there's no particular origin for the feud, but it's hard to believe there isn't *something*."

Law shrugged. "We just get on each other's nerves. There's no real cause."

"Oh, no, there is," Rohan said.

"There *is*?" Law exclaimed, and he was not a person who exclaimed.

All faces swung toward Rohan, who said, "Yeah, you ruined her first play."

"*Excuse* me?"

"You didn't know that?" Eve said, a quizzical look on her face.

"No?" He looked at Sawyer for backup.

Sawyer just shrugged. "I thought everyone knew that."

"*I* didn't, if it's any consolation," Nora said.

"*Excuse* me?" Law said again, because it was all he could think to say.

"I just thought it was well established and you didn't want to talk about it because it was kind of a dick move," Sawyer said.

"Will someone please tell me what the hell is going on?"

"She was fifteen," Rohan said, taking pity on him. "She was directing *Romeo and Juliet* out on the town green. Sadie Saunders was playing Juliet. Or she was *supposed* to be playing Juliet, but you guys skipped town."

Oh.

Oh my God.

Law remembered that weekend well. He had randomly won tickets to a concert in Toronto. It had been one of those radio station promos where they put you up in a hotel. He hadn't taken over the bar yet, so he'd had more time for fun back then, and he and Sadie had been in the flush of . . . what? New infatuation? Nah, more like new lust. Sadie was fun, but he'd never been bowled over by love or anything, and he was pretty sure the same had been true for her. But she'd been a year older than he was, and a lot cooler. So their little fling that summer had been a blast. But if he really scraped back into the recesses of his brain, he did sort of remember arguing with her about a play she'd agreed to be in on a lark. Having to work pretty hard to convince her to come to Toronto. The details were vague but coming back to him. Oh, wait, Sadie had been flattered, he remembered because the director—that would be Maya—had told her she had the classical beauty needed to play Juliet.

"I had concert tickets," he said, like he was up before a judge.

"Wait," Nora said. "You dated Sadie?"

"A long time ago. Casually." He wasn't sure why he felt the need to qualify the past. Yeah, he had dated Sadie. What was the big deal? Everyone liked Sadie. Having dated her would only reflect well on him.

"Yes," Rohan said. "And they took off the day of the play, so Maya had to cancel it. She'd made the sets and costumes herself and all that. That was her first play, so it was still all kind of homespun. She was inspired by the Leonardo DiCaprio movie version, so she'd painted a big backdrop of that Mexico City Jesus statue."

Well, shit. "She didn't have understudies?" Law remembered a production of *The Tempest* when Prospero broke his ankle during the dress rehearsal and Alan Hemming had to fill in. Maya had been worked up because the high school teacher had been all of thirty if he was a day, and Prospero was supposed to be wise and old.

"She does now," Rohan said. "She's never done a play since without understudies. In fact, she memorizes the entirety of every play she directs but isn't in so in theory she can step in and play any role."

"She's blown me off more than once because of play memorizing," Nora said. "I always kind of thought it was overkill, but I get it now."

Oh God. How many hours had Maya sat at his bar, memorizing lines? He'd always thought she'd been working on the roles she'd been playing. But she'd been memorizing *entire plays*?

"Yeah," Rohan said to Nora. "She was really affected by that first disastrous show. She'd been planning to film it as part of her college application package."

This just kept getting worse. Law never would have tried to lure Sadie away that weekend if he'd thought— But that was the problem, wasn't it? He hadn't thought. He suddenly remembered arguing with Sadie in the car about whether *Romeo and Juliet* was a stupid story or a romantic one.

It was like finding out your favorite superhero had an origin story you had somehow missed. He'd always thought he and Maya fought because...they just did. He barely remembered a time when Maya wasn't sniping at him.

But think: she'd been away at college for four years.

Had she sniped at him before that?

It was hard to say. She'd been a kid. She hadn't really registered for him.

Until she turned nineteen and came into his bar and started snarking at him. Sting Day. A day he had imbued with origin-story mythology, but apparently he'd gotten it all wrong. *Holy shit.*

He looked over at her, but she wasn't paying any attention to him. She was bopping around with Holden.

"Oh my gosh, is Holden teaching Maya the 'Petal Power' choreography?" Nora exclaimed. "I gotta get my big pregnant ass in on this." She grabbed Eve. "Come on. We can come back for drinks later."

"So hey," Rohan said, drawing Law from his thoughts. "Pearl told me this place was written up in a *Globe and Mail* article?"

"Yeah." Law had to force himself to focus on what Rohan was saying. His brain was occupied with *freaking the fuck out* over the bomb that had just been dropped on him.

"I'm working on a publicity plan for *Much Ado about Nothing*," Rohan said, "and I was thinking I'd try to get a theater critic out here by shamelessly dangling Holden's name. But then I thought maybe I should email that journalist, too, and build on this idea that Moonflower Bay is a cultural hot spot, you know?"

"That's a good idea."

"Do you remember the name on the byline?"

"Yes!" Anything he could do to help make the play a success. He grabbed a pen. "I'll write it down for you."

"Thanks."

"No problem." It was, it turned out, the least he could do—do his part to ensure the success of Maya's latest play, since apparently he was responsible for the failure of her first one.

Maya was learning that trying to coax what she wanted from Holden in rehearsals—including getting him to learn his lines, which was what she wanted most of all—was not the most effective method. He responded better to "spontaneous" conversations in social settings than he did to overt direction. Which was annoying, given that she was literally his director, but it was what it was. So she'd taken to strategically hanging out with him, often at the bar. And although the bar when a band was playing wouldn't have been her first choice, Holden had seen the sign advertising Final

Vinyl, the 1980s–1990s cover band Benjamin often had in, and here they were.

She surprised herself by having a great time. Sometimes when there was a band, people would shove some of the tables aside and make a dance floor, and they had been dancing up a storm. During a break between sets, Maya went up to speak to the band. She knew the lead singer a little—he lived near Port Frederick, and she'd been trying to get him to be in one of her musicals for years.

"Hey, guys, I know this isn't your era, but any chance you know any Two Squared?"

The bassist, who was younger than the other guys, cracked up. "I do. I secretly loved them when I was a kid."

She hitched her head toward Holden. "Well, that there is Holden Hampshire."

"No shit?" His eyebrows shot up. "We can do 'Petal Power.' I'll give these guys the chords over the next break." When the lead singer groaned, he said, "I'll sing, dude. It won't kill you."

During the break, she and Holden hit the jukebox. He was a Spice Girls fan, too, it turned out. "I mean, I sort of have to be, don't I?" he said. "You don't grow up in a band like Two Squared and not respect your elders."

When the band came back on, the bassist took the mic. "This one is in honor of a very special guest." Holden smiled and waved as the whole bar went crazy, and the band ripped into a rock-and-roll-ified version of Two Squared's biggest hit. Holden taught Maya and the girls the dance moves, even going so far as to modify them for Nora, who wasn't able to boing around as much due to her belly. Holden could be all right when he wanted to.

It was fun. Goofy, invigorating fun. Maya realized she hadn't laughed like this in a long time. Impending financial ruin could do a number on one's sense of humor.

"I gotta go," Nora said when the song ended. "My feet are killing me."

"Yeah, I'm done, too," Eve said. "It's almost midnight, and I'm about to turn into a pumpkin."

"Party poopers!" Maya said affectionately as she hugged them and caught her breath. The band, reverting to its 1980s roots, cued up a ballad—"Every Rose Has Its Thorn," which brought her back to that evening on the roof with Benjamin, when they'd bantered about that song.

It suddenly occurred to her that maybe what Holden needed in terms of his Benedick character development was lessons from Benjamin. Say what you wanted about Benjamin, when the banter was flying, he could keep up.

"Dance with me?" Holden asked.

She tried to wave him off. "Thanks, but I'm gonna sit this one out."

"Come on!" He started pulling on her arm. "You know you want to." He started singing, but in a funny exaggerated way. He'd had a lot of beer, and he was happy. She did love this song. It lent itself to funny, exaggerated singing, but it was also just a cool song. Those big-haired metal bands from the 1980s knew what they were doing.

"Okay, okay." She let herself be propelled to the center of the makeshift dance floor. Holden took her into his arms, and they started swaying.

"This is nice," he said into her ear.

"Mm-hmm." She tried to look over at the bar, but she didn't have a clear sight line.

"I heard there's a town tradition of throwing flowers into the lake?"

"What?"

"Flowers? The lake?"

"Oh, yeah. But on nights with full moons." They'd twirled around enough that she could see the bar now, but there was no one behind it.

"Oh, bummer."

"Well, I mean, it's not like there's a rule." She herself had been known to be loose with her interpretation of the tradition.

"I was thinking maybe you could show me."

"Sure. After this song?"

"Or you could show me your place."

"You're in my place."

Oops. She hadn't meant to say that. For some reason she didn't want him knowing she'd evicted herself for him. She didn't like people knowing how close to the edge she was. Well, except the girls. And Benjamin. Which was sort of strange. She *hated* the idea that Benjamin might think of her as weak, or incapable.

Happily, Holden was too tipsy to understand what she meant. He pulled back, his face scrunched in confusion, and she took the opportunity to redirect. "I'm actually staying with a friend at the moment. My place has been undergoing some renovations."

"Ah. I could show you my place, then."

You mean you could show me my own place. She tried not to laugh. "Sure. I'd love to see your place." It would be easier to work on his lines there. Though maybe he'd had too much to drink for that.

"You on the pill?"

What? She jerked in his arms, and they both stumbled. He righted them and shot her a smile. She threw her head back and laughed.

"What?" He laughed along with her, but uncertainly. He thought she was laughing at him, and he wasn't used to that.

"Honey, you're drunk."

"So?"

"I'm your director."

"So?"

"So that's two avenues in which I could take advantage of the situation."

"Please do."

She stopped laughing and pondered him. Holden was ridiculously good-looking. And fun, when she wasn't trying to get him to do his job—she'd truly had a great time this evening goofing around with him and the girls.

And now it seemed that he was propositioning her. What even was her life?

But aside from the moral yuckiness, he just...didn't do it for her.

He was looking adorably bewildered, so she kissed him on the cheek and was about to tell him to go home, when someone intruded on their circle.

"I brought you a glass of wine." Benjamin. Speaking to her but looking at Holden.

"Thanks, but I don't have my wallet with me." That was a lie. She had it—it was in her purse—but it was empty. She was living on credit card fumes. "So I've been taking up space in your bar without buying anything," she said cheerily to deflect from the fact that she *hated* doing that.

Law withdrew his attention from Holden and transferred it to her. But only for a second before he was back to scowling at Holden. "I don't know why your boyfriend here didn't buy you a drink."

She was about to correct the record with a *He's not my boyfriend* retort, but she stopped herself. She, to her continuing surprise, did not even harbor one little speck of attraction to Holden, but Benjamin did not need to know that.

"Oh, right," Holden said, "Sorry. You want a drink, Maya?"

She smiled sweetly at him. "I'd love a drink, thanks."

Holden pulled out a twenty, but Benjamin just stood there. She'd assumed he would hand over the wine, but that did not seem to be the plan. He might even have—she wasn't sure if she was imagining it—pulled the glass a tiny bit closer to his chest as Holden tried to pay for it.

Nope, not imagining it. In fact, he leaned his torso back, rotated, and handed her the wine. "On the house."

"Uh, thanks. That's nice of you." It was, even though he was being weird.

"But isn't your wine always on the house?" Holden asked. "Or at least the second glass?"

Huh? She turned to Holden. "What do you mean?"

"Well, it sort of seems like when other people order a glass of wine, they get a glass of wine. But when we're here working on lines and you order a glass of wine, you get a glass of wine but then you keep getting it topped up."

"That's..."

True? Also surprisingly observant for Holden?

She'd assumed that was what Benjamin did for regulars. She searched her memory. The problem was her friends weren't really wine drinkers. It wasn't like he was going to take someone's entire pint glass and refill it with beer for free. That was different from a little top-up of wine, wasn't it?

While she pondered, Benjamin turned his death glare onto Holden. "I charge appropriately."

I charge appropriately? What did *that* mean?

Holden rolled his eyes. "Whatever, dude." To Maya he said, "I'm going to hit the bathroom."

As soon as Holden was gone, Benjamin leaned forward. "Crystal Palace season opener next Saturday," he whispered.

She blinked, adjusting from the history of drink pouring to... "Is that your way of suggesting a truce?" She had been so stressed about the play, she'd lost track of time, but the season was due to start.

"It might be," he said.

There wasn't precedent for this, for him inviting her over. The way they normally played the truce game was she *told* him when she was coming over.

When she didn't answer right away, he asked, "And will you be coming over for it?"

Well, regardless of all this weirdness, she wasn't missing the first match of the season. "Yes."

"And do you want to watch it live?" he asked. "It's on at ten a.m. our time."

They had never done that. They always watched archived matches late at night. "Yes," she said, striving to keep her tone mild. "I want to watch it live." How extraordinary.

He snorted. "Don't sound so excited."

She was excited, though. She was extremely excited.

To his annoyance, Law started seeing Holden Hampshire everywhere after that night in the bar. When he ran across the street for something at Jenna's, there Holden would be, chatting with Jenna and other customers. Or he'd show up at the bar, order a drink, and proceed to start mouthing his lines like a simpleton.

The next Friday, Law met Brie for lunch at Sadie's Diner. Brie had given her notice in Toronto and was in town looking at rentals. He needed her to sign an employment contract, and he'd suggested she do it over lunch—and there was Band Boy again.

"Hey, Lawson's Lager House, right?" Holden said, looking up from the phone that seemed to be his constant companion—when he wasn't slow dancing with Maya.

Law grunted in assent. But, realizing he was being rude, he said, "Brie Goodwin, this is Holden Hampshire. Holden, Brie." At least Brie would be immune to Holden. She was too cool to care about a washed-up "celebrity" like Holden.

Brie cocked her head. "Holden Hampshire as in Two Squared?"

"Guilty."

She laughed in delight. "I loved you guys back in the day."

Dammit. Law shoveled fries into his mouth while Brie effused— did *everyone* love this guy?—and Holden affected modesty.

"What does Two Squared mean?" Law asked once the other two were done with their exchange. "How'd you get that for a name?" It was a stupid one.

"Well, see, there were four guys in the band," Holden said, and Law refrained from pointing out that "band" might be too generous a label for the song-and-dance show he'd seen when he YouTubed the group. "And four, is, like, two to the power of two."

"That's it?" That was even dumber than Law had imagined. He'd expected something less literal.

"Two to the power of two is another way of saying two squared," Holden said. "You know, that little number in the upper right of a regular number?"

"I am familiar."

"Does he *live* in Moonflower Bay?" Brie, all agog, asked after Holden left.

"No, no. He's in town rehearsing a play. We have a great little theater company, and the director has lured him here to star in a show. It will be on before you get here, which is too bad. They're doing *Much Ado about Nothing*, which I don't know that much about, but she's pretty much a Shakespeare expert and..."

Brie was looking at him kind of funny. Maybe she wasn't a theater fan.

"So the job," he said, forcing himself to concentrate on the topic at hand. He pulled the contract out. "I think this reflects what we talked about." What they had talked about was her having the title "manager" and gradually taking over admin and supervision at the bar as well as covering a fair chunk of the shifts. But they'd also talked about her helping with the restaurant, and he'd built in a bonus structure that would compensate her for her insight and assistance on that front. "If you want to take the contract with you and read it and mail it back, that's cool."

She had picked it up and was scanning it. "Nope, this looks great. Honestly, I kind of expected a small-town gig like this to be sealed on a handshake." She rummaged in her purse for a pen.

As she slid the signed contract across the table, he couldn't deny he was a little nervous. Her salary was less than she'd made in Toronto, on account of the lower cost of living here, but more than he otherwise would have paid. She was clearly worth it, but it was a significant expense.

"Can I get you two anything else?"

Law eyed the smiling Sadie, who had come to clear their

plates. He didn't get out much, so he hadn't seen her since the big revelation about *Romeo and Juliet*. He was tempted to ask her about it, but he couldn't right now. What would be the point, anyway? They had done a crappy thing a long time ago. There was no getting around that. There was also no need to make her feel bad.

After lunch, he and Brie went back downtown so he could point out Jason Sims's house, which was still for sale. "This is the place I have my eye on for the restaurant."

"It looks great." She glanced at him. "But you're not sure?"

"Not sure there's enough room out back for seating and a pizza oven," he said in a complete deflection from the truth. He didn't want to tell her he was in a holding pattern until he found out if Miss I've Applied for Dozens of Grants in My Lifetime had kicked his ass.

She contemplated the house from their vantage point on the sidewalk. "You're going to keep doing pizza at the bar, right?"

"I don't see why not. The oven there is already built. It's not like I can move it."

"So maybe *don't* do pizza at the restaurant? Keep that the signature food for the bar. You want to make sure people keep patronizing the bar, and bars and pizza kind of go together anyway. Then you can come up with something else for the restaurant?"

That was an interesting take. "I am kind of becoming known for my grilled-cheese sandwiches. I do them outside the bar on presses during town festivals."

"Perfect. You have a built-in audience, and that's exactly the kind of food I hear you talking about wanting to serve. Not fussy but capable of being classed up. You can use local cheeses and herbs and stuff."

"Hey, can I ask you a favor? The restaurant isn't a secret per se, but I'm trying to keep the news under wraps until it's a little farther along."

"Of course."

"Thanks. You want to see the rest of Main Street?"

"Sure."

They strolled, and he pointed out local landmarks and businesses of note.

"What's with all the moonflowers?"

"A town tradition. Everyone grows them. There's a superstition that if you throw one into the lake under a full moon and make a wish, your wish will come true."

"That is disgustingly charming." They walked in silence a way until she said, "Speaking of disgustingly charming, is this a florist? What an adorable name."

They'd stopped in front of A Rose by Any Other Name. "Yeah, it's . . . " Maya was in there. That was rare. "This place is owned by the father of the theater director I was telling you about. Come on, I'll introduce you."

He realized his error when he was halfway through the door. Holden was in there, too. Super close to Maya. In fact, both of them were behind the counter.

"Hi," Maya said, her brow furrowed—she was confused by his appearance.

"We're interrupting. You're running lines."

"I don't think it's called interrupting when you enter a place of business that's open," she said.

"Oh, hey, we meet again," Holden said. "And we're *not* running lines." He grinned.

They weren't? Then what were they doing huddled so close together?

"Because I have mine all memorized." He did a little fist pump, and Maya tilted her head and raised her eyebrows slightly, suggesting she might not share Holden's view on the matter. "High five, Brit!" Holden lifted his hand for Brie to slap.

She looked at him blankly. "It's Brie."

"Like the cheese," Holden said.

"Yes, like the cheese," Brie said in a deadpan tone. Law liked

Brie. He'd made a good move hiring her, even if it freaked him out a little.

She finally took pity on poor Holden, who was standing there with his palm up, still waiting for his high five. After slapping it weakly, she offered the same hand to Maya. "Sorry, we haven't met. I'm Brie."

"Maya." Maya darted her gaze back and forth between him and Brie, for God knew what reason.

"I've heard all about your theater. Sounds like a cool play you guys are working on." Brie turned to Holden to include him in the sentiment.

Maya kept doing the eye-darting thing, but eventually her gaze stayed on Law. "Are you looking for my dad? He and my mom are visiting relatives in Brampton today."

"Oh no, I'm not looking for your dad."

She blinked. "Was there something you wanted, then?"

He felt dumb, suddenly, for thinking they had the kind of relationship where he could just pop in and say hi. "Yeah, give me two wishing flowers."

She raised an eyebrow but went to the fridge to get them.

"I thought you said that was for full moons," Brie said.

"Well, it can't hurt." Brie shook her head at him laughingly, and he added, "What? You can't think of a wish?"

"That will be ten dollars," Maya said curtly. Clearly she was pissed at him. Or extra pissed, given that "pissed at him" was kind of her baseline, their recent thaw aside.

He wanted to ask if she was still coming tomorrow for soccer. He had Carter opening so he'd have a buffer between when the match ended and when the bar opened. But of course he couldn't ask her, not with an audience.

As they strolled toward the lake, Brie said, "I didn't know if I should introduce myself as the new bar manager back there. I assume that part isn't a secret? I'll be here soon enough."

"Oh no. Just the restaurant part. And I know I'm being kind

of cagey about that, but small towns can be gossipy. I need to..."
Decide if I'm mortgaging the damn bar. "Get it off the ground
before word really gets out. But some people know. My friends
know. Maya, who you met back there, knows."

"Maya is not your friend?"

"What?"

"You said your friends know, and you said Maya knows. Which
suggests that Maya isn't a friend?"

"Oh. Right." That was another thing that was hard to explain.
"No, she's not really a friend." *Was she?*

"Ex-girlfriend?"

"No! God, no."

"Sorry, none of my business. She just seemed a little frosty
back there."

"That's just what she's like." Around him, anyway. He thought
back to her laughing and dancing with Holden the other night.
They'd reached the little beach. He handed Brie a flower and
pointed toward the pier. "Let's walk out there to throw them."

"Aren't these supposed to be moonflowers?"

"Traditionally, yes. But the town has gotten more popular with
tourists, especially around the two big summer festivals, and everyone was stealing the moonflowers, so now the town steers people to
buy flowers from A Rose by Any Other Name. And you can't sell
cut moonflowers, since they grow on vines, so this is sort of like a
copycat flower. It's an amaryllis, I think." He paused. "And yes, I
do realize how absurd that sounds. This town sometimes straddles
that fine line between charming and bonkers."

"Now you tell me," she joked, "*after* I've signed the contract."

He gave a moment's thought to telling her about "the matchmakers," but decided not to. He had no idea what her relationship
status was, and as her boss it wasn't his place to ask. Anyway, if
she was going to be working downtown, she'd find out about them
soon enough.

When they reached the railing at the end of the pier, she gazed at the water. It was a sunny day, and the lake was at its bluest. "Amazing." She held her flower out. "You're going to do it, too, right?"

He supposed he was. He'd bought two flowers. She flung hers into the water as he pondered. He hadn't done this for years. His mind went blank. Brie turned to him expectantly. Okay, clearly he should wish for the restaurant to be successful. But that seemed so big. So amorphous.

He tried to narrow it down. To put it in Spice Girls terms, what did he really really want?

His mind flashed forward to tomorrow morning. Crystal Palace versus Liverpool.

Raising his hand, he threw the flower and wished for Maya to not be so mad that she didn't show up.

Chapter Fourteen

❧

*W*hen Maya arrived at the bar Saturday morning, she was thirty minutes early. She'd planned to run over to Jenna's to pick up something—she usually tried to arrive at truces with some little offering or other even though she and Benjamin both knew she was going to drink his wine. Although no wine for morning matches. There was no precedent for this. But when she'd come downstairs from her room at the Mermaid, she'd found Pearl and Eiko chatting in the lobby with Eve. They hadn't noticed her creeping down the stairs, so she'd quietly fled through the kitchen.

Once she was out back, she'd nearly run into Karl, who was, for God knew what reason, poking around in the passageway between the inn and the bakery.

Were these people *everywhere*?

Well, yes. That shouldn't be surprising. They just seemed *extra* everywhere right now.

As she'd crept carefully past the passageway, Karl had looked up, but not right at her, so she'd hightailed it past and, instinctively, jogged over to the bar.

And now she was having a bout of indecisiveness. She was already here. She should just go up, right? Rather than risk Karl seeing her?

But was it rude to be so early?

She shook her head. When had she ever been worried about being rude to Benjamin?

She pulled on the door.

Locked. Hmm.

The back door opened onto a vestibule containing an old-school pay phone and a chalkboard list of what was on tap. From there, you could open another door to get into the bar or head up a flight of stairs to Benjamin's apartment.

She'd assumed he always kept the outside door open, because she had literally never encountered it locked. And since he kept the inner door to his bar locked, and presumably the door to his apartment locked, this door was kind of superfluous. But on the other hand, this vestibule was often filled, when the bar was open, with drunk people up to no good.

Okay, well, she'd carry on with her plan to go to Jenna's.

But then Karl stepped out of the passageway. He was carrying a ladder—she didn't even want to ponder why— and thankfully, it was blocking his view of her. She flattened herself against the wall and got out her phone to text Benjamin. 911—I'm downstairs, and I need you to come let me in.

She wasn't sure he would recognize her number. They were on some group chats together, but they'd never texted one-on-one. She had him in her contacts as *Pizza Jerk*. But presumably he wasn't expecting anyone else at his back door this morning.

A few moments later, she could hear him clattering down the stairs like a herd of bison. Yeah, she probably should have said, "I need you to let me in *quietly*."

He appeared on the other side of the glass door, and...welcome to the third See Benjamin's Chest Day of the summer. She ordered herself to be cool and put her finger to her lips to signal quiet.

"What's wrong?" he whispered urgently as he yanked open the door. She hustled inside, but because she was looking over her shoulder as she did so, she didn't realize he hadn't moved back—typical Benjamin, not giving her an inch—so she ended up banging against his chest.

Which, in addition to being bare, was damp.

As was his hair, she discovered, as she tilted her head back to look at him. No, not damp, fully wet. As if to punctuate her observation, a drop of water fell on her cheek.

To her complete shock, one of his arms banded around her waist, and he pulled her against his chest. "Are you okay?" he said urgently.

It took her a minute to get her bearings and therefore to answer. He was just so...hard. But also accommodating. Comfortable to lean against even though he was...her nemesis. The Pizza Jerk. Or something. While her vocabulary was failing, his other hand came to her face, tilting it to the side, like he was trying to see her better in the dimly lit vestibule.

His hand on her face shocked her out of her stupor. "Of course I'm okay." She tried to look anywhere except at his eyes. Being the object of such intense, direct scrutiny from him was suddenly uncomfortable—which made no sense, because they spent a lot of time having staring contests. She squirmed, trying to push back against his embrace, but he didn't give way. "Why wouldn't I be okay?"

"On account of the fact that you texted me 911?"

Right. She bit back the urge to apologize if she'd worried him. "It wasn't 911 *per se*. It was Karl. I didn't want him to see me coming here."

He snorted and let go of her. Stepped back to make the room she'd been actively trying to acquire a mere moment ago but now found she didn't want at all.

"Do *you* want Karl to see me coming here?" she asked.

He muttered something under his breath that she didn't catch, but then raised his voice and said, as he mounted the stairs, "All right. C'mon."

"Why was this door locked anyway?"

"It's usually locked when the bar is closed. I unlock it when I know you're coming. And if you haven't noticed, you're half an hour early."

"You keep this door locked?"

He shot her a bewildered look over his shoulder. "Have you not noticed this town has its share of meth heads in and amongst the moonflowers?"

Of course she had. It just seemed uncharacteristically considerate of him to run down and unlock it in advance of her arrival, rather than telling her to text when she was downstairs. But probably he didn't want to get into the habit of texting her. She'd made that *Pizza Jerk* contact for him, to keep things organized in group texts. But he likely had no idea which string of numbers was hers. Anyway, if they started texting regularly, they'd spend all their time typing rants at each other. Ranting in person was much more efficient.

Inside, Benjamin grabbed a full coffeepot. "You want some?"

She nodded—and she may or may not have admired the way the muscles in his back rippled as he reached up to a high shelf for a mug. "Sorry I didn't bring anything. Oh, but wait!" She rummaged in her purse and pulled out a couple fortune cookies and dropped them on the counter. "Never let it be said I skimp in the hospitality gift department."

He rolled his eyes. "I'll be right back."

She took her coffee and strolled into the living room, taking the opportunity to examine his sweet apartment in the bright light of day. There were archways between the rooms, a charming little historical touch that broke up the large space. And he had good furniture—mostly midcentury teak stuff, but then his big, amazing, fluffy, pale-blue couch. The first time she'd come up here, she'd thought it was weird that his apartment was so nice while the bar was kind of rough. The bar was spotless, but between the wood-paneled walls and the wooden floors and booths, it was sort of dark and heavy feeling. But now she wondered if the fact that it looked like it was 1955 inside the bar was more a function of the family legacy thing than it was a reflection of Benjamin's taste.

She strolled across the cushy living room rug to the front window. It was silly, but she liked to look at her apartment from his apartment. Well, really, she liked to do the reverse, to look at his apartment from hers. Since they were both up late due to their jobs, she was often still awake when he closed the bar. So she'd see his place dark, and later the lights would come on. She'd imagine him puttering around as he unwound and got ready for bed. After a while the light in this room would go off, and sometime later the light in another window she assumed belonged to his bedroom would go off, too.

It felt kind of weird that she hadn't spied on him in recent weeks, because she'd been living in the Mermaid.

Had Holden spied on him from her apartment?

Nah. Holden wasn't that observant. She smiled. She had developed a certain affection for her leading man, but she definitely no longer had stars in her eyes. That was probably helped along by the fact that he kept propositioning her. She'd assumed, that time they'd been dancing, that his suggestiveness had been a result of his drunkenness, but it turned out that no, he genuinely wanted in her pants. She had no illusions that it was anything other than that he was bored in this town, and she was convenient. They'd made sort of a joke of it—him asking and her rebuffing. But he kept trying—like yesterday, when he'd popped into the flower shop unexpectedly.

Who would have ever thought she'd be in a position to turn down sexual advances from a member of Two Squared?

"What's so funny?"

She turned. Benjamin's hair had clearly been towel dried, because it was merely damp now. He was wearing a bright-green Heineken T-shirt. It was worn-looking and, she was sure, incredibly soft. You could tell by looking at it. It also made his eyes, which were a few shades darker, pop like crazy.

She pointed over her shoulder at the window. "Do you ever see Holden from here?"

"No. He never opens the curtains." His lip curled. She wasn't sure if that little sneer was inspired by the idea of someone eschewing daylight or by Holden specifically.

She moved from the window and sat on the couch before she realized he was still standing, looking at her. He opened his mouth like he was going to say something but then shut it.

"Sorry I alarmed you with that text," she said, but then had to stifle the urge to clamp her hand over her mouth. She never apologized to Benjamin, even on the extremely rare occasion when it might be called for.

"No, I'm the one who should—"

He didn't clamp his hand over his mouth, but he did cut himself off rather abruptly.

Whatever. It was the first match of the season, and they were watching it live! She shook her head, scooched around so she could really get comfy on his perfect sofa, and let the excitement course through her. She'd been so incredibly busy rehearsing—and managing Holden—that she hadn't had time to savor the anticipation.

"I see you dressed up for the occasion," he said.

"I sure did." She was wearing her Crystal Palace dress. It was nothing special, just a soft, comfy knit sheath dress. She'd paired it with her red glitter Cons, which she'd laced for the occasion with bright-blue laces. "Ahh! I'm so excited!"

He smiled at her a little too sincerely.

"What?"

"Nothing." He picked up his remote and cued up the match. "It will be interesting to see how Hendricks works out."

"Huh?"

"The new guy traded from Tottenham?"

"I know, I'm just surprised *you* do."

"Eh, you've got me kind of invested in this band of hooligans."

"Well, the conventional wisdom is that it was a bad transfer—they call it a transfer, not a trade."

She expected him to razz her about her insistence on the UK terminology, but he didn't. "I don't know. I feel like Hendricks could go either way. Yes, they lost Diaz, but he didn't have that great a season last year, really. He had some big, theatrical moments, but when you actually look at the numbers, I'm not sure he was worth what they were paying him."

She blinked. She was struck dumb.

"What?" he asked.

"I just..." She was not used to talking to him about football. There was no one in this town who cared about the Premier League. There might be some passing interest toward the end of the season, but other than that it was a typical Canadian town, all hockey all the time with perhaps a small chaser of the NBA.

"What?" he said again, looking a little alarmed.

"Nothing!" Why was he suddenly so *worried* about everything? "Honestly, Benjamin, I'm a little gobsmacked to find that you actually enjoy this."

Instead of responding, he said, "Why don't you call me Law like everyone else does?"

"Because everyone else does." Crap. That had come out on its own. "I just..." Ugh, how to salvage this? "Law seems like a friendly nickname, and you and I are..."

"Not friendly?" he said cheerfully.

That was true. Or it had been. Lately they seemed to be swinging back and forth between their usual mode of "not friendly" and...something else. Something that felt friendly? She looked at his angular jaw, the morning sun making the auburn in his stubble glint. No, *friendly* was not the word.

She was overthinking this. "Right. Anyway, I don't know, I don't like calling you what everyone else does."

"Well, I'm sorry to inform you that my mother calls me Benjamin."

"Really?" Calling him the same thing his mother did felt...not right. "Does anyone call you Ben?"

"Not really. Maybe telemarketers trying to be friendly. And it's how I introduce myself when I'm meeting someone new and I need a first and last name—Ben Lawson. But that's pretty much it for Ben."

Hmm. She let the name rattle around in her brain. *Ben.*

When Maya got up to get some more coffee a while later, Crystal Palace was ahead by one, and she twirled across the living room instead of walking, all stripes and glee. It drew Law's attention to her blue-and-red dress. Apparently he'd been wrong that night in Bayshore when he'd had the notion that she never wore dresses in real life. This one was made out of T-shirt material, so it was casual. But it was kind of formfitting, which seemed...not casual.

"Does anyone ever wonder where you are when you come here?"

She paused under the archway that separated the dining room from the living room. "Not really. I live alone. Well, when I'm not living in the Mermaid. I did kind of have to sneak out this morning because Eiko and Pearl were in the lobby."

"Weren't you worried someone would see you in your dress? Everyone knows you love Crystal Palace."

She looked down at herself. "Well, but this isn't, like, an official dress. It's just a red-and-blue-striped dress I happened to find at Old Navy a couple years ago."

Still. She looked very...spirited.

"And really," she went on, "does the average person around here know that Crystal Palace's colors are red and blue?"

Fair point, he supposed.

"Anyway, it's not like it's a secret that I'm here."

"You were the one texting 911 to try to get in here unseen this morning."

He thought they might be ramping up to argue, but she made a funny face and said, "You're right."

He cupped his hand to his ear. "I'm sorry, what did you just say?"

She rolled her eyes and turned for the kitchen, calling over her shoulder, "You were right. Once. Don't let it go to your head."

He kind of loved when she said that to him. Not the *You were right* part so much as the *Don't let it go to your head* part. He had no idea why.

"But anyway," she called from the kitchen as she refilled her coffee, "I was avoiding Karl. I think we can both agree that Karl and his minions do not need to know I'm up here. Not only would they get the wrong idea, they would *delight* in getting the wrong idea. Do you want to become one of their projects?" She skipped back in and set her mug and the fortune cookies she'd previously left in the kitchen on the coffee table.

"Nope." He sure as hell didn't. "Do Eve and Nora know you're here?"

"No."

"Why keep it from them if it's not a secret?"

"Do Sawyer and Jake know I'm here?" she countered.

"Touché." They had come close to getting busted by Jake last winter. Law still remembered the panic of waking up to someone knocking on his door. "But why?" he wondered out loud. "Why do we care?"

"We care because they wouldn't understand."

"They wouldn't understand soccer?"

"*Football.* They wouldn't understand why two people who hate each other are secretly holed up watching *football* together."

Right. Except he didn't hate her. Never had. And he was still grappling with the bombshell news that if he hadn't ruined *Romeo and Juliet* all those years ago, maybe she wouldn't hate him, either. Maybe everything would be . . . different.

She flopped down next to him, turned her whole body so she

was facing him, and flashed a grin. "It's kind of like we're having an affair, isn't it?"

He smiled back automatically and had the jolting realization that she had smiled at him face-on a lot lately. He used to think about how he'd never gotten one of those, only observed them from the side. Though this one was really a smile of amusement: people would think they were having an affair, ha ha, how ludicrous.

"Sneaking around," she went on, "holed up in your apartment at all hours. Ha! It *totally* seems like we're having an affair."

He wanted to say that no, it did not totally seem like they were having an affair.

Because if they were having an affair, he could kiss her right now.

Which he suddenly wanted to do more than anything.

Her smile disappeared. "But actually, I guess there's not really any danger of people thinking that now that you have Brie."

Huh? "Yeah, I guess I will be home more once she starts." Was that what she meant? People wouldn't see him with Maya at the bar as much, therefore there would be less fodder for gossip? He really didn't think anyone was gossiping about them, though.

"Once she 'starts'? What are you doing? Auditioning her?"

"I thought about doing that—a probationary period." It had seemed like a way to mitigate the risk of hiring someone who might not be a good fit. "But since she's moving from Toronto, that seemed kind of cruel."

"She's moving here from Toronto?" She whistled. "Wow."

"I know. I'm lucky. Anyway, the tryout period became a moot point. When I met her, I just knew."

"You just knew," Maya echoed, her voice flat.

"I think that's how it works sometimes."

"So I hear." She didn't sound convinced. "Where'd you guys meet?"

"Online." It turned out you could hire people through LinkedIn.

"I was kind of amazed at how many responses I got. Once you cast your net wider than just this area, and get more methodical than word of mouth, it's amazing what you can turn up."

"I bet." She frowned. "Though I clearly am doing it wrong."

But she was casting plays. He was hiring bar help. It was different. "Well, even with the huge volume of responses, Brie was obviously the best of the bunch."

"Obviously."

He eyed her. Her mood had taken a nosedive, and the way she was responding with flat, one- or two-word responses was kind of odd.

"So she's moving here." Maya looked around the apartment with her brow furrowed. "When does she arrive?"

"Three weeks."

She whistled again. "Wow, you don't mess around."

"Well, it's going to take two weeks for her to get out of her current situation, and then she's going to take a breather."

"She's going to take a *breather*? After her *current situation*?"

"Yeah. I feel like it would be rude to try to force her to rush it. It's not like I *need* her. I've been fine without her up until now."

She laughed, but it sounded hollow, like a bad actor laughing onstage. And Maya wasn't a bad actor. "So I guess I'd better enjoy today's match while I can."

Huh? "What do you mean?"

She looked as confused as he felt. "Does Brie like football?"

"I have no idea. Odds are not."

"But she's going to be cool with me coming over and hanging out for hours on end?"

"I don't see why she would care. It has nothing to do with her."

She squinted at him. "Have you sustained a head injury?"

"Have you?"

"Benjamin. I understand that we live in modern times, where some of us are so evolved that we never feel a speck of jealousy. But do you honestly want your brand-new girlfriend to not care that you spend a suspicious amount of time cozied up with me on your couch partaking in an activity she isn't part of?"

"My girlfriend? What are you *talking* about? Who's my girl-friend?"

"Uh, hello? Brie? The one who's moving here to be with you? The one you're strolling Main Street and making wishes with?"

Holy hell.

"The one you were huddled with in the corner of the bar?" she went on.

He wanted to point out that *she* was huddled with Holden at the bar all the time. But he couldn't, because he was laughing. Throwing his head back and letting it shake through his chest. He tried to stop when he caught a glimpse of Maya's continuing confusion, but he was powerless against the tide of laughter. Until her confusion started to shade into hurt. That sobered him right up.

"Maya. Brie is moving here—'here' being Moonflower Bay, not this apartment—to become the manager of the bar. I hired her. She's my *employee*."

Her mouth rounded into an O, but no sound came out. She was doing the gears-turning thinking face, and eventually the sound caught up with the shape. "Ohhhhh."

He could see how this had all happened. Brie hadn't introduced herself with anything other than her name at the shop yesterday. He'd been so disconcerted to find Holden there *not* running lines. Which meant he was just hanging out. And then Brie hadn't said anything about the job because she'd been overinterpreting his directive to keep the restaurant stuff quiet.

Maya started laughing, which somehow functioned as permission for him to start again. It was strange to be laughing together. Good strange, though. It made him imagine—

"How's the mermaid queen thing going?" she asked, jolting him back to reality.

"What?" He stopped laughing but could not quite extinguish the residual smile.

"You know, your pledge to get someone else elected?"

Right. That killed the smile. Back to business as usual. "Okay, well, I told you I thought I'd try Sadie, but I decided that if I'm opening a restaurant that's going to compete with hers, I should leave that alone."

Maya snorted. "Yeah, maybe don't start playing pranks on your closest rival."

"So I tried to find someone who would be up for it. I asked Eiko, but she said no." Karl was often elected king, and Law had suddenly thought, hey, why not Eiko as queen? The town old folks were already the de facto monarchs in town.

"Whoa, whoa, rewind. You're *asking* people if they *want* you to get them elected?"

"Uh, yes?"

"You're getting consent? What about me? Where was my consent?"

He was pretty sure she was kidding. His smile had died on the vine earlier, but hers hadn't. Still... "Yeah, I'm, uh, sorry about that."

He was sorry about a lot of things, it turned out. He had almost apologized earlier, for *Romeo and Juliet*, but he'd stopped himself. Chickened out. He'd been so looking forward to watching the match, and he was afraid if he apologized for that, they'd have a huge fight and she would leave. Maybe forever—and that was...not something he could live with.

But he could apologize for this instead. "It just seemed...funny? I don't know. In keeping with our..." He couldn't find the words. He waved his hand back and forth between them. *Feud*, the word everyone else used, didn't seem right. At least not anymore.

"'Thing'?" she supplied.

"Yeah." *Thing* was suitably vague.

"And honestly, I really only did it actively that first time. After that, everyone started asking me for ballots. I think it's because you're, uh, really good at it. You sort of seem like you *are* the mermaid queen, which I know sounds dumb, but...Anyway, I didn't realize you hated it so much. I thought you were just…" Ugh. Words. Hard. "Anyway, no more. I don't have it locked down yet, but I'm going to figure it out. I promise you won't be mermaid queen this year." He would go up there and sit on that damn throne himself if he had to.

Something happened to her face then, something subtle, but he was looking closely enough to notice. It was a slight furrowing of her brow, but it was almost immediately erased. He didn't have time to puzzle out what it might mean, because Crystal Palace scored and she was up on her feet, arms extended over her head.

He watched her celebrate by wiggling around in her dress. She looked so carefree, it made him want to press pause. Freeze the scene so they could both stay here in their secret soccer truce-bubble.

She sat back down abruptly with a sigh of happiness. All this up and down brought to mind a marionette, except not because Maya was no one's puppet. She pulled her own strings.

She looked at him, and he realized he'd been staring—probably too intently. He forced himself to look away, and his gaze landed on the fortune cookies. "Can I have one of these?"

"Please do."

He contemplated his fortune while he chewed. A PERSON OF WORDS AND NOT DEEDS IS A GARDEN FULL OF WEEDS.

The marionette comparison was actually pretty apt, Law thought nearly two hours later. The match had been close, and every time Crystal Palace pulled ahead, she leaped to her feet. When they fell behind, she slumped theatrically on the sofa.

"Noooo," she moaned, watching through her fingers as Liverpool scored, putting Crystal Palace down by two goals with ten minutes left.

"Tell me about how you got into them," Law said, because apparently they talked during matches now. After establishing that Brie was not, in fact, his new girlfriend, they'd chatted on and off about all kinds of stuff: the business Karl's Junior Achievement kids were launching, names Jake and Nora were considering for their baby. "I know it has to do with your time in the UK, but no offense, you never struck me as very..."

"Sporty?" she suggested, peeling one hand off her face to look at him with one eye.

"Yeah, so do you arrive on British soil and they plug you directly into the Premier League matrix?"

She laughed. "No. You're right. I'm not sporty. I went on the exchange purely for the theater angle. Royal National Theatre, Royal Shakespeare Company, all that. But my host family was into Crystal Palace. The fan bases for the London clubs are very localized—so, like, you cheer for your neighborhood club. I have to tell you, I was not pleased being dragged along to a match, but once I got there—wow. Those stadiums are huge. It's its own kind of theater. I understood nothing about the game at that point, but I was hooked immediately."

"You should take up hockey. You've seen the bar on nights the Leafs play. You'd have lots of company then."

"I like having my own thing." She let the other hand fall from her face and tilted her head as she studied him. A half smile bloomed. "This company is okay, too."

He sucked in a breath. As compliments went, it was mild. But it felt like she'd bequeathed him a precious gift. The question was, would this détente, this goodwill, last?

Did he want it to?

He liked battling with her.

But he also liked...whatever this was. He liked her staring at him with a cat-that-ate-the canary smile and saying not-mean things to him.

Man, his standards were low.

Cheers erupted from the TV, and they both turned. "Ahh!" She was on her feet again, celebrating as Crystal Palace tied the score. She remained standing, bouncing in place as play resumed.

There were ten seconds left when Crystal Palace got possession. He jumped to his feet, too, tension snaking through him as Hendricks, the player they'd been talking about before, took a shot. Time seemed to slow down as they watched the trajectory of the ball. The goalkeeper leaped to try to block it.

"It went in! It went in!" She jumped up and down and...

...threw herself into his arms?

It took him a second to adjust to what was happening. To the soft dress and the pull on his neck as her arms wound around it. To her. It took him a second to adjust to *her*, and didn't that just about sum up the entirety of his history with Maya Mehta?

Then they were kissing. He wasn't sure who started it. Just that it felt like it was what was supposed to happen now. Her team had won. But it wasn't only that. If this had been purely an impulsive her-team-won kiss—or an *I thought you were someone else* kiss—it would have been quick. It would have been followed by an equally quick retreat and probably by awkwardness and apologies.

This kiss was not ending. She was moving her lips across his hungrily, like she hadn't kissed anyone in a long time. God knew he hadn't. So he turned off his brain and let himself sink into her. Her lips were soft, softer than he'd ever imagined any part of her could be. She was usually all brittleness and angles, but now, here, somehow she was pliant and lax as she sighed against his mouth. She was still holding on to his neck, and he added his arms to the mix, wrapping them around her and pulling her against him as he pressed his tongue against the seam of her lips, which opened for him unhesitatingly. And then he was inside the mouth that had yammered at him so ceaselessly for so many years. It was soft, too, as soft as her lips had been, but hotter. Needier. It seemed—

As suddenly as it had started, it was over.

She let go of him and took a big step back, leaving him disoriented and breathing heavily. Her hair was messed up, more of it out of her topknot than in it. He had done that.

"Oh, wow," she said, eyes wide. "I'm sorry. I don't know what—"

"Shh." He held up a hand to silence her, though it was probably futile. But he didn't want her to apologize. Or make a speech about how this had been a mistake.

She surprised him by doing neither, though she did not heed his request for silence—of course she didn't. "Are you going to tell anyone about this?"

That wasn't what he'd expected. He'd expected a discussion. A litany of questions he couldn't answer.

"Please promise you're not going to tell anyone about this," she said, with more urgency.

"I don't kiss and tell." He hoped she wasn't asking because she thought he was that kind of guy. "I would never do that," he added for good measure.

She looked at him for a long moment, smiled as if she liked that answer, and said, "I gotta go."

What? That was it?

He followed her to the door. Was she really going to leave without insisting that they analyze what had just happened?

It seemed she was. She paused with her hand on the doorknob. "Thanks for . . . " She pressed her lips together like she was trying not to smile, but the corners of her lips turned up. " . . . everything."

"Hold on."

What? What was he doing? He was getting what he wanted. He didn't *want* to talk about that kiss, so he should keep his mouth shut. His mouth, apparently having other ideas, asked, "Did you really think I was someone else last time?" *Did you think I was Holden?*

She looked at him without speaking for several long moments. Long enough for him to regret the question. Because did he really want to know the answer? But then she shocked him by saying, evenly, "No."

He didn't know what to do with that no, other than to stand there and let it course through him, a single syllable ricocheting through his body like a victory.

After a few beats of silence, she turned to go.

"There's a match on Thursday—same time," his mouth said. His brain caught up and seconded the motion. *Yes. Let's do this again.*

"*Much Ado* opens Thursday." He knew that. He had a ticket and an ironclad promise from Carter to cover the bar. "And I'm afraid we'll be rehearsing all morning." She grimaced.

"Replay after the show?" Damn, he sounded desperate.

"I'd say yes, but we're having a cast party. Normally I'd pick football over a cast party any day, but Holden wants a party."

"After that," he said, having apparently abandoned all attempts to appear cool. "Just the highlights reel, maybe?"

"But that will be like three a.m."

He shrugged. "I'll be up."

She grinned. "Okay, yay!" She opened the door but paused before actually leaving. "Come to the party if you want. It's going to be in the lobby of the theater."

"Did you just invite me to your party?" He made a show of acting shocked. "Did you just, of your own free will, invite me somewhere?"

"Once. I invited you somewhere once. Don't let it go to your head."

He wanted to kiss her goodbye.

Holy shit. *He wanted to kiss her goodbye.*

He didn't, but it was a close thing. She slipped out and left him alone to contemplate the paradox of how someone's mouth could be so sharp and so soft at the same time.

Chapter Fifteen

Hey. It's Law. You want to have your cast party at the bar on Thursday?

Uh, what? Maya looked up from where she was doing a little tweaking of the set. Looked out at the empty seats. She wasn't sure why. It wasn't like she had an audience who could help her interpret the text.

> *Maya:* That's a really nice offer. Why would you do that?
> *Law:* Because I'm a nice guy?
> *Maya:* No you're not.
> *Law:* Because I'm a patron of the arts?
> *Maya:* No you're not.
> *Law:* Okay, forget it. I just thought you'd have more room to spread out, and you wouldn't have to get the party catered if it's here.

Was this because they'd kissed? Was he going to start being nice to her now? She didn't know how she felt about that. She didn't want things to get complicated, and with him, *nice* meant *complicated*. That kiss had been the result of football-related excitement. Maybe a little bit the result of the slight thaw in their feud, but that was it. It didn't *mean* anything.

> *Law:* Anyway, half the town will be at your party, so
> this way I'll actually get some business.

Ah. That made more sense. This was a self-interested move on his part. But it would also save her a lot of money.

> *Maya:* Sure, that sounds great. Thanks.
> *Law:* First round of drinks on me.

And dang, he was back to being nice.

It had been a long time since Maya had been this nervous. She always felt a little twinge of anticipation before a show, but it was usually excitement more than nerves. It fed her rather than paralyzed her.

But as she peeked out at the packed theater on opening night, she almost passed out. There were the usual town denizens. Her parents and Rohan were in the front row. Behind them sat Nora and Jake and Sawyer—Eve always helped with costumes for Maya's shows, so she was backstage.

And all the old meddlers. Her heart swelled.

But aside from all those folks, amazingly, there were also *about a thousand* people she *didn't* know. The box office take as of this morning had been her highest ever, and from the looks of things, they'd had same-day takers for the unsold seats.

She motioned for the cast and crew to huddle up. "We have a full house." A full house! That had literally never happened. The old theater was bigger than the current demand for it. There were murmurs of excitement, and Holden looked a little green around the edges.

"I know this afternoon was a little dicey." That was understating it. They'd gathered to go through a couple of the roughest scenes, and they were...still rough. Holden had called for a line prompt twice, which was one thing at the best of times, but in a scene where rapid-fire back-and-forth banter was the whole point, it ruined the momentum. "But in my experience, a rough final runthrough is always a good sign. It's always when you're struggling that suddenly, with the addition of a live audience, the play sort of bursts through." Sometimes. Here was hoping. "All the ingredients are there. You've worked so hard. You're all great, and I have so much confidence in you."

Thank goodness she was a decent actor.

Everyone cheered, and her stage manager, a high-school drama geek named Ingrid who was responsible—and cheap—gave the two-minute warning. Maya pulled Holden aside. This was a bit of a gamble, but sometimes you had to trust your gut. "Holden, you know how we talked about how the Benedick-and-Beatrice scenes depend on pacing and momentum?" He nodded. "If you forget a line tonight, I want you to not ask for the prompt but make something up."

"*Really?*" She had shocked him.

"Yes. Preserving the scene is more important than getting it exactly right. If you forget, throw something out there. Try to make it make sense. Then, hopefully, after my next line, you'll be back on track." *Please, God, let him get back on track.*

Let him not get off track to begin with? No, that was probably too much to ask for.

Where were a lake and a full moon and a wishing flower when you needed them? Where was a fortune cookie that read YOUR PLAY IS GOING TO BE BOTH GREAT AND LUCRATIVE?

"Okay, no prob," Holden said.

No prob.

Here was hoping.

"Places, everyone!" Ingrid called—and here went nothing.

Much Ado about Nothing was great.

Of course it was. Maya's plays always were. She knew how to tell a story. How to keep you interested. And her shows often had flashes of humor you didn't see coming—kind of like her.

Law often needled Maya about her penchant for Shakespeare, but he supposed there was a reason the dude endured all these hundreds of years later. As with every Shakespeare play Law saw, it took a while to adjust. When a messenger came running onstage to open the play, panting and talking about lions and lambs, he thought, as he always did, *Huh?* But invariably, once he stopped trying so hard and sat back and let the language and the spectacle wash over him, something would click in his mind. He'd find himself understanding what was happening before him—and invested in it.

The main couple was great—they were young and earnest, as the roles seemed to call for. Easily manipulated. Law rolled his eyes as the dude let himself get talked into believing his fiancée had been untrue. But the villain doing the manipulating was a force of nature. He was a teacher from an arts school in London who'd appeared in lots of Maya's summer shows. He was evil but funny—Maya played him for laughs with his mannerisms and costumes.

But the stars of the show were Maya and Holden. Their characters purported to hate each other, but everyone could see they didn't. Watching their cluelessness—they were easily manipulated, too—give way to realization was hilarious.

Maya's performance was no surprise. Even though she always said she was a director first and an actor second, she was great at pretty much every role she attempted. He heard other people in town talking about how she lost herself in a role. How you'd forget it was Maya you were watching. That wasn't the case for him. He was always aware, somewhere pretty close to the top of his con-sciousness, that he was watching *her*. The Maya-ness never faded. If anything, it intensified. *There's Maya playing Lady Macbeth*, say, or, *Wow, Maya can really belt it out as Mary Poppins*. But at the same time, paradoxically, it never detracted from his ability to get swept up in the story.

Holden was also killing it. His cheerful, somewhat self-impressed demeanor allowed him to inhabit the role of Benedick, who shared those traits. And then, sometimes, Holden would bust out these pop-star dance moves that would have the whole place roaring with laughter.

But even as Law recognized how well cast Holden was, and how good a job he was doing, something wasn't sitting right. Something heavy and bitter was accumulating in Law's gut as Benedick and Beatrice bantered. He wasn't sure if it was possible to fake that kind of chemistry, even for talented actors. He thought back to Maya and Holden goofing around at the bar the other night, and then, suddenly, in each other's arms dancing.

But then he thought of asking Maya if she'd really been thinking of someone else that time she'd kissed him and of her looking him right in the eye and saying, *No*.

Man, he was so confused.

There was a standing ovation at the end, a long one. He slipped out before it was over.

Chapter Sixteen

⁓

*M*aya was distracted as everyone swirled around congratulating her and each other. Her brain was glitching on the night's best piece of news: the box office take was thirteen grand.

Thirteen grand.

That was twice as much as she'd ever made on a single show.

She had expenses on that, of course, but thirteen grand was better than her most optimistic imaginings.

"Hey, boss!"

She turned and was nearly flattened by a tackle-hug from her secret weapon.

"You were great, Holden." He really had been. Everything she had seen in him when she'd first imagined casting him had come through beautifully. And more to the point, his name had drawn the crowd of her dreams.

"Did you notice I made up a line when I forgot?"

"I did." She stifled a giggle. "I was there." Standing right in front of him, panicking and praying that he'd right the ship. And he had. After responding to her "Against my will I am sent to bid you come in to dinner" with "Fair Beatrice, I find I am not hungry," she had been able to adjust her next line on the fly and they'd gotten back on track. "You handled it beautifully."

He stuck his arm out. "May I escort you to the bar, fair Beatrice?"

The party was fun, and good for her ego, too, as everyone came up to fawn over her. But she couldn't help wishing she had a fast-forward button so she could go upstairs for the football match. She'd avoided checking the score all day so she could preserve the surprise.

She kept looking around for Ben. He was here, obviously, but they hadn't interacted yet. She wanted to tell him not to tell her the outcome of the match.

Holden bought her a glass of wine, her first. She'd been so thirsty when she arrived that she'd guzzled a couple glasses of water. "Heyyyy, boss. Beatrice. Bossy Beatrice. Ha!"

He was clearly well past his first.

"Hey now, don't get too happy." She tried to make it sound teasing, but she meant it. "We have a show tomorrow night. Stamina is important."

"Yes, Mom." He rolled his eyes.

He could be such a baby sometimes. She had learned his ways. He was used to getting what he wanted when he wanted. He lived in the moment and took the path of least resistance. She wasn't sure whether that was because he was a celebrity or whether it was just Holden.

She sipped her wine. It was the wrong one. But whatever, it was fine.

"My agent got me an audition for Ryan Alexander's new movie," Holden said with a grin. "Not a lead, but a solid secondary character."

"That's . . ." She'd been going to say "great," because that's what she was supposed to say. But by all accounts, Ryan Alexander was a grade-A ass. The Me Too noose was tightening around him, to hear it told. That wasn't even insider information—Maya's

Canadian stage circles didn't overlap with the Hollywood studio–based film world. It was stuff she'd picked up reading the *Hollywood Reporter*.

Also, Ryan Alexander's movies sucked. "I'd be careful of him, Holden."

"Huh?"

"I wouldn't be surprised if some shit hit the fan with him in the near future."

"What does *that* mean?" he said peevishly, and suddenly there was Ben. He silently took the glass of wine she was holding and handed her a different one.

"It means he's a misogynistic creep at best and a predator at worst," she said to Holden, and then, to Ben, "Thanks." He nodded and retreated.

"What does that have to do with me?" Holden said, his tone a touch belligerent. "He's not going to prey on *me*."

"Right. He's not. Forget it." There was no use in trying to reason with Holden— in general, but especially when he was drunk.

"No. You clearly have an opinion on the matter, like you do on everything, so let's hear it."

She wasn't sure what he meant by "everything," unless he was talking about the fact that she was the director of the play he was in and therefore it was literally her job to have an opinion, but she let it slide. "I just think that when you know someone is a bad person, you shouldn't associate yourself with him. But more pragmatically, I wouldn't want this to come back to bite you. Think of all those people who've had to apologize for working with Woody Allen."

"I don't know why you have to get so worked up about everything."

Wow. And here she'd thought Holden was a happy drunk. She'd rather be fending off his advances, as annoying as they were, than fighting about this. "Can we drop it? You're a really talented guy. You have a lot of potential as an actor. I just don't want to see it wasted, is all."

She started to turn away, but he grabbed her arm, which caused most of the wine to slosh out of her glass. Ugh. He was like a mosquito, a super-persistent mosquito who wouldn't quit buzzing around, and—

"You will get the fuck out of my bar right now."

—he was about to be swatted. But not by her.

The last thing she needed was Ben meddling in this. "It's fine. We were just—"

He either didn't hear her or was choosing to ignore her. He had Holden, who was protesting that he'd been misunderstood, by the arm. "How do *you* like being grabbed?"

She didn't need a scene. She needed Holden to show up for work tomorrow without a monstrous hangover, to be charming and remember his lines—or enough of them, anyway—and to help her earn another thirteen thousand dollars. "Seriously, Ben. Back off."

Ben let go of Holden, so that was something at least. "I invite you to leave my bar."

"Or what? You gonna call the cops?"

Holden sounded like such a little boy. It was embarrassing. Anger flashed hot in Maya's chest. At Holden for being such an ass, but also at Ben for making a scene. She had been handling it.

"No. I am going to walk twenty feet over there"—Ben hitched his thumb toward the bar—"and get my buddy the police chief to come have a word with you."

"Dude, *chill*." Holden rolled his eyes but turned to go.

"Sleep well!" she called after him. "Great job tonight!" She whirled on Ben. "What the hell was that?"

"What the hell was *that*?" he countered, making a flailing gesture in the direction Holden had gone.

"I asked you first! What gives you the right to swoop in like that?"

"He was treating you like shit."

"So? *You* treat me like shit." She regretted it as soon as it was out of her mouth, before the wince the vicious accusation triggered on his face. Her mind flashed back to that day at the dunk tank, when he'd steadied her as she was falling. Then to when he'd added her wine for intermission to his wholesale order.

"Okay, *one*, I do *not* treat you like shit. Defending myself against your relentless attacks is not the same as treating you like shit."

He was right. But she couldn't quite make herself retract her previous statement. She was still angry. What if he'd driven off Holden? What if Holden was so pissed—angry-pissed and/or drunk-pissed—that he couldn't or wouldn't do tomorrow's show? Maya had never canceled a play, not since that first, ill-fated one, and she wasn't about to start now. *Especially* on account of *him*. Again. "And what's number two in your little speech?" What could he possibly say that would make this better?

He was looking around the bar instead of at her, which made her do the same. They had an audience—not the good kind. Everyone was staring at them. And it was quiet, except for the music coming from the jukebox.

Ben reached for her but his hand stopped an inch before it landed on her arm, and he sort of zoomed it out in front of him before retracting it. He could hardly take her by the arm when he'd just come out swinging because Holden had done that. The resulting arm flail made him look like he was doing a very bad modern dance.

It took some of the fight out of her, and when he jerked his head indicating he wanted her to follow him, she was inclined to go. His earlier statement implied he had more to say. She wanted to know what it was.

So she followed him to the kitchen, goose bumps rising like they were back in the dunk tank.

"*Two*," he said, whirling on her, "if I treat you like shit, which I *don't*, it's because treating you like shit is *my* job. Not Holden Hampshire's."

She laughed. She couldn't help it. That was a ridiculous argument. Her amusement annoyed him, though. He scowled and advanced on her.

"So," she said, still chuckling, "if *you* treat me like shit—"

"Which I *don't*." He punctuated the "don't" by pressing his palm against the wall next to her head. That stopped her laughter.

"Hypothetically," she squeaked. Squeaking was not a good look here. She made a concerted effort to lower her voice even as the goose bumps spread. "Run with me here. If you"—she poked his chest with her index finger—"treat me like shit, it means you have that market cornered? *That's* what you're saying? No one else is allowed to? You"—she poked again—"were protecting your turf, so to speak?"

"Exactly," he snapped, wrapping his other hand around her extended finger and moving it away from his chest. He had done that move before—interrupting a poke by physically removing her finger. It annoyed her. "Except I *don't* treat you like shit," he added.

He was so annoying.

Also annoying? The way her nipples had hardened into stiff little nubs. The way her breath got shaky as he rotated the hand that was holding her finger, pried the rest of her fingers open, and laced his through hers.

The way, as he moved their joined hands to the wall on the other side of her head, she knew what was going to happen next.

The way she allowed herself to remain caged in, one arm pinned to the wall, like this was *normal*. Like this was something they did.

In the movies they would have gone from yelling at each other to making out in a matter of seconds. But she knew instinctively that wasn't how they rolled. Their feud was a large, long-standing, heavy thing. Slow to turn. Like a warship retreating.

"What are you doing?" she whispered, even though she knew exactly what he was doing.

He dipped his head so their faces were inches apart. "I'm going to kiss you."

"Why?"

"Because that's a thing we do now, I think?"

It was a question, and though he moved even closer—she

could feel his breath against her lips—he was waiting for her to answer it.

"Yeah," she breathed. "I guess it is."

This time, she vowed as his lips came down on hers, she wasn't going to freak out and pull away. She was going to...see what happened.

What happened, it turned out, was that she was going to act like a starving woman being given a meal, and she wasn't even going to be embarrassed about it. She wrapped her free arm around his neck—he was still pinning her other arm to the wall—and as their tongues tangled, she moaned. Her body was alive all over, overtuned to the sensations of the wall behind her and the air in front of her. She didn't want that air there, so she tried to hook one of her legs around him to draw him closer. It was a clumsy attempt, and she stumbled, but he got the message and righted them, letting loose a low hum and pressing his body against hers. She gasped so loudly when his erection ground against her stomach that it broke the seal between their lips. He pressed openmouthed kisses along her jaw and down the side of her neck. She tilted her head to give him better access.

"Your pulse is racing," he bit out as his mouth slid around to the front of her throat.

"How very observant of you," she managed. Her lungs, constricted by the half corset she was wearing as part of her Beatrice costume, were starting to ache.

He chuckled and went to work on a spot at the base of her throat. He was right. Her pulse was thundering. So much that it almost hurt. She wanted him to move off that spot. She wanted him to move *down*. She was wearing a blouse under the corset. She grabbed the neckline and pulled, exposing a good amount of cleavage.

"Oh my God," he bit out, and hearing him like that, at her mercy, made power surge through her.

She shifted against him, standing on her toes to try to get his erection where she wanted it. "You have quite the hard-on."

"How very observant of you," he panted, dipping his tongue into her cleavage. Having his mouth there made her nipples, so close to his mouth yet so far, even harder.

She stumbled, and this time it wasn't her own doing. He'd backed her against the wall next to the kitchen's swinging door, but they'd migrated a bit as they'd been feasting on each other, so she was blocking the door—the door that someone was trying to push open.

Since she'd been standing on her tiptoes, she pitched forward. He caught her with a mumbled curse and pulled her against his chest, probably to cover the fact that her boobs were half hanging out, and shot out an arm to block the door from opening. "What?" he barked at the intruder.

"Mill Street keg's empty." She recognized Carter's voice.

"Give me a minute."

He stepped away from her after the door closed, and she wanted to wail. Her body was all wound up. She glanced at the fly of his jeans. His was, too, which was strangely comforting. They were in this together.

"How do I fix this?" He was trying to put her blouse to rights. It was loose and flowy and had fabric tape that could be used to adjust the neckline. She batted his hands away, fixed her shirt, and took a deep breath—or as deep a breath as she could manage. The corset was a short, underbust variety, and since it was purely for visual purposes, she'd had Eve lace it loosely. Or so she'd thought.

"You want to escape out the back?" he asked. "I'll make your excuses."

She gave half a thought to going across the street to find Holden to make sure everything was okay with them, but she found she didn't want to. She could text him. "Nah. I can't leave my own party."

He nodded as he adjusted himself and reached for an apron—he did not normally wear an apron—hanging on a peg nearby. He was covering the evidence of his arousal. She smirked.

"Good?" he asked after she'd fixed herself and smoothed her hair.

"Yeah," she said. "Good." And even though she'd come into this kitchen discombobulated and pissed off, and even though she was now disheveled and turned on with no relief in sight, she really was.

The rest of the party was interminable. Law had no idea if Maya was still planning to come upstairs for the match. He wouldn't blame her if she didn't want to anymore. A lot had happened today: her play, her fight with Holden—that absolute asshole.

Their, uh, interlude in the kitchen.

He adjusted his apron. He kept having to do that, every time he caught a glimpse of her standing there in that corset chatting to someone or other, like it was no big deal.

Oh, that corset.

It was messing with him. Her costume was some kind of old-fashioned-lady outfit. It was surely more specific than that, but to him she looked like a fancy version of his idea of a serving wench. She was wearing a long, flowing blue skirt and one of those puffy blouses he associated with Shakespearean plays. Nothing about her outfit could reasonably be called risqué. It covered her from midcalf to neck—at least when she didn't have the blouse gaping to make way for his mouth. But that brown leather corset over the whole thing, cinching in at her waist—God help him. Here he'd had the idea that corsets went *under* clothes.

He tried to act normal, to pull pints and mix drinks. He kept his eye on her glass of wine and topped it up once, but she wasn't drinking very much, he supposed because she was taking her own advice to Holden about the need to stay sharp for the show tomorrow.

Sawyer, who Law thought had left when Eve had a while ago, startled him by sidling up to the bar. He turned. Jake was there, too. Uh-oh. Was it bromance intervention time? He'd been on the other side of these kinds of "chats" enough that he could recognize the signs. The two of them without Eve and Nora, huddled at the corner of the bar, looking at him all intensely, like they were all-seeing, endlessly patient Jedi masters and he was an untested, ignorant kid.

"Well, that was interesting," Sawyer said.

"What was interesting?" Law tried, though he knew it was probably futile.

Jake raised his eyebrows, and Sawyer said, "You throwing Holden Hampshire out on his ass."

Law had to tamp down a smile. "I'd do it again. That guy *is* an ass."

"I don't disagree," Sawyer said, "but people were taking bets on whether you and Maya were going to come to physical blows or make out."

"Well, neither," he lied, "but if I had to pick one, it'd be come to blows." And that was the critical difference between this intervention attempt and the ones he'd been on the other side of. Sawyer and Jake had been sleeping with their respective ladies but insisting it was just sex, that there was nothing actually happening, blah, blah. Meanwhile, it had been obvious to anyone with a pair of eyeballs that they were head over heels and needed to get out of their own way.

"So you dragged Maya away for ten minutes so you guys could have a fistfight?" Sawyer asked.

"No, no. God, give me some credit. We just went to the kitchen to . . . argue."

With our tongues in each other's mouth.

"You sure about that?"

"Are you kidding? She is not going to say a civil word to me until the grant competition is over. And when I win it, she will never speak to me again." He tried to smirk. "I look forward to it."

Sawyer stared at him like he was trying to administer a lie detector test by ESP. "Well, you might have to watch your back when it comes to the grant. That play was great."

"It was, wasn't it?" Law said before he could think better of it. Sawyer narrowed his eyes.

Law picked up a spoon and clinked it against a glass. "Last call!"

he hollered. Finally. It was only one fifteen, and a little earlier than he usually did last call, but whatever. He was done with this day and this conversation.

Last call triggered a line at the bar that had Carter and him working steadily for the next fifteen minutes—and got Sawyer and Jake off his back.

As things started to slow down, Maya appeared. She set her empty glass down. "I'll take my bill, please."

He printed it and slid it to her as he took a couple more orders.

By the time he had circled back to take her payment, she'd settled on a stool. "You only charged me for one glass."

"First round was on me, remember?"

"Yeah, but you always top up my glass before it's empty, and you only ever charge me for one glass."

He shrugged. Busted. He was surprised she hadn't called him on it earlier. Like, *years* earlier.

"Why do you do that?"

He didn't know what to say. Lately the answer was that he realized how stressed she was financially. A glass of wine here and there made no difference to him. But that was a new realization, so how did he explain the long-standing preferential treatment?

Well, he knew how to explain it to himself, if he was being honest, but how did he explain it to *her*?

Thankfully, Carter came over saying they didn't have enough change in the till, so he said to Maya, "Sorry, I have to deal with some closing stuff. Maybe we can talk about this later?"

"Sure." She smiled. Her easy agreement was disconcerting. "We can talk later."

And then she got up and left.

Did that mean no soccer?

Well, whatever. He was beat, his body battling the opposing forces of exhaustion and agitation. It was time to call it a night. To end this day in which he'd lived an entire lifetime. He sent Carter home, cashed out, and yawned through the cleaning.

When he left through the back door, he jumped about a mile when he found Maya sitting on the bottom step in the vestibule looking at her phone. "What are you doing here?"

"I thought we were going to talk later. It's later."

"How'd you get in?" He'd locked the exterior rear door a while ago. People had to come and go from the front in the last hour the bar was open—a safety measure he'd instituted so he could keep an eye on everyone, make sure the drunks got taxis or rides.

She raised her eyebrows like he was a simpleton. "I never left."

Oh. "Right." So she'd been hanging around back here while he thought he was alone in the bar. The idea made him . . . uncomfortable and comfortable at the same time.

"I've been sitting here using your secret Wi-Fi to read about the match." She'd been sitting a little way up the staircase, so when she stood, she was taller than he was—which meant that damn corset was right at his eye level. The top edge of it was an upside-down V. He supposed the point of it was to shove her breasts up and out— that was what corsets did, right? But of course you couldn't see anything because of the puffy blouse.

He took a deep breath and blew it out slowly. They were going to talk now. Fine. That was fine.

He locked the door to the bar, double-checked the exterior door, and gestured up the stairs. "After you." She started up, which gave him a close-up view of the back of the corset. It laced up and was tied in a bow, but a lopsided one. One end was dangling down quite a bit farther than the other, like it *wanted* him to grab it and pull. His fingers felt like they were vibrating. He thought suddenly of her swimsuit, the sailor-themed one with the buttons. He had wanted to grab one of those buttons, too.

He ordered his brain to concentrate on more pressing questions. Namely, what the hell was he going to say about the wine situation?

Actually, maybe that wasn't the topic. Maybe she'd want to talk about what had happened in the kitchen. She'd surprised him the other day by *not* insisting they talk about *that* kiss, but he could

sort of see how if making out was going to be a regular thing—
Please let it be a regular thing—they might have to establish some
guidelines.

"Ben?" She paused outside the door to his apartment.

"Hmm?" And since when did she call him Ben?

And since when did he like it?

"What would happen if we just . . . didn't talk?"

"What do you mean?" he said to her butt, because she was at
the top of the staircase and he was a few steps behind her. Or said
to where he imagined her butt might be under her voluminous skirt.
He had to revise his earlier thought about her costume being too
modest to be risqué. There was something intensely erotic about a
garment that concealed so much.

But then he thought again about that swimsuit, which had not
concealed *anything* but had given him the same feeling.

"I mean, what if we go in there, and we make a rule that we
don't talk?" she said.

"We've spent months in there not talking."

He wasn't sure why he was arguing. He'd *just* been fretting over
what to say to her. But suddenly the idea of sitting silently side
by side on the sofa while they watched soccer felt like a big step
backward. He didn't want to regress. He *liked* talking to her, even
when talking took the form of fighting.

Maybe especially when it took the form of fighting?

Aww, shit, he was getting confused. Skirts, swimsuits, corsets.
Talking, not talking. Everything was all jumbled up in his mind.

"That's not what I mean," she said slowly, like maybe she was
working through her own brain jumble. "I meant . . . a different kind
of not talking."

Oh. Oh, *shit*.

"Ahh!" She shrieked and grabbed for him, because he'd started
to fall down the stairs. Her statement had caused him to rear back,
not in revulsion, which he supposed rearing back usually signified,
but because he was just so shocked.

But he needed to get over himself, because every cell in his body wanted him to get his ass inside and start not talking.

He grabbed the railing and pushed himself up to stand next to her. There wasn't enough room on the small landing for two people to fit comfortably, but that was fine because when had she ever made him comfortable? He let himself brush against her as he leaned past her to unlock the door. She sucked in a breath, held it, and looked up at him with what he could only describe as bedroom eyes. He'd heard that phrase before and thought it ridiculous, but nope, turned out it was a real thing. Her pupils were blown, and her eyelids drooped a little. But then she opened her mouth, like she was going to talk. As he pushed the door open with one hand and pointed inside, he laid the palm of his other hand across her mouth—gently, because he didn't want to seem like, say, a deranged kidnapper. He just wanted to get a message across. She'd said she wanted to go inside and *not* talk, and unless she had changed her mind, that was damn well what they were going to do.

Chapter Seventeen

❧

*H*ooboy.

Maya sucked in a breath as Ben pressed against her from behind.

It was pretty clear what was going to happen, but as was becoming their custom, there was no frantic coming together, no crashing of mouths, no tearing off of clothes. They were still turning the warship, maybe?

When Ben laid a hand over her mouth, it made all the little hairs on the back of her neck stand on end and a clenching sensation take hold between her legs. His hand was resting against her so lightly, it almost tickled. She wanted to put her own hands over his and press down, increase the pressure.

Interesting.

She wanted him to touch her, to *really* touch her. She wanted to touch him. She wanted to *jump* him.

Even more interesting.

But no. He was being cool, with his smooth, understated pointing gesture. He wanted her to go inside. He took his hand off her mouth. She wanted it back.

Extremely interesting.

He was holding the door for her. What could she do but walk through it?

She entered the dark apartment and made for the living room. She heard him throw his keys on the kitchen counter, and the *snick* of the little lamp he had on a sideboard in the dining room as he turned it on. She was pretty sure he'd passed a switch for the overhead light on his way in. That must have been intentional, right? Mood lighting?

What now? She made her way to the window, like she always did, to look out at her apartment. There were no lights on. She could feel her mind starting to fire up, wondering if Holden was there, already asleep, or if he was out doing something guaranteed to be bad news for *Much Ado* and therefore for her.

She should turn off her brain.

She laid her forehead on the glass. In her mind, the pane was going to be cold. Like, it was going to cool her feverish mind or something. But no. It was August.

If she wanted to turn her brain off, how would she do that? Her theatrical training suggested the answer was to get out of her head and tune into her body. God knew she'd sat through enough "relax your toes, relax your ankles, et cetera, et cetera" exercises in her day. Was there a part of her that was tense that she could make a conscious effort to relax?

Yes. Her lungs. Her ribs. She could get this corset off. It had been bugging her all evening and now, suddenly, it was torture. She reached around to try to undo the bow. She wasn't even sure if she could get it off by herself.

Well, she didn't have to get it off by herself, did she? That had been the whole point of coming up here. She could kill two birds with one stone—a sexual overture *and* the ability to breathe!

She lifted her head off the windowpane and turned. Ben was staring at her. He'd stopped under the archway that divided the dining area from the living room, light from the lamp behind him backlighting him. She couldn't make out his expression, so it was hard to know what he was thinking. What if she was overreaching? When he'd said, *That's a thing we do now*, he'd been talking about kissing. Maybe that was all he wanted to do.

But how would she know unless she asked? She was getting that stage-fright feeling again. Way worse than before the curtain had opened earlier. But the show must go on, right? "Can you help me get this corset off?"

He didn't answer, merely stared at her. Just when she started to feel that she'd made a terrible mistake, he walked to a side table next to the sofa and turned on another lamp. "Sure. But I want to be able to see."

She didn't know if he meant he needed the light to illuminate the laces, like task lighting, or if he wanted it to see *her*.

He stood by the lamp for what seemed a maddeningly long interval. Just when she was about to tell him to get a move on, he strolled over. She was going to need to turn around for him to unlace her, but they were back to having one of their staring contests. She was glad he'd turned on the light, because now she could see that while he was staring at her like he always did, he was also biting down on his lower lip. She did the same, almost against her will. And on they stared.

Until she realized she'd been holding her breath. When she let it out, she almost felt dizzy. She was going to have to lose the contest. So she shot him a little eye roll that seemed to amuse him, and turned around. Finally, *finally*, she felt the pressure of his fingers. But not the heat of them, separated as they were from her by a layer of linen and a layer of leather. It felt like a lost opportunity. She wanted his skin on her skin. "Hurry," she panted, but it was no use. He was going to do things in his own time.

Which meant slowly, apparently, agonizingly slowly. The apartment was so silent that the sound of the laces dragging against each other as he undid the bow hissed through the air between them.

The feeling of being almost but not quite free was excruciating, suddenly. Of having his hands on her but not *on* her.

She still couldn't get a full breath in. "Hurry, hurry," she said again, more urgently. "I can't breathe."

He went into overdrive, loosening the bottom laces with lightning speed. When he got her fully unlaced, he pulled off the corset and flung it aside, turning her around as he did so. His hands came to rest lightly on the sides of her lower ribs, as if to soothe. "Better?"

She nodded. Better, yes, but she still didn't have his hands on her skin. They were resting on the blouse that had been under the corset. So she grabbed a handful of fabric on each side. He began to let go of her, but she said, "Don't move."

He raised his eyebrows and shot her one of his stupid smirks. "And here I thought that was a help-me-so-I-don't-suffocate corset removal."

"It was, but…" She pulled her blouse partway up, past his hands, which were as warm as she'd imagined. He was still looking at her with amusement. "I am good at multitasking."

The stupid thing about her costume was that she had to wear a bra under it. The corset stopped under her boobs, and the white linen blouse was too sheer for her to go braless under it, especially under the stage lights.

So while this would have been an excellent opportunity for her to peel off her shirt and flash him in all her topless glory, what was actually going to happen was she was going to peel off her shirt and flash him a giant, unsexy, padded "nude" bra. And it was white-lady nude, so she couldn't even go for a monochromatic version of the giant, unsexy padded bra look.

But the show must go on.

So she finished taking off the blouse and, as quickly as she could, undid the bra.

There, that had wiped the smirk off his face. He was a little slack-jawed, even. "Are you—"

"Remember how we weren't going to talk? Let's go back to

that." Because they were certainly capable of talking themselves out of this. They probably *should* talk themselves out of this.

"Okay," he said, "but—"

"Shh." She put her hands on his and guided them up so he was cupping her breasts.

"Oh shit," he said.

"Will you *shut up*?" She let go of his hands, wrapped her arms around his neck, and tugged his head down and kissed him. That should do it.

It did. He kissed her back, right away, no hesitation. She sighed into his mouth. This was starting to feel normal. Like it *was* a thing they did. Not boring-normal, though, as evidenced by the heat that gathered inside her when his hands, which had been resting lightly on her breasts, started to really get in on the action. He slid them back and forth, his palms rough against her sensitive flesh. As much as she'd been having trouble getting in a full breath before, now she was all sighs, sighs shading into moans. His mouth came back to hers, swallowing one of those moans, and his hands kept going, kneading and then grazing her nipples, and it was almost too much.

His tongue, his hands, *him*. Too much and not enough at the same time, and didn't that sum up just about everything to do with Ben Lawson?

She twisted, trying to rub herself against him, but his arms were in the way as he continued to work her breasts. She hummed her frustration into his mouth and pulled on his neck to lever herself to the side. There. There was his erection against her hip. Another pull on his neck and she launched herself off the ground. One of his hands came around to grab her butt, instinctively, it felt like, like at the dunk tank. She squirmed in his hold until his hardness was lined up with her center and ground herself shamelessly on him, her thin skirt letting her really feel the bulge beneath his jeans.

"Oh shit," he said again, and she laughed against his mouth. She had reduced him to one short phrase.

Which was good, but not ideal. "Shh." She kissed him again.

It didn't work this time. He groaned and pulled his head away. He kept holding her up with his body, taking a step so she was backed against the window, which created more friction where their bodies were joined. It was *glorious*.

"Sorry," he rasped, "but we have to talk. A little bit."

"Why?" She tried to lick his neck.

He took evasive maneuvers. "There has to be a logistical discussion at the very least."

"A *logistical* discussion? Wow, you really have some moves." She tried another approach, reaching for the hem of his T-shirt. She couldn't get it very far up, given the way he was bracing her against the window with his body, but she got her hands on his skin at least. Her fingers traced taut stomach muscles.

He hissed like she was hurting him but followed it with more talk. "Yeah. Birth control? STIs?"

"Here's your discussion: Do you have condoms in this apartment?"

"Yeah."

"Okay, end of discussion."

He rolled his eyes, but he was grinning. She tried again with the shirt, and this time he helped her, lifting one arm at a time while using the other to keep holding her up.

His shirt dispensed with, he stepped away enough to slide her back to her feet, but then he was back, smiling against her mouth as they kissed. He started walking backward, pulling her with him, their arms around each other like they were slow dancing. They were clumsy, trying to walk as a unit but not stop kissing, which led them to step on each other's toes and trip over their own feet.

His smile was contagious. She was super turned on as her breasts slid against his chest, but some of the urgency had bled out of their encounter, making way for levity. They laughingly stumbled their way into the bathroom, where he yanked open the medicine cabinet and found a box of condoms. He grabbed her hand, giving up on the lip-locked stumble-walking, and led her into his bedroom, the mystery room she'd wondered about for so long.

She didn't have time to really take it in, because he sat on the bed and pulled her onto his lap. Once she was there, he flopped onto his back, taking her with him. She squealed—which, let the record show, was not the same as talking—as she landed on his chest. He went right for her lips, palming her cheeks to angle her face so he could invade her mouth. They kissed and kissed.

She *loved* kissing him. She could do it forever, letting their tongues tangle lazily and then more urgently as heat bloomed between her legs.

Eventually one hand floated off her cheek. He growled into her mouth as his hand slid over the curve of her butt.

Okay, maybe she *couldn't* kiss him forever. The heavy hand on her backside was a tease. It hinted at the potential for so much more pleasure. She thought of his hands in the bar, filling pints, polishing glasses. And now those hands were on her. Remarkable.

But they weren't really on *her*. They were on her clothing, and again, she didn't want that. She wanted *skin*.

He must have felt the same, because he grabbed a handful of skirt and pulled. She helped him, working the fabric up so her legs were exposed. She squirmed, bending one knee so she could grind herself against him, but she was only wearing thin cotton underwear and his jeans were stiff against her sensitive flesh. She knew how to fix that. She sat up, undid his jeans, and rolled over so she was on her back. He got the message, standing up and shucking his jeans. He paused, standing there in a pair of gray boxer briefs, his eyebrows raised. He was asking if he should take them off, too. Since he'd finally gotten the hang of the no-talking thing, she answered by getting her skirt all the way off and shimmying out of her underwear. She boosted herself up on her elbows so she could see him better. *Your move.*

He peeled his underwear off, too, and *hello*.

It had been a long time since she'd seen a penis in the flesh. Just seeing it jutting out, as if it were straining toward her, made her feel a little weak, like she was a lady in a gothic novel, but also, paradoxically, powerful, like she was a siren who could make men do her bidding.

A mermaid queen, maybe?

She tested her powers by crooking a finger at him.

He stalked toward her and climbed onto the bed, laying himself over her but using his arms to hold his weight off her. "You gotta take the lead here."

"Shh!" She pinched her fingers and thumb closed over his lips.

He batted her hand away. "I'm serious. You drive this."

Ugh. She sighed. "How do I know what you want to do?"

"I want to do what you want to do," he said quickly.

"What if I want to do something creepy? What if I have a weird fetish that I'm about to whip out? Oh, what if it's *actually* whips? What if—"

"Okay, you were right. Hush." He stopped her mouth with his.

"Oh!" She turned her head to evade his kisses. "I'm sorry, what did you say?"

His mouth chased hers. "Not talking is better."

"No, what did you actually say? What words did you use?"

He snorted even as he kept trying to kiss her. "I said you were right. Once. Don't let it go to your head."

She secretly loved it when he parroted her own lines back to her. It meant he'd been listening to her all along.

She let herself get lost in his kisses again, but this time there was nothing between them, and it felt so *good*.

But soon, too soon, he was gone. On the move. She made a noise of dismay that totally didn't count as talking and tried to grab him, but he was too fast. He wrapped his hands around her ankles, and before she could process what was happening, dragged her so her butt was right on the edge of the bed and her legs were hanging over.

Then he knelt on the floor between them.

And *wow*. Was he really going to go there, just like that?

Yes, yes he was. He pressed his lips to the crease where thigh met torso. As he lavished attention on the damp skin there with his mouth, he stroked her folds with one hand.

She swallowed a gasp. Part of her was irritated that he found her already slick with wetness. She didn't like him knowing he had that much power over her. But when he lowered his mouth and licked her seam, she told that part of her to shut up.

If Maya refused to talk—who would have ever thought he'd live to see the day when he was *trying* to get Maya to talk to him and she *wouldn't*?—Law was going to have to make sure they did something she enjoyed. Go slowly and watch her closely—he was good at watching her closely.

Not that it was going to be any hardship. Well, the *slowly* part might be a little torturous, but it was a good kind of torturous.

She felt so good, so soft and slippery and ready.

She tasted good, too, the tangy sweetness of her most sensitive, vulnerable flesh under his mouth. The intimacy of doing this with *her*, the woman who lived to antagonize him. It almost made him dizzy.

He explored gently, lightly, with his tongue, so she could adjust to what was happening. When she inhaled sharply and held her breath, he tried to angle his head so he could see her, but she was flat on her back looking up at the ceiling. He couldn't see her face.

He stopped, pulled away a bit, intending to slide up enough to check on her. But he didn't have to, because as soon as he broke contact with her, she moaned—it wasn't a happy moan—and bucked her hips, chasing his retreating mouth.

Okay, then. He chuckled and settled back between her legs, smiling against her. Damn, he kept doing that, touching her body with his lips and smiling at the same time. It made him feel like a fool, all this smiling at moments that should be serious and focused, but he couldn't make himself stop. It wasn't long before she was moaning again, and these were *definitely* good moans.

He had to force himself not to take his dick in hand. Listening to her was killing him. It shouldn't have been a surprise that she wasn't holding back, that she wasn't a quiet lover. She sighed and moaned and writhed as he kept up the measured assault. He might have wondered, given that she was such a good actress, if it was all real. But that was the convenient part about having sex with someone who disliked you. She wasn't going to do you any favors by faking it.

And as if to hammer home the point, she let loose a moan that sounded like it was shading into a sob, and her flesh started pulsing against his lips. He stayed with her. A sense of . . . something washed over him as she rode out the waves of her release. It was a triumphant feeling, like when he bested her in an argument. Except they weren't arguing.

It was also a little like the feeling he got during a truce, when they *stopped* arguing and coexisted in the same space for a while. Except right now they were doing a hell of a lot more than coexisting.

It was a feeling of . . . rightness. A feeling he didn't have a word for.

She interrupted his mental vocabulary session by throwing the box of condoms at his head. A corner clipped his temple. "Ow!"

"Shh!" she scolded.

While he retrieved the box, she scooted back up on the bed and reclined against his pillows looking like a self-satisfied queen. He thought suddenly of when she'd played Cleopatra in one of her plays. She definitely looked like a woman with an empire under her command. Which he supposed made him the empire. He was surprisingly okay with that.

He made quick work of the condom wrapper, sheathed himself, and crawled up to join her. She didn't waste any time—she reached for him and wrapped her legs around his waist. He buried his face in the crook of her neck, and oh, the feeling of being surrounded by her, her soft, warm skin everywhere, her ankles hooked at his lower back. He needed a minute to get himself together or he was going to blow right here, before he even got to be inside her.

It didn't help matters that she only let him be for a moment before she squirmed around so his face in the crook of her neck became his face in her breasts. He groaned, took one in hand, and flicked his tongue over the small brown peak of the other. And groaned again when a hand snaked around his dick.

She guided him to her entrance, and he didn't need any more encouragement. He pulled away from her breasts and studied her face as he slid in. She stared at him, her pupils still blown despite the fact that he'd turned on the bedside lamp—he'd been turning on lamps since they arrived, because damn, for all he knew this was going to be his one and only chance with her, and he wanted to be able to *see*.

He stared at her.

A smile bloomed, lighting up her face. It made his breath catch.

Eventually she moved, rolled her hips a little. It woke him up, and he moved with her, letting his own hips move forward and back, but slowly, as seemed to be in keeping with the rhythm of everything between them this evening.

He wasn't going to last very long, but his ego wanted her to come again. He was aware that it might be too soon, but why not go down trying? He made room for his hand to slide between them and used two fingers to seek out her clit. He had no idea what was going to work here, but he tried to mimic what he'd done with his mouth earlier, asserting a moderate amount of pressure and setting up a regular stroking motion even as he kept moving his hips, sliding in and out and letting himself grind into her at the top of each stroke until he was buried to the hilt. Pleasure radiated through him as pressure gathered. They kept up the eye contact. With lovers past, he'd always found intense eye contact awkward, but with her it wasn't. He had the sudden, absurd notion that maybe all their years of staring contests had been about preparing them for this moment.

Her breathing shortened, and she adjusted her hips, relocking her ankles at his lower back. The change in angle let him slide in a little deeper and, oh shit, he couldn't hold back anymore. He'd meant to keep up the pressure on her clit, but he faltered as his orgasm barreled down on him. She slid her own hand down and picked up where he'd left off as she continued to roll her hips and stare at him. The smile was gone, replaced by a slight furrowing of her brow. She was concentrating—on this, on them, on her own pleasure. Had he ever seen anything so hot?

With a groan, he ground into her one last time and emptied himself into the condom. She kept going, her breathing growing shuddery. He teased one of her nipples. It seemed to be the nudge she needed. She cried out and her eyes slipped closed—she lost the staring contest—as she surrendered.

And there was that feeling again, that vague sense of rightness he couldn't quite name.

He rolled off her, grabbed a tissue from the nightstand to deal with the condom, and rolled back. She hadn't moved, just remained splayed on her back, half propped up on his pillows. He copied her posture, stretching out next to her and staring at the ceiling as his breath returned to normal. He wondered when the no-talking rule would be lifted. Wondered what to say when it was. *Thanks*? *Can we do that again soon? You are the sexiest person I've ever seen*?

"When was the last time you had sex?"

The question, and the sudden shock of her voice ringing out over the silent, charged air, startled a laugh out of him. "It's been a while."

"What does that mean? Like, it's been two weeks or it's been two years?"

"It's been…" He thought back to the tourist Sawyer had been harassing him about. She'd left town after last year's Mermaid Parade. "About a year." Probably not a great look, but he was beyond caring.

"Really?"

He kind of liked that she was so shocked. "When and with whom do you think I'm having sex? You live across the street from me. You're in my bar all the time. You're in my *face* all the time."

She cracked up. "Point taken."

"What about you?" Did he really want to know, though?

"About the same. You remember my production of *Grease* last summer?"

"Yep." She'd been one of the Pink Ladies in that one, the beauty school dropout with the blue hair. She'd rocked that hair.

"Well, let's just say Danny Zuko was *really* good at the hand jive."

It was his turn to crack up. "Ah, so you *do* sleep with your leading men."

"Only the ones who aren't douchebags," she joked, but then she grew serious. "No, not really. I usually have a policy against it. It's kind of gross to be in charge of someone, even in a small-potatoes theater like mine, and get involved with them. But I don't know, Danny Zuko was persistent. And hot. He was quite a bit older than I was, too, and unlike a lot of actors, he had no problem taking direction from a younger woman. So..." She shrugged.

"But you and Pearl are always comparing Tinder matches."

"Yeah, but that's just a hobby. I never actually meet up with any of them."

That was...pleasantly surprising. "How come?"

She shrugged. "It never works. You can't tell through a screen or through DM if you have chemistry with someone."

Did they have chemistry? Would she have slept with him if they didn't? "Hey, I wanted to apologize for something."

Shit. He did want to apologize, but his mouth had been faster than his brain. He actually wasn't prepared to apologize for *that*. He needed to...practice that one.

But handily, there was more than one thing he could stand to apologize for.

"Yeah?" She rolled over, and she was kind of hugging herself.

"You're cold," he said, and before she could protest, he grabbed a quilt he had folded at the foot of the bed and shook it out over both of them. He settled himself on his side, facing her but not touching her. "You remember when we had dinner in Bayshore?"

"I'm still full from it, I think."

"You remember afterward, we were talking about the town grant? I offered to look at yours."

She snorted.

"I didn't mean it the way it sounded, all condescending. I was trying to be nice. Anyway, I'm sorry. But you were right. If anything, when it comes to grants, it should be me asking you for help."

Another snort. "That's not going to happen. You're going down, my friend."

He laughed. He also didn't miss that she'd called him "my friend." "We'll see about that. You have no idea how community-minded I've been lately while you've been in rehearsals." She shook her head, but she was laughing. "What are you going to do with the money on the very off chance that you win?" He tried to make the question casual, but he really wanted to know how bad things were.

"Not have to close the theater."

God. It still killed him to hear that she was seriously entertaining the idea of closing the theater. "That's kind of vague."

He thought she was going to take offense, but she surprised him by saying, "It is, isn't it?" She squinted at him like she was trying to decide what to say. "I didn't get a grant I'd been counting on last year." She blew out a breath, as if that had been a hard admission—which he got. The rest came in a single, rapid-fire sentence. "I haven't been paying myself and I was looking at having to default on the mortgage and lay off Richard and Marjorie this fall."

Aww, shit. Well, there was his answer to how bad it was.

"Holden was supposed to be my Hail Mary," she went on. "And he was. He is. If I sell out the rest of the run, which looks likely,

I'll avert immediate disaster. But if I win the grant, I can actually get ahead for once. My proposal is to use it to create some fund-raising infrastructure—a consultant, direct mail and social media campaigns, that sort of thing. The idea—the hope—is that an initial influx of cash will help create a more sustained flow of income."

"You have to have money to make money."

"Exactly. Although I'm not sure why I'm telling you all this."

"Maybe because we just slept together and you're feeling uncharacteristically vulnerable?" He was teasing, but not really.

She did one of her little eye rolls. "What about you, on the extremely slim chance that you win?"

"I found a location that I really want for the restaurant, but it's for sale, not for rent. I'd budgeted several months' rent into my plan, but not a down payment on a purchase. For that I'd need to mortgage the bar building."

"Ah. The weight of family legacy."

She saw the problem immediately—of course she did. "Yeah. I'll still need a mortgage even if I win the grant, but it won't have to be very big. It won't mean losing the bar if the restaurant fails."

"Does your dad own the bar building?"

"Nope. He passed it on to me. I just don't want to...mess up what he made. What my grandpa made. I don't want anyone to lose their jobs." He chuckled. "Even Carter, who I'm perpetually on the verge of firing anyway."

"And here I thought your main motivation with the grant was that you just didn't want me to win it."

"No, no." He was pretty sure her idea was going to win out on its own merits. Which might not be the worst thing. He wanted to win, but he *also* didn't want the theater to close.

"It's interesting that we're talking about this calmly and ratio-nally instead of yelling at each other," she said.

"Well, as noted, I think maybe the fact that we're in bed naked is a factor in that."

"But we're still competing, right?"

He supposed they were. "May the best man win." He stuck his hand out.

She ignored it. "I am not a man."

"I am aware." *Extremely aware.* "It's just a saying."

"It's a sexist saying."

"May the best person win?"

She still didn't shake his hand. "I should go." She made no move to get out of bed, though.

"Or you could stay." *Please stay.* "We forgot about the match."

"It's already almost three. Rain check? I'm super tired." She let loose a huge yawn.

"Have a nap. I'll set the alarm, and you can sneak out the back." Assuming they were still hiding this. Whatever *this* was.

She looked at him for a long moment before saying, "Okay."

He wanted to take her into his arms. Or at least for her to shake his hand over his *May the best person win* pronouncement.

Instead they lay there side by side and stared at each other until they both fell asleep.

Doing a walk of shame in Moonflower Bay was a fraught activity at the best of times, given the prying eyes everywhere. Doing it dressed as Beatrice from *Much Ado about Nothing* was a whole other level of shame. Maya could only hope, as she slipped out the back door of the bar, that there wouldn't be too many people around. Pearl would be up, starting the day's pies, which she still did even though she'd retired from the customer service side of the bakery, and she often left the kitchen door propped open. But it must have been Maya's lucky day because the bakery was all closed up. She didn't see a soul as she power walked along the backs of the Main Street businesses.

Safe. She breathed a sigh of relief as she unlocked the kitchen door of the Mermaid.

And ran right into Eve and Sawyer.

Dammit. The Mermaid wasn't a bed-and-breakfast. There was no reason for Eve and Sawyer to be up this early.

But what did Maya know? *She* was never up this early, on account of her job. How did she know what her friends' morning routine was?

Eve raised her eyebrows. "Well, hello there."

"Hi. I was just...out for an early-morning walk."

Eve's eyes flickered down her body. Maya was wearing the Beatrice skirt and blouse and carrying the corset. She gave half a thought to claiming she'd been with Holden, but Eve would never buy it.

Holden. She hadn't even thought of him once since last night. Ben had managed to wipe her brain clean of all her worries. How had he done that?

Well, she knew how he'd done that. Her face heated.

Still, she had to make things right with Holden. But maybe not at six in the morning.

"You're up early," Eve said with exaggerated perkiness.

"Mmm," Maya said noncommittally. She bustled past them, mimicking Eve's fake-cheery tone and saying, "Have a great day!" She had no doubt she was going to have to face the music at some point, but she wasn't going to do it in front of Sawyer, aka one of Ben's besties.

"At some point" turned out to be a whopping thirty minutes later, when Maya responded to a knock on her door by opening it and finding not just Eve but Nora, too, on the other side.

"Ugh, just kill me now," she said, swinging open the door to let them in and making her way back to the bed. She flopped onto it.

"Nah," Nora said to Eve. "We should wait until after she's told us her secrets to kill her, don't you think?"

"Definitely," Eve agreed.

Both women crowded into the tiny room and joined her on the bed. No one said anything for a few seconds.

"Would you believe I slept with Holden?" she tried.

"I would not," Eve said.

She searched her mind. "Jordan? He was my mer-king last year."

"Nope," Nora said.

Maya sighed. But then was cheered when she realized she could tell them a partial truth. "Okay. We actually have this thing going where we watch football together."

"What?" Eve said. "What are you talking about?"

"We watch Crystal Palace matches. The only way to watch them in Canada is through this app he has. So we call a truce and watch football together sometimes."

"How long has this been going on?" Nora asked.

"Um, like . . . since last winter?"

"*What?*" Eve screeched. "That is quite the secret you've been keeping."

"It's not a secret."

"Then why haven't you told us?" Nora said.

"It never came up?"

"It never came up that you're hanging out alone with Law at his place?" Eve said.

"Okay, listen. I didn't want to get into it. Because it wasn't how it looked."

"How was it, then?" Nora asked.

"It was football! He has the specialized app for the bar!"

"Why don't you just watch it at the bar?" Eve picked up the questioning. "Why are you watching it in his apartment?"

"Because . . ." She was digging a hole here. "It's just . . . a thing we do."

"You said 'was,'" Nora said.

"Huh?"

"You said it *wasn't* how it looked. Past tense."

They were as bad as the town meddlers. "Okay, yes, we slept together."

"Oh. My. God," Eve said.

"In one sense, it's not really that surprising, is it?" Nora said to Eve. "The way they're constantly bickering?"

"I know," Eve said. "There's all this tension between them all the time. Still, it's a *tad* surprising."

"Hello, I'm right here," Maya said.

They were no longer listening to her. "It's probably not that much of a stretch for it to be *sexual* tension, right?" Nora said to Eve. "Jake said they had a massive blowout at the bar last night after we left."

"I can hear you, you know."

"So the next question," Eve said, finally deigning to turn her attention to Maya, "is how long have you been sleeping with him?"

"Last night was the first time." They looked like they didn't believe her, so she raised her right hand and said, "I swear on the grave of William Shakespeare."

Eve whistled, indicating that she'd gotten the message.

"How are you feeling?" Maya nodded at Nora's belly, hoping to change the subject.

Nora swatted her. "Nice try. I feel like shit, but that is a topic for later."

"Look," Maya said. "It just happened. I don't know any more than you do at this point."

"Is it going to happen again?" Nora asked.

I sure hope so. "I don't know. I left before he woke up." She'd woken before the alarm, all tangled up with him, and she'd panicked, extricated herself without waking him, and bolted.

"Are you guys together now?" Eve asked.

"No!" Maya didn't know much, but she did know that.

"So is this a 'friends with benefits' thing?" Nora made the air quotes with her fingers. "Because I think it's well established by now that those don't work in this town."

Right. Eve had told Nora as much less than a year ago. "Yes, but you and Jake were *friends*. Eve and Sawyer were *friends*." She looked at Eve. "Sort of. Eventually. Anyway, my point is you can't be friends with benefits if you're not friends to begin with."

That momentarily silenced them. She seized the opportunity to say, "You know what? I hardly got any sleep last night. I'm not saying that's not my own fault, but I have to be at the theater in a few hours. And I love you guys, but get out."

Chapter Eighteen

The next time Law saw Maya was after her Saturday show, when she came into the bar and pulled out a stool like everything was the same as it ever was.

Which maybe it was?

She, dressed in her Beatrice costume with that damn corset all laced up like it *hadn't* just been flung to the floor at his place forty-eight hours ago, was acting like nothing had changed.

So they were going to pretend that Thursday night hadn't happened?

Of course they were. He'd known that yesterday morning when he'd woken to the six a.m. alarm he had set to find her already gone.

So. Okay. He could do that.

No, actually, he couldn't.

But what could he do about it now? Here in his half-full bar with Karl sitting only three empty spots away from Maya? What could he possibly say? *I am and have always been insanely attracted to you, so would you please at least acknowledge what happened?*

"Rough night?" He set a glass in front of her and uncorked a bottle of her wine.

"You could say that." As he poured, she picked up one of the wine menus. When he was done, her hand shot out and stopped him from retracting the bottle. They each held an end of it for a moment in a tug-of-war while she transferred her attention between the wine label and the menu.

He was about to be busted.

Which, fine. It wasn't like this was a secret. She would have noticed the preferential treatment if she'd been paying any attention at all.

"This isn't on the menu."

"That is correct."

"There's a different Riesling on the menu."

"Your powers of observation astound me."

"Why isn't this one on the menu?"

"It's a limited release. If I put it on the menu, I'd run out."

"So you sell it only to me."

He lifted a shoulder and let it fall.

"And you undercharge me."

"No, I charge you the friends-and-family rate." Which wasn't a thing, but whatever. He turned to evasive measures. "How's the show been going?"

"The show has been going shockingly well. There have been a few blips, but Holden seems to perform better under pressure than he does normally."

"So you and Holden are..."

She raised an eyebrow. "Are you asking if your little scene the other night drove a wedge between me and my star?"

"I guess I am."

"He's been a little frosty, but I think he's mostly shaken it off. He's still doing his thing, drawing the crowds. This was night three of a sold-out house. That has never happened."

"That's great."

He was genuinely happy for her. But he didn't need to express it like that. That would be giving away too much in the war he was going to assume they were still waging until he had evidence to suggest otherwise. So instead he went with a joke. "So probably you're here to tell me you're withdrawing from the grant competition because you don't need the money anymore?"

He expected sass, but she leaned forward and whispered, "Actually, I'm here because I was wondering if you wanted to have sex again."

Oh shit. He had to grab the edge of the bar to steady himself, he was so shocked by the question. The answer, however, was right there at the top of his consciousness: *Yes, indeed I do.* "Now?" he asked.

She mimicked his earlier half shrug but infused it with a big dose of coyness.

"Carter!" he shouted. He made an effort to lower his voice when Carter, who was scheduled to go home soon, looked over, alarmed. "Any chance you can close?" God, Brie couldn't get here fast enough. If this thing with Maya was going to become an actual thing, he needed more nights off. Carter made a thumbs-up sign, and Law grabbed his keys and phone from behind the bar and made a "Let's go" motion.

"But I'm not done with my wine." Said the woman who had just implied that now would be her preferred time for getting it on.

He came around the bar, picked up the glass, and leaned over to whisper in her ear. "The nice thing about sleeping with the bartender is you can take your wine to go."

She grinned, and they headed for the back door.

Which was blocked by Sawyer and Eve.

Dammit.

Maya saw them at the same time he did and did a funny little pirouette. "Front door," she muttered.

He followed her, but once they were on the sidewalk out front, she said, "Actually, maybe we should go to my room at the Mermaid.

How do we know they won't see us sneaking up the back stairs? And since we know they're here, they won't be at the inn."

"Good thinking. You have condoms at your place?"

"I do."

Which was how he found himself power walking down Main Street holding a full glass of Riesling that wasn't on his menu. As they mounted the stairs at the Mermaid, he said, "Do you want to talk about this at all?"

"Do I want to talk about what?"

Oh, for God's sake. "I don't know. The fact that we were enemies a week ago and now we're sleeping together?"

"What is there to talk about? We're enemies who sleep together." She smiled. "Enemies with benefits."

"Is that like friends with benefits?"

"No, it is not. Because enemies are not friends. Did you fail reading comprehension in grade school?"

"I know, I just—"

"Friends with benefits never works. Friends are too…friendly. They end up catching feelings."

He couldn't argue with that. Case in point number one: Sawyer and Eve. Case in point number two: Jake and Nora. "But 'enemies' feels so harsh. Are we actually *enemies*?"

"Is one of us going to win the town grant over the other one? Does one of us steal parking spaces and have an oven that belches smoke, both of which infringe on the business operations of the other?"

She was so dramatic. They hadn't really argued about anything—not really—for quite some time. But whatever. She was right that they weren't friends. *Friendly* did not at all feel like the word to describe his feelings for Maya.

"Wow," he said as she ushered him into her room. It was an explosion of pink: cotton candy pink on the walls and fuchsia floor tiles.

"Ah, yes, behold the Barbie Dream Room. Decorated by Eve when she was a kid."

"I've heard about this." He spun slowly in place. "Why didn't she redo it when she renovated the inn?"

"That is a very good question," Maya said as she threw her keys on the dressing table. "The answer, I'm pretty sure, has something to do with emotions and possibly also teenage Eve and Sawyer getting it on in this room. So I prefer not to think about it."

He chuckled. "Yeah, that's a wise move."

"This room is—" Her brow furrowed abruptly, like she had just thought of something unpleasant.

"What?" he asked.

"Maybe we should have gone to your place."

"Why?"

"Forget it." She turned her back to him. "Stop talking and unlace me."

"I'm not going to do that," he said as he pulled one of the dangling ends of the corset cord and undid the bow.

"Seems like you already are," she said, her tone arch.

"No." He reached his fingers into the mass of laces and wiggled them in order to loosen everything in one go, gratified by her resulting sharp intake of breath. She wasn't as blasé as she seemed. "I'm not going to not talk this time. I want us to talk."

"We just *did*. If you want to have some big analysis of this, I don't think—"

"No." He slid one of the laces from its hole, the resulting swishing sound making his dick plump up. "I want to *talk* while we're doing this." He yanked the other lace, which made an even louder sound as it scraped against the eyelet. "I want to tell you that this corset is making me crazy. I can't tell if I like it better on"—he held it closed against her torso—"or off." He pulled it open and tossed it onto the bed.

"Oh," she sighed as realization dawned. "*That* kind of talking."

"Yeah, you're good at talking. As much as I enjoyed myself the other night, which for the record was very much, silence is not really your thing."

She pulled the flowy blouse off with a matter-of-fact efficiency that should not have been sexy. "And here I thought you preferred me silent."

He glanced at her breasts before forcing his eyes back up. "It's a situational thing."

"Is it?" She took off her bra. "While we're putting things on the record, this is necessary under this costume. This is not the kind of bra I normally wear."

"For the record?" He tried to keep his eyes on her face, but damn, knowing her breasts were finally free was like a magnetic force pulling his gaze down.

"Yeah. Next time, I won't be wearing this ugly thing." She flung the bra onto the floor.

That was enough to pull his gaze up. "Next time?" He raised an eyebrow. He wasn't sure why. The impulse to challenge her was stronger than his instinct to produce a contract for her to sign promising there would be a next time.

"After the show tomorrow?" she asked. "After I change after the show, I mean?" Was he mistaken or was there a touch less breezy confidence in that question?

"Yep." He had no idea if Carter would be able to close tomorrow, but he'd shut the whole damn bar down if necessary.

"Not that I'm really much of a lingerie person," she said as she kicked the bra, which had landed at their feet, away. Again he thought he detected a note of uncertainty in her tone. "I'm a plain-black-undies-under-my-jeans kind of person. I mean, you know that, right? Like, you know what you're getting?"

His chest flooded with something he was pretty sure was affection. "I know what I'm getting," he confirmed. In fact, as much as he enjoyed the Beatrice look, he couldn't wait for the return of Maya. Maya of the Converse sneakers and Shakespeare T-shirts.

He stripped off his T-shirt. Maybe if he lost some clothing, she'd feel less vulnerable. She smiled. It must be working. He unbuttoned his jeans. She stepped out of her skirt, and the smile grew.

Then it turned a little wicked. "I'm having a brain wave," she declared. And God help him, she grabbed the corset from where it had landed on the bed and wrapped it around herself.

"Oh shit." His half-hard dick sprang to attention.

"You say that a lot." She turned around and, holding the corset to her chest, presented him with the laces again.

"You sure? You couldn't breathe in this thing the other night."

"Don't tie it tightly, but it's, uh, possible those breathing problems had another source."

He was glad she couldn't see the grin that felt like it was going to crack his face open.

She turned around after he tied her back up, and the smile slid right off his face. *Oh shit.* Yeah, he supposed he did say that a lot, but only because sometimes the things she did and said—and the mere fact of her—felt like ... *Oh shit.*

The corset nestled underneath her breasts and extended down to her hip bones. There was a strip of bare flesh between it and the tops of her panties, which did indeed seem to be made of black cotton. His lungs seized like it was *him* in the corset.

Really, it was more of a wide belt. There was no reason for him to be having a meltdown because of a wide belt. He cleared his throat. "And here I thought corsets, uh, covered you up."

"Regular ones do. This is called a waspie. It's a type of underbust corset."

"Underbust," he echoed.

"Yeah, it's just for the aesthetics of the costume. It doesn't push things up and out like a more traditional corset would." She cupped her breasts and moved the flesh together and toward him as if to demonstrate the concept of "up and out." Her breasts were gorgeous. Then she let go. They fell a little bit once gravity kicked in. Still gorgeous.

"Right, but it still, ah ... accentuates things." God. Listen to him. *It accentuates things*? Were they having a costume fitting? He cleared his throat again. "I think it's possible we're overcorrecting here."

"Huh?"

"With the talking."

She cracked up. "So you're saying I'm right." She came toward him, planted one palm on his chest and pushed. He resisted.

"No. I'm saying we're both right." He gave up resisting and let himself be propelled backward until his calves hit her bed. He sat.

And she sank to her knees between his legs.

Oh shit.

At least he hadn't said it out loud that time.

"Your turn," she said cheerily as she took his dick out of his pants.

"Oh shit."

She smirked.

But only for a moment, because she took his length into her mouth—that was Maya for you, getting right to the point. But then she popped off and tilted her head back to look at him. "Is this cool?"

"Yes. This is very cool."

As if *cool* could begin to describe the feeling of her smiling, taking him back into her mouth, hollowing her cheeks, and sucking.

"Oh *shit*," he said again as an electric shock traveled up his dick into the deepest part of his body—into his soul, it felt like. She laughed around him, the vibrations changing the sensation into something less intense but no less great. She set up a rhythm that soon had him holding his breath and pushing back against the wall of pleasure encroaching on him.

This could not be over this fast. He moved her off him, gently, resting his fingers lightly on her temples to guide her back. She sat back on her heels, gazing up at him as she wiped her mouth with the back of her hand, and he had to use one hand to physically press down on his dick to keep from coming at the very sight of her.

"Not cool anymore?" she asked gently.

He shook his head and let the hand that was still on her temple slide down her cheek. She turned her head into his palm, like she had that night earlier in the summer.

"Very, very cool," he said. "So cool I'm about to embarrass myself."

She smiled. "Well, I'd better get up there, then."

"Condom?" Ben asked.

"In the bedside table." The bed nestled against the wall on one side, and Ben was on the outer edge, so she climbed up from the foot, sliding in between him and the wall and propping her head on one hand.

"I thought you hadn't had sex for a year?" he said while he rummaged around in her nightstand. "And yet here they are, so handy."

"Hope springs eternal?"

He chuckled and, condom in hand, turned to face her. He was so bloody handsome, it wasn't fair, all sleek muscles and a smattering of chest hair, which, like his facial stubble, was brown with hints of auburn.

"Sorry, but this is starting to bug me." She sat partway up and rotated her torso. "Can you take it off again?"

He made quick work of the laces and, when he pulled the corset off, she sighed in relief.

"I tied it too tight," he said.

"No, it's not that comfortable even when it's loose. It's the nature of corsets, I guess." She turned around to find him frowning. Did he not like her without it? That was more disappointing than it should have been.

Both of his hands landed on her rib cage and started massaging.

She looked down. There were vertical indentations in her skin where the corset's boning had been and a larger, horizontal one where the band of the megabra had cut into her. It suddenly clicked that his frown had been a look of concern. "It's okay," she said. "It's part of the job."

The frown deepened as he pressed a little harder and lengthened his strokes.

"Oh my…" Her eyes slipped shut. Who knew having your *rib cage* massaged could feel so incredibly good?

She heaved a huge sigh, and he said, "That's right."

"Don't stop," she said, goose bumps rising as her skin prickled with pleasure.

He didn't stop, but he did lean down and kiss her, even as he kept kneading her skin. She sighed into his mouth, letting a wave of…something engulf her. It was pleasure but more.

Relief. Bone-deep relief. It unspooled inside her even as desire coiled up between her legs. She let her hands slide up and down his back as he kept working both her mouth and the flesh at her torso that she had never realized was so tender. After some time—she had no idea how much, as her world had shrunk to the size of this little pink room—he pulled away. She tried to stop him, emitting a mew of protest and holding on to his neck.

"Be right back." He dropped a kiss on the tip of her nose, a gesture that startled her. It suggested a kind of familiar intimacy that made her feel like she might cry as something inside her lurched with want. Not sexual want, or not *only* that. Just…the idea of someone who kissed your nose and said, *Be right back.* It was a more affectionate gesture than she would have expected from him.

He was rolling a condom on. She used the moment to get herself together. She was not going to get all up in her feelings about a peck on the nose.

He turned toward her but remained where he was, his head cocked as he gazed at her.

"What?" she asked, suddenly nervous, though she wasn't sure why.

"You are gorgeous," he said.

She rolled her eyes even as warmth exploded in her chest at the unexpected compliment. She made a dismissive gesture.

"Oh, come on. I have been known to be right once or twice. Even you've said so."

She felt herself blushing. "You're not so bad yourself."

That was an understatement, she thought, as he grinned and crawled back over to where he'd been before, sitting on his haunches and resuming the weirdly sensual rib cage massage.

"Ugh," she said, noting that she sounded almost annoyed. "Why does that feel so *good*? How can that—" She had no words, just a moan of pleasure, as he widened the sweep of his fingers, letting his thumbs drag over the bottoms of her breasts. He chuckled and lowered his mouth to hers, cutting off her ability to speak, which was fine because words had failed her already anyway.

Soon the pleasure took on an edge as he brushed higher on each upward stroke, grazing her nipples. She feasted on his mouth, feeling like she couldn't get enough. He'd moved to stretch out over her but was keeping his weight mostly off her with his elbows on the bed.

She needed more pressure, more skin, more of *him*, so she wrapped her legs around his waist and tried to pull him closer.

He got the hint and took one hand off to position himself between her legs.

"Is this cool?" he asked, echoing her earlier question.

"This is very cool," she said, echoing his answer.

She gasped as he pushed in. The feeling of being filled was so all-consuming, so good. The pressure, the stretch. "Hooboy," she whispered.

He smiled, a great big one that lit up his whole face. "You sound like a granny when you say that. You swear like a granny."

"It's my dad. My mom swears a lot, but my dad is kind of against it. I guess I take after him."

"Maybe let's not talk about your parents right now?"

She laughed, even as want seized inside her. "Would a granny do this?" She grabbed his ass, and he cracked up as he thrust into her again. "Would a granny do this?" She lightly slapped one butt cheek before moving her hand, clamping it on the back of his head, and pressing his face against her cleavage and sort of comically shaking her boobs in his face.

She'd meant it comically, anyway, but when he groaned and fastened his mouth onto a nipple, it wasn't funny anymore. He lavished attention on her breasts even as he slid in and out of her. The feeling of fullness, of heaviness, started in her breasts, too, and soon she was whimpering because he was back to being too much and not enough at the same time.

He lifted his head and searched her face, probably to check that the mortifying noises she was making weren't signs of distress. She shot him a little smile and stuck her tongue out. He smiled back and shortened his thrusts so she was getting pressure on her clit. Desire—*more* desire, which she wouldn't have thought possible—flooded in suddenly, almost violently. It was like a shove right to the edge of a cliff. She was left panting, teetering, as they stared at each other.

"Oh shit," he said suddenly, his eyes widening. He lost his rhythm, his hips stuttering. He didn't break eye contact, though, and he put his hands back on her ribs, where they'd started. They landed on her skin, and she fell off the cliff. She struggled to keep her eyes open as she came—and came and came, shudders racking her. A groan ripped from his throat, but he kept his eyes open, too.

It wasn't until several seconds had passed, seconds they spent panting and staring at each other, that he rolled off her and onto his back next to her. She looked at the ceiling and pondered the cosmic injustice of the fact that Ben was the best lover she'd ever had. It was going to be hard to pull off this enemies-with-benefits thing.

But she had to. They had to.

It was a terrible thought. It actually scared her as it came over her with growing surety. *I can't give this up.*

"I should go," he said, jolting her from her overdramatic thoughts.

"Really?" She wasn't sure why she was arguing. It wasn't like they were going to cuddle. It was just a bit whiplash-inducing to be coming so hard with a guy one minute and then watching him heaving himself out of bed the next.

"I'm always afraid Carter is going to burn the place down when he closes," he said.

Chapter Nineteen

&

On Sunday, when Maya came into the bar close to closing, Law didn't even say anything to her, just slipped her the key to his apartment and said, "I'll be up as soon as I can. There's a bottle of your wine in the fridge."

When he arrived thirty minutes later, it was to find her lying on his couch watching soccer in leggings and a T-shirt. She had said she wasn't going to be wearing her heavy-duty stage underwear this time, but she'd been in costume earlier, downstairs.

"What happened to Beatrice?"

"I brought pajamas to change into." She'd said she wasn't a lingerie person, and that accorded with his sense of her, but he had to laugh at the fact that her pajamas were basically the same as her normal uniform, except with leggings instead of jeans. But she was barefoot, which he didn't think she'd ever been in his house before. Of course, she'd been *naked* in his house before, but in those instances, by the time she'd *gotten* naked, he'd been too distracted by other body parts to pay attention to her feet.

She had also never lain on his sofa before. They always sat.

"Carter closes when we watch late-night football."

"Yeah, but in those cases, we're in the building."

"So we can perish when it burns down?"

He smirked. "I'll throw you out the window. I'm going down with the ship."

"Well, you can't stay here anyway. I'm sorry to report that Eve is onto us."

"Really?" he asked as he dressed.

"Yeah, she and Sawyer caught me coming in the other morning. Man, am I going to be glad to get my apartment back."

Dressed and put to rights, he paused with his hand on the door. "I'll see you tomorrow?"

She knew what he was really asking. Or at least she *thought* she knew. She hoped. "I'll come by after the show?"

"Yeah." He grinned. "You do that."

There was something about the combination of her sprawled out, her bare feet poking out of her leggings. She looked like she knew this place. Like it was comfortable and familiar to her. Like she belonged here.

As he approached the sofa, he noticed her toenails were painted. They stopped him in his tracks. Because they were cute as all hell, perfect little glossy pops of lavender, but also because of the mere fact of them. Unless she was in costume, she always wore a pair of Converse high-tops from her extensive collection. No, wait. She had worn flip-flops on his boat and sandals in Bayshore. Had her toenails been painted those days? He had no idea, which suddenly seemed like a massive lost opportunity.

Her feet were pretty. He almost laughed at himself. He was certain that *feet* and *pretty* were not words he had ever used in the same sentence before. But she *did* have pretty feet.

Something was happening in his chest. A seizing of sorts, like all the muscles in there had gone on high alert. It reminded him of the way he'd felt when Karl had announced the grant. It was a surge of want. A feeling of *I must have this.*

"Not that I'm staying over," she said quickly, and it took him a minute to catch up to the fact that she was still talking about pajamas. She said it like she was trying to reassure him, like she was afraid of coming across as too presumptuous. He wanted to say, *Stay.*

He knew she wouldn't, though. Whatever they were doing, in her mind, it didn't involve staying over. That was why he'd forced himself out of her bed so quickly last night, after the deed had been done.

"Just that when I sneak back to the Mermaid, if I'm caught by Eve and Sawyer, it's not completely obvious that I haven't been home all night," she went on. "This is really more like loungewear."

All right, so she wouldn't stay over. But maybe he could get her to put her legs on his lap while they watched soccer, because to his surprise, he also wanted that. He wanted her to lounge on him, like that was a thing they did. He inched closer to the sofa, trying to figure out how to sit down in a way that wouldn't disturb her. If he slipped in at the end, she'd only have to retract her legs a little to make room. And then he could sort of absently grab them, and—

She sat up.

Dammit.

He sat down, and she scrambled farther away, keeping the same distance between them they usually did. Or they used to do.

This was all very confusing.

"What are you watching?" he asked.

"League highlights reel for the week. I think I'm too tired for a full match."

"Long day?"

"I always get really tired on the Sunday night after a run of shows. I think it's all the adrenaline. When it's over, my body knows it can crash." She yawned, and pointed to her mouth as if to say, *See?*

He yawned, too.

"It's contagious, sorry." She laughed. "Anyway, I thought a full match might put me to sleep, and..." She wagged her eyebrows in an exaggerated fashion. "Let's just say the primary purpose of this evening's visit isn't football."

"You don't say?" He wagged back.

"Yeah." She turned back to the TV. "I think this only has ten more minutes."

"You want anything to drink? Did you find the wine?"

"I'm gonna pass, thanks. That's also likely to put me to sleep at this point."

He wanted to tell her to lie back down and sleep. That it was okay to do that here. He would even stop fixating on the idea of her legs on his lap and give her the whole couch. But of course he could say none of those things, so he just sat next to her, hyperaware of the space between them, and watched soccer highlights.

As before, he could tell when she fell asleep by the way her breathing changed. And when she started to list to the side, he was there to catch her.

He moved closer and put his arm around her, encouraging her to lean into him.

She started to mumble and pull away.

"It's okay," he whispered. "Sleep." But then, figuring that was likely to wake her up and send her packing, he clarified. "Nap." That had worked last time she was here.

It worked again. She sighed and snuggled against him, and that feeling of rightness came over him. It was like a drug, this feeling he sometimes got around her, calming and invigorating at the same time.

Bang, bang, bang.

Law woke up with a start. Someone was at the door. *Shit.*

Maya stirred in his arms. "What time is it?"

Bang, bang, bang.

They were tangled together on the sofa. He had woken up at some point after they'd initially fallen asleep and scooched them down so they were lying flat and covered them with a blanket he had on the back of the sofa. He had thought at the time he would probably pay for that decision this morning, when she woke up and things were weird because he'd basically facilitated a cuddle.

"Is someone at the door?" she asked, all adorable confusion. "Did we fall asleep?"

"Yes to both questions," he whispered. "That's probably Jake." As they'd learned, Jake had a key to the building and didn't see anything wrong with letting himself in and trying to break down Law's apartment door. "Maybe we should just—"

Come clean, he'd been going to say, but she shot off the sofa, said, "I'll hide in your bedroom," and ran down the hall.

Right. She was right.

He peeked at the time as he went to the door. Nine.

"What?" he said, opening the door a crack to reveal both Jake and Sawyer.

"Maya didn't come home last night. Eve and I were worried about her," Sawyer said, his eyes twinkling in a way that did not telegraph worry.

"She's fine."

Sawyer widened his eyes comically. "She is? How do you know?"

"I just do."

"You want to go for a boat ride?" Sawyer asked. "We"—he motioned to Jake—"were talking about how we never get out on the lake anymore."

"Okay." This was good. If he left the premises, Maya would be able to sneak out. He had no doubt he was in for a serious bro intervention, but that would be the case regardless. And he could take it, especially if it prevented Maya from being embarrassed by being caught here. He grabbed his keys, wallet, and phone, and stuffed his feet into shoes. After firing off a quick text to Maya— It's Sawyer and Jake. I'm leaving with them to get them off the scent—he was out the door.

They didn't jump down his throat right away. Maybe they were waiting for him to navigate the boat out of the marina and down the stretch of river they had to traverse to get into the lake. Once he'd done that and they were still silent, he figured they were waiting until they were farther out on the open water—until he literally could not escape—before going in for the kill.

Except they didn't. They just started talking about how nice the weather was. Or Sawyer did. Jake, as was his way, made vague noises of agreement.

It was driving Law batty. Finally, unable to take any more, he said, "Okay, okay. Maya was with me last night."

They both swung around to look at him. He cut the engine. "It's not what you think. We're just sleeping together."

"Hmm, that sounds awfully familiar, doesn't it, Jake?" Sawyer said.

"It does."

"I know it sounds the same as you guys, but it's *not* the same," Law said.

"How is it not the same?" Sawyer asked.

"You and Eve were palling around, taking Clara to university when you got together." He turned to Jake. "And *you*. You and Nora were practically making each other friendship bracelets." He tapped his chest. "I, on the other hand, don't *like* Maya."

"Right," Sawyer said. "You skipped that part."

"What does that mean?"

"At the risk of sounding like a twelve-year-old, you don't *like* Maya; you *love* her."

"I do *not*. Gross."

"*Now* who sounds like a twelve-year-old?" Jake asked.

"We have this thing where we watch soccer late at night," Law said.

"Yeah, and you've been doing that for *months*, I hear," Sawyer said.

"When I came over last winter early in the morning on New Year's Eve, he had someone up there," Jake remarked mildly.

"Yeah," Law said. "You totally busted me when you came over to get a pizza for *Nora*, who was holed up at *your* place."

Jake held up his hands like *So what?* And really, Law didn't have any kind of moral-equivalency argument, given that Nora was now Jake's wife. "My point is, Maya and I are both night owls because of our jobs. We're basically forced to spend time together."

"Except that's not right at all," Sawyer said. "You're up there watching soccer all night voluntarily. That's your apartment. What is she doing? Breaking down the door and handcuffing herself to you?"

"Of course not. Anyway, it really was just soccer for months." He did hear how crazy that sounded. "It's only recently that we..."

"Caught feelings?" Sawyer said cheerfully. "Because honestly,

I think we're all looking at all those years of you guys sniping at each other with new eyes."

"Listen. This is a matter of proximity." That sounded wrong, though. "Convenience." That sounded *really* wrong. But okay, those weren't the right words. He was bad at vocabulary when it came to Maya, as evidenced by his inability to articulate what that warm feeling he'd been calling "rightness" was. Still, he wasn't so clueless he couldn't recognize what things *weren't*. "We have sex. That's why she was at my place this morning."

Except that wasn't true, was it? They *hadn't* had sex last night. She'd fallen asleep on him—he'd encouraged her to—and they'd cuddled.

So whatever, they'd had one interlude with no sex. That didn't mean anything.

"Convenience. Sex," Sawyer said, echoing Law's words back to him.

Law tried not to visibly wince. "There's no love in this equation, is my point."

"How do you know?" Sawyer asked.

"You're supposed to hear choruses of angels, right? Like, the earth moves and you get all shaky." To be fair, he did get shaky when Maya was around, but it was from anger. Or...it used to be.

"Well," Jake said, "you get choruses of Gorgons. Close enough."

Holy shit, was it? Was it possible that...No. He couldn't even think it. It made him...Well, it made him shaky. *No.* "Anyway, it doesn't matter. She hates me." Maybe. "Dislikes me." Sort of. "She's never going to want to *actually* be with me."

They stopped harassing him in favor of sharing a silent look between them that was more annoying than continued harassment would have been. "What?"

"Should we tell him?" Sawyer asked Jake.

"Tell me what?"

Sawyer turned. "You can tell yourself whatever you want, dude. But Maya told Eve that she's into you. Like, for real."

"*What?*" He shot to his feet and had to grab the steering wheel so as not to fall in the water. "What did she say? What words did she use?"

Sawyer chuckled. "I don't know. Eve mentioned it in passing, I didn't pay it much mind because I thought you'd be indifferent." He looked at the sky. "Wow, it's really a beautiful day, isn't it?"

Maya's pajama hack totally worked, because as she sneaked out of the bar after Law, she ran into her brother, who didn't suspect anything was amiss.

"Hey, kid."

"What are you doing downtown so early?"

"I'm doing the store today. I told Mom and Dad to take the day off."

"Well, aren't you the model child?"

He shrugged. "Honestly, I'm kind of bored. I've never not worked. Not since I was fourteen." It was true. Her brother had always had part-time jobs. "Hey, come in with me for a sec, will you? I just got some amazing news."

"Sure." She felt a little bad that she hadn't seen more of Rohan since he'd arrived. Her Herculean efforts to get the play into shape had meant long days. And the...other stuff she had going on had meant long nights. "What's up?"

"Don't freak out," he said as he unlocked the shop, "but the theater critic for the *Globe and Mail* is coming to the play on Saturday afternoon."

She blinked about a thousand times, running his words through her brain again to make sure she'd heard them correctly. "Are you *kidding*?"

"It's wild, right? But no! I got in touch with both the theater critic and the food critic and made this—semibullshit—case for Moonflower Bay as an up-and-coming cultural and culinary spot. I included the link to the story they ran about Law's pizza, and links to some local coverage of the Mermaid Parade, and the theater guy emailed back. He's coming to see the play and the parade on Saturday."

All she could do was blink. She had never even dreamed something like this was possible. The exposure it would give her would be...like another Holden. Without having to actually deal with Holden.

"I know the timing sucks in the sense that Saturday is the second-to-last show," Rohan said as he booted up the computer. "So it's not like the article will drive ticket sales in any meaningful way, but..." He shrugged. "Maybe people will see it and want to come to some shows next season?"

"Ahhh!" She ran around behind the counter and threw her arms around her brother. "This is amazing! Thank you so much!" Rohan was such a natural entrepreneur. *He* should come up with an idea on the fly and apply for the grant.

Except not. Because that grant was hers.

Unless it was Ben's. Which would make her mad.

Kind of.

She needed to work on her application some more. "I gotta go."

"Oh, hey," Rohan said as she was on her way out. "I forgot to tell you that I was talking to Jenna the other day, and she told me that Eve told her that Law is into you."

"*What?*" Maya ground to a halt halfway out the door.

He chuckled. "That sounds like junior high, doesn't it?"

She forced her legs, which, like the rest of her body, were doing a weird buzzing thing, to carry her back into the store. "Say that again."

"Uh, Jenna told me that Eve told her that Law likes you? I think Sawyer said something to Eve?"

"Into me or likes me?"

"Huh?"

"The first time you said he was 'into me.' The second time you said he 'liked' me. Which is it?"

"I don't know. I didn't pay that much attention."

"Okay, how long ago was this conversation?"

He shot her a bewildered look. "I don't know."

"You can't remember what she said. You can't remember when she said it. What's the matter with you?"

"Look," he said, starting to sound annoyed. "I didn't pay that close attention, okay? I thought you didn't like the guy. I didn't think you'd care." He raised his eyebrows. "But maybe I was wrong about that?"

"No, no, I *don't* like the guy."

"You sure about that?"

No.

She needed to regroup. "I have to run." She had to go to the source. Which was Eve.

Who was in the kitchen at the Mermaid having coffee with Nora.

"What is this? Is morning coffee a regular thing? I have to start getting up earlier."

"Hey!" Nora smiled. "I heard the show was great last night."

"It was! Holden is turning out to be the best decision I ever made." He'd been less friendly after his spat with Ben at the bar, but that was fine. She didn't need Holden to be her friend. And as a bonus, he'd stopped propositioning her.

Eve pointed to an empty stool and got up. "I'll get you some coffee."

"No coffee for me, thanks. But I do want to ask you something. So, ah . . ." There was no way to bring this up without looking like, to quote Rohan, she was in junior high. "Rohan says that Jenna told him that you"—she nodded at Eve—"told her that Sawyer told you that Benjamin told him that he likes me."

Eve paused in the middle of climbing back onto her stool. "Come again?"

Nora cracked up.

"I'm hearing that Benjamin likes me. Do you think he likes me?"

Eve raised her eyebrows. "Do *you* like *him*?"

"No! I just want to know if he likes me! And if he does, I want to know why you didn't bother to tell me!"

"I thought if I told you, you'd get all worked up." Eve made a gesture that seemed to say, *Like you are right now.* "You got all up in my face last time we talked about this." Maya winced. She had been a little strident. "And since I thought you were indifferent, I didn't bother saying anything. Honestly, I didn't even really pay that much attention when Sawyer was talking about it."

"You're right." She was being a jerk. "I'm sorry. I'm really tired. I'm going upstairs to power nap, but first, I have amazing news!"

After she told them about the *Globe* critic, she went upstairs and texted Ben. Rohan got the Globe and Mail critic to come to the show Saturday!

He wrote back right away. That's amazing! Congrats!

It was only later, as she was drifting off to sleep, that she realized how odd it was that when she'd had good news, the impulse to text Ben and tell him about it had been automatic.

What was going to happen to them when she won the grant?

Or when he did?

Chapter Twenty

When Maya woke up several hours later, it was to a series of texts from Holden proclaiming in increasingly urgent tones that he needed to talk to her.

And then there was a soft knock on her door. "Maya?" It was Eve. "Holden's downstairs saying he needs to see you. I tried to send him away, but he's being really insistent."

"Yeah, okay, tell him I'll be down in a few minutes." Maya sighed and heaved herself out of bed. She'd been looking forward to a few days off—it was Monday, and the last two shows didn't start until Saturday—the traditional matinee before the parade. Which was supposed to mean a break from Holden. But apparently it wasn't to be.

"What's up?" she asked as she entered the little parlor off the lobby.

He blew out a breath and ran his fingers through his hair. He looked uncomfortable.

"What's the matter?"

"You remember that audition I told you about?"

"The Ryan Alexander movie?"

He nodded. "It's on Saturday."

"*This* Saturday?" The Saturday the theater critic was coming? Another nod, but he was looking at his feet now.

"Well, it can't be. We have shows Saturday and Sunday."

"Right, well, this is a huge opportunity for me, see. A chance to take things to the next level, careerwise."

No. This wasn't happening. "Holden, you made a commitment. You can't just bail on me!"

"I know, I know. But this offer…"

"We signed a contract." Dread took root in her gut. This whole thing with Holden had seemed too good to be true—and look, it had been.

"You have to understand," he said. "You've got a real cute theater company here."

Okay, no. The dread that had been growing in her gut was pulled out by the roots and replaced with anger. "A *cute* theater company?"

"And I have to thank you for this opportunity," he went on as if he hadn't heard her. "My agent said Ryan was really impressed I was doing live theater. He said Ryan said the movie is going to have the same kind of battle-of-the sexes vibe as *Much Ado*."

Oh, hell no. "Don't you *dare* compare my play to anything Ryan fucking Alexander is touching."

His eyes widened. It was true that she didn't swear a lot. If you believed Ben, she was known for her *hooboy*s. But honestly. She might not be a big, fancy Hollywood director, but she didn't want to be. And more to the point, she wasn't an asshole. And her theater company might not be powerful and prestigious, but it sure as hell wasn't *cute*. At least not in the condescending way Holden meant.

"You don't have to get all pissy about it," he grumbled. "I was doing you a favor anyway."

"No, Holden, you were doing a *job*. A job I hired you for that you are now apparently bailing on."

He stopped staring at the floor, stopped fidgeting, and looked her in the eye. "I'm sorry."

Maya flattered herself that she was a pretty decent actor. She'd had good training, anyway. One of her main teachers had said actors use themselves as vessels for emotion. Talked about cultivating an emotion and letting it in—but then letting it out. That last part, he'd said, was key to not taking the emotions of a character home with you.

She had done that here, to a point. She'd cycled through bewilderment, disbelief, dread, and anger pretty quickly, one emotion sliding away to make room for the next so fast she almost didn't feel them.

Until Holden left.

Everything poured out of her to make room for a wave of despair. She was going to have to cancel the last two shows—and lose the exposure the *Globe and Mail* article would have provided.

She'd had a huge opportunity handed to her today, and now it was being snatched away.

"Everything okay?" Eve popped her head in. "Holden took off like a bat out of hell."

"He's leaving."

"What do you mean?"

"He's going to LA. He's bailing on the rest of the run."

"Oh, honey. You want me to—"

No, She didn't want Eve to do anything. She didn't want Eve at all, surprisingly.

She wanted Ben.

It was a quiet Monday afternoon at the bar. Things were always quiet early in the week before festival weekends. It was like people were saving up their party mojo. There were only a handful of customers in the bar, and they were all looked after, so Law was using the opportunity to forge ballots in favor of Pearl for mermaid queen. Not having been successful in his quest to find a willing volunteer, he'd decided to resort to fraud. The old folks stopped at nothing to get what they wanted, so what was one little detour to the dark side on his part?

He had a stack of ballots and a bunch of different kinds of pens and pencils, and he was huddling next to the cash register. *PEARL*, he wrote in red ink using block letters. *Pearl B*, he wrote in pencil in what he hoped were kid-like bubble letters. Then, in blue cursive: *Perl Bruneda*—this particular imaginary person was a bad speller.

He wasn't exactly sure how he was going to sneak his pile of fake ballots into the ballot box, which was kept under Karl's watchful eye at the hardware store, but he'd cross that bridge when he came to it. Karl was being weird, anyway. Usually he and Pearl and Eiko made a big deal of announcing the king and queen the weekend before the parade, but for some reason this year they'd decided to keep the voting open to the last minute—which suited Law and his scheming ways just fine.

He was so immersed in his subterfuge that he was startled when his phone buzzed with a text from Eve, which was a bit unusual. They were friendly enough but didn't have much occasion to text each other directly. Holden is bailing on the play. There was a shouting match. He left, and Maya ran off.

> *Law:* What? But the Globe guy is coming on Satur-
> day.
> *Eve:* Exactly.

Oh shit. He clattered to standing, but then he didn't know what to do. His limbs were vibrating with the need to move, to find her, but he wasn't sure where she would have gone. If Holden had really left town, maybe to her apartment?

He was still frozen, mind racing, when the door opened. It was

Maya. Standing there in all her mermaid queen glory—in all her Maya vulnerability.

He looked at her, and suddenly he knew that whatever else happened, she was his.

If he could talk her into having him.

That feeling of rightness that he'd had trouble making sense of? He knew what it was now. He understood what Sawyer and Jake had been trying to say.

She came right to the bar, right to him. She looked so sad.

"Holden's leaving," she said, her voice quavering. "I have to cancel the last two shows." Her eyes started to fill.

"Aww, sweetheart." He had no one to cover the bar, but he did not give one flying fuck. He fished out his apartment keys, handed them to her, and stuck his fingers in his mouth and let out an ear-piercing whistle. "Sorry, folks," he shouted, "bar's closing."

There was a murmur of disbelief and, as people started realizing he was serious, grumbling.

"Ben!" Maya exclaimed. "Don't close the bar."

He shot her a quelling look and made a shooing motion toward the back. "Go on ahead. I'll be right behind you."

The line echoed in his head. *I'll be right behind you.* He wanted to say more. *I'll help you. I'll hold you up.* Or maybe even, more pragmatically, *I will go to wherever Holden fucking Hampshire is, and I will drag him back here by his sorry little ass.* But this was not the time for that.

This was the time to get these people out of his goddamn bar. He clapped his hands to move them along. "Take your drinks with you. On the house if you haven't settled your checks."

Carol Dyson, who owned Curl Up and Dye, the beauty salon that functioned as a kind of satellite gossip node in town, secondary to the hardware store, eyed him as she gathered her things. This was going to be all over town in a matter of minutes. Interestingly, that was another thing that should have bothered him but about which he could not currently find a single fuck to give.

Five minutes later, he was locking the bar and bounding up the stairs. He paused outside his apartment and fished his wallet out of his pocket.

A PERSON OF WORDS AND NOT DEEDS IS A GARDEN FULL OF WEEDS.

He'd kept the fortune from the night Maya first kissed him—well, from the night she first kissed him and didn't claim she'd thought he was someone else. He looked at it for a long moment before shoving it back in among his credit cards and pushing the door open.

She was sitting on the sofa staring into space—and she was crying.

"Oh, hey now." He crossed the room quickly.

She remained slumped on the sofa, looking up at him as she spoke. She didn't even bother to try to hide her tears, which, frankly, alarmed him. She was usually so unflappable. And if she had any weaknesses or vulnerabilities, she didn't show them, especially to *him*.

Although she was here, wasn't she? She'd come to him instead of Eve or Nora or her family.

"Holden's leaving."

"I heard."

"I don't know why I'm so upset," she said. "It's not like I had to cancel the entire run. It was a longer run than usual, and I did really well on the shows he was here for."

"I think you're so upset because—" He stopped himself. She didn't need him telling her why she was upset.

"Because of the guy from the *Globe*," she finished.

"Yes, but..." That wasn't what he'd been thinking.

"What?" she said quietly. "What were you going to say?"

He paused for a moment and searched her face. He still wasn't used to this new Maya who *wanted* his opinion. He lowered himself to sit, but as always when they sat together on this sofa, he kept some distance between them. He mirrored her position, letting his head fall back and looking at the ceiling, so they weren't looking at each other. He didn't know if that move was to protect her or him. "Well, Holden was a big deal. Mind you, he was also a big dick."

She snuffled a little, like maybe she was laughing through her tears, which would feel like a huge victory. So he rotated his neck and turned his head to check. She had done the same. If the topic weren't so serious, they might have made a funny picture, plastered against the sofa with their heads turned, like tortoises stretching their necks toward each other.

If that had been a laugh, there was no evidence of it now. She was still crying. Or, rather, tears were still falling. She made no noise. It was like her eyes were leaking. They were unnerving, these silent tears. Maya was, in most respects, kind of dramatic. If he'd imagined her crying, it would have been different. Not so dejected.

She was looking at him expectantly, though, so he plowed on. "It was a pretty big coup to get Holden. You sold a lot of tickets based on his name. And now you're saying you have to cancel shows. That's a big deal. And it's on you. It's not your fault, but you're the one left wearing it. And that's aside from the fact that one of the shows had the goddamn *Globe and Mail* coming to it." Anger was electrifying his voice, making it raspy with emotion, which was not normally something he would allow. He didn't generally like Maya to know she was getting to him. But she was letting him see her cry, so he let his voice continue to telegraph the disgust he felt. "You're the one left with the fallout, while he swans off to do *whatever the fuck*."

Maya's tears kept coming, but there was something else happening now, too. Her eyes were wide, and her mouth was half fallen open in astonishment, half smiling. She was surprised by his anger, but she liked his interpretation of things. So he kept going. "And that's not you. You are a hustler—in a good way. You put in the work. You don't let people down. But he forced you to. And there's no way around the fact that he's costing you a ton of money. So yes, you might be ahead, but it's still a loss against what could have been. It's money and reputation all mixed up, and it's a shitty situation."

She let loose a little sob, but then she tried to swallow it.

Ah, shit. He didn't know what to do with these tears. He understood where they were coming from, but Holden Hampshire wasn't worth it. He didn't *deserve* them.

He hated that she was crying, but he *also* hated that if she needed to cry, she was trying to stifle it.

"Shh," he soothed.

She shook her head and started to look away, like her pride was belatedly kicking in. He'd thought before that she would never want him to see her cry, and it was as if all of a sudden she was remembering this first principle.

He was flip-flopping on first principles, too, it seemed, because he didn't *want* her to look away, to lose this particular staring contest. He didn't want to stop seeing her pain, if she had to have pain.

So, moving slowly, like she was a wild horse he didn't want to spook, he laid a hand on her forearm. She turned back to him, her eyes still wounded. He opened his arms, knowing it was probably futile but doing it anyway. When they sat on this couch or when they lay together in bed, they always left space between them.

When she came into his arms, immediately and unhesitatingly, *he* suddenly had to blink back tears. It—her, the fact of her, here in his arms—felt so hard-won.

He had the sudden thought that, just like he hadn't wanted either of them to lose the staring contest just then, he didn't want either of them to lose, *period*.

"Why are you being so nice to me?" she said, her voice muffled because she'd buried her head against his chest.

Because this is what you do when you love someone. You hold them up when they need you.

He held her and let the feeling fill him up—the feeling he'd been calling "rightness" but now knew was love. It was astonishing to realize that he had loved her for a long time. There had just been an extra layer in there making things confusing, like steam on a pair of glasses obscuring his vision.

He laughed.

She pulled away, searching his face. "What's so funny?" She thought he was laughing at her.

I'm laughing because I love you. Yeah, now was not the time for that. That would come later.

Now was the time for an apology. The real one, this time. The big one. And then a proposal. A totally obvious proposal that had been under his nose the whole time.

A PERSON OF WORDS AND NOT DEEDS IS A GARDEN FULL OF WEEDS.

Time for deeds.

"I need to apologize."

Maya studied Ben's face. "You're laughing because you need to apologize." It had been hard to pull back from his embrace, which had felt like such a haven, even though, objectively speaking, she knew that a hug was not going to solve any of her problems. But now he was laughing at her?

"I don't know," he said. "It's confusing. You confuse me sometimes."

She knew the feeling.

"I'm sorry I ruined *Romeo and Juliet*."

She tried to pull away—all the way, this time. "We don't have to talk about it. It was so long ago."

He held on to her. Not hard, not enough that she couldn't get away if she wanted to. And since she didn't want to, not really, she let herself be held.

She let herself be held. When was the last time she'd done that?

"We do have to talk about it, though," he said, firmly but gently.

She closed her eyes against his scrutiny. Usually her mission was to stare back at him, to not back down. But this was so embarrassing. That she would hold a grudge so long, that she would let it spiral so out of control.

"I did a shitty thing, and I'm sorry."

She opened her eyes. "You weren't in the play." Sadie was the one who'd actually bailed on the show, so it followed logically that if Maya was going to spend years punishing someone, it should have been Sadie. And yeah, she might not be the president of Sadie's fan club, but the woman made the world's best pancakes.

Also, Sadie did not have all-seeing eyes the color of moss. And a stupidly impressive work ethic. And the ability to own her mistakes. And to hold her like she had the power to make sure nothing bad ever happened to her again.

Hooboy, she was in trouble.

"Yeah," he said, "but I remember Sadie telling me she was in a play. I didn't really even know what that meant, since that was your first play."

"Well, how would you have known?" Why was she arguing with him? She had been marked by having to cancel that play, and she *had* blamed him, so why was she attempting to reason away what he was trying to say?

Because letting him apologize meant admitting how much he'd hurt her. How vulnerable she had been—and still was—when it came to him. She'd spent *years* sparring with him, showing him her strongest self. It was hard to just...stop.

"Well, I did know," he said. "But I will say that I only remembered all this recently. I remember that weekend, of course—I'd won concert tickets in Toronto—but the circumstances around it had faded. It wasn't until Rohan told me the story a couple weeks ago and it all came back that I pieced together that it was *your* play." He rolled his eyes. "Which is dumb. Of course it was your play. Who else's would it have been? Sadie was supposed to play Juliet. We argued about it on the way to Toronto. I wanted to ask her if she'd actually read the play. I was like, 'You know you die in the end, right? Over some teenage jerk?'"

She laughed. Leave it to Ben to make her laugh in the middle of an apology. He wasn't wrong about the play. "Romeo and Juliet are both jerks."

"So why stage it?"

"Everyone loves it. It's a crowd-pleaser."

"Like *My Fair Lady*."

Yes. She loved that he remembered that. He did that—remembered little things she said.

"I talked Sadie into blowing it off," he said. "The concert tickets came with a hotel room. I really wanted to go, and I didn't realize how much damage us going would do here. To you. It was careless. And for what it's worth all these years later, which I realize might not be a lot, I'm sorry."

It was amazing what a simple apology could do.

Also amazing was how, now that she had it, she realized she didn't need it. That Ben Lawson had been kind to her for so long. Which was a confusing thing to ponder, but if you looked at what he did, at his actions, the conclusion was unmistakable. He stocked special wine for her that he barely charged her for. Put the Spice Girls on his jukebox. Came to all her plays. Let her watch football at his house in the middle of the night.

Steadied her when she was about to fall—literally, like that time at the dunk tank, but also metaphorically, like . . . right now.

But she didn't know how to say all that. So she smirked and said, "You and Sadie, eh? What was up with that?"

His eyes widened. He was surprised she wasn't going to make a bigger deal of the apology. "Yeah, I don't know, except she suddenly asked me out that summer. She was a year older than I was. You remember she went to Western before she came back and opened the diner?" Maya nodded. "She was still in school at that point but was home for the summer. She seemed so worldly." He rolled his eyes, like he was annoyed with his own bullshit.

"What happened with you two?"

"Nothing. We only went out for a month that summer. She was..."

"What?"

"Boring," he said immediately, then winced like he'd verbalized something he hadn't intended to. "Please don't tell anyone I said that. Sadie is really sweet. There's just..."

"Not a lot under the surface?" That had always been Maya's impression, but she figured she wasn't the most reliable judge of character when it came to her runaway Juliet.

He nodded but made a face like he was chagrined to be agreeing.

"What show was it?" she asked.

"What?"

"The concert you won tickets to."

"Does it matter?"

"Yes. If you ruined my play to go see, say, Beyoncé, that's one thing."

He chuckled. "No, it, uh, wasn't Beyoncé."

"Tell me who it was! Let's see, this would have been, what?" She tried to send her mind back. "Twelve years ago?"

It was his turn to close his eyes. Ooh, he didn't want to tell her. Which meant she absolutely had to know. "Ben Lawson, I won't forgive you until you tell me who it was."

He sighed, opened his eyes, and mumbled, "It was the Jonas Brothers."

A shocked laugh ripped from her throat. "What? Mr. I Don't Know About Boy Bands! And this would have been original Jonas Brothers, not latter-day, married-to-women-out-of-their-leagues Jonas Brothers." She threw her head back and let herself laugh unreservedly. It felt good.

"It was free!" he protested, but he was laughing, too. "It was the trip as much as the concert." But he sobered quickly. "It was stupid, though. I ruined your play for the Jonas Brothers. But somehow, all these years, if I'd thought about why you hated me, I wouldn't have put two and two together. I wouldn't have connected it back to that."

"I don't *hate* you." Not anymore. Had she ever? Truly? "And I'm not sure it was ever hate, anyway. I..." She hardly knew how to explain it, even to herself. "I was mad, for sure. But, I don't know, I moved back here and we had a couple legitimate business spats, and the animosity sort of accreted. And then we just..." She waved her hand back and forth between them.

"Started feuding?" he supplied, an odd cheeriness in his tone.

"Yeah, and now it's like a habit more than anything." It was her turn to wince. "That sounds terrible."

"No, I know exactly what you mean. It's like we didn't hate each other so much as we enjoyed fighting with each other."

Why was he using the past tense? Did that mean they weren't going to fight anymore? The thought was oddly disappointing.

Also, forget fighting, were they going to keep sleeping together?

And if not, which would she miss more?

"Anyway," he said, "I really am sorry."

She sighed. She'd been trying to brush off the apology, but she was going to have to engage with it, wasn't she? "It's okay. I mean, I was mad at the time. I was actually really hurt." That was hard to admit. "But really, that should have been directed at Sadie. I just...Arg. In a way, you guys did me a favor. After that play, I made sure I always had understudies. If I wasn't acting in a play, just directing it, I learned the whole play so I could step in myself if need be." She had learned a good lesson that day. "I got really obsessive about my backup system, until..."

"Holden."

Right. Amazingly, though she had come up here crying, feeling like she was going to break into pieces on account of Holden, she'd forgotten about him while they were talking. That was the power of Ben. "I should have had someone else learn the part. But I thought, well, Holden *moved* here for this, so he's going to be reliable. And who's going to understudy Holden Hampshire, anyway?" She blew out a breath. She was so frustrated with herself. "What am I going to *do*?"

"You're going to come to the beach with me."

"What?"

He stood and extended his hand. "Come on. I have an idea, but it's too beautiful a day to talk about it inside."

"What about the bar? You can't just leave the bar closed."

"You know what? It turns out I can."

Chapter Twenty-One

⌐

𝓛aw could leave the bar empty and locked in the middle of the afternoon. He could take a loan against the bar building and open a restaurant. He could apologize to the woman he loved for hurting her, albeit unknowingly, in the past.

He could do all these things, it turned out.

So the *next* thing was easy. "I think we should apply for the grant together."

Maybe he should have dropped the bomb on their way to the beach, rather than wait until they were right at the edge of the water, because she started so violently he feared for a moment that she was going to trip and get wet.

But she steadied herself and turned to him. Bewilderment gave way to incredulity, and he could tell she was gearing up to argue.

Bring it.

"What on earth are you talking about?"

He smiled. "I'm talking about a joint application. Think of it as risk pooling. No, it's more than that. We've been bickering about business-related stuff all this time, but what if we flipped the script?

A restaurant and a theater. They complement each other. Why not stick our lots in together?"

"But you're probably going to win. So if we shared, you'd be giving up half the grant."

"That's not true. You're going to win." He truly believed that.

"I am not! You already have a successful business."

"It's apples and oranges. I sell beer. People will always pay for beer. You're a nonprofit. This town is organized around its festivals. And what's at the center of every festival?"

"A pack of meddling old people?"

"No. A play. Your plays."

She sucked in a breath.

He gestured across the beach, which was fairly crowded but thankfully not populated by any of the old folks. He'd brought her here hoping to make a point he was struggling to articulate even to himself. "Sandcastle Beach. The site of so many battles. Think of all the years we spent competing. Think of all the *energy* we spent. What if we had worked together? Can you imagine the sandcastle we could have built?"

"What are you saying? Is this a metaphor? My brain is too tired for metaphors right now."

He smiled. "The new restaurant will need business. You want to keep theater attendance up in the post-Holden era. What if we offered dinner-and-theater packages? Maybe we could each draw customers we might not have had without the other. If we work together instead of against each other, we might find that we're more than the sum of our parts."

"We're more than the sum of our parts," she echoed, a note of astonishment in her tone.

"So I'm thinking, what if we divide the money into thirds? You use a third for building repairs. I'll use a third as a down payment on Jason's house. So each business is getting a new lease on life, so to speak. Then we take the final third and use it for stuff that will benefit us both—and the town."

"But you're going to need more than thirty grand to buy Jason's house. You'll still need a mortgage."

"Right. The grant was never going to be enough to allow me to buy the place outright, and—"

"But you said it was enough to—"

"Will you let me talk, woman?" He rolled his eyes, but he smiled as he did it. She rolled hers back, but she stopped talking. "I've learned something from you this summer." Her mouth fell open, but she didn't interrupt him again. "I learned that sometimes you have to take a risk. I've been thinking about that Junior Achievement panel. You *did* start something from nothing when you opened that theater, and I admire the hell out of it. Sometimes you just have to take a risk." *In more ways than one.* But one risk at a time. "Watching you taught me that."

"Sometimes you just have to take a risk," she echoed, astonishment and happiness battling it out on her face. "But that third of the grant, that shared third, if we play it right, can mitigate the risk for both of us."

"Exactly."

"We could do behind-the-scenes packages. Meet the actors at the bar afterwards. Or your chef caters a meal backstage for people who buy VIP tickets."

"See—you have all the good ideas."

"Well, this whole collaboration was your idea."

"Yeah, but that was obvious. It was staring us in the face."

"*I* didn't see it."

"Well, maybe you're not as smart as I am." He winked.

"Are we going to fight now about who has better ideas, except in a new twist, we're each arguing for the other?"

"Maybe." He for one hoped this peace treaty wasn't going to be the end of *all* fighting. Giving up bickering with Maya would be like giving up seeing the world in color. "There is one flaw in my plan, though."

"There is?"

"You were going to use the grant money to set up a fundraising program."

"*If* I won. Honestly, I was already a little worried about that being the centerpiece of my application. Fundraising will support the theater, not the town. It's not actually very community-minded."

"But the theater is a big part of this community."

"Are you trying to talk me out of what you were just trying to persuade me of seconds ago?"

"No! I just want you to see what you're giving up."

"I see it. And I'm not really giving it up. I'm just postponing it. We get the grant, we do the joint stuff, we add volume to both of our businesses, I can use *that* increment of new profit to set something up fundraisingwise."

He couldn't hide his grin if you paid him. "Okay, then."

"All that time we spent fighting about the pizza oven, we could have been leveraging the pizza oven for the common good," she mused.

"It kind of blows the mind, doesn't it?"

"You know what? I secretly love your pizza. Nora has been smuggling it to me since she moved here."

"*Really?*" Another thing that blew the mind.

"Really. So..." She trailed off, all coy and adorable. "I think this means I should get my pizza for free from here on out. Because we're basically business partners now, right?"

And ideally a whole lot more, but, again, one thing at a time. A chat on the beach wasn't enough to make his case on that front. For that he needed an action plan.

A PERSON OF WORDS AND NOT DEEDS IS A GARDEN FULL OF WEEDS.

But for these deeds, he needed help.

Handily, he lived in a town full of helpers.

Maya was looking at him kind of funny, so he got his head back into the game—this game, the business-partners game. If they were going to mix business and pleasure, which he sincerely hoped they were, they needed this part cleanly squared away. He would never want her to think one was contingent on the other. He would design dinner-and-theater packages with her and leave it at that if that was what she wanted. His heart would break in the process, but he would do it. So he held out his hand for her to shake. "Yes—business partners. And yes—all the free pizza you can eat."

She shook his hand, but she seemed a little underwhelmed.

"We can win it, right?" he asked. Maybe that was what she was concerned about. He hadn't been keeping up on who else was applying.

"Are you kidding me?" she said, shaking off her seriousness. "What's more community-minded than joining forces to provide arts and dining for the town and to lure in tourism dollars?"

He liked that idea. He also liked the idea of just…having her around while he made the big restaurant leap. Between Maya and Brie, he sort of felt like he couldn't go wrong. Smart women saving his ass. "There is one more thing we have to discuss."

She smiled widely, which was a bit confusing, because he wouldn't have thought this topic would inspire that reaction. "And what would that be?"

"Holden."

The smile evaporated. "What's there to talk about?"

"Where he's gone so I can go drag him back by his hair?" And who would have ever thought Law would find himself in a position of *wanting* Holden Hampshire around?

"LA," she said dejectedly.

"Give me his number."

"You're not going to get him back."

"I know, but I'd like to have a few words with him." She raised an eyebrow. "I promise I'll be civil. I just want to talk to him." The eyebrow went higher. "Do you trust me?"

"I…do." She sounded surprised. She gave him the number.

"Don't cancel the last two shows yet, okay?"

"You're not going to get him back here."

"I know, but let me try. It's only Monday. You have the rest of the week to cancel."

"Yeah, but if I'm going to cancel on people, it seems better to give them as much notice as I can. And I have to get Marjorie going on issuing refunds."

"Give me twenty-four hours."

"What are you going to do? Send in the Mafia and threaten to break his legs? This isn't like throwing him out of your bar."

"You just *said* you trusted me."

"Fine," she harrumphed.

"Okay, now we gotta get moving on this application. We have to start over, and it's due a week from tomorrow. I really should go open the bar. So let me take a crack at a first draft and I'll email you?"

"So there you go; that's the whole sordid story." Maya flopped back on her bed in the pink room. She had invited Eve and Nora up that evening for a summit.

Maya could handle Ben when they were fighting. Or when they were having sex. But she didn't know what to make of this new, collegial, business-partner version of him. His plan to do a joint grant application was great, of that she had no doubt. But was it a platonic plan? Were they done sleeping together? "So I guess we're just going to be *friends* now? He's going to *email* me?"

Eve laughed. "You make it sound like the worst torture imaginable."

"The thing is, Ben sees me. Like, he really sees me."

"Whoa, whoa. You're calling him Ben now?" Nora asked.

"I think when a person sees you, you're supposed to use the nickname," Eve said.

"We're happy for you," Nora said. "He's a great guy."

"You're talking like we're *together*. That is not what's happening here. He's all, 'We're getting the grant together, we're business partners, I'll email you.' So, like, what? Are we just never going to talk about our interlude of sleeping together?"

"You know what's a good way to talk about something?" Eve appeared to be directing her question to Nora rather than Maya.

"Talk about it?" Nora answered.

"Bingo," Eve said. "Or, you know, email works, too."

"Okay, shut up," Maya said. "I know that. But it's not that simple. Try to remember, ladies. Cast your minds way back to a time when you were scared and uncertain."

"I know, sweetie." Eve lay back next to Maya to stare up at the cciling in solidarity.

"I'm coming in," Nora said. "Make room." She made a *beep beep* noise like a truck backing up.

"Oh, shut up. You're one of those cute pregnant ladies who look exactly the same except for the bump," Maya said as she moved over.

Once they were all lying on the bed, Nora said, "Hey, have you and Law had sex in this room?"

Eve cracked up. "Oh my God! The pink room is on its third romance!"

"Hello, as we *just* established, I am not having a 'romance' with Ben," Maya said. "To date it has been more like arguing plus sex."

"Yeah, but have you had sex in *this room*?" Nora punctuated the question with a little physical prodding, tapping her finger on Maya's shoulder.

Maya laughed. "Hooboy, have I ever."

The girls whooped.

Maya turned to Eve. "Actually, if this room really is three for three, you should start charging more for it."

"Maybe it only works when I let people live in it for free," Eve said. "If you think about it, both of you were temporarily homeless when you moved in here."

That was a funny coincidence. "You should rename it. I don't think 'the pink room' really telegraphs, *Move into this room and you will get laid.*"

"I actually used to think of it as the Pink Room of Pain," Eve said. "You know how there's the Red Room of Pain in *Fifty Shades*?"

They all laughed. "It's actually always reminded me of a vagina," Nora said. "I mean, I know given my line of work I see a lot more of them than you two do, but all this pink! Pink walls!"

"The Vagina Room!" Maya exclaimed as the three of them cracked up. "There you go, Eve. That there is marketing gold."

"How about the Lucky Room?" Eve asked.

Maya sighed. If only.

Chapter Twenty-Two

℮

𝓑rie, God bless her, agreed to come to town early when Law called her up and told her the whole story. He explained that he needed to disappear for a few days because he had to work on a project to show the woman he was in love with that he was dead serious, and was there any chance she could come to town earlier than planned?

She'd said two things: "Sure" and "This is that woman from the flower shop, isn't it?"

"Yep," he'd agreed easily. "The woman from the flower shop."

And then he'd texted Holden Hampshire, that asshole. This is Ben Lawson from Lawson's Lager House. Can you do me a favor that's actually a favor for Maya? A way to make what you did less shitty?

He'd followed that up with meetings. Eve and Sawyer and Nora and Jake, first, who had embraced their assignments readily, if with a large dose of teasing.

And then Pearl, Karl, and Eiko. Of course, they'd all come through. That was the upside to life in Moonflower Bay. The meddlers could be counted on to meddle for good when you wanted them to. There was an existing meddling infrastructure just waiting to be activated.

Brie arrived Tuesday morning, and he showed her around the bar.

"I know this is quick, and I know I'm asking a lot, but I need you to hold down the fort through Saturday. I've got Carter, who you'll meet when he shows up later, all prepped. He knows you're here, and he's going to be working as much as he can."

Then he took Brie upstairs. Like Maya had done with Holden, he was lending out his apartment. Brie had done him a solid by dropping everything and coming, and he owed her.

Also, he didn't want to see Maya.

Well, he *did* want to see Maya. It was *all* he wanted, basically. But he had to sacrifice her for the short term in order to make things right—really right—for the long term. He hoped.

"I'm sorry this is sort of a trial by fire," he said to Brie.

"I'll figure it out. And I can text you if I have any questions, right? It sounds like you're going to be helming a major logistics push in addition to doing the grant stuff. I don't want to bug you, but I assume you're not going totally off the grid?"

"Definitely text me anytime. And thank you. I appreciate this."

"No problem." He started to thank her again, but she waved him off. "Go."

So he went—to his parents' house to hunker down.

On Tuesday afternoon, just under the "Give me twenty-four hours" plea Ben had made, Maya received a very surprising text.

> **Holden:** Hi. Have you blocked me, lol?
> **Maya:** I should have blocked you.
> **Holden:** Right. Okay, so I'm sorry for how I handled things. I've had a change of plans. Benedick will be there Saturday.

Holy crap. Ben had done it—whatever "it" was.

She wasn't prepared for this. Her first impulse was to fire off a Screw you, I don't need your charity text, but she made herself ponder the offer with her businessperson hat on. Which, she reasoned, probably meant it was okay to text her business partner.

Maya: Holden just texted and said he can do one more show. What did you do?

Ben: I had a chat with him.

Maya: Did you break any of his bones?

Ben: I did not.

Maya: Did you have anyone else break any of his bones?

Ben: Still no.

Maya: I want to tell him to eff off, but I shouldn't, right?

Ben: Well, you know how much I loathe the guy, but if he does Saturday, you don't have to cancel that show AND you get the Globe review, right?

Maya: Yeah, I know. You're right.

Ben: Uh, what did you just say?

Maya: You were right. Once. Don't let it go to your head.

Ben: Hold off on canceling Sunday, too. You never know how things will work out.

Maya: Why? Are you going to break his bones in person on Saturday?

Ben: I can say with 100 percent certainty that I will not break any of Holden Hampshire's bones.

Ben: 90 percent.

Maya: But if I wait to cancel Sunday, I'll only be giving those people twenty-four hours' notice.

Ben: Trust.

So she trusted.

They spent the next few days writing the first draft of their proposal—and bantering. But not the same way as usual. It was more like... bantering about spreadsheets? And also not in person, because Ben was gone.

She went to the bar Tuesday night, only to find Brie working alone. She went up the back stairs and knocked on his door—no answer. And there were no lights on in his apartment. Judging by Ben's texts, he was working hard on the application. But he wasn't doing it at home.

Well, okay. He was allowed to be somewhere else.

And it wasn't like he wasn't in touch. The next day, he started emailing her ad budgets and research on theater-dinner packages in other places.

> **Maya:** Wow, you aren't kidding around here. Don't
> you think we're a slam dunk to get this thing?
> **Ben:** Probably, but this is research we're going to
> have to do anyway, once we have the money,
> so we might as well do it now and use it to
> bolster the application.
> **Maya:** Right.

Not wanting him to be able to say she hadn't pulled her weight, she'd thrown herself into tweaking her plans for next season.

> **Maya:** I was going to go back to My Fair Lady for
> the musical next year, but what if it's Chicago
> instead, and you do Chicago-style hot dogs or
> deep dish at the restaurant?
> **Ben:** Great—plays with food tie-ins. Love it.
> **Maya:** Or there's always Titus Andronicus, where
> Titus captures the sons of his enemy, Tamora,
> bakes them into a pie, and feeds it to her. You

> know I do like to do a Shakespeare every year
> if I can.
> ***Ben:*** Hmm. I'm going to say no on that one.

And on they went, ideas flying. But it was *only* ideas that were flying. Conspicuously absent were innuendo and conflict. And the more progress they made on the grant, the more she would have given for one or the other—or, ideally, both.

> ***Maya:*** Where are you anyway? I haven't seen you in
> the bar.

That was a legit question, right? He didn't owe her an accounting of his whereabouts, but it was okay for her to notice his absence. In a friendly way.

> ***Ben:*** Brie's doing the heavy lifting while I work on
> this thing. I've gone to my parents' place so I
> can concentrate.

That was accompanied by a picture of his computer on his lap on a Muskoka chair overlooking the lake.

So yeah, he hadn't bailed on Maya, the grant coapplicant. But it sort of felt like he *had* bailed on Maya the person.

When Law arrived at his parents' place, he sat them down and told them everything. He had to. He could hardly show up, announce his intention to stay in their guest room for a week, and spend his days hovering over spreadsheets instead of at the bar.

But more importantly, he wanted to. Not in the sense that he was looking forward to it, but in the sense that it was long overdue. And hell, he was apparently in the midst of overhauling everything else about his life, so no time like the present.

"I wondered if something like this was in the works," his dad said after Law explained about the restaurant plans, hiring Brie, the grant—and his intention to take out a mortgage on the bar building.

"You *did*?"

"With the pizza, and the sandwiches, being so successful, it seems like the next logical step."

"It *does*?" He was aware that he sounded like an idiot, with his astonished two-word questions, but he was just so damn shocked. "You're not upset?"

"Why would we be upset, honey?" his mom asked.

"Because I'm mortgaging the place you guys built? That Grandpa built?"

"We took a mortgage out on the building in 1991 to raise some cash," Mom said.

"You *did*?" And there he went again with the two-word questions.

"It was either that or close it," his dad said.

"Okay, then. This is different. The bar is doing fine. It's doing well."

"Well, then this is a good time to expand, isn't it?" Dad said.

"Did you think we were going to be angry about this?" His mom reached across the kitchen table and patted his hand.

Yes. "I don't know." He turned to his dad. "You're always talking about the legacy of the place."

"Yeah, because I'm proud of it. I'm proud of what I did with it—keep it afloat. And I'm proud of what you're doing with it."

"Even if you don't always approve of what I'm doing with it? You were skeptical about the pizza."

"I'm not in charge anymore. I admit I have wondered at times about some of your choices, but it was never that I didn't approve. I'm more conservative than you are, but you clearly know what you're doing. You have an entrepreneurial streak I never did. You remind me of your grandpa that way."

"I *do*?" That was a huge compliment. "But," he said, not sure why he didn't stop talking and take yes for an answer, "you always used to joke that the bar was your second child. You don't care that I'm risking it?"

"It's not that we don't care," his dad said. "It's that we trust you. Because you're our child. The bar is not our child. That was a joke—maybe a bad one, in retrospect."

His dad, never a very demonstrative guy, reached out and copied his wife's gesture from earlier, laying his hand on top of Law's. Suddenly choked up, Law had to swallow hard. He blamed Maya for making him all weird and emotional lately. But he also noticed that his dad's eyes were extra shiny.

"Speak for yourself," his mom said to his dad. "I personally trust Maya way more than you, Benjamin." As she turned toward Law, her twinkling eyes telegraphed that she was teasing. "If your new business is tied to hers, I don't think you can go wrong. That play last week was phenomenal."

She was kidding, but it was true. Somehow, having Maya on his team made everything seem easier. Made his dreams seem more in reach.

"Why don't you invite her out for dinner tomorrow?" Mom said. "You two can sit outside and work on your application."

Nope. As much as sitting with Maya on his parents' patio over-looking the lake sounded like heaven right now, he couldn't do it. He couldn't see her until Saturday. "So about that. There's actually something else I have to tell you."

When he was done relaying his second big piece of news of the evening, his mom got up, kissed the top of his head, and headed out of the kitchen.

"Where are you going?" He'd thought she'd be all aflutter about his plan. Or that she'd tease him, at least. "Aren't you going to say something?"

"Oh, my darling, yes. I will be back momentarily, and I will say many things. But first I need to go buy some theater tickets for Saturday."

Chapter Twenty-Three

❧

*I*t hadn't occurred to Maya that maybe she shouldn't have trusted Holden's sudden about-face. But at ten to two on Saturday afternoon, she started wondering if she'd been betrayed. Again.

Maya: Where are you? Curtain is in ten minutes!

He had said he wouldn't be able to make the preshow cast meeting, and frankly, she hadn't wanted him there. But they were on imminently.

"Let me take that, hon," Eiko said, reaching for her phone. "I'll keep it safe for you during the show."

Huh?

"It's stressing you out," Eiko added.

"What are you even doing here?" Maya looked around. What was *everyone* doing here? Eve and Nora had come backstage to keep her company and calm her nerves while she did her makeup, but here they still were, and they had Sawyer and Jake with them. And her brother was lurking. He'd been acting as a jack-of-all-trades through the run, but as far as she knew, there was nothing that needed his attention right now. And... "Karl? Why is Karl here?" She turned in place. It felt like the whole town was here.

But on the other hand, a handful of people in town knew about the Holden drama, so word had likely gotten out. Everyone was probably here thinking they were "helping" or "showing support" or whatever spin they wanted to put on their nosiness.

She clapped her hands. "Hey, folks! I'm going to have to ask everyone who isn't part of the cast or crew to go take your seats."

No one moved. They all just looked at her, many of them with strange smiles. Pearl—what on earth was Pearl doing backstage?—was grinning so wildly, she looked a little unhinged.

"Listen, I appreciate all the support, but—"

Someone tapped her on the shoulder. Ah, her tardy star. That explained the odd facial expressions. Everyone was still starstruck by the jerk. A burst of annoyance exploded in her chest.

"It's about time!" she snapped as she whirled and came face-to-face with...

Benedick. Definitely Benedick, dressed as he was in the military officer's garb of the opening scenes: double-breasted, gold-buttoned jacket; tight-fitting breeches tucked into knee-high boots; a scabbard at his hip.

It just wasn't Holden.

"Ben...," she said, trailing off.

"...edick?" he finished with smiling eyes.

"What are you doing here?" she asked weakly, though she supposed it was obvious.

"Saving the play?" His usual public-facing, breezy confidence was nowhere in evidence.

Maya was not a swooner, generally. She was more of a get-on-with-it-er. But her knees suddenly felt like they'd gone on strike.

"I know my lines and everything." He winced. "Mostly."

"That's where I come in!" Eiko stepped up. "I made cue cards, so we have backup. I was going to crouch in front of the stage, but it turns out I can't really crouch thanks to my crappy hips, so Jake is going to be the croucher."

"That's why I've been hiding all week," Ben said. "I've been memorizing my lines."

"Eve and I made a Benedick costume that fits Law," Pearl said.

"One minute!" Ingrid, the stage manager, called, walking through the crowd with a clipboard and shooing the hangers-on into the wings.

Maya eyed Ben warily. "Are you sure we shouldn't—"

"The rest of the cast worked with me on the blocking—that's what you call it, I think?" he said. "But you do get that you're gonna have to carry this thing, right?"

"Places, everyone!" Ingrid called.

Ben started backing away. He wasn't in the opening scene.

"But wait!" she called after him.

"You can't blame me if the *Globe and Mail* review is less than stellar," Ben said with a perplexing degree of calm. "I mean, you *can*. You probably will." He stopped walking and grinned. "I look forward to it, actually."

She . . . was out of words.

"Oh!" he called. "There is one more thing." He was still backing away, so the distance between them was growing as he spoke. "I'm in love with you." He snorted, like he found the idea half-delightful, half-off-putting. "Completely and totally hung up on you, actually." When she didn't answer—if she thought she'd had no words a moment ago, she'd had *no idea*—he added, "Break a leg!"

And then he disappeared.

And the curtain opened.

The first exchange in the play was between the governor of their fictional town and a messenger. Maya listened to them talk and tried to pull herself together. The bright lights prevented her from seeing beyond the first few rows, but in those rows were friendly faces. Eve was backstage working on costume changes, but there was Sawyer sitting with Nora. Pearl, Eiko, and Karl were there, too.

Jake, the town's odd-job guy, was, as promised, crouched in the space between the stage and the first row.

And front and center were Ro and her parents. Her attention caught on her dad, and he noticed, because unlike the rest of the audience members, who were watching the actors who were speaking, he was looking at her.

He smiled and gave her a big, dorky thumbs-up that made something in her chest catch.

Everyone was here. All her people. Her village.

For a moment it felt like they were all staring at her, all at once.

Which, actually, they now were. It was her line, and she was just standing there like an idiot. She took a deep breath. "'I pray you, is Signior Mountanto returned from the wars or no?'"

Beatrice was asking about Benedick. Her nemesis. Her love.

And there he was, striding onto the stage. *Her* nemesis. *Her* love.

Who was "completely and totally hung up" on her.

It boggled the mind.

Some of the other men joked around, as the script called for, but Ben/edick didn't have a line right away. He just stared at her—which worked for the script, because Benedick and Beatrice were basically obsessed with each other. He was looking very pleased with himself, no doubt because he had successfully ambushed her backstage, both with his presence and with his declaration.

And then they were off, doing what they'd always done. Bantering.

He wasn't as polished as Holden. He could have projected better. He didn't always know where to stand. He sometimes glanced at the cue cards, but always in advance of his next line, so he was never stuck with nothing to say.

But they had chemistry. They had chemistry for *days*.

And chemistry, it turned out, was everything.

Because what underlay chemistry was love.

And love could sustain you.

Law honestly hadn't known if he could pull this off, but Maya saved him.

Practicing his lines by himself, or with some of the other cast members who'd come out to his parents' house to help, had been one thing. Saying them live onstage with Maya as his foil was another. The first had been a slog. Homework. The second? Magic. Their first scene together was full of rapid-fire banter, and once they got going, it was as natural as...bantering with Maya. He had *fun*, which was not something he could have predicted.

And then, oh, and then.

There was a point, early in Act II, when they had to dance together at a masked ball—after some more bantering. It was a wild, reeling sort of dance that he stumbled through. He managed not to actually trip, though—until she twirled right up against him and whispered his own words from before back to him: "I'm in love with you, too. Completely and totally hung up on you, actually."

He fell down.

Luckily, she managed to work it into the play, mocking him to the audience in such a way that it seemed like it had been choreographed.

It turned out that Benedick had the last line in *Much Ado about Nothing*, and as Law approached it, he felt like he'd run a marathon. He was sweaty and exhausted. But also exhilarated. He took a deep breath and delivered the play's final line, "'Strike up, pipers.'"

He was cueing the celebratory music, both because the bad guys had not prevailed and because there'd been a double wedding. A wedding that had come complete with a kiss. "'Peace,'" he'd gotten to say to Maya, "'I will stop your mouth.'" And then he'd kissed her.

He had a feeling that getting her to stop talking by kissing her was going to become a regular move for him.

The "pipers" heeded his call, but of course, in Maya's creative production, that meant a pop version of the play's earlier song started blasting through the theater's speakers.

They were supposed to dance, to do some Two Squared choreography, but a man had to draw the line somewhere. So he folded his arms, raised an eyebrow, and leaned against a "tree" to watch the others frolic.

Maya came over to him and tried to get him to dance, but he wasn't having it.

"Come on," she whispered, pulling on his arm as the crowd cheered.

"Dream on." He would die before he did Holden Hampshire's choreography. The guy had done him a solid with the decoy texts, but dancing was not happening.

"Please?" she wheedled as the crowd kicked it up a notch, hooting and clapping rhythmically. "Because you loooove me?"

"Nope," he said, but his face was about to crack open from smiling.

"What if I told you—"

"Peace," he interrupted. See? This line was already coming in handy. "I will stop your mouth."

And he did.

After the curtain call, they were mobbed. Law hadn't thought about this aspect of things, so focused had he been on the dual projects of the play and the grant.

They were swarmed by the cast and crew first, and since everyone wanted to talk to either him or Maya, they were drawn away from each other. He kept glancing at her, trying to figure out a way to get back to her.

Then the townspeople started pouring in, including Karl and Pearl and Eiko. They were carrying a crown and trident, and they were making a beeline for Maya. How was that possible? He had literally stuffed the ballot box with votes for Pearl.

"Sorry," he said, interrupting Sawyer, who was jawing about how he'd known all along that Law and Maya would end up together. Law forced his way through the crowd, ignoring everyone's exclamations and congratulations. He had to get to her before the old folks did.

They beat him by a few seconds. They'd started talking to her, but her attention shifted to him when he broke into their circle. "Hi," she said.

"Hi."

They stared at each other with goofy grins on their faces. To think that she was his. That he was hers. That they were done with the feud. Or maybe that the feud was never going to end? That part of things was confusing. But why should it be otherwise? Confused was his default mode when it came to her.

Pearl started trying to hand the mermaid crown to Maya, and that tipped him out of his slack-jawed paralysis. "Okay, so here's the thing. I tried to get someone else elected mermaid queen. I really did."

"But everyone just wants you, hon," Eiko said. "We saved the coronation for now because we didn't want to upstage certain other people's plans." She shot a bemused look at Law. "But you won in a landslide, Queen Maya."

Which, again, was impossible. He had personally stuffed a hundred counterfeit ballots into the box. He'd even bought a gallon of paint so he could slip them in while Karl was distracted mixing it. He turned to the old folks. "I will fight you over this. I respect you all, but I will fight you." He swung his attention back to Maya, who looked like she was trying not to laugh. "I swear to God, I didn't do this. I tried to *undo* this."

"It's okay." Maya took the crown from Pearl. "I actually secretly like being the mermaid queen."

Huh? "You *do*?"

"Yeah, I just never wanted you to know I liked it."

Wait. *What?*

"I mean, when have I ever seen a starring rôle I didn't love?"

"All right, then," said Karl. "That's settled."

The old folks started herding Maya toward the backstage exit. He followed. What else was he going to do?

And hey, he'd get to watch her as mermaid queen again. He couldn't think of a better way to end this day.

Well, he *could*, but that would come later.

"Can we get a minute alone?" he said as they all approached the float.

"Nope," Karl said. "The rest of the parade is ready to go, and the route is lined with people."

"The Mermaid Parade waits for no one," Pearl said.

"Yeah, but it usually starts a bit after the play." Maya turned to Law. "I usually have an hour to shift gears."

"Not this year!" Pearl trilled, winking at Eiko.

"But . . . ," Maya protested.

"Maya and I need to talk," Law said decisively.

"You can talk the rest of your life." Eiko tried to hand him the trident. "Hell, you can talk on the float."

Huh? "*I'm* not getting on the float."

"I don't see why not," Karl said. "You were elected king."

Oh, for God's sake. "I was not."

"You were, though," Karl said.

"Children." Pearl gestured at both him and Maya. "I say this with love, but you two are kind of dumb. The whole town saw where this was going, if not years ago certainly earlier this summer. You were *both* elected in a landslide. The people have spoken."

He looked at Maya, who shrugged and made a why-not face. Eiko opened his hand like he was a doll and stuck the trident in it, and Karl moved a step stool to the edge of the float.

"We don't have the right outfits," he tried, though he wasn't really sure why he was objecting. If Maya wanted to be mermaid queen, he was good to go.

"Your costumes are fine," Pearl said. "We can make an exception this year."

"Maya and I are applying for the grant jointly," Law said, remembering suddenly that they did have something to surprise the old meddlers with. Ha. If these people thought they pulled all the strings in this town, they had another thing coming.

"Of course you are," said Eiko, patting his arm briefly before snapping her fingers and pointing at the steps. "Get up there."

"We've been wondering when you would land on that strategy," Pearl said.

All right. He was defeated. Law followed Maya up to the matching clamshell thrones. He grabbed her hand before they sat, and the crowd cheered. All their friends were there. He made eye contact with Sawyer and Jake, who both grinned.

He suddenly thought back to his last boat ride with the guys. "Did you tell Eve that you liked me? Like a week or so ago?"

"No!" Maya sounded appalled. "Did you tell Sawyer *you* liked *me*?"

"I did not. In fact, I actively denied it."

She cracked up. "We got played, didn't we?"

"We did indeed."

"Rohan was in on it, too, I'm pretty sure." She pointed to her family as she sat on her throne. They were all waving enthusiastically at her.

"I guess the meddling spanned the generations this time," he said, spotting his own parents and waving at them sheepishly.

"The trident is mine," Maya said once the float started moving. She grabbed one end of it, but he held on to the other, resulting in a little tug-of-war. "I got possession of it last year, and I'm not giving it up."

"Oh, so I get nothing?" he countered, though he let her have it. "How is anyone supposed to be able to tell that I'm the mer-king?"

"You could take your shirt off. Usually the mer-king doesn't wear a shirt. Unless it's Karl, in which case he wears that T-shirt with fake muscles on it."

"I'm not taking my shirt off."

"Suit yourself." She shrugged. "I mean, it's not like I'm a theater director or anything. It's not like I have professional training and years of experience in what makes for a good visual—"

"Peace. I will stop your—"

"No!" Maya said. "I strongly suggest you don't come over here. Don't even stand up. It's too easy to lose your balance."

"Aww, you loooove me."

"No, I just don't want you to fall to your death and know I could have prevented it. I'd do that for anyone. I don't want blood on my hands."

"Close enough," he said. "I guess that means I'll have to stop your mouth later."

"Yeah, okay." She smiled. "And *I* guess that means for now you'll just have to listen to me talk."

He was extremely okay with that.

"Actually, I have some notes for you."

"Notes?"

"It's a theater term. The director gives notes to the actors after a show—things that can be improved or done differently. Because I assume your whole swoop-in-and-save-the-play move wasn't a one-time-only thing? There's still a show tomorrow."

Right. This was the flaw in his plan. Even though he was the one who'd told her not to cancel tomorrow's show, he hadn't really allowed himself to think beyond his wild attempt to save the play and get the girl. But now that he had done both those things, he was gonna have to get up onstage and do it all again tomorrow, wasn't he?

"You know what they say?" Maya said, looking like she was trying not to laugh.

"Um, I think they say, 'Thanks for saving the show the big fancy theater critic was at, but you're off the hook now'?"

"No. They say the show must go on."

He reached over and grabbed her hand. "And so it must."

"Are you ready for my notes?"

"Bring it."

Epilogue

❧

A year later

*B*ang, bang, bang.

Law rolled over and checked the time on his phone. Seven a.m. "Are you *kidding* me?"

"Whaaa?"

"Shh," he soothed the befuddled Maya—they had only gone to sleep three hours ago. She'd had a show last night and then, well…He had heard the phrase *honeymoon phase* to describe new relationships, and if that was a real thing, they were still in it. Maybe the length of the honeymoon phase was proportional to the number of years the couple had spent picking at each other? "Go back to sleep," he murmured, resting his hand momentarily on her cheek as he got out of bed.

Their visitor must be Jake, though they had not been the recipient of an early-morning visit since last summer. Now that Law and Maya were together and shacked up at his place—their place, now—his friends had calmed down on that front.

He threw on some clothing and hustled out to yank open the door before whoever it was knocked again and further disturbed Maya. "What?"

There was no one there. Just a newspaper lying on the ground next to a tray from Lawson's Lunch holding two cups of coffee. He stooped down to grab it all. It was the *Globe and Mail*, and it was open to a random— Oh, hang on. It was open to a review of *Titus Andronicus*, Maya's play that was opening tonight. Holy shit!

Her shows were popular enough now that she staged a preview the night before opening. He used the occasion, too, to test-run the accompanying food. They only sold preview tickets to locals, though—it functioned like a dress rehearsal of both food and theater in front of a friendly audience. But it looked like someone had tipped off the same *Globe and Mail* critic who had come to *Much Ado about Nothing* a year ago. That review had been mixed, praising the staging but lamenting the "underwhelming last-minute stand-in for the promised big-name Benedick." Apparently saving a show and locking down the love of a lifetime looked "underwhelming" from the outside. Whatever.

But this review…He jogged back to the bedroom, leaped onto the bed, and shook her.

"Stop it." She rolled over.

"You'll want to see this."

"What happened to 'Go back to sleep'?"

Instead of answering, he started reading the review. "'One could be forgiven for assuming that *Titus Andronicus* as staged by the mighty-but-small Moonflower Bay Theater Company would be an overreach. One would be wrong.'"

That woke her up. She bolted to sitting. "*What?*"

She was not wearing a shirt, and he could not help but stare. He still wasn't used to this. The idea that she was *here*, after all those—

"Ow!" She had slugged his shoulder.

She did it again. "Read!"

"Okay, okay! 'The bloody tale of mortal enemies culminates in Roman general Titus murdering the children of Tamora, queen of the Goths, and serving them to her in a pie, so as one might imagine, in lesser hands the resulting production could tend toward the overwrought. In the steady, nuanced hands of director Maya Mehta, though, it does not. There's no melodrama here, just theater that is smart, bracing, and exhilarating.'"

"Ahhhhh!" she screamed.

He smirked. "I think maybe that's the first time anyone's ever called you subtle."

"Ahhhhh!" she repeated, as if to illustrate his point.

He went back to the review. "'I'm not sure the same can be said about the dinner half of the optional dinner-theater package.'"

"*What?*" She was indignant on his behalf. She grabbed the paper and read silently. "Oh, this is actually okay. He says, 'Because, really, there's nothing subtle about the meat pie—or mushroom, should your own personal vision of revenge be less carnivorous— served before the show at the new and punching-above-its-weight Lawson's Lunch. (A boxed version of the same dinner can also be preordered and picked up at the theater after the show—not a bad option considering the town's two charming beaches make an ideal backdrop for a leisurely late-night nosh.) Chef Michelle McAdams, formerly of the well-regarded White Rhino in nearby Bayshore, hits you over the head with organic lamb, locally foraged chanterelles, fennel, and mixed herbs in a perfectly flaky double crust. Thoughts of revenge evaporate with the first divine bite.'"

Well. He grinned. He would take that.

"We did it!" she said.

"We did." And they had. They'd won the grant. Law had gotten the mortgage and bought and renovated Jason's place. Lawson's Lunch had been popular with locals the moment it opened, and it had been at capacity nearly every day this summer. The theater was thriving, too. With her take from the *Much Ado* run, Maya had been able to do a massive repair and refresh. They even had plans in the works to close off half the balcony and build a second, cabaret-style venue that would house stand-up comedy, concerts, and smaller-scale plays—and have an integrated bar serving drinks and snacks. "But we already knew that. We didn't need the *Globe and Mail* to tell us that."

"Still," she said, "it's nice to have, isn't it?"

"I guess so, but you know what's even nicer?"

"What?"

"You naked in my bed."

"It's not your bed anymore, it's our bed," she shot back, and he smiled. One of the best things about his permanent cease-fire with Maya was that she still sassed him whenever the opportunity presented itself.

"You naked in our bed," he corrected smoothly, taking his shirt off and crawling toward her.

She put her shirt on.

"Oh, for God's sake." He tried to grab her as she hopped off her side of the bed, but she evaded him.

"Who dropped that paper off?" she asked. "Who has keys? Jake and Brie?"

"Who even knows at this point?"

"I have to find the girls."

He followed the familiar strains of the Spice Girls into the bathroom. Maya, he had learned, started each day with a shower and the Spice Girls—she played the music on her phone that she left on the bathroom counter. He eyed the lineup of fortune cookie fortunes taped to the mirror. She kept her fortunes, it turned out, and he had added his about deeds-and-not-weeds to her collection.

"What are you doing?" she squealed when he pulled the shower curtain back and got in with her. "I gotta find the girls and show them that review."

"You'll see the girls tonight." Would she ever. She would see everyone tonight. She just didn't know it yet.

"Yeah, but I want to tell them . . . Oh." She let her head fall back against his chest as he hugged her from behind.

He ground himself against her shamelessly. "I think the girls can wait, can't they?"

"You're right."

"I'm sorry, what did you just say?"

She turned in his arms. "Oh, shut up."

Maya was giddy as she arrived at the bar for the opening-night cast party. The scene was familiar. Comforting. Ben looked up —right at her—as she paused in the doorway, taking everything in. He saw her before anyone else did, and he winked.

Everyone else caught on as she let the door shut behind her, and a cheer erupted from the crowd. She made her way slowly to the bar, stopping to hug Ben's parents, then her own, who were at a table with all the old folks—as Maya had predicted, her dad had segued right into being a professional meddler when he retired.

Eventually she reached the bar, where her friends were. The girl gang had expanded to include Brie and Michelle, the maker of the magical meat pies.

Brie was behind the bar, as was Ben, who was at the other end, closer to Sawyer and Jake. Jake wore nine-month-old Penny, who was fast asleep, in a sling. Amusingly, Maya and her friends had started mimicking the bromance habit of hanging out together with the bartender, except now they had their own bartender.

Maya took off her Tamora headpiece and set it on the bar. "This thing is heavy." She'd been running late after the show, so she hadn't bothered changing out of her queen of the Goths costume, though maybe she should have. The leather armor was making her hot.

"Hi!" Eve said. "We thought you were never going to get here!" The other girls lobbed enthusiastic greetings and congratulations at her—except Michelle, who hadn't noticed her arrival because she was bent over the bar looking intently at something with Rohan.

Rohan, who, it turned out, *did* want A Rose by Any Other Name. Kind of. He'd kept their dad's shop, but he'd also purchased an old barn and was renovating it for destination weddings and events—Michelle was advising on catering. So basically, Maya's entrepreneurial brother was building an events empire.

"Yeah, sorry I'm late," she said in answer to Eve's question, but she wasn't sorry. She'd stayed back on purpose, looking out at her empty, spiffed-up theater, which had been full earlier in the evening, and reveled in her good fortune. *Their* good fortune. She looked over at Ben, who was still watching her from behind the bar. What a difference a year made. It was amazing what love and hard work and perseverance could do.

And, let's be real, it was *also* amazing what a hundred thousand dollars could do.

Ben came out from behind the bar and wrapped her in his arms. "The show was so great," he whispered. "You were so great."

Before she could say anything—she'd been going to say that the dinner part of their dinner-theater partnership hadn't been so bad either and that she sincerely hoped her personal revenge pie with a side of pizza was waiting for her as promised behind the bar—he let go of her abruptly, stepped back, and handed her a fortune cookie.

"What's this?"

"What does it look like?"

"It looks like a fortune cookie." It wasn't wrapped, though. It looked like a fancy, homemade fortune cookie.

"Your powers of observation astound me."

She rolled her eyes at him. "Should I open it?"

"Great idea."

It was only then that she registered that the entire bar had fallen silent, just like that night last summer when she and Ben had argued about Holden. Hmm. She broke open the cookie. The fortune in it was handwritten—by Ben, judging by the handwriting. "'Get thee a good husband, and use him as he uses thee,'" she read out loud. "That's..." Hang on. *Hang on.*

"*All's Well That Ends Well*," he said.

"I know. I just..." Did this mean what she thought it did? Did it mean what she *hoped* it did?

"Maya," he said. "Queen of the Goths. Queen of the mermaids. Queen of my heart. You're better at words than I am, so I'm just going to get straight to the point."

He dropped to one knee.

"Hooboy!" Adrenaline surged through her, stronger than any she'd experienced onstage, as her whole being cried out, *Yes!* But she should wait for the actual question. His line was next.

"Will you marry me?"

She grinned. "I think so."

"You *think* so?" He raised his eyebrows at her.

"I mean yes. Of course." *Of course.* "I'm just trying to think if I can extract any sort of concession here. How about, yes, I will marry you if you come around to my way of thinking on the tables in the cabaret, because—"

And he was up, stopping her mouth. He did that.

She didn't hate it.

For a bonus story from Jenny Holiday that you'll love, please turn the page to read *Once Upon a Bride*.

Jay Smith likes to be in control. His every choice is made with his carefully planned future in mind. So when the lobby in his accounting firm needs a makeover, Jay takes charge—and decides he needs a designer. What he does *not* need is Elise Maxwell, the first woman to tempt him to break all his long-held rules. But independent for the first time in her life, Elise isn't looking for a boyfriend. She's finally cut off her overbearing, old-money family, and she's determined to establish a successful design business—all on her own. She certainly doesn't want someone telling her how to do her job. Not even someone as irresistible and fun to tease as Jay...

FOREVER

Chapter 1

The guy did not look like his picture. That was the first thing Elise Maxwell noticed about Jay Smith when he emerged into the waiting area of Cohen & Smith Accounting, walked right over to her, and said, "Ms. Maxwell, I've been waiting for you," in a way that suggested that he had, in fact, been waiting for her. Like, for *her*, specifically. She didn't even know how he had recognized her. Yes, she probably looked like an interior designer—she tried hard to make sure her personal style reflected the good taste and eye for detail her profession demanded—but there was at least one other woman in the waiting area who could have fit the bill. Who could have been Elise Maxwell, aspiring interior designer.

Except she needed to quit it with the *aspiring* part. What was her best friend Gia always telling her? *Just because you haven't had any big, lucrative jobs yet doesn't mean you're "aspiring."*

Tell that to her bank account, but yes. Elise appreciated the sentiment. So Elise Maxwell, interior designer, stood and shook the hand Jay "I Don't Look Like My Picture" Smith extended.

Elise had not seen a picture of Jay's hand, but she had not imagined it being...like this. Big and warm and somehow striking the perfect sweet spot between firm and gentle with its grasp.

Most of the time when guys did not look like their pictures, it went in the opposite direction. Like when a guy's Tinder profile showed him shirtless holding up a fish and you thought, *Well, maybe I can excuse the stupid fish because look at those arms! And when we get married, I'll appreciate all those fishing trips, because don't smother me, dude.* But then you met him in person, and it turned out that those arms were from six years and two gym memberships ago.

This was...not that. The photo of Jay Smith, partner at Cohen & Smith, that accompanied his bio on the firm's website showed an accountant. It sort of went with his name: nondescript. In the portrait he wore a suit and glasses, and his hair was slicked back. And the picture was in black and white.

Jay Smith in the flesh, however, was not black and white. His hair was a deep rich brown, and instead of being neatly pasted back, it looked like he'd been raking his fingers through it all morning. His eyes, which were not obscured by glasses at the moment, were turquoise. Like, seriously, colored-contact levels of saturation. Elise had done an accent wall the other day that was pretty much that exact color.

"Bahaman Sea Blue," she said before she could stop herself.

He flashed a smile that was equal parts amusement and bewilderment. Lines appeared around his eyes as he did so. She wondered how old he was. Older than she was, but she couldn't tell by how much.

"I'm sorry," she said. "I just did a job that involved some paint the exact color of your eyes. Benjamin Moore Bahaman Sea Blue."

Then, to try to save herself, to make it seem less weird that she'd just informed him of the color of his eyes in the Benjamin Moore palette, she pointed to the pale-pink button-down shirt he wore and said, "Millennial pink."

He grinned, and those lines came back. What the hell was going on with those lines? She kind of wanted to...stroke them?

No stroking prospective clients, Elise.

But seriously, those eyes—the crazy color and the lines around them—made her realize how long it had been since she'd been on a date. Or...done other things. Between dealing with all the family drama, finding an apartment, and getting her business off the ground, she'd barely had time to sleep, much less engage in any extracurricular activities.

She hadn't missed those activities—she'd thought. Or at least she hadn't missed them until she was suddenly confronted with Jay Smith's laugh lines.

"Millennial pink," he repeated. "Is that a Benjamin Moore color, too?"

"No. Just a zeitgeisty thing. It's a color millennials like." Though he was rocking it super well, paired with a skinny black tie. "It's very of the moment."

"Well, I'm thirty-seven, so I guess I am a millennial."

That confirmed her sense that he was older than she was. But only by seven years. Somehow he *seemed* older than he actually looked. He was commanding. In a good way.

Not that that mattered.

No stroking prospective clients, Elise.

He turned and gestured vaguely at the waiting area. "So this is the 'before' picture, I guess."

Yes. The firm was hiring a designer to redo the lobby. It wouldn't be the most exciting job, but having something like this on her résumé would be huge for her. Cohen & Smith wasn't a major global player like Ernst & Young, but according to her research, the firm had a reasonably big reach in Toronto. If she did a good job, there might be referrals. And for someone with exactly $717 in the bank and a burning desire to not go crawling home to Daddy, referrals were precisely what was needed.

"What's your diagnosis?" he asked, still looking around the

space, which matched her impression of his corporate portrait: nondescript. Beige sofas, beige low-pile carpet, boring landscape paintings.

"Well, it could use a refresh."

"I know it could use a refresh. That's why I'm interviewing designers."

Technically he was still smiling, but there was an edge to his tone that hadn't been there before. In doing her research on the firm and its partners, she'd read a profile of Jay in *Canadian Business*. He reportedly had an IQ of 150 and was known for valuing honesty and transparency. For being hard but fair. For not suffering fools.

So she tried again with that in mind. "Your company's slogan is interesting. Most accounting firms would say something vague and kind of interchangeable about service and integrity. Yours is 'Toronto's Accountants.'" He nodded, and she took it as permission to continue. "I read in an interview that you don't have national or international ambitions for the company."

"Right. When my partner and I started the firm, we made a distinct choice not to try to chase the Big Four, but we also aren't a small mom-and-pop shop. Most of our clients are well-to-do individuals or medium-size businesses headquartered here. We thought it would be a sweet spot, and that turned out to be true."

"And you do a lot of local charity work," she said. "Your mission statement references the generation of wealth coming with an obligation to funnel some of that wealth back into the city."

"Someone's done her homework." The respect in his tone thrilled her, probably disproportionately. The last thing she needed was to get herself into a position where she was seeking approval from a man. She'd done that with dear old Dad. Done it and was done *with* it. Elise and her $717 were on their own now. As scary as it was sometimes, she wouldn't have it any other way. She wished she could have her independence *and* maintain a relationship with her parents, but that was a game she couldn't win. Not unless she was content to contort herself into the mold her parents had cast for her the day she was born: old-money North Toronto socialite. Just like her mom. God forbid she should actually want a career of her own.

Anyway, the fact that Jay's praise delighted her so much wasn't about that. It was that she was getting somewhere with him. So she pressed on. "I *have* done my homework. And the results make me wonder why the physical space of your business looks like every other accounting firm in the world. Like every other dental office, even. Sitting out here, you could just as well be waiting to get your molars drilled in Yellowknife as get your taxes done in Toronto." He winced at the dental office comparison, so she decided to wrap things up and deliver her prescription in a nutshell. "What I would do with this space is make it match your corporate values."

He looked at her for a long time, his face impossible to read— those laugh lines had disappeared along with his smile. There was some of that edge again, in his demeanor this time rather than in his voice, but there just the same.

And stupidly compelling just the same.

Just when she was starting to sweat, to fear she'd gone too far on the whole honesty front, he grinned. "And I presume you have some ideas about how to do that?"

"Absolutely."

Elise Maxwell looked exactly like her picture—namely, almost supernaturally pretty. Jay let his eyes roam as she settled into the guest chair at his desk and unzipped a leather portfolio. She had honey-blond hair, sparkling hazel eyes, and a heart-shaped mouth that almost looked like a cartoon. He might even call it millennial pink. He glanced at his shirt for comparative purposes. Nope, her lips were darker.

The picture on her website had been a full-body one of her dressed in a crazy floral-print minidress but with plain black tights and flat shoes. Today she wore a dark-green-and-black-striped tunic over skinny black pants and black patent-leather heels. Elise Maxwell managed to convey fun and creativity, but with just the right dose of reined-in professionalism.

So did her plans for his lobby, judging by the pile of sketches and images she was arranging on the desk between them. Not that that mattered, because he'd decided to hire her before he'd even seen them—right after her devastating little monologue about how the waiting area looked like a dental office. Still, he had to let her talk him through her vision. Hell, he *wanted* her to talk him through her vision. And here he'd thought he'd drawn the short straw when his partner, Kent, had stuck him with the job of overseeing the lobby redesign.

He ordered himself to pay attention to her work instead of to her. *Ogle the designs, not the designer.* Not that it mattered. She was too young for him.

"So one idea is to embrace the Toronto part of your mission," she said. "You want to be 'Toronto's Accountants,' so why not show it? Not in a hokey, boosterish sort of way, though." She slid a stack of photographs closer to him. "These are reproductions of some shots by an up-and-coming local photographer. I know you've supported the Toronto Arts Foundation. Buying some large prints from this woman would align with that mission, too."

Damn. He'd been thinking of sprucing up the lobby as a neces-sary but annoying task. Never in a million years had he imagined it could also advance some of the firm's corporate responsibility goals. Plus, he was no artist, but these photos were *great*. They were of some iconic Toronto scenes—a streetcar, the midcentury city hall building—but taken from odd angles so the familiar looked a little strange. Strange in an appealing way. Nothing you'd ever see in a dental office.

"Obviously that's just the art," she went on. "I don't think you want to go crazy with color or anything. You still want to convey the sophistication and seriousness people will expect from someone they're trusting their finances to, so I'm not suggesting you paint the lobby hot pink."

He had the sudden, alarming notion that if she told him to paint the lobby hot pink, he would do exactly that.

"But I do think you should abandon beige," she said.

"Abandon beige?" He chuckled. It was an interesting, amusing turn of phrase.

"Yes. So many corporate spaces are beige. I get it. It's safe." She pulled a foam board out of her portfolio. It was covered with squares of color and swatches of fabric. She pointed to one of the squares—a pale, icy blue. "But something like this could be good for the walls. Unassuming enough to allow the art to speak for itself, but it still has a little personality."

She moved on to some of the fabric swatches. "These are just some initial ideas for upholstery for sofas and chairs."

"And what about flooring?" He realized with a start that he, who had literally never spent more than thirty seconds thinking about flooring, was on the edge of his chair waiting to hear what she'd say about the carpet in the waiting area. The *beige* carpet in the waiting area. "The carpet out there is only a year old," he added, suddenly wanting to push her a little, to see more of the contrarian spirit that had animated her in the lobby earlier.

"I get it. That carpet disguises stains. People track in snow and salt in the winter." She was trying to be diplomatic. "Design has to be functional."

He raised an eyebrow. Diplomatic didn't look good on Elise Maxwell. He liked her better when she was making impassioned speeches that made her cheeks go pink. "I always thought design was about making things look pretty."

"It is. It can be. And there's nothing wrong with wanting things to be pretty. But what good is useless beauty?"

"Is beauty ever just useless, though?" For example, he could look at Elise Maxwell forever.

Whoa. Where had that come from?

And not that she was merely beautiful. She was clearly a talented, thoughtful designer, too.

Ogle the designs, not the designer.

The too-young *designer.*

There was no ring on her finger, but there was no way a woman like Elise Maxwell didn't already have the names of her future kids picked out. Hell, she probably had their future bedrooms designed, too.

"Is beauty ever just useless?" she echoed thoughtfully, giving his throwaway question serious consideration. Then she smiled— a full-on delighted, high-wattage smile, which wasn't helping his cause. "An accountant *and* a philosopher."

He dipped his head self-deprecatingly.

"My point," she went on, "is merely that I understand the beige carpet impulse. But whatever function it was serving could be served equally well with a more beautiful solution. Engineered hardwood, for example, can stand up to a lot, and though it would be more expensive to install, it would last a lot longer. You probably have a cleaning service that's vacuuming that carpet every night, at least in the winter. They could just as easily mop a floor. It would look better, and let's face it, your design choices send a message to your clients. What kind of message is beige carpet sending?"

"'Welcome to the dental office'?"

She chuckled. "Exactly. This doesn't seem like a very beige sort of company. And you—"

She cut herself off. He wanted to know what she'd been going to say, suddenly. *Needed* to know. So he raised an eyebrow and made a *continue* gesture. When she still didn't say anything, he summoned his best cranky boss tone, the one Kent was always telling him was scaring the interns, and said, "Tell me what you were going to say."

She sucked in a breath. Apparently that tone worked on prospective interior designers, too, because she answered him. "I was going to say that you don't seem like a beige sort of man to me." She bit her lip. He watched her top teeth scrape against a perfect plump of pink-but-darker-than-millennial-pink lower lip. "You don't seem like a beige sort of man to me at all."

Well, *shit*.

Too young, too young, too young, his mind chanted, even as his renegade mouth opened and said, "You're hired. And I want you to do my office, too."

Chapter 2

℮lise walked out of Cohen & Smith with grace and restraint. She was the picture of professionalism as she stepped onto the elevator, nodding at its other occupant. As she crossed the marble-floored lobby, her heels clacked, and she made sure to keep the spaces between the clacks even and long, like she was a bridesmaid walking down an aisle.

She even managed to walk like a normal person—a normal person in a little bit of a hurry, maybe—once she got outside to the sidewalk. But the farther away from Jay's building she got, the more she sped up. By the time she burst through the doors of a coffee shop around the corner, she had abandoned all pretense and was literally skipping.

"You got it!" Her friend Wendy looked up from her computer. Wendy worked downtown and had insisted on lying in wait near the interview for moral support purposes.

"I got it!" Elise couldn't resist a little twirl as she sank into the chair opposite Wendy. She pulled out her phone. "Hang on, I just have to text Gia."

"No, you don't." Grinning, Wendy turned the computer around to reveal a group FaceTime session populated by Elise's bestie among besties, Gia, a model who jet-setted around the world and was currently in Berlin, and Jane, the fourth member of their tightly knit crew, who was at home on the west side of town.

"Ahhh! Hi!" Elise's squeals were echoed by the girls on the screen. "And!" She laughingly infused some drama into her voice. "Not only did I get the lobby job, he asked me to do his office, too!"

"Did you get a deposit?" Jane asked. Elise's friends knew all about her financial troubles.

"Because if not," Gia said, "you know I will gladly wire you some—"

"I've told you guys, I can't take your money! That wouldn't be any different from taking Daddy's money."

Wendy held up a palm. "Okay, that's objectively not true. It would be completely different."

"The whole point of starting my own business is that it's *mine*. It's not propped up by family money—not that there's any of *that* being offered."

Not remotely. Her father had been happy to give her an unlimited allowance as long as she spent it on frivolous things. He'd even been tolerant when, after graduation, she'd started working part-time helping an interior designer who did a lot of homes in their neighborhood. But that was because he'd considered it a hobby, one she would drop when she got married.

Once Elise decided she'd had enough of Persian rugs and monogrammed towels in Rosedale and announced her plan to start her own business, the shit hit the fan. It hadn't helped that she'd recently turned thirty and had failed to settle down with any of the entirely suitable boyfriends she'd had.

"Right," Gia said. "But unlike your father, we believe in you. It would be a loan. You can pay it back when your business takes off."

Elise grinned even as she got a little choked up. She loved her girls so much. Without them she never would have had the guts to break out on her own. Her whole life, she'd had things handed to her: an expensive education, designer clothes, an address in a tony neighborhood. Watching her awesome friends work for what they had—work *hard*—had been an inspiration. Their unwavering support meant everything.

"Anyway, I don't need it! I'm stopping by tomorrow to sign a contract and pick up the deposit."

"So he went for your whole Toronto-themed thing?" Gia asked.

"He did! I even kind of insulted his current decor, but he didn't seem to mind."

"Who's *he*?" Wendy asked.

Elise and Gia talked or texted almost every night, so Gia knew some of the nitty-gritty details about the job that Wendy and Jane didn't. "One of the partners. This guy called Jay Smith."

"Was he as boring as he looks?" Gia asked.

Elise felt her cheeks warming.

Tell me what you were going to say.

Her mind had been replaying that sentence since she left Jay's office. On the surface of things, it had been an entirely unremarkable sentence. But the *way* he had issued the directive—in a tone that was half impatience, half entitlement even as he'd looked at her like what she had to say was the most important thing in the world just then—had stuck with her.

"He was...not boring."

The girls shrieked in unison.

A wolf whistle rang through Jay's office. He turned from where he was tying his bow tie in front of a mirror on the wall and grinned at his friend Stacey, who had let herself in.

"Haven't you ever heard of checking in with reception?" he teased.

"*Please.*" She came over and finished tying the tie for him. "Reception is for keeping out the people you *don't* like."

He laughed. "You look nice. How's the trial going?" He knew Stacey from when she'd been working in the government, prosecuting tax fraud. They'd met when one of his clients, back when he'd been working at a big firm, had been audited. Years later, when she'd branched out to open her own tax law practice, he'd lured her to this building.

"Terrible!" she trilled. "But there is an open bar with my name on it at the Four Seasons, so let's blow this popsicle stand." He glanced at his watch, and she must have anticipated an argument because she said, "Jay. You know I admire your work ethic. Your famous control over your empire and all that. But it's time to party."

She smirked, but her expression quickly morphed into a more affectionate one. She was always needling him about what she saw as too much work and not enough play. But since she was a close friend, she knew that he'd worked hard to get where he was. That his legendary discipline was what had made him into the man he was: one different from the men he'd grown up with. One who was putting a stop to the cycle of toxicity that was his family legacy.

"I am fully prepared to party. I just need a few minutes. We're redoing the office, and the designer is coming over with the contract. She'll be here shortly."

"Can't you just have her leave it with the receptionist I so blithely ignored?"

He could. There was no reason not to. He could leave the check and tell the receptionist to tell Elise he'd courier the signed contract back tomorrow. But...

"Nope."

Stacey cocked her head at him.

He couldn't interpret her expression, which was unusual. "What?"

Instead of answering, she performed an exaggerated sigh, walked over to the sitting area in his office, and plopped down on the sofa. Which was beige. Of course. What the hell was the matter with him that he had never really even noticed, much less taken issue with, all this beige?

His assistant, Patricia, popped her head in. "Elise Maxwell is here."

"Send her in."

Stacey really did look great. She was dressed in a black ball gown that had a pretty, sparkly overlay of some sort. Elise, though. She wasn't as dressed up, but she was...something. There was a put-togetherness about her. And that compelling mixture of out-there style juxtaposed with more classic, restrained pieces. This time, she was wearing a royal-blue dress that buttoned up like a shirt. On its own it was kind of conservative. But she was wearing a wide red fabric belt, and her hair was up in some kind of twist with a big red flower stuck into it. You could have told him she was going to the same gala he and Stacey were or to a board meeting at a bank and he would have believed it—she would have fit into either setting. Well, she would have stood out in either setting, but in a—

"Ahem." Stacey was making a production of clearing her throat as she stood.

Right.

"Elise Maxwell, this is Stacey Tran. Elise is our new designer. Stacey is—"

"Jay's ex-girlfriend." Stacey stuck out her hand and ignored the look Jay shot her. He'd been going to say that Stacey was a friend. Because that was true. Yes, they'd dated for two months several years ago, but they'd parted amicably and that part of their relationship was ancient history. Neither of them gave it any thought, much less brought it up—usually.

"Oh!" Elise shook Stacey's hand but seemed flustered. Not the same woman who'd given him the speech about how boring his office was. Her eyes flickered over to him and widened a little as she took him in.

Right. Her appearance had made him forget, momentarily, that he was wearing a penguin suit. "We're going to a gala—a charity thing."

"Well." She pulled some papers out of her handbag. "I'll leave this, then, and let you get going."

"No, no." Grabbing a pen from his desk, he moved to the sitting area. "I'll sign it now." Stacey smooshed up *right* next to him on the stupid beige sofa, which was a little weird, and Elise took the chair across.

"Don't you want to read that first?" Stacey was giving him her skeptical lawyer face.

He had flipped to the last page. But she was right. He was not the kind of person who signed contracts without reading them—normally. Stacey had been joking when she'd referenced his "empire," but he *had* clawed himself out of his impoverished background and made a successful life. He had done that by being devoted to details. You could change the course of a project—or a life—by paying attention to enough cumulative details. Some people might call it micromanaging. Some people might call him uptight. He did not give a shit about some people.

So he went back to the start. The document was labeled "Operation: Abandon Beige."

He cracked up. Stacey, unapologetically continuing to invade his space, read over his shoulder.

"Yeah, I'm just going to go ahead and sign this." And he did, details be damned.

He handed it back to Elise, who took it with one hand while gesturing with the other to the Scrabble game that rested on the coffee table between them. "You play?"

"When I can get someone to play with me. Kent—my partner and cofounder—and I used to pull all-nighters early in the life of the company, and we'd take Scrabble breaks. But these days I can't pry him away from his phone—it's all Candy Crush or whatever."

She laughed. "Right? Why is it so hard to get people to appreciate classic board games?"

"I take it you appreciate them?" Stacey asked, her voice and her eyebrows high.

Elise smiled. "I do. I have quite a board game collection, actually. But I always have to guilt my friends into playing with me."

Well. A gorgeous, talented woman looking for someone to play board games with her. That was...something.

Clearing his throat, Jay stood and moved over to the desk to grab Elise's check. "This is for you."

"Thanks." She walked over and took the check and then the hand he had extended for her to shake on the deal.

"Your hand is freezing," he said before he could think better of it. He hadn't meant to be overly familiar—he wasn't one of those guys—but it had just popped out because of how true it was. It was like shaking hands with a snowman.

She smiled. "Yeah, I'm one of those clichéd women who's always cold."

He wanted to give her the coat of his tux, but that was something you did *after* the party. And she wasn't coming to the party with them. Which was a little disappointing, actually.

"If it works for you," she said, "I'll pull together some more samples than just the ones I showed you yesterday—assuming you're still good with the photographs—and we'll start there? Maybe we can meet next week."

"Yes," he said. "Definitely still good with those photos." He turned to Stacey. "You should see these amazing photos she found."

"So I'll call your assistant to set something up?" Elise said. "Same woman who scheduled the interview, right—Patricia?"

He pulled a card out of his breast pocket and wrote his cell number on it. "No, just text me directly."

Stacey coughed, but when he looked over at her, she was all wide-eyed smiles.

He turned back to Elise. "Let's meet at your office." It would be fun to see how the designer did her own space.

She cleared her throat. "I, ah, don't have a studio. I work out of my apartment."

"Oh, that's fine." But wait. Was he overstepping? He wasn't trying to invite himself over to her house. She must have a home office, though, right? Her brow furrowed. Okay, she clearly didn't want to meet at her place. "We can meet here. I was just thinking it might be good to get away from all this..." He gestured vaguely around the space. "Beige."

She chuckled and reached for the business card he was still holding.

Her hand brushed against his as she did so. Before he could think better of it, he closed his hand around the tips of her icy fingers, struck with an almost involuntary impulse to warm her up. But as quickly as he did so, he pulled back because, hello, that was wildly inappropriate.

"Meeting at my place sounds great." Her cheeks had gone pink. Even though her hands were cold, her face looked...warm. "I'll text you."

"Well!" Stacey clapped her hands together. "By my calculations, Jay, we only have forty-five minutes of open bar time before the program starts, so chop-chop."

Right. *Stacey.* The gala. He grabbed his keys and gestured for both women to precede him out the door. No one spoke as they were waiting for the elevator. When they got on, it was occupied by a woman named Annabelle. She worked in another company in the building, and they had a friendly elevator-and-parking-garage relationship.

"Looking good, Jay," she teased, and he dipped his head in acknowledgment, a bit embarrassed. He'd had kind of a crush on Annabelle when he first met her, and she knew it.

Annabelle got off on another floor. "That was another of Jay's ex-girlfriends," Stacey said.

What? "That's just plain not true." What the hell was Stacey's problem today? Had she gotten started on the open bar early? He turned to Elise. "I asked her out once. Years ago. She said no. And because I'm not an asshole, that was it. Now we chat in the elevator like normal people." God. Why was this so embarrassing?

"Okay..." Elise looked uncomfortable as the elevator hit the ground floor. And maybe he *was* an asshole, because why had he felt the need to give her that big disclaimer in the first place?

And why did his chest suddenly feel tight, like he was having trouble getting in a good breath? It must be the stupid bow tie. He concentrated on filling his lungs as he held the elevator door open for the women.

As they emerged onto the street, Elise turned to him. "I'll text you to set up the meeting."

"We're going to hail a cab," he said. "Can we drop you somewhere?"

"Thanks, but no. I'm meeting a friend who works downtown."

And then she was gone. And he could breathe again.

He turned on Stacey once they were in the cab. "What the hell was all that?"

"What was what?" She took out a compact and examined her reflection in its mirror.

"You're not my ex-girlfriend."

"I am, though."

"Stacey. I've known you for seven years. And we dated—not very successfully—for, like, two months in there near the beginning."

Stacey smiled at her reflection. "I was testing the waters."

"What does *that* mean?"

"I wanted to see what the reaction would be."

"What the hell are you talking about? Whose reaction?"

"Yours. Hers. Either." She turned to him. "You like this woman."

He sighed and slumped against the seat. There was no use denying it. Stacey could sniff out laundered offshore bank accounts buried under mountains of decoys. She didn't miss *anything*. "She's way too young."

"She looks like she's thirty at least."

"Which is too young."

"Jesus Christ, Jay, for a guy who's generally one of the good ones, you can be such a misogynistic jerk sometimes."

"*Excuse* me?" Jay would admit to his faults, but he was fairly certain misogyny wasn't one of them. No, that was one of his *father's* faults. And Jay was *not* his father.

"How arrogant do you have to be to just assume that every woman you meet under the age of forty-five wants kids? To just assign that stance to her? Some women—even young ones—don't want kids. Don't you think it's better to find out before you just write off—"

"And what am I supposed to say? 'Hello, I like you, but I don't want kids. Might you, too, not want kids?' *That's* a great way to approach a first date."

"Why not? It's not like things are working out with your chosen demographic."

He tried to object, but Stacey held up a hand. "Don't interrupt."

Resigned, he settled in to listen to her little speech.

"I mean, yes, you can date older women exclusively"—she gestured at herself—"but it's not like you've found one of us to ride off into the sunset with."

"But that's just bad luck," he said, though it was probably useless to argue. "That's just life." She raised her eyebrows at him. "Anyway," he pushed on, still knowing it was pointless, "I'm closer to forty than thirty now. The gap is shrinking." He made a face, going for humor. "Soon I'll be able to date women my age."

She was not amused. "Are you *listening* to yourself? Could you be any more inflexible?"

Okay, now he was getting annoyed. What business was it of hers who he chose to date? He didn't want kids. So he made it a priority to avoid women who were likely to want them. Women who hadn't yet aged out of being able to have them. There was nothing wrong with that. That wasn't inflexibility. That was honesty.

But whatever. He wasn't getting into it with Stacey. Arguing with a lawyer was never a good idea.

"Or . . ." She drew out the word in overly dramatic fashion. "You could, you know, actually examine this whole rabid stance against having kids and stop letting it rule your life."

"No." He wasn't going to bicker fruitlessly with her, but he couldn't let that stand.

"You're not your father."

"What the *hell*, Stacey?"

"Or Cam's father."

He looked at her sharply. He'd been thinking, back in his office, that Stacey *knew* why he pushed himself so hard, why he maintained such discipline over his affairs. But *knowing* about that was different from *talking* about it. She'd gone too far.

And she knew it. "I'm sorry." She laid a hand on his arm. "I'm not trying to be mean. I just sometimes think you're too wrapped up in a certain vision of yourself. One that is…less fulfilling than it could be."

The phrase *abandon beige* popped into his head.

"And honestly?" Stacey went on. "I know you won't believe me, but I think you would be a great dad. I wish you would just give yourself a chance."

Elise wondered if Jay had a thing for older women or if it was just a coincidence that his two ex-girlfriends—or ex-crushes, or whatever—she had happened to meet were both closer to fifty than forty.

And both stunningly beautiful.

And self-assured.

There had been no *aspiring* with either of those women.

They probably had proper offices that didn't also double as their living rooms.

Their tiny living rooms.

But whatever. She smoothed her shirt—she'd gone with a classic white blouse and a pair of jeans, given that the meeting was at her place and she didn't want to look like she was trying super hard, even though she was, in fact, trying super, super hard—and reminded herself that it wasn't a crime to be in the early phase of her career. Everybody started somewhere. Not that long ago, Jay and his partner had taken a risk by starting their own company, and she was doing the same thing.

She surveyed the space. The flowers on the coffee table would just get in the way of their work, so she moved them. Then she restacked the magazines and games she stored on the bottom level of the coffee table. She wanted everything to be perfect.

Even though she was expecting Jay, she jumped a little when the doorbell announced his presence. She lived on the third floor of a Victorian that had been converted to apartments, so she had to hoof it down to the front door to let him in.

"Hi," he said, and *oh*. It was Friday at two o'clock, and they must have casual Fridays in his office, because he was dressed in jeans and a blue polo shirt. Nothing special, yet the blue made his impossible eyes even more impossible—they looked like they were going to twinkle right out of his skull. And standing on her porch backlit by the sun, he looked like a Disney prince. He was so—

Okay, enough. *No stroking clients, Elise.*

"Come on up." When she ushered him into her apartment, she said, "You didn't look at my portfolio the other day, so you don't know that I'm a new business owner. That's why I work out of my place—I'm trying to keep the overhead low initially."

She was cueing up a rehearsed speech for when he asked what she had done before she struck out on her own, but he just said, "That's smart."

Then, looking around, he said, "This place is amazing."

She smiled. It *was* pretty amazing. She'd worked hard to make it so. Elise would admit to being a bit of a perfectionist. Her friends were always needling her about it like it was a bad thing, but she didn't see anything wrong with having a vision and sticking to it. That was how you ended up with results like this. Ironically, though, this was not how she would have designed a public-facing office. Her apartment was all exuberance and color, whereas in a place where she'd meet with clients, she would probably have leaned more classic.

But she was stupidly gratified by his praise. It felt like he'd seen a glimpse of the real her, and he approved.

He walked farther in and stopped in front of the sofa. "Hold on, though. Is this a *beige* sofa?" The appearance of those crow's-feet said he was teasing.

She bit back a smirk and picked up one of the brightly colored pillows from the sofa. "The judicious use of beige has its place. You couldn't have all these crazy pillows on top of a sofa that was already a bonkers color."

"I don't know," he teased. "I thought I signed up for Operation: Abandon Beige, and now I find out that the largest piece of furniture in my designer's house is actually..." He made a show of sitting down on the sofa and sort of comically manspreading over it. "Beige?"

She threw the pillow at him.

And immediately regretted it. In addition to stroking clients, *throwing things at them* was not a great idea.

But it was okay, because he cracked up and threw it back at her.

She caught it, suddenly breathless like she was catching some kind of...sports thing instead of a pillow. She wasn't sporty enough to finish that metaphor properly. "You want something, some water before we get started? Or coffee?"

"Nah, I'm done for the day—done for the week. I decided to make you my last meeting."

She wasn't sure what that had to do with declining coffee. "Wine?" She jokingly looked at her watch. "It *is* after noon."

He looked at her for what felt like a beat too long—yet also not long enough—before saying, "I'd love a glass of wine."

There was no reason for Jay to still be at Elise's house three hours later. He'd loved everything she'd shown him and had approved it all. She clearly had enough creativity and talent in her little finger to create the best damn lobby in Toronto. If this had been any other designer, he would have given her carte blanche to do what she wanted. And that would have been a big item off his to-do list. Would have let him get back to his job. To micromanaging things he was actually qualified to micromanage.

But damn, he wasn't going to do that. Because watching Elise Maxwell work was such an enormous turn-on, it was ridiculous. She was clearly passionate about design. She had a vision for his office, and she was willing to fight for it. He liked that. A lot.

So he kept asking questions. Sometimes he took issue with some detail, just so he could watch her defend said detail even as she quite sincerely took what he was saying into account.

"I'm going to have to veto that one." He sipped his third glass of wine as she showed him a wallpaper sample she was suggesting for the small lavatory inside his office. "Way too crazy."

He was lying. It was not too crazy. The pattern of dark-green horizontal stripes was, in reality, just the right amount of crazy. She'd somehow picked up on his penchant for green without his having said anything.

Her brow furrowed slightly as she tilted her head and stared at the sample like she was seeing it for the first time. There was something about the wrinkling of the usually smooth skin on her forehead that made him shift in his seat.

"This"—she pulled out another sample, this one covered with tiny palm trees—"is too crazy. The stripes, by contrast, are classic with a little twist. Masculine yet fun."

"Masculine isn't usually fun?" he teased. But damn, he needed to cut this shit out. He'd hired her to do a job. He couldn't be getting all suggestive. He was not that kind of man.

He suddenly had a flash of his brother Cameron's dad "flirting" with the receptionist at the used car dealership he'd worked at. That's what Angus had called it—flirting. Even though Jay had only been nine or ten at the time, he had been pretty sure the receptionist, who always responded to Angus's overtures with pained, tight-lipped smiles, wouldn't have called it that. And he knew his *mother* wouldn't have, either, based on the fights he'd overheard over the years.

So he could like Elise from afar—honestly, there was no way to make himself *not* do that—but anything more was a bad idea. He set down his wine. Time for cooler heads to prevail.

"Oh no," Elise said. "I misspoke. Masculine is fun." The way she said *fun*, all low and sort of stretched out, suggested that maybe he wasn't the only one having trouble keeping things strictly professional.

But still. She was working for him, and that meant he was morally prohibited from hitting on her. End of story. So time to lean on that legendary self-discipline Stacey had been haranguing him about the other day. And discipline wasn't discipline unless it was hard, right? Even if he was interested in breaking his rule about not dating younger women—which he *wasn't*—nothing could happen with Elise until she was done with the job.

She did that lip-scraping thing again.

Shit. He'd been going to suggest a rousing round of Boggle after their work was done—it was visible under her glass coffee table, and he hadn't played since he and Mrs. Compton from the trailer park used to battle it out. But that wasn't a good idea. He had to get out of here. Now.

"I have to go."

She blinked as he stood. "Okay."

He'd been sitting on a sofa, and she on a chair next to him. As he came around toward the front door, they ended up doing one of those stupid back-and-forth dances where they were trying to get out of each other's way but were in fact getting right in each other's way. She laughed. It lit up her face even as it sliced through his chest.

She laid her hands on his forearms, jokingly, making a production of moving him to one side and keeping him there so they could get past each other.

Her hands were freezing, like they'd been the other day in his office. Maybe it was the fact that they weren't in his office with Stacey watching like a hawk. Or maybe it was the wine. *Something* made him pull her hands up so they were in a prayer position and then enclose them in his.

"I told you I'm always cold," she said apologetically.

He smiled. "It's not a character flaw."

Also, *cold* was not the word he would use for her, on balance.

All right, though. *Down, boy.* He was on his way *out* of here.

It was harder than it should have been to let go of her, but he did. She walked him down to the main door. He opened it to find an older man standing on the porch, hand raised like he was about to ring one of the doorbells.

"Daddy?" Jay hadn't been looking at Elise, but the shock was audible in her voice. "What are you doing here?"

He could tell from the way she asked the question, from the way the bold confidence he loved—*liked*—about her had been replaced by hesitancy, and by the scowl on the man's face that this was not a warm father-daughter relationship.

"And who are you?" the man said to him. There was an edge to the question, a possessiveness, that got Jay's hackles up.

Elise jumped in. "Jay Smith, this is my father, Charles Maxwell. Dad, Jay is a client."

"Is that what they're calling it these days?"

Whoa. Jay didn't know what was going on here, but he knew he did *not* like it. He knew Charles Maxwell—or knew of him. He was one of the richest men in Canada, and the second-generation head of a boutique hedge fund company—and, by all accounts, a real asshole.

Which meant Elise came from serious money. So it was interesting that she was living in a small apartment in this not-great part of town. And that she was working out of said apartment because she was concerned with keeping overhead low.

Jay stuck out his hand. "Partner at Cohen & Smith." His firm wasn't huge, but it wasn't nothing. Charles Maxwell would have heard of it. He made his tone completely flat so that when he said, "Pleasure to meet you, sir," he could have been conveying the opposite sentiment. "Your daughter is extremely talented. She's doing quite the job on our office. You must be proud."

When Charles Maxwell only flared his nostrils, Elise said, "Can I help you with something, Dad?"

"Your mother insisted I drop by and give you this." He held out a check. He wasn't even subtle about it. It was like he was *trying* to embarrass her. Jay's fingers flexed, almost of their own accord.

She held up her hands like he was robbing her. "I don't want your money."

"You wanted it six months ago when you gave me that ridiculous presentation about starting your business."

"And that would have been a loan," she said haughtily. "A loan I no longer need."

"That's not what your bank account says."

"And how would you know that?"

"I have friends at Scotiabank."

She gasped. "That was a gross invasion of privacy, not to mention illegal."

All right. Jay had no doubt Elise Maxwell could hold her own against her villain of a father, but he couldn't stand here and not say anything—that wasn't the way his mama had raised him. "Sir, I think you should leave."

Charles Maxwell's eyes slid over to him and back to Elise. There was no warmth in them. His mind landed on his recent conversation with Stacey. Jesus Christ, he *would* make a better father than this asshole.

Theoretically.

Elise's father turned and left without a word, which Jay was thankful for, because he wasn't sure it was a good idea to get into a fight—verbal or otherwise—over his interior designer's honor. He would have done it in a heartbeat, but he was trying to be a responsible, professional client here. That was why he was leaving in the first place. And he was pretty sure responsible, professional clients didn't land punches on their designers' fathers, no matter how much they deserved it.

"Oh my God," she said after her father had cleared the porch steps and the walkway. "I'm so sorry you had to see that."

Her voice was muffled. He turned to find her with her head in her hands, clearly mortified.

"Hey." He moved instinctively to touch her but checked the impulse. "No problem. Believe me, I know shitty fathers."

"Really?"

She looked up, so apparently relieved that he kept going. "Really. In fact, I had two of them, so I'm pretty sure I've got you beat."

"Two!" Some of her spark was back. "Gay parents?"

"Nope. There was my father, and then when he left, there was my younger half brother's for a couple years, too. A bonus shitty dad, if you will." But he didn't want her to start feeling sorry for him, so he added, "Luckily, I have an amazing mother who more than made up for it." Which was only sort of true. The amazing part was absolutely true, and she'd done her best, but Jay knew those early years with his dad, and then the time later with Cam's dad, had fucked with him. There was no way for them not to have.

"Still. I'm so embarrassed."

"Embarrassed? Why? I don't know the whole story, but from where I'm standing, it sort of looks like your father doesn't approve of you starting your design business, but you're doing it anyway. That's something to be *proud* of."

He wanted to ask so many more questions. Why didn't her father approve? What about the mother who had reportedly sent him with the check? How much money was in her bank account?

Why were her hands always so cold?

And what could he do to warm them up?

But no. None of those questions were anywhere near to being his business. So he smiled and said, "Have a good weekend, Elise. I'll see you next week?"

She nodded. She was coming to the office next Tuesday, after work, to supervise the start of the flooring installation. He was stupidly excited.

Dangerously excited.

Once he'd rounded the corner and was out of sight of her house, he got out his phone and glanced at the time. Five thirty. His brother, who was at home in Thunder Bay after a deployment as a reservist in the Canadian Forces, worked as a bartender. Hopefully he wouldn't be at work yet.

"Hey!" Cameron picked up right away.

He wasn't in the habit of calling his brother, so he was glad of the warm reception. Cam and Jay, though they'd been close when Cam was young, didn't have the best relationship these days. But it sort of seemed that after a rough young adulthood, Cam was in the process of straightening himself out. He had joined the reserves. He was working a steady job while waiting for his next deployment. He had a girlfriend. Jay wasn't a huge fan of Christie. She seemed kind of self-absorbed. But whatever. It wasn't his place to have an opinion. He was just glad things seemed to be improving between Cam and him.

"What's up, Bro?" Cam asked.

"Do you think I would be a good father?" It was out before he could think better of it, but fuck it, that was what he wanted to know, wasn't it?

"Oh my God, did you get someone knocked up?" Cam cracked up. "I thought that was my thing." Cam had indeed gotten his high school girlfriend pregnant. Jay sometimes wondered about what had happened to her—and to the baby—after her parents hustled her out of town. But there was no way he could ask his brother that without totally alienating him.

"Ha. No. I'm just...wondering."

Cam must have heard something in his tone, because he sobered right up. "You would make a great father."

"Did you know that children who come from abusive situations are thirty to forty percent more likely to become abusers themselves?"

"I did not, but I'm not surprised. Shit that happens when you're a kid can fuck you up." He laughed, but this time there was no genuine mirth in it. "Look at me." Before Jay could protest that Cam seemed to be getting his act together, he added, "Which is funny because of the two of us, you have way more cause to be a fuckup. They were both gone before I was born."

They referred to Jay's father and to Cam's father, Angus, who'd left when their mom was pregnant with Cam. After years of emotional abuse and manipulation, he'd hit her one day—in front of eleven-year-old Jay—and she'd finally sent him packing. Cam's dad shoved their mom so hard that day that Jay had worried constantly about the fate of his unborn baby brother until the moment his mom came home from the hospital and placed him in Jay's arms.

It was funny. He had one emblematic memory of each man, and in both cases, it was the day he left. Jay's dad had not left after a fit of physical violence like Angus, but in some ways the wounds he had left ran deeper. That day was still crystal clear in Jay's mind. His dad and mom had been fighting—more than usual. His dad had packed his shit into his truck, shrugging off his mom's pleas to stay and try to work things out.

"What about Jay?" she'd said, once she'd finally accepted that he was going.

His dad had asked for a word with him alone, which his mom had granted.

Jay had tried so hard not to cry. Crying in front of his dad was never a good idea. It was a sure way to earn his disgust.

So he had been shocked when, despite the tears he could not hold back, his dad looked him in the eye and said, "Sorry, kid. It was inevitable. We Smiths are leavers. My dad left my mom. I guess it's my turn now. So how do you want to play this? Do you want to pretend that we're going to have a relationship? And I'll see you one or two more times before I tap out? Or do you want to just call it here?"

"I want to just call it here," he had responded. It had been a lie. Even though his dad was an asshole, he was still his dad. But, ironically, Jay had thought that was the answer that would make his dad think more highly of him.

Jesus, that was fucked up. As an adult, he could see just how much.

He consoled himself that he was ending that cycle. If you didn't have kids, you couldn't leave them. That's what people like Stacey didn't understand.

"Anyway," Cam went on, pulling Jay from his memories. "You've always said you don't want kids. So what's happening?"

"Nothing."

It was the truth. Nothing was happening. What was the *matter* with him? Okay, he had a crush on a woman who was too young for him based on the rules he'd established for himself. But how had he gotten from *that* to this overwrought stroll down memory lane?

Even *if* he allowed something to happen with Elise—not now, but when she was done with the job—it was *still* nothing. If he allowed this attraction to go somewhere, it didn't mean they were going to have kids.

He thought of Elise's tendency to scrape her teeth against her lower lip.

He had been thinking about that a lot lately.

Maybe Stacey *was* right. Maybe he could relax his rule just a little. Just this once.

"You've met a girl!" Cam the mind reader said triumphantly, sounding every bit the annoying younger brother. "What's her name?"

"Never mind."

"Never mind? Hmm. Jay and Never Mind sitting in a tree...I don't know, dude, it doesn't sound too good. Maybe you should keep looking."

Shit. Now that he had given the idea a few seconds of airtime in his mind, he couldn't shake it.

He couldn't shake *her*.

And suddenly he didn't even want to try anymore. He just wanted to give in.

But not now. Not while she was still working for him. He was willing to bend one rule, but not that one. He wasn't the kind of man who exploited his position of power like that. So he would have to wait. Exercise some discipline.

"Seriously, what's her name?" Cam asked.

"I gotta go," Jay said.

Because, yep, he needed his phone to text Elise and ask her how long she thought the job was going to take.

Chapter 3

Elise was officially crushing on Jay.

There was no other explanation for why she was standing in her bedroom trying on her seventh outfit of the morning.

And downing Advils like they were candy when normally, given her current level of pain, she would have called off this afternoon's meeting.

Nothing was sitting right on her today. She was always bloated before her period, but this was more than that. This was the fact that the pain, when it was this bad, made her feel dull all over—her skin, her expression, *everything*.

And she so very much did not want to be dull in front of him.

So, yeah, she could only conclude that she was officially crushing on her client.

Which was dumb for many reasons, foremost among them that she didn't want a man in her life right now. She was at a critical stage in getting her business off the ground. She was making a go of it independently—both financially and emotionally—for the first time in her life. Jumping into a relationship would compromise that.

Her phone buzzed with Gia's custom ringtone. Have fun today with Hottie McHottie Accountants Unlimited.

The message was followed by a string of eggplant emoji. Gia was onto her. Still, she wasn't going to cop to it.

> *Elise:* I don't know what you're talking about.
> *Gia:* Oh get over yourself. You want him. I can tell.

Gia's job took her all over the world. But clearly their frequent FaceTimes had been enough for Gia to read the situation. She'd no doubt seen right through the way Elise kept casually bringing up Jay. But for some reason, Elise still felt compelled to deflect.

> *Elise:* You haven't even met him. Or seen me in
>   person for like two months. You can't "tell."
> *Gia:* Doesn't matter. I know you. And I am an expert
>   in these matters.
> *Elise:* What matters? Matters of the heart? Because
>   I just met him!
> *Gia:* No, silly. Matters of the LOINS. I am an expert
>   In matters of the loins.

Elise laughed. That was true. Gia...enjoyed company of the male persuasion. A lot.

> *Elise:* Well, I'm not looking for a relationship right
>   now. Right now, it's all about Elise Maxwell,
>   independent woman.
> *Gia:* Well you don't have to MARRY him. Just use
>   him and move on.

That was certainly Gia's method. Elise didn't judge it, but it hadn't ever been her thing.

Elise: Anyway, it doesn't matter. I can barely stand
    up today.
Gia: Oh, bebe, I'm sorry. How bad is it this month?
Elise: 6.5, maybe 7.

She was lying about that, too, though she wasn't sure why. Maybe because to cop to the pain being a solid eight would dampen what was left of her spirits.

And what was left of her spirits really, really wanted to see Jay.

An hour later, Elise was poised in the doorway to his office. Seeing him bent over his desk, his attention fully absorbed in something as he absently scratched his stubble, made those spirits . . . stir. She'd learned that when Jay focused on things, he *focused* on them. At her place last week, he had looked at the samples she'd shown him like he was trying to set them on fire with his eyes. Like nothing mattered more than the little square of tile she was proposing.

"Ms. Maxwell is here," his assistant announced before she shut the door behind Elise.

Jay looked up, and for a moment Elise felt herself the object of that intense concentration. It was as if he'd transferred it from his work to her. But then his expression changed, lightened, and a smile transformed his face, making those absurdly gorgeous eyes dance.

"Hi," he said, and it made her shiver.

God, she was crushing so hard, it was pathetic. "Hi." She tried to stop herself from grinning like an idiot. She did not succeed.

Take that, pain.

Still, as much as she was enjoying this little distraction from the agony in her insides, she needed to clear the air from last week.

"Before we get started, I wanted to say again how sorry I am you had to witness that unfortunate episode with my father."

He stood and gestured her over to the soon-to-no-longer-be-beige sofa. She winced as she sat. Sometimes when she was in an especially bad stretch, the compression of sitting made things worse.

He'd been aiming for a chair, she thought, but was suddenly next to her on the sofa. "Are you okay?"

"Yes, yes." She pinned on a smile she feared looked as fake as it felt, then busied herself taking out the samples they'd agreed on. Today's meeting was about looking at them against the new flooring and making final decisions on what to order.

She could feel his attention, that intense, singular focus she craved from him even as it made her squirm.

"Listen," he said. "We're not responsible for our parents. I mentioned my father the other day. And my brother's father?" She nodded and watched his nostrils flare. "They were abusive assholes. They probably still are, if they're still alive. But I'm not responsible for their shitty behavior. All I can do is try not to be like them."

"Oh! Do you have kids?" She was shocked by that. But really, she knew nothing about him.

"No, no. I just meant in general." He searched her face. "No kids for me."

That last bit was said more like a grand philosophical proclamation than a statement about his current family status.

He was looking at her like it was her turn to talk. And it was. He'd shared something pretty personal, talking about his childhood.

"My father wasn't...abusive," she said.

"Maybe not physically..." He trailed off as if he was filling in the blanks himself.

"He just really did not want me to start this company," But she was filling in those blanks, too, suddenly. She'd always known her father was a bully. But could his behavior be considered abusive?

"What does he want you to do instead?"

The question pulled her from her thoughts, and she huffed a bitter laugh. "Nothing. He wants me to be like my mother, basically. A lady who lunches. A socialite. Not that there's anything wrong with that," she added quickly. Her mom wasn't a bad person.

"That's just not you," he said with a certainty that thrilled her. She sometimes struggled with becoming a person who was different from the Elise everyone in her family saw.

"It's funny, because if you were going to pick a stereotypically girly, old-money type of career to have, you'd pick interior design. It's not like I'm trying to be a brain surgeon or something."

"Do you have siblings?"

"One brother, who's two years older."

"What does he do?"

"He teaches at a fancy private boys' school."

"So your brother is allowed to have a career, and you're not?" When he said it like that... "That's pretty screwed up, isn't it?"

"Well, look, I won't presume to know anything about your life, but I can say with a hundred percent confidence that in this regard at least, your father is an idiot if he doesn't see the boatload of talent you have. Not to mention drive. I see a lot of intergenerational wealth at my job. What I hardly ever see is someone walking away from it to make their own way."

Heat exploded inside her like he'd flipped a switch on a gas fireplace. She was tempted to brush off the compliments, to down-play what she was doing. But you know what? Screw that. He was right. So as squirmy and unsettled as it made her, she just said, "Thank you."

"Can I ask you a question?" Jay's nostrils were flaring again, like they had when he talked about his father and his brother's father.

"Of course."

"When we were texting the other day, you said this job was going to take two more months. Any way we can hurry that up?"

Oh. That wasn't what she had expected. Was he already tired of working on this project with her?

"Well, we can try to speed things up. We can put a rush on some of the pieces if you like, but a few of them I don't think we can get any faster. But if time is of the essence, we could make some substitutions."

And there was that weird, intense look again. It was like he could raise her temperature just by looking at her.

"No, that's okay," he finally said. "I can wait two months."

But he said it with a hint of resignation. Like he *was* tired of working on this project with her.

That was disappointing.

In the following weeks, Elise continued to be disappointed.

Which was ridiculous.

How could she be disappointed by the fact that Jay was the perfect client? He was interested and engaged. He deferred to her in most cases but argued just enough to keep things interesting—and when he did push back against her ideas, he made thoughtful points that forced her to further refine her point of view.

He just wasn't giving her that sexy-intense look anymore. Or holding her cold hands. The spark that had been there between them—the spark she'd *thought* had been there, but maybe she'd been imagining it—had gone out. Well, not on her end. On her end, she pretty much had to walk around with a metaphorical fire extinguisher at all times. But he had stopped giving off the sexy-intense vibes, leaving only the regular-intense vibes. And the dude *was* intense. A perfectionist, whether they were talking about the edges of the wallpaper in the bathroom or he was asking Patricia to send something back to someone whose work had not measured up. He was never rude. Quite the opposite, in fact—he was scrupulously polite. But insistent. He knew what he wanted, and he was going to get it.

It was stupidly sexy.

So she had an unrequited crush. She had allowed herself to acknowledge that fact, even if she still wouldn't admit it to Gia. She'd decided it was harmless as long as it stayed unrequited. The last thing she needed right now was to start depending on a man. She'd had a lifetime of that. She could worry about relationships down the line, after she'd proven herself. But a little one-sided crushing—what could it hurt?

And with Jay, although the flirty banter had gone, she could honestly say that, in a surprising twist, they had become friends. After she'd confided in him about her father, he'd done the same. It was as if, by sharing those early secrets, they had skipped all the getting-to-know-you stuff that usually accompanied new friendships. Now, seven weeks after he'd hired her, they were following sessions to approve the work of tradespeople with lunch around the corner. Or wrapping up a meeting with a quick game of Scrabble. It was awesome—in general and because she'd never had a friend she didn't have to force to play board games with her.

"What is your opinion about hockey?" he asked at one of their lunches. They were sitting side by side on stools at the counter of an old-school-soda-fountain-turned-hipster restaurant.

It was weird being friends with a guy. Elise's close friendships had always been with women.

"That's the one they play on ice, right?" She winked to show she was joking and was gratified when he laughed. Jay was so wickedly intelligent, it made her proud to be able to amuse him.

"Kent has a pair of Leafs tickets for tonight he can't use." Kent was the Cohen of Cohen & Smith. "I was going to see if you wanted to come."

"I would totally go to a Leafs game, depending on what was happening at halftime."

"There's no halftime in hockey."

"Are you going to revoke my Canadian citizenship?" she teased, and she got another chuckle. "So what *do* they have in hockey?"

"Three periods."

"So that means there's two halftimes." She was kidding there. But not about going. "I'll totally go to the Leafs game with you." She really could not imagine anything she'd like to do more, suddenly.

He stared at her for a long time without speaking. For a minute she thought it was going to turn into one of his sexy-intense stares— oh, how she missed those despite the pep talk she'd just given herself about not relying on a man—but then it dissipated. "Nah. We'd better not."

Huh?

"It's really cold in hockey arenas," he added, and she had the distinct sense that he was reaching for an excuse. Why had he brought it up to begin with if he didn't want to go with her? Her pride prevented her from pushing him on it, but disappointment lodged in her chest, and she was relieved when the lunch was over.

They'd taken to texting, too. Later that evening, she got one from him that was simply a picture of the game Battleship.

She let out a delighted laugh. See? They clicked. As *friends*. She typed a reply. Now there's a game I haven't thought of in years. Is that yours?

> *Jay:* I bought it this evening at an antique/junk store.
> *Elise:* What happened to two-halftimes hockey?
> *Jay:* I told Kent to give the tickets to a junior accountant who's been pulling tons of overtime this month.

Even though she truly did not care about hockey, Elise found herself absurdly glad that Jay hadn't gone without her.

> *Elise:* But you went antiquing instead? That seems sort of random.
> *Jay:* My friend Stacey dragged me out.

So much for absurd happiness. Jay hadn't gone to the game without her, but he was spending the evening with his stunning, legal-genius ex-girlfriend.

> *Elise:* Well, hopefully you can get her to play that excellent game with you. I haven't played Battleship for years. I'm jealous.

In more ways than one.

> *Jay:* Nah, Stacey's on a date—aka phase two of her
>   evening. I was just the opening act.

Elise watched the little dots that indicated he was still typing.

> *Jay:* Platonic opening act.

She grinned. There were more dots.

> *Jay:* So basically I'm trying to invite myself over to
>   play Battleship. If you're not busy?
> *Elise:* I'm not, and I would love that.

This was a bad idea.

But as Jay climbed the stairs behind Elise—without even trying not to stare at her yoga pants–encased ass as it swayed—he couldn't seem to talk any sense into himself.

After that call with his brother, during which Jay had all but decided to put the moves on Elise after the job was done, he had spent seven long weeks being nothing but benignly friendly to her. And along the way, they'd become genuine friends. He loved hanging out with her. She was smart and funny. She possessed a vivacity that felt almost like a drug. Like when he was around her and her vibrant clothes and her Operation: Abandon Beige, he was...honed. Better than he usually was. Smarter. More aware. More alive.

And he was almost there. They were probably a week away from signing off on the whole job. He couldn't wait one more week?

It was funny. Most people who resolved to do something difficult weakened when drunk or when tired. When their defenses were down.

He weakened when faced with vintage two-player board games.

But anyway, it was just Battleship. His self-discipline was legendary. Surely it could hold him in check for a game of Battleship.

It was just that he hadn't been over to her place since that first week. Being alone with her in a private space had seemed unwise.

Elise led him into the living room. "Wine?"

"Yes," he said instantly. Which was also unwise.

"I almost changed before you got here, but I decided we've reached the stage in our relationship where I don't have to look professional," she called from the kitchen, where he could hear her uncorking a bottle. She reappeared with the bottle and two glasses. When they'd had lunch, she'd been wearing a black dress and canary-yellow tights. Now she was in those skintight yoga pants that had mesmerized him on the stairs and a bright-orange tank top covered with a royal-blue cardigan.

Jesus Christ, she looked amazing. He took a big drink of the wine she handed him. She flopped on the sofa next to him, and his fingers practically vibrated from want.

She turned her head toward him—just her head, as she was still sprawled against the back of the sofa—and grinned. "My father is writing me out of the will."

He almost choked on his next sip. Her happy expression was so at odds with her pronouncement. "Don't look so broken up about it."

She shrugged. "I was thinking about what you said a while ago, about intergenerational transfer of wealth. I haven't done anything to earn that money. Hell, *he* didn't do anything to earn that money. His grandfather was the guy who made it all—my father just maintains it."

"That's how the world works. The rich stay rich."

"Well, aren't you a radical accountant?" she teased.

He liked it too much when she teased him, so he bit back a smile and shrugged. What he'd said was true. A lot of his work was about helping rich people make sure their kids stayed rich after they were gone. About protecting assets. Which was why he was so devoted to the firm's philanthropic efforts.

"Well," she declared. "I want to earn my money."

"Good for you."

"Which isn't to say I'm not scared shitless." Her voice had gone kind of shaky, which had the effect of prodding at the same protective instinct that had made him want to punch her father the last time he'd been here. "I've always had a safety net, you know?"

"What does your brother have to say about all this?" Elise seemed to have a good relationship with her brother, Andy, but didn't the guy bear some responsibility here? How could he just sit back and be the recipient of such stunningly inequitable treatment?

She snickered. "He says he'll give me half of everything when our parents croak."

Okay, then. Jay lowered his metaphorical weapons. He wasn't going to have to track down this Andy dude and give him a talking-to, after all.

"But whatever. Inheritances are nice, but I'm not sure you should plan your life around them."

"I wish my clients were as smart as you."

She bit her lip like she was trying not to smile. "You think I'm smart?"

"I do."

She looked down, all embarrassed suddenly, and it did something to him. "What?" he said gently, nudging her shoulder with his.

"No one has ever said that to me before."

Well, that pissed him right off. "What about this gaggle of girlfriends you keep telling me about?"

"Well, yeah, they're great, but we go so far back, it's automatic loyalty from them, you know? They're biased. If you asked them to make a list of my qualities, they'd be all *smart, creative, pretty*—"

"That's all true." *Shit.* That had just popped out.

She'd been rattling off her list of adjectives in a jokey,

sclf-dcprecating way, but when he interrupted her, she stopped talking, and her eyes widened.

He was so mixed up. He wanted to kiss her. Hell, he wanted to bend her over the beige sofa that had been the source of so many jokes. But he also wanted to warm her hands up. And give her father a piece of his mind.

And play Battleship. And Scrabble and Boggle...and everything.

He closed his eyes for a moment, to block her out. He couldn't think with her *right there*. He needed to get his addled brain back under control. He needed her not to be so goddamn compelling. He needed her not to—

Kiss him?

Oh, *shit*.

That was what he got for closing his eyes against Elise Maxwell.

He was nearly undone when her soft, almost hesitant lips came down on his with a shaky little puff of breath.

He'd been making a list of things he *didn't* need, but suddenly those things were mere wisps of memory. They were so small, so insignificant, compared to the need barreling down on him.

For a few seconds, he kept his eyes closed and allowed it to happen. Made his hands into tight fists by his side and let her lips move over his. Let her hair fall against his face—she was half kneeling over him—a honey curtain that smelled like goddamn lemons.

She was only touching him with her lips, but it was like all the crazy colors of her—of her sofa cushions and her clothing and *her*—were assaulting him, every part of him all at once.

Then she sighed a little. Her tongue touched the seam of his lips, and this was going to be it. He had already compromised his principles by being here at all. Now he was going to move beyond compromising them and throw them out the goddamn window. So much for a lifetime of careful discipline. This was how little it took to prove what kind of man he was.

But just as he groaned in surrender, she laid a palm against his cheek. In addition to being too soft for his stubbly face, it was cold. It delivered whatever was the opposite of a burn.

It shocked him back to his senses.

He grabbed it and pulled it down, then gently levered her away from him.

"Oh my God. I'm sorry." She tried to pull her hand from his, but he held fast. "I misread this. I'm so sorry." She closed her eyes against him, like he'd done with her a few moments ago, but in his case, it had been to try to stem the tide of lust. She, by contrast, was embarrassed. Mortified, even, he'd venture, given how red her face had turned.

He *hated* that. So he decided to tell her the truth. It wasn't like it could make things any *more* awkward than they currently were. "No. No, you didn't misread."

Those pretty hazel eyes flew open, then darted down to their still-clasped hands.

He could feel his own face heating to match hers as he let go of her hands. "I mean, why else am I at the home of my interior designer on Friday night drinking wine and getting all cozy on the sofa?" He smirked, trying to lighten the bombshell confession he'd made. "The *beige* sofa?"

She pressed her lips together, doing that thing where she tried to suppress a smile. "Because you wanted to look at my samples?"

He wasn't sure if she'd meant that as a double entendre or if he just had a dirty mind. Screw it, he was going to go with the dirty version. "I *do* want to look at your samples. Jesus Christ, Elise, I want to do more than look at them."

Wary but interested, her eyes moved over his face like she was reading a book. "Why do I sense a *but* coming?"

He nodded and ran his fingers through his hair. "But you're working for me. I hired you to do a job."

"Is *this* why you keep asking me how long until the project is over?"

"It is."

She laughed—hard—as she flopped back down next to him on the sofa. "Well..." She stretched the single syllable out like she did sometimes. It drove him mad. "I can report that the Decorators & Designers Association of Canada has an extensive code of ethics, including a section about interacting with clients. It's all about protecting client information, not agreeing to things you're not qualified to do, how to handle disputes." She spread the fingers of one hand and used the pointer finger from the other to tick off the ethics violations as she listed them. When she was done, she lifted both palms into the air and said, triumphantly, "Nowhere does it say anything about..." Her hands came down and sort of fanned the space between them.

"About what?" He knew exactly what she meant, of course, but he wanted to hear what she would say.

"About wanting to jump your clients." She grinned. "Or about *actually* jumping them."

Well, hot damn. "Are you saying you want to jump me?"

"Why is it so easy to be honest with you?"

"I don't know. I *am* known for my low bullshit threshold," he said. "I'm not usually like this."

"You mean you don't usually proposition your employers over Battleship?"

"Okay, you're not my employer, but we'll argue about that later."

He got a little thrill—an actual physical shiver—at the prospect that she was planning to mount a defense against his stance that they couldn't hook up until they were done working together.

"And no, I don't usually proposition anyone, over Battleship or anything else. I'm usually kind of... passive."

"Says the woman who turned her back on everything that's been given to her in favor of charting her own path. The woman who marched into my lobby and insulted it."

She nodded. "I think that answers my question about why it's easy to be honest with you, even though in some ways it feels like that's unusual for me. Everyone else in my life knows me from way back. You met me just as I was becoming someone else."

It made sense, but he did take issue with her terminology. "I don't think you're becoming someone else. I think you're just becoming more yourself."

She smiled. She liked that analysis. "So you're really not going to...look at my samples?"

He sighed. "Look, I know it sounds overly rigid, but I just think it's suspect. Maybe I'm not technically your boss, but I hired you. I can fire you. You're at a delicate point in the life of your business, so I should keep my hands to myself for the time being."

"That's very responsible."

"I notice you're not rushing to agree with me."

"I *don't* agree with you."

He chuckled. "I know it sounds uptight. I'm known for my low bullshit threshold, as I said, but I also get called uptight a lot. I'll own that."

"It doesn't sound uptight." She heaved a big sigh. He loved how heavy with disappointment it was. "It sounds disciplined. Smart." She rolled her eyes like she was disgusted with her own conclusion. "So what do we do?"

"We sublimate until the job is done." He opened the Battleship box. "And you get ready to have your armada sunk."

Chapter 4

༄

The next week was the longest of Elise's life. Also the happiest. And it wasn't just due to Jay. As his office and lobby neared completion, a growing sense of pride in her work took root. She'd gotten two additional jobs in the building as a result of her work on the Cohen & Smith project, and Jay swore up and down that he hadn't put anyone up to it, that her work sold itself.

But okay, her happiness was mostly due to Jay. It was a strange position they were in. They had basically admitted that they were going to have sex. Just not yet. Which made for a heated dynamic. He kept calling himself uptight, but honestly, it was sexy as hell, both the waiting itself and watching him exercise such relentless discipline. Because she would have crumbled the moment he crooked his finger.

There was just something so incredibly hot about that kind of control. It literally made her feel weak in the knees sometimes.

"How many more days?" he asked gruffly, turning from where he'd been standing by his door. They'd just received delivery of the guest chairs, and he'd been seeing the delivery guys out. "You said two months, and it's been two months."

She sighed. She'd been doing a lot of that lately. She thought about telling him that the project was as good as done, but she had tried variations on this argument all week, and she knew he wouldn't go for it. "The area rugs are slightly delayed. They're supposed to come in Friday"—that was two days from now—"and then you can..."

"Then I can what?"

She swallowed hard. "Then you can sign off on everything."

He leveled an intense look at her—the sexy-intense look had returned since their little chat at her apartment—and she thought he was going to call her on the fact that *sign off on everything* wasn't how she'd intended to end that sentence. He didn't, though. He merely walked over to the sitting area in his office—which was looking really good, if she did say so herself—and said, "Scrabble?"

She laughed. "Yes." If she couldn't do what she really wanted to do, Scrabble was the perfect consolation prize.

They chose tiles, and as she assessed hers, she had to laugh again. Did she dare lay down the word that was jumping out at her? Well, hell, why not? They'd basically spent the week eye-fucking each other as they rode the job out, adhering to his letter-of-the-law no-sex-while-working-together hang-up.

So, trying not to blush—and, judging by the rising temperature of her cheeks, failing—she laid down CLIT.

Then she lifted her gaze to him. He was already looking at her, eyebrows raised like she was a naughty schoolgirl.

"What?" She batted her eyelashes. "It was my best option."

He did not speak, but his nostrils flared. He looked down at his tiles for a moment. Then, slowly, he got up and walked to the door. Was he going to *leave*? Crap, maybe she'd gone too far. She should have been more sensitive about respecting his boundaries. She should have—

Click.

The sound of him locking the door was, objectively, not very loud. But its reverberations echoed through her suddenly aching body as if it had been a bomb.

He stared at her as he walked back—still at the same measured pace—to the sofa. She felt like she was being stalked. Like they were in a nature documentary where the predator's approach was being shown in slow motion. Except instead of getting killed, she was going to...get her comeuppance.

In a really good way.

She exhaled a shaky breath.

Once seated, he kept his attention half on her, half on the board as slowly, so slowly, building off her L, he laid down three of his tiles: LICK.

She gasped, which was silly because she had started this.

He was looking at her with a maddeningly calm expression. But the nostril flaring was back, in a big way.

Well, hell, if she was in, she was all in. So she looked directly at him and said, "Yes, please, if you don't mind."

She should have been embarrassed to be so bold. She'd never outright asked for anything like that before, but suddenly the idea of him with his head between her legs had lodged itself in her brain, and she was pretty sure it was going to stick there for a good long time.

"Not only do I not mind, I insist." He smoldered at her. *Smoldered.* It was the only word for it. "The rugs will be here Friday, you say?"

Well, crap. She'd thought for a moment there, with the door locking, that he was going to give in. But no, he was still hung up on the rugs. "Give or take. You can, ah, let me know when they arrive, and I'll clear my schedule."

He nodded, the picture of seriousness. But then his voice lowered an octave from where it had been as he asked, "And then I can lick your clit?"

A strangled cry erupted from her throat as she slumped back against the sofa. "So actually hooking up with me contravenes your personal code of ethics, but somehow talking about licking my clit is allowable professional behavior?"

She'd been kidding, but his brow furrowed. Deeply. "Shit. You're right. This is sexual harassment territory."

She held her hands up. "No! I was kidding! I'm the one who started this! Harass me!" He still looked unconvinced. She could practically see him beating himself up. She did *not* want him to get spooked and shut down the sexy talk. It was all she had to hang on to until those damn rugs arrived.

So she said the first sexy thing that popped into her head, aiming to get them back on track. "But you're going to fuck me, too, right, not just go down on me?" She shocked herself.

She *liked* that she had shocked herself, though. It was reassuring, in a weird way, to be this far outside her comfort zone. If they'd been all moony and romantic with each other, she would have started to panic. That would have been too much like boyfriend territory.

She must have shocked him, too, because he inhaled sharply. "Elise," he said, all low and irritated, kind of like he was talking to a kid. But also *not*.

"What?" She feigned innocent confusion. "You don't want to fuck me?"

"I want what you want," he said, speaking through his hands, which had come up to cradle his face, like the world was too much—or maybe *she* was too much. It made her feel powerful.

"*I* want what *you* want." Because she did, suddenly. She had the distinct sense that putting herself in Jay's capable hands would be... severely rewarding.

He looked up sharply at that, his eyes practically sparking. He liked that. Suddenly she could imagine all that control and discipline he exerted over his life flaring up in other contexts. She squeezed her thighs together against the throbbing that had started between them. "You like being in charge, don't you?"

"I've been known to get a little bossy."

"Hmm." She shifted in her seat and reached for her tiles. If she wanted to keep up with the apparently dirty turn the game was taking, all she had was COY. She had a random mess of letters—two Ys, an O, an E, and very few useful consonants. But COY could work. She took her time laying down the word, trying to embody it. "Bossy sounds just fine to me."

His eyes narrowed as he studied her. "And yet, you don't seem like the type who follows the path laid out for her."

"Are you talking about my rift with my family?" He nodded. "Because that's completely different."

"Oh, so you just smile and good-naturedly take orders in other contexts?"

"Depends who I'm taking orders from."

But then she realized that her teasing tone was all wrong. Jay knew about and respected her quest to remake her life. And that was the key word, wasn't it? *Respect.* She was pretty sure the gentlemanly side of Jay, the part that was making them wait until she was officially not working for him anymore, was somehow worried that he was going to accidentally oppress her.

"Jay," she said, turning serious. "I'm really excited to have sex with you. I'm not going to lie—part of that excitement is about the fact that what you're calling your 'bossiness' turns me on. A lot. But don't make this into some big psychological thing that it isn't. Context is everything."

"Jesus Christ, Elise." He tipped his head back and looked at the ceiling. "I'm not going to make it to Friday."

She chuckled. Who knew she would enjoy torturing him so much? "I was just being honest." Which was still an unfamiliar sensation. "I'm still kind of marveling over how I can just say whatever I want to you. It's weird."

"You said that, but I'm still having trouble believing that it's all that unusual for you."

Jay pretty much said whatever he wanted most of the time.

But it was different for her. Probably in part because women were socialized to be deferential, to not make waves. And in part because *she* in particular had been socialized that way. It wasn't as if she had a lot of practice with people valuing what she had to say. Of course, with her friends she could be honest, but that was different. They didn't look at her with a singular focus, like they were hanging on every word that came out of her mouth.

"It *is* unusual! It's like…radical honesty." *Radical honesty.* She liked that phrase. She liked the *feeling* of radical honesty— so much she laughed from sheer delight. "I've never really done that."

"Well." He waggled his eyebrows. "It suits you. Even if it does sort of torture me." Then, after a wink, he turned his attention to his tiles. "I've got nothing. I'm going to have to do an exchange."

As he swapped new tiles for old, she smiled at him, her client and her friend. Her soon-to-be lover. If this damn job ever got done. But given his immovable stance, there was nothing to do but take her turn at Scrabble. She studied her tiles. She had nothing that would continue the sexy theme they had going. But she could build off the Y in COY to play YET. Oh well, the suggestive streak couldn't go on forever.

He raised his eyebrows. "As in, are the damn rugs here yet?"

Or maybe it could. She cracked up. That was another great thing about Jay. He could shift so effortlessly between filthy and funny.

"Pretty much."

The rugs came two days later, just after lunch.

They had been the longest two days of Jay's life.

When Patricia poked her head in and said, "There are some rugs here. Do you want them placed now or do you want to hang on to them and do it after hours?"

Jay shot up from his desk. *Rugs.* His new favorite word. "Either way. You handle it."

"Okaaay..."

He supposed it seemed a strange request. He was known for being a perfectionist-slash-micromanager. And he hadn't involved Patricia in any aspects of the design project. No, that project had been *his*.

Had been—past tense.

"Cancel the rest of my appointments for the day."

"But you have the Carlises coming in at three!" The alarm in her voice was palpable. The Carlises were multimillionaires—and high-maintenance multimillionaires at that.

"Something came up," he called over his shoulder as he strode out of the office.

He used one hand to obsessively punch the button for the elevator and the other to slide his phone out of his back pocket. The rugs are here. Where are you?

Jay's text arrived at the worst time. Elise had been hoping her estimate had been off and that the rugs would be even more delayed. But no. Here it was Friday, and the rugs were right on time. What was she going to say to him? She winced as she sat up enough to type a response.

Elise: Home.

Home in bed, more specifically. She'd had to cancel a consult this afternoon, and she was lying in the dark waiting for enough time to pass that she could take another dose of painkillers. How ironic that she was *literally* in bed when those stupid rugs arrived.

Jay: I'm on my way.

Ugh. She wanted to scream. To punch things. But she was too wiped out to do either. She tried not to let herself sink into a pit of self-pity every month, but this wasn't fair. She started typing but then erased it. What could she say? *I'm sorry, kind sir, but my rogue uterine lining will make it impossible for me to entertain any gentlemen callers this evening.*

Jay: In a taxi. Faster than dealing with parking.

Well, okay. She'd just tell him in person. Let him see the real her. Their relationship had been characterized by radical honesty, right? He wasn't going to be her boyfriend, but she hoped he wasn't thinking of them hooking up as a one-time thing. Even though they had yet to have sex, she was pretty sure that once was not going to be enough for her. And if he felt the same, which she hoped he did, he was going to have to know that she spent a couple days every month curled up in the fetal position racked with pain. And hopefully he wouldn't be too put off by her "lady issues," as her father had called them.

The sound of her buzzer sliced through the apartment. When she'd been apartment hunting, part of the appeal of this particular one had been that it was in a heritage house that was more than a hundred years old. It had character.

But it did not have a doorman. Or even an intercom system. Damn, what she wouldn't give right now to be in a high-rise like her friend Wendy.

The buzzer went off again.

She heaved herself off her bed, her eyes tearing, and started plodding down to the front door.

Something was wrong with Elise.

Jay knew it the moment she opened the door. It took him only a nanosecond to go from cursing her for taking so long to answer the door to being seized with worry over what was the matter.

"Hi." Her voice was scratchy—and not in a good way. Her face was pink—and not in a good way. She held one arm tightly across her stomach like she was trying to keep her guts contained.

"What's wrong?"

Was she *crying*? Worry flash froze into panic. "Elise. Sweetheart. What's wrong?" He rested his hands on her shoulders and crouched so he could see into her eyes. Tears were indeed gathering in them.

She sort of sagged against him as she whispered, "I can't have sex with you."

"Okay," he said immediately, even as, on the inside, every single one of his cells stood up and howled in protest. "I'll go, but I need to know you're okay before I do. Can I call one of your friends?"

She smiled weakly. "I can't have sex with you *today*." The clarification calmed his riled cells somewhat, but he was still confused. And worried. "You want to come up, and I'll explain?"

Upstairs, she sank immediately onto the sofa. This was the first time he'd been here that she hadn't offered him something to drink. She was a natural hostess—usually.

"I have endometriosis." A hint of her old sassy self appeared on her face. "I'm in a lot of pain right now in my...internal sexual regions."

"Endometriosis," he echoed. That had something to do with periods, he thought.

She answered his unspoken question. "It's when the lining of your uterus grows on the outside instead of the inside. On other organs, usually. And whereas in the inside, it, uh, builds up and sheds every month...Is this too much squicky lady talk?"

He shook his head vehemently. "No. Not at all." To his surprise, he desperately wanted to know what was going on. He wanted to know everything about Elise.

"Yeah, well, so the stuff on the outside thickens and builds up like it would before a period, but then there's nowhere for it to go. Scar tissue builds up. It hurts. A lot."

"Can they do anything for it?"

"They have. It's actually better than it used to be."

That was hard to imagine. His skepticism must have shown in his face, because she smiled. "Yeah, I've had surgery for it, and that helped, at least initially. It seems to be getting worse again now. But it used to be just horrific. For years. Nobody believed me."

"What?" Okay, that was just dumb. Anyone could see she was in pain, and if this was a milder version of what she'd experienced before? It boggled the mind.

"Yeah, doctors would tell me it was just bad period pain—which I've since learned is really common with endo. Then one day in university I was hanging out with my friends when it was really bad. Gia was sort of used to it, because we spent so much time together. But Wendy was so alarmed, she called an ambulance. I tried to talk her out of it, but I'm glad she prevailed, because there was a doctor at the emergency room who finally took it seriously. I got some scans, a diagnosis, and, later, a bunch of my insides hacked out."

Wow. It was a lot to take in. His heart broke for her, enduring all this pain, at the same time that he was pissed at the people who hadn't taken her seriously.

"I'm really sorry, Jay." She sounded so defeated. "I know we were both, uh, primed for this."

"Sweetheart, don't be sorry." He wanted to sling an arm around her, to hold her close, but he wasn't sure if that would hurt. So he settled for laying a palm lightly against her cheek. There was still the low hum of attraction he always felt around her, but for the most part, his lust had dissipated. It had been replaced by something that was both softer and stronger. "There's plenty of time."

"You'll wait?"

"Uh, *yes*."

He would wait forever, he realized with a start.

Wow. But that was a thought to be examined later.

She blew out a breath that seemed like a sigh of relief.

"Did you think it was the day the rugs arrived or nothing?" he asked.

She shrugged.

Maybe it was that her defenses were down because of the pain, but he thought he had seen a flash of vulnerability, of uncertainty, in that shrug. "Nope," he said. "We're just going to extend our torture a little more. How long do these bouts usually last?"

"Two or three days."

"And what would you normally do while you're not feeling well?" He kind of wanted to march her back to the emergency room and demand relief on her behalf, but of course that wasn't the correct course of action.

"I'd lay in my bed and watch stupid TV to try to distract myself from the pain."

"All right, then. You mind company?"

The smile that lit her face changed it, chased away the shadows. She looked like her old self. "I would love company."

"What's on?" He followed her into her bedroom. She was sort of shuffling, clearly still in pain, and it damn near killed him to watch.

He'd never been in her bedroom. Like the living room, and like her personal style, it was a mixture of exuberant and restrained. The walls were a bright, almost lime green, but pretty much everything else—lamps, rugs, a small desk—was quiet neutrals or subtle patterns. The bed, sitting on a raised platform, was a mossy jumble of white linens and pillows. It looked like an unkempt cloud in a green sky.

She picked up a remote and aimed it at a small TV mounted on the wall. It came to life displaying her Netflix queue. "I was watching *Grace and Frankie*. But we can switch to something else."

"Nah. That sounds perfect. My mom is the world's biggest Jane Fonda fan, so I've been meaning to check this show out. Mom used to try to make me do her old Jane Fonda workout videos along with her, but thankfully there wasn't enough room in the trailer for both of us to do it." He kicked off his shoes and bounced around in a parody of aerobics, then dived onto the empty bed, hoping to elicit a laugh.

It worked. The bed dipped as she eased herself on, but her smile became a wince. Slowly she arranged herself next to him. They were lying side by side, almost—but not quite—touching. She turned her head and aimed a smile at him that was so incandescent it took his breath away.

Yeah, this was not how he had imagined this afternoon going. At all. But somehow, impossibly, he wasn't the least bit disappointed. In fact, this felt... exactly right.

Elise had never had so much fun while enduring so much pain. Well, *fun* wasn't the right word. Jay's steady, solid, caring presence— his persistence—felt like *mercy*, like a grace she hadn't earned. She luxuriated in it, which should have been impossible given that luxury shouldn't be able to coexist with pain. But somehow, with him, it did.

After a bunch of episodes of the show, the room started to grow dark as evening descended, and he insisted that she eat something. She tried to demur, but he wouldn't have it and quizzed her about her usual comfort food. And after she listened to him bang around in her kitchen for fifteen minutes, he returned with a grilled-cheese sandwich.

And she felt better after eating it. Stronger.

The downstairs buzzer rang as she was finishing her last bite. Jay jumped up from his spot next to her. "That's for me. That was the last of your bread, so I ordered a pizza for myself." He paused. "Was that okay?" His brow furrowed like he was worried he had overstepped.

"Of course." She grinned listening to him tromping down the stairs, thrilled that he was apparently planning to stay on into the evening.

When he reappeared a few minutes later with some pizza on a plate, he was also holding Yahtzee.

"Now *this* is a classic," he said appreciatively. "I don't think I've played this for thirty years."

She scooched herself up against the headboard and made a bring-it motion with her fingers.

"You up for it?"

"Yeah, if I get too wrecked to lift my hand to roll a pair of dice, just take me out to the pasture and shoot me."

He frowned. He *was* so uptight sometimes—his friends and colleagues were right. But she loved it, as it was so often in service of her. She thought back to their confrontation with her father, when he'd gotten all weird and snippy, then to his insistence that they not sleep together until the design job was done.

Jay was a very good kind of uptight.

"I'm kidding." She patted the bed. He sat, though he still looked overly serious. So she grabbed the game and said, "Youngest and prettiest goes first."

That did it—he grinned. "But of course."

After the game—annoyingly, she lost—she lay back down. He would probably leave soon. She really, really didn't want him to. Having him here had made the day so much more bearable.

"You tired?" he asked.

She tried to say no, but a yawn overtook her. Busted.

He would leave, now that he thought he was keeping her up.

And sure enough, he sat back and uncoiled his legs—he'd been sitting cross-legged for Yahtzee. But he merely shuffled around until he was lying back against one of her pillows. She'd been lying on her side on top of the duvet, but now he was tugging on it—he wanted her to get under the covers.

He was going to tuck her in. Of course he was. He did stuff like that.

But to her astonishment, when she got under the covers, he did, too.

He moved right up next to her and opened his arms.

Tears threatened, and her throat tightened. This probably wasn't a good idea. This was pretty boyfriendy. But she was tired, in pain, and powerless to resist. So she surrendered. She nestled herself into his embrace and went to sleep.

Chapter 5

ℰ

$\mathcal{B}$y Sunday the pain had receded, but Elise had had to postpone the booty call to spend the day with the girls.

"Now don't get too excited," she said as she showed the security guard in Jay's office building her temporary badge. "This isn't like a residential job. It's not going to hit you over the head with its fabulousness."

"I beg to differ," Gia said. "I can already feel myself getting faint at the fabulousness that's in my future."

Gia had flown in late Saturday. She did that sometimes. She would parachute in for a quick best-friends-fest, and the four of them would gorge on each other's company. Gia had stayed at Elise's place last night, and today they had all gone from breakfast to the spa, and now they were headed up to the empty offices of Cohen & Smith so she could show them her work.

They all crowded onto the elevator, chattering a mile a minute.

These intense doses of her best friends, where they dropped everything and just reveled in each other's company, were among Elise's favorite ways to spend time. Usually.

She had been more than a little distracted today.

But she wasn't going to be one of those women who bailed on her friends for a man. And she really did want to show off her first big solo design job.

"Hold the elevator!"

Elise reflexively did so, sticking her hand out to stop the door closing.

"Thanks."

Oh crap. It was that woman Stacey. Jay's ex-girlfriend. Or not. Depending on who you believed.

"Hey!" Stacey seemed a little too happy to see her. "Elise, right?"

"Yes, hi. I'm just taking my friends up to Cohen & Smith to show them my work. Jay said I could."

She wasn't sure why she added that last bit. Jay had given her a key to the office long ago and told her to come and go as she pleased, but it wasn't like Stacey needed an explanation.

"I'm sure he did." Stacey was looking way too amused for a casual elevator encounter.

Elise was starting to get annoyed. So this woman was Jay's ex. So she was stunningly beautiful and accomplished. Just because she had a history with Jay didn't mean she had to lord it over Elise.

Her irritation must have shown on her face, because Stacey said, "I'm sorry I was so weird and bitchy that day we met."

Uh, what? That was the last thing Elise had expected.

"It was because I get kind of possessive of Jay. And not because we dated, but because we're old friends. I mean, we *did* date, but he was right, it was only for, like, five minutes. I mean, the way he kisses." She made a face like she'd smelled something bad. "Like, chill out, dude. It's like he only has one degree of intensity, and that's, like, a hundred. But you know, right?"

Elise's face heated. "Um, no, I don't know, actually."

Stacey grinned. "Well, you'll see." Elise started to protest, but the elevator stopped at Stacey's floor. She paused halfway out. "You're *exactly* his type."

"What...type is that?" Elise couldn't help asking.

"Smart. Capable. Independent."

Well, crap. Elise was shocked that she came off that way to someone like Stacey. Shocked and pleased. Maybe she was moving along faster than she'd realized on the whole self-transformation project.

She was trying to think how to respond when Stacey stepped fully off the elevator. As the doors started to close, she winked and said, "I'll be seeing you around, Elise."

Her friends—she'd forgotten about them for a second there—were silent until the elevator closed fully and started moving again. Then they lost their minds, exclaiming, talking over each other, and—*crap*. She was going to have to do some explaining.

The offices were dark. She'd kind of hoped someone might be burning the Sunday-night oil, thereby saving her from the interrogation she was about to be subjected to, but no such luck.

"Can I at least show you the lobby first?" she asked weakly as she held the door for everyone.

"No, you cannot," Jane said. "I can't concentrate on your brilliance until I know who that woman is and why she thinks you would know how your client kisses."

Wendy sank into one of the chairs in the lobby. "I concur."

Gia did the same. "I don't know who that woman was, but I do know that Elise likes this Jay guy. A lot."

Elise sighed. Gia was already onto her, which she'd known. And now that the other two sensed that something was afoot, they were never going to let it go.

So she sat, too, and told them everything. About the sexual tension, the postponed booty call. But also about how awesome his confidence in her work made her feel. About his take that her rift with her parents said something about her character. She didn't spare any detail. The more she talked, the more embarrassed she became that she'd kept all this from them in the first place. It was just that this...thing with Jay wasn't like any of the relationships she'd had in the past. It felt different. Private.

"Look at you!" Wendy exclaimed when she was done. "New apartment, new company, new boyfriend."

"Oh no." Elise hurried to correct her. "He's not my boyfriend. We're just going to sleep together."

Hopefully several times.

"I see," Jane said. "You guys lie around playing board games and cuddling, but he's *not* your boyfriend."

"Yeah, I would almost buy that, except for the cuddling," said Wendy. "You don't cuddle with your fuck buddies."

Crap. Wendy would know. She was the queen of long-term casual relationships.

"You *especially* don't cuddle with your fuck buddy when you're not actually fucking," said Gia.

Panic started to seize Elise. "Oh my God, you guys. I can't have a boyfriend."

"Why not?" Jane asked.

"I'm in the middle of establishing my business, and, well, this sounds dumb, but I also feel like I'm establishing *myself*, you know? As an independent person. For the first time in my life."

"So?" Wendy asked.

"Well, I've spent my whole life dependent on my father. Now I'm going to switch to a boyfriend?" If that was even on offer, and there was no evidence it was. So she wasn't sure why they were even having this conversation.

"Oh my God, Elise, you are so dumb sometimes," Gia said.

"Not according to *Stacey*." Wendy cackled in that way she had.

"Look," said Gia. "You don't *want* a boyfriend? I'm cool with that. I, of all people, am cool with that." It was true. Gia was unapologetic about her allergy to commitment. "But don't cast Jay in the same mold as your father. From what you've said, Jay...Ugh, I can't believe I'm going to say this." She made a gagging gesture. "Jay lifts you up. Helps you."

Was that...true?

"It's okay to let someone help you," Jane added.

Elise didn't know what to say. They were all silent. Just for a moment, but it must have been too much for Wendy, because she stood, clapped her hands, and said, "Well, this has been a great talk. Let's see some decor and shit."

The "great talk" was still rattling around inside Elise's head when she said goodbye to Gia at the airport. Gia had tried to order Elise to call Jay, insisting that she would take a cab, but Elise wouldn't hear of it. She always drove Gia to the airport at the end of her visits. Maybe she had some thinking to do about the little bombs her friends had dropped on her earlier. Maybe they had made some points that were worth considering. But she absolutely refused to be the kind of person who ditched her friends for a guy. Even if she was becoming someone else, she refused to be *that* girl.

As she sat in her car outside the terminal, she told herself that it was too late to text him. He wouldn't be expecting it anyway. She'd texted him yesterday when she found out Gia was coming to town and outright told him she wouldn't be able to see him until Monday. And they'd both known what she'd meant by "see."

But damn, she wanted him. So desperately.

She also *missed* him, which was a little alarming—it had only been forty-eight hours since he'd left her place. He'd slipped out of her bed Friday night close to midnight, whispered to her not to get up as she half dozed, kissed her on the forehead, and let himself out.

Oh God. Was she falling for him?

And could that be...okay?

The girls had made a pretty convincing argument that it could.

But anyway, she was getting ahead of herself. She had no idea what his thoughts on the matter were. They'd agreed to have sex tomorrow, and she was more than fine with that, even if nothing else happened.

She glanced at her phone. Ten fifteen.

Really, though, what could it hurt to text? If he was asleep, he wouldn't answer. Right?

She was a fool. She opened her message app. Are you available to receive a rug delivery?

She laughed at herself. The line was so awkward and cheesy, yet somehow perfect.

The reply came instantly, and it sent a shiver up her spine.

> *Jay:* Hell yes.
> *Jay:* I'll be right there. I just need ten minutes to get
>   myself organized, and then I'm out the door.
> *Elise:* Actually, I'm already in my car. Is it okay if I
>   come to you?

That would give her something to do. Forward motion. And it would get them together sooner—she didn't need ten minutes to get ready to go.

> *Jay:* Of course. You haven't been here, have you?
>   I'm at 12 Bellair, unit 1803.

She glanced at herself in the rearview mirror. She was really going to do this.

> *Elise:* Should I pick up some condoms?
> *Jay:* I have some.
> *Elise:* I'm clean, actually.

She wasn't sure why she sent that last text. It wasn't normal to forgo a condom when you were having casual sex. Which was what they were having. Right?

> *Jay:* Right. Me, too, but pregnancy . . .

Yes. She forgot that other people had to worry about that. She sighed.

> ***Elise:*** Not a concern. That surgery I had took with it one ovary, and apparently the other side isn't in great working order.

He didn't reply, which seemed weird. Had he somehow been put off by the notion that she was unlikely to be able to conceive? Since she'd known for years she almost certainly wouldn't be able to have kids—biologically, at least—it was something she'd come to accept. She'd become rather matter-of-fact about it, even. But okay, infertility probably wasn't a topic to introduce into a hey-we're-going-to-have-some-hot-sex logistics text thread. She should probably do some damage control.

> ***Elise:*** Sorry to drop that on you. Not even sure why I brought it up. It's not relevant. It's not like we're going to get married.

They *were* going to get married, was the thing—if Jay had anything to say about it, anyway.

He was standing in front of his bathroom mirror. He had high-tailed it in there to brush his teeth when the first booty call text arrived. Now he was staring at himself like he was looking at a fantastic mythological animal, at some exotic creature he didn't recognize and couldn't name.

The revelation had arrived in his head fully formed, an automatic response to her breezy assertion that they weren't going to get married. It came with a rush of possessiveness. In keeping with the animal metaphor, he felt like some kind of primitive ape beating its chest, pointing at his mate and claiming her. *Mine.*

As revelations went, it was a big one. But not as big as the one that hit him right on its heels, an aftershock a thousand times more powerful than the original: he wanted to marry her *regardless* of her fertility status.

Holy shit.

Elise Maxwell, the woman he wanted more than anyone else, had just told him she couldn't get pregnant. This should have been the best news he'd ever received. And it was. But she could have just texted him about her desire to have fourteen kids, and he *still* would have wanted to marry her.

What. The. Fuck.

He almost laughed, it was so absurd. They would have had some shit to work out if that had been the case, but he would have been online in an instant, cruising through listings for relationship counseling. Which he was pretty sure meant...

He was in love with Elise Maxwell.

Of course he was. It was so obvious now that he did laugh. Stared at his reflection, at this man who looked familiar but had suddenly become a stranger, and cracked right up.

He had always experienced love, or affection, or whatever it was he'd had with his past girlfriends, as a more gradual thing. There would be an initial attraction, then a getting-to-know-you process. Feelings developed gradually. Like immersing yourself in a cold pool one body part at a time, taking time to adjust to the new sensation before progressing any farther.

This was...not that. This was jumping into the deep end and not even realizing you'd jumped until you were already there, sputtering for breath and swimming for your life.

So much for his decades-long insistence on women who'd aged out of their childbearing years. He'd met Elise, and all that discipline had just tumbled down like a poorly constructed Jenga tower.

Although it turned out the collapse didn't matter. The universe had given him *exactly* what he wanted, in the form of exactly *who* he wanted. He must have been a saint in a past life.

She was his dream woman. She was everything he wanted—and nothing he didn't want.

He was going to marry Elise Maxwell.

Though that was too creepy and intense a declaration to make so soon. So he would amend that thought: from here on out, he was making it his mission to be the kind of man that Elise would want to marry. Someday. Eventually. There was no hurry—another side effect of the no-kids thing was that there was no ticking clock hanging over them.

Oh, they were going to have so much fun. A lifetime of fun.

It was a weird feeling, imagining with such calm certainty a future in which he was married to a woman he had yet to have sex with.

His phone buzzed, drawing him out of his fantasies.

> *Elise:* On my way.

Shit. He hadn't replied to her last text, so consumed had he been by his own swooning.

> *Jay:* Sorry I disappeared for a minute there. Re birth control: we can do whatever makes you comfortable.

He grinned and added a final thought.

> *Jay:* And hurry.

By the time the doorman was calling up to Jay's to tell him she was on the way up, Elise had lost some of her nerve. Her time with Jay had been one extended, scorching bout of foreplay. But then it had been derailed by her period. Would it be like an actual train derailment, where the momentum was all gone and they had to somehow get themselves going again? A bit of self-doubt started to worm its way into her mind.

Okay, more than a bit. A *lot* of self-doubt. At her worst, on the worst days of the worst months, she felt broken. The feeling always passed. But she'd let him see her like that, at a low—if not at her absolute worst—which somehow felt more intimate than the prospect of having sex with him.

The elevator made its way up to the eighteenth floor, each peppy *ding* an ice pick that chipped open the pit in her stomach a little bit more.

There was also the part where she hadn't done this for a *long* time. And, to be honest, she hadn't ever slept with someone she *liked* so much.

Which was a dumb revelation, because she'd had long-term boyfriends before.

There was just something about Jay that made the stakes feel ridiculously high. Jay blew every other man she'd ever met out of the water.

She paused outside his door. Well, *paused* wasn't the right word, really. It was more like *balked*. She had her hand up, poised to knock and everything. But what was she going to say to him? What if she—

She hadn't knocked, but the door suddenly swung open almost violently. He surged forward for a second, before he registered that she was standing right there. Then he reared back so as not to crash into her. But he'd overcorrected, and he had to grab the door frame so he didn't fall over backward.

It should have been funny. She probably would have laughed. She was pretty sure that's why she had opened her mouth—to laugh. But then he grabbed her and pulled her to him, making her reconsider.

Maybe she'd actually opened her mouth so she could stand up on her tiptoes and press it over his. So she could slide her tongue inside without any prelude so that they were finally—*finally*—kissing.

He groaned and took control. One hand came to the back of her head, the other snaked around her waist, and he feasted on her. His lips were hot and demanding, and as his tongue battled hers, her mind lurched back to the Dirty Scrabble game. To his threat to lick her clit, specifically. It suddenly felt like he already had: moisture pooled between her legs, and she rolled her hips in search of desperately needed pressure. Her first attempt was thwarted by their height difference, and she only managed to grind up against the front of one of his thighs. It was pressure, but not focused enough, not hard enough. It was almost *worse* in a way, because all it did was ratchet her need up even higher. "Unnh." The frustrated moan slipped out as she tried again to mash herself against him.

"Look at you," he muttered as he pulled her into the apartment, which put some distance between them, distance that she *did not want*. "So frustrated. So beautiful." He kicked the door shut.

She bared her teeth at him because *frustrated* hit it on the nose—though it occurred to her that this move probably wasn't reinforcing the whole *beautiful* thing.

"Aww." He took her hand. "How can I make it better?"

She would have thought he was being annoyingly smug, that he was playing her, except she'd felt the evidence of his arousal just now. She might not have aimed properly to get what she wanted, but the hard, insistent length of him had dug into the soft flesh of her belly. His pupils were blown out, too, black circles surrounded by the thinnest slice of that Bahaman Sea Blue, and she could see the pulse racing at the base of his throat.

He wanted her as much as she wanted him. The difference was that he had a better rein on his lust. He wasn't having a tantrum like she was. He was still exercising his famous restraint. Discipline.

It was almost unbearably hot. She suspected he could do more for her with the crook of a finger than other men could with their full arsenals.

"I don't know," she said. She hadn't been trying to make her voice breathless, but what came out was sort of Marilyn Monroe–

esque. She had no doubt he would do whatever she asked to "make it better," but suddenly the idea of narrowing down this vast, un-swimmable sea of lust she was floundering in to a single, specific, actionable request seemed an impossible task.

He must have known somehow, because he tugged her toward him again. He leaned over and put his lips on the side of her neck, moving them against her skin as he spoke. "Do what I say, and I'll make it better, okay?"

"Yes." The thought and the vocalization came simultaneously, and something flared in his eyes. He liked that. She did, too.

He started walking, but he kept her plastered to his chest, so she was walking backward as he moved forward. She stumbled a bit, and he righted her and kept going, silent and staring. All that famous focus, turned toward her. Would he lose control eventually, or would he keep his iron-fisted restraint? She wasn't sure which option she preferred.

He made a right-angle turn halfway down the hall, flipping on a light that illuminated a bedroom. He kept going, never slowing his pace, until she hit a bed with the backs of her legs. He pushed her gently so she ended up sitting on the bed.

"Take off your clothes," he said. Then he stepped back and, in one fluid motion, pulled his T-shirt over his head.

She stared, let herself just look her fill. Leer, really. Shirtless, he was both the same and not the same as other men. He had all the same parts, of course—a very fine-looking, lightly muscled chest with a smattering of dark hair chief among them. But he also looked different. She struggled to articulate why, but there was something about him that was strangely, sharply familiar. Like he was *hers*.

"Take your clothes off," he said again, interrupting her silent ogle-fest. He sounded almost peevish. Even though she still had the strong feeling that he somehow *belonged* to her, which should have suggested that *she* was the boss here, she jumped to do his bidding. She slid out of her skirt, but then she checked herself halfway through unbuttoning her blouse. His eyes rose from where he'd been watching the progress of her fingers working the buttons to her face. His eyebrows kept going until they stopped, perched high, expectantly, and maybe a little impatiently. When she still didn't move, he said, "I thought we established you were going to do what I say."

"I'm going to." Her voice came out low and raspy. Goose bumps rose on his chest as she spoke. See? She *did* kind of own him. She bit back a grin. "But this isn't going to be some *Fifty Shades* thing. I'm not going to be your silent, submissive doll."

He didn't break eye contact. A muscle twitched in his jaw. "Good. I like when you get lippy. I hired you because of that little speech about how my lobby looked like a dental office."

She licked her lips, trying to see if she could make that muscle twitch again. "I believe I said a dental office in Yellowknife."

Success.

"You bait me on purpose, don't you?"

He didn't wait for an answer. He just pushed her down gently so she was lying on her back as he climbed onto the bed, caging her by hovering over her on his hands and knees. He wasn't touching her, though, and suddenly she was back to where she'd been in the doorway, drowning in a sea of too much—yet not enough—sensation. He leaned down with his head only and kissed her. It was slower than before, but deeper. Dirty and relentless, like his tongue couldn't get deep enough. Yet he was also, maddeningly, taking his time. When she clasped her arms around his neck and tried to pull him down on top of her, he wrenched himself from her grasp, making her cry out and arch up after him.

He grabbed her forearms, peeled her off him, and pressed her arms down on the bed above her head. Then he slid his palms up her arms until he reached her hands, which he guided up to the headboard. They were clumsy, and she banged a knuckle sharply against the ironwork and winced. He brought the hand to his mouth and, still with the unrelenting eye contact, kissed it tenderly. She shuddered, and he did it again, dragging his lax, open mouth against the bends of her fingers. Then, slowly, he extended her arm again and said, "Grab on to the bars, okay?"

She glanced up at the offending headboard, which was a series of unremarkable wrought-iron spindles. He nodded at her hands. She found herself wanting him to...*not* ask. To order. So she caressed the spindles but didn't grab on. "This headboard is ugly."

He didn't falter. "You can get me a new one. Later. Grab on to the bars."

She still didn't do it—though she did smirk to show she was playing with him—and she rolled her hips almost involuntarily. She expected him to take things up a notch, to get more forceful or loud with his command—that's what she'd been aiming for—but he did the reverse. Leaning over, he put his mouth right next to her ear, but he said nothing. He slid one hand into her opened blouse and shoved the soft cup of her bra up on one side, just grazing her nipple with the base of his palm. The friction made her gasp. He lifted his hand then, leaving the one breast cold and exposed. He was no longer touching her anywhere, which suddenly seemed wildly unfair. But he hadn't moved his head, so he was still right there with his lips. She could feel his hot breath on the shell of her ear. He repeated his earlier command, but it was quieter this time. "Grab on to the bars."

She grabbed the bars.

"Good girl." The hand came down on her breast again, and she cried out in relief. "Grab on and don't let go. Don't let go until I tell you to."

He hadn't asked this time, but she nodded anyway, writhing and twisting fruitlessly after him as he slid down her body.

When he was gone, she was so...exposed. She was stretched out, her body taut with desire.

She'd taken her skirt off already, but she still had her underwear on. She hadn't been planning on seeing him this evening, so it was just a ratty old cotton pair. She spared half a thought wishing she'd worn something nicer, but he jerked her underwear down in the same rough way he'd pushed her bra up. Like he wasn't registering her clothing at all, except as a barrier to be removed.

His thumbs pressed on the front creases of her thighs as he exhaled a shaky breath. He was still in control, but was it slipping? He had her so turned inside out, she didn't know if she wanted to bolster that control or hasten its demise.

He rotated his hands and pushed her thighs open. "God." Another one of those breaths that teetered on the edge. "I've been thinking of nothing else since we played Scrabble."

When he paused so close to her body that she could feel the heat radiating from his face, she knew what he intended to do. She responded by pushing her pelvis up off the bed to close the distance between them.

At first he just laid his lips against her, and they both moaned. But he pulled back. She barely had time to register her disapproval before he enacted the Dirty Scrabble scenario, dragging his tongue over her clit.

"Oh my God!" she bit out. With anyone else, she would probably have been embarrassed by how wet she was, but the radical honesty thing they had going apparently extended to nonverbal interactions, too. He kept up the lazy licking as she writhed under him. Soon she was bucking wildly as pleasure pooled deep in her core. As if he knew she was close, his hands clamped down on her hips, stilling her pelvis by pinning it to the bed.

She tried to push back against him, but he growled his displeasure. "Be still," he ordered, searching her face. "Don't move." She nodded, but he added an "Okay?"

She'd been thinking, earlier, about how she wanted him to tell, not ask, but she appreciated that he was the kind of man who sought verbal consent. It signaled a level of care that she wasn't sure she had ever experienced with anyone in bed before. And somehow that made the experience even sexier.

"Yes," she whispered, and he lowered his head again. He kept his hands on her hips—not that she had intended to contravene his instructions. It was hard, though, to keep still. It was like having restless legs at night but without the relief of being allowed to move them. The noises he made as he ate at her—growls of pleasure interspersed with incoherent swearing—were so wonderfully obscene, she couldn't stand it. As much as she was a convert to this delectable form of torture, she needed more.

"Jay!"

She hadn't meant to yell, but apparently she couldn't control things like volume and tone anymore. She could barely control her body—but that part seemed okay, because he was doing a spectacular job of it for her, putting it where he wanted it and doing such deliciously filthy things to it.

But of course her cry had come out sounding alarmed. So he stopped. Let go of her hips as his head popped up from between her legs, his handsome face knit in concern.

She heaved a ragged breath and rushed to reassure him that she wasn't calling things off. "I need you inside me now."

He smiled a wicked, wicked smile. "You do, eh?"

She nodded frantically, her whole body vibrating.

His hands traced up the sides of her body from her hips and undid her bra, which clasped in the front, and kneaded the flesh of her breasts. She was on her back and stretched out, so there wasn't much there. She wasn't very generously endowed, and this position wasn't showing what she did have to her best advantage—another thing she would have been embarrassed by in other circumstances. But here, now, she didn't care, just thrust her chest up at him the best she could, taking care not to lift her hips or let go of the headboard. She was still, for some unfathomable reason, following his orders.

Well, actually the reason was fathomable: doing what he said felt so amazingly *good*.

He took one tight, aching nipple into his mouth, and she practically screamed. It felt so incredible, even as it highlighted how *not enough* it was.

"I need you inside me." She tried again, infusing her voice with as much neediness as she could muster and not caring what she sounded like.

"I suggest..." He spoke around her nipple, his teeth gently grazing the too-sensitive flesh. "You ask me nicely."

"Please, Jay. Please."

Oh Jesus Christ. The way she lay there, her body splayed and stretched as she continued to hold on to the headboard. The way she begged him so nicely... Fuck.

Jay had had a lot of sex in his life. A lot of different *kinds* of sex. He liked it all—you might call him an enthusiastic agnostic in matters of the bedroom.

But maybe that was because he'd never had exactly *this* kind of sex, with *this* woman.

He had found religion.

And it involved bossing Elise Maxwell around. For example: "Spread your legs wider."

She spread her legs wider so fast it unbalanced him.

But it wasn't a simple case of some mild dominance, as it also involved getting her to mouth off. So when he said, "So pretty. I could just lay here and look at you forever," he had an ulterior motive.

The compliment embedded in the statement was the absolute truth, but really, he *couldn't* lie here looking at her forever. He was shaking with the effort of not touching her. He was trying to bait her.

It worked. She lifted her head, even as she maintained her grasp on the headboard. "That's the worst idea I've ever heard."

He quirked an eyebrow. "Yeah?"

She just glared at him.

He chuckled and ran a hand lightly over the pink folds that had been exposed by his previous command that she spread her legs. But the joke was on him, because his control was hanging by a thread. But...

Birth control. He had to hold on to his senses long enough to take care of her, to ensure her comfort. "What are we doing for birth control?" he rasped as he dragged the tip of his cock over her. "Condom?"

"I can't get pregnant," she bit out between gasps. "I'm clean. So if you are, too, we're good."

He was. And oh God, the idea of being inside her bare. Skin to skin.

"Are you okay?"

He opened his eyes. He hadn't realized he'd closed them. Or that his jaw had locked. His reaction to the fantasy-come-true scenario she'd suggested probably looked, outwardly, like pain. Relaxing his face, he felt a goofy grin blossom of its own accord. He was trying to project confidence and authority here, not goofiness, but apparently he had no control over his facial muscles. "I am *fantastic*."

It was her turn to smile, a giant, guileless, joy-filled one that sliced right through him, raising a lump in his throat.

They remained pinned in place for a moment, staring at each other and grinning stupidly.

This was the beginning.

The start of a new life.

There had been nothing wrong with his old life, but this one was better.

Her smile disappeared. "Do I need to let go of this headboard to get you to move?"

That knocked him out of his mooning. He did not want her to do that. He wasn't sure why—he had no master plan here—except that they both seemed to be getting off on these mild power games.

He grabbed his dick and guided it to her entrance, keeping a close eye on her face the whole time. "You sure?" he whispered.

He'd meant about the no-condom thing, but the way she said, "Yes," so quietly but so assuredly, made him think she was answering a bigger question.

He slid in, pushing past the initial resistance he encountered, and *fuck*. She might always be cold, but inside she was a furnace. And... "So tight," he gasped.

"Well, you're kind of huge," she shot back.

She must have seen the beginnings of hesitation on his face. Before he could ask if he was hurting her, she said, "Huge in the best way."

He inched himself in the rest of the way, stopping when he was fully seated, needing a moment to adjust to being inside her. To being in this new life.

Elise moaned—or maybe it was he. Either way, he suddenly *had* to move. Obeying the primal urge, he pulled out halfway and sank back in, trying to keep his strokes even.

"I need—" Her eyes widened when he filled her fully the second time. "Oh!" She shook her head back and forth like she was frustrated. He loved the sight of her honey hair fanned out over his pillow.

He leaned in to get a whiff of the addictive lemon scent that always lingered in her hair. "What do you need, sweetheart?"

"I was going to say that I need pressure on my clit to come, but now I'm not sure."

He grinned as he found the sensitive nub with his thumb. "Well, let's just cover all the bases, shall we?"

"Oh my God!" She started grinding her hips up to meet his, circling them a little at the top of every stroke.

Using the hand that wasn't working her clit, he reached down for one of her legs. "Now wrap your legs around me, sweetheart."

She hooked her ankles together around his lower back, and he let loose, pumping his hips into her sweet heat. It wasn't going to take long, so he concentrated on making sure she was keeping up with him. "You feel so fucking good, Elise. I want you to come all over my dick. Can you do that?" He rubbed his thumb in circles over and around her clit as he spoke.

She nodded frantically, but said, "I want to touch you."

He shook his head. He wanted her to keep holding on to the headboard. He wasn't sure if he could talk, though. Almost unendurable pressure was gathering at the base of his spine. "Keep...holding on," he managed to gasp as he fucked her against the bed.

She did not obey him, his Elise. Despite their games, they both knew who was in charge here.

On a giant inhalation, her hands flew off the bedpost and landed on his sweat-slicked back. Her whole body almost seemed to levitate as she clung to him.

And oh, the addition of those hands. Her touch, suddenly there where it hadn't been before. It was the single most erotic moment of his life, somehow. He was going to come, hard. But her eyes had slipped closed.

"Look at me," he said. "Look at me when I come inside you."

Her eyes, almost all pupil, flew open. He started to shudder, and she screamed.

Chapter 6

❧

*S*till think I'm uptight?"

Elise wasn't sure how long they'd been lying there panting and staring at the ceiling. She was about to answer Jay's question with a vehement no when she had a sudden realization. "Hey! I'm not cold."

She rolled on to her side to face him, and he did the same. She pressed her room-temperature, bordering-on-warm palms against his chest briefly and then did a silly jazz-hands gesture with them.

He smiled and enclosed her hands between his.

She and her warm hands thought about his question. "You are uptight in the best possible way." There was something about the way he asserted himself in the bedroom, ran the show with his signature intensity focused entirely on her, that undid her a bit. No, it undid her *a lot*. "Anyway, *I* never said you were uptight. You're always talking about how people say you're uptight, but I am not one of those people. I think you're driven. You have high standards. It's a good thing."

He looked way too self-satisfied at her pronouncement, so she pulled her hand out of his grasp and swatted him. He grabbed it back and then shocked her by bringing it to his mouth and kissing her palm tenderly.

Then he shocked her again—he seemed to be really good at doing that—by saying, "I want to meet your friends."

She quirked her head, merely from surprise, but he must have thought she was recoiling, because he said, "Too soon?"

"No, no. You just...sound serious."

He shrugged. "I'm decisive. I don't waste time when I know what I want."

"Jay Smith, are you asking me to go steady?" She kept her tone light to show she was teasing.

But she kind of wasn't. She was holding her breath. Because she wanted him to be. She could see now *exactly* what Gia had been saying. Jay made her better. Happier. And in fact, because of the whole radical honesty thing they had going, he helped make her *more* herself.

He didn't seem to think she was teasing, either, because he just said, "More like telling. But yes. I'm not into sharing." Then his face lightened a little, and he smirked. "I'm uptight that way."

He wasn't into sharing. And he was talking about *her*. That was...totally thrilling. "So, what? You're my boyfriend now?"

Please say yes. She held her breath. Funny how fast one talk with her girlfriends and one scorching session between the sheets had her changing her tune on the topic.

"Yes. I'm your boyfriend now."

She hadn't thought she was looking for one of those, but now that he, *he* specifically, was here, she understood that she'd been looking for *him*.

She exhaled.

"Unless you don't want me to be," he added.

She shook her head, suddenly weirdly shy. "I want you to be." Her voice had gone embarrassingly squeaky, so she burrowed into his chest. She didn't want to have to look at him while she asked her question. "You don't mind that I'm basically out of commission for two or three days a month?"

"No." She felt the surety with which he uttered the word. It rumbled through his chest. "I mean, I mind because I don't want you to be in pain, and I think we should try to figure out a way to cut down on that, but I don't mind in any elemental way."

This. This was what the girls had meant. Jay was going to be someone she could rely on. But what she hadn't seen was that that wasn't the same thing as being *dependent* on someone.

"Having sex all the time is going to be exhausting, anyway," he went on, laughter in his voice. "It will be good to break for a couple days for board games."

"And you don't mind..."

"What?" He levered her off him, and, using his hands to cup her face, forced her into eye contact with him.

God, this was so mortifying. But radical honesty, right? "You don't mind that I can't have kids?"

He smiled so tenderly. "Which means you're basically my dream girl, because I never wanted them."

"But why?" It seemed an important question, suddenly. He had said that once when they were talking about their parents, but she needed to make sure he meant it. That he wasn't settling.

"I'd be terrible at it."

"I don't think you would be. Are you sure? Do you understand what you're missing out on? Or if you only want me because I *can't* have them, that makes me feel kind of—" She shook her head. "I'm sorry. It's way too early to be talking about this stuff."

"Will you stop?" For the first time since she'd met him, he sounded truly annoyed at her. But then he shook his head fondly and softened his voice. "I want you. Full stop. Whatever package of qualities come with you, that's what I want."

Wow. Tears gathered in the corners of her eyes.

"And for the record, it's not too early to be talking about this."

"We only just slept together for the first time. We've known each other two months."

He shrugged like time was a minor detail not to be concerned with. Like it didn't apply to them. And maybe it didn't. The thought was buoying. No, it was exhilarating. "So this is it?" she asked.

"This is it."

"I always kind of worried about the kid thing being a barrier," she confessed.

"Do *you* want them?" Was it her imagination, or did he stiffen a little?

"I've always known it wasn't going to happen for me, so it's not really a question I've spent much time worrying about."

He smiled—a big, wide, delighted smile that gradually turned hotter, more wicked. "Well then, Elise Maxwell, I'd say we're ideally suited. Hiring you was the best goddamn decision I ever made in my life."

All she could do was sigh happily. And also sort of frustratedly, because the way that smile had morphed before her eyes was making her achy again. Restless.

But then his phone buzzed. "Shit. I'm sorry, I should get that. It's probably Patricia. She's freaking out because I told her to cancel my morning appointments tomorrow so we could..." He waggled his eyebrows. "Sleep in."

"Right." She somehow doubted they were going to get any sleep, either tonight or in the morning. But a lazy morning holed up with Jay playing hooky was pretty much the best thing she could imagine.

"Ha!" He threw his head back and laughed, tickled by whatever he'd read on his phone. "It *is* Patricia."

"So late on a Sunday night?"

"I do feel a little bad about that. I'm not acting like myself, and it's throwing her for a loop." He winced. "I'm afraid my not being there tomorrow morning is creating more work for her. I also had her cancel everything on Friday when the rugs suddenly arrived, so I could hightail it to your place. So basically we're two for two on me bailing on work for booty calls, and she's having to compensate."

"But were they really booty calls?" she teased. "The first one was more of a Yahtzee call."

He didn't laugh, just stared at her for a long moment before saying, "No. They weren't booty calls. They were everything calls."

Everything. That was the thing about Jay. He could give her screaming orgasms, take care of her when she was hurting, admire her professional talents, and sink her battleships. He *was* everything. On the one hand, she should feel like they were moving too fast. But on the other hand, she *didn't* feel that way. He was right somehow: by some alchemy she didn't understand, it *wasn't* too early to be talking seriously about the future.

"Well, poor Patricia." Elise felt bad. But not bad enough to tell him to go to work tomorrow. She wanted her lazy morning.

"I'll give her some time off to compensate." Still looking at the phone, he barked a laugh.

"Everything okay?"

"She reports that the big rug in my office has a tear in it."

"Oh." That *was* funny, given all the sexually charged meaning they'd jokingly invested in the rugs. Still, it was brand new, and it hadn't been cheap. "We'll send it back."

He whipped his gaze to hers, interrupting his typing. "No, we won't."

"It's defective!" she argued. "You can't just spend two grand on a rug that's defective from the get-go."

"I can do whatever I want. I'm the client. That rug has symbolic value, and it's staying."

She was flattered, but he wasn't being reasonable. "Come on. You're not the superstitious type."

"Elise." He set his phone aside. "Listen to me very carefully. The rug stays." Something flared in his eyes. "I'm going to be buried with that goddamn rug. Just roll me up in it and heave me into the ground."

All right, then. Elise fanned herself with her hands. She had a feeling that being cold wasn't going to be a problem anymore.

"Now," he said, pushing his phone farther away, so far that it clattered off the bed onto the ground, "let's try the whole keep-your-hands-on-the-headboard thing again."

Epilogue

❧

Four months later

The text came in when Elise was out with her friends. She and Wendy and Jane had planned a night of drinks and dinner. Gia had flown in at the last minute, which was a bit of a surprise because she'd visited only a week ago, and she was in the middle of a job in California. But whatever, Elise would take Gia whenever she could get her.

> ***Jay:*** I sent the rug back.

Normally she wouldn't answer a text while she was out with the girls, but this particular one was impossible to ignore. They were sitting at a bar having cocktails, and she turned away to try to reply without drawing too much attention to herself.

> ***Elise:*** What? The ripped one?

She tamped down a little spurt of panic. It was just a rug. She was the one who'd tried to talk him into returning it in the first place. It didn't have any inherent meaning. Just because it was a silly symbol of their relationship didn't mean it had any actual *power* over their fate.

"Is that Jay?" Gia asked.

"Judging by how alarmed she looks," Wendy said, "I'm gonna go with Daddy dearest."

Jane laughed, but then she stopped, like she was trying to hide it. Elise looked at her friends. What was up with them? If Wendy really thought Elise's father was texting, she'd be all up in her face about it, rushing to defend Elise from what she perceived as the enemy.

Her phone dinged again.

> *Jay:* Yeah. I thought it was time to get a new one.
>   Come over and see if you like it.
> *Elise:* You got a new rug without consulting me?

That might have come off a little shrewish, but she *was* his designer. And he was in the advantageous position of not being charged for design services these days.

> *Jay:* Come see it. If you don't like it, I'll return it.
>   Bring the girls.

"Seriously," Wendy said, "Who is texting and making you make those faces?"

Elise looked up. "It is Jay. He got a new rug at the office, and he wants me to come over and see it." Which, said out loud, sounded like a dumb thing to be texting about. The girls didn't know about the rug subtext. They'd all enthusiastically endorsed her whirlwind romance with Jay, but Elise was maybe guilty of not telling them every single detail. Which was a new one for her. But...She felt her face heat as she thought back to Jay working her over so expertly and thoroughly this morning before they got out of bed. Some things were private.

She picked up her phone. "I'll tell him I'll see it later."

"Let's go see it!" Jane said with a strange amount of enthusiasm.

Elise narrowed her eyes. "It's eight on Friday night. We're all together"—she shot Gia an affectionate look—"so we're not going to an accounting firm to look at a rug!"

"Mmm, look at a rug." Gia snorted. "Sounds like it could be a euphemism for something dirty."

Wendy hopped off her bar stool. "Let's go. This place is boring anyway."

"And Cohen & Smith is not boring?" Elise grinned. "Besides the decor, I mean. The decor is the opposite of boring."

Wendy slapped down a wad of cash and was halfway to the door when the others shrugged. They all knew there was no point in trying to talk Wendy out of anything.

Fifteen minutes later, they were in the elevator, on their way up to Jay's office. "Hey, maybe after we're done here, I can show you guys the bank job." She'd redone the HR department of a major bank, which spanned three floors of Jay's building. It hadn't been the most exciting job because she'd had to work within a narrow corporate-approved color palette, but it had led to another job doing the CEO's house, which *had* been an exciting one in that she'd been given carte blanche—and a huge budget. Still, she was proud of her work in the bank offices. It was a living testament to how far she'd come, and if they were on-site anyway, she wanted to show it to her best friends.

"For sure!" Gia said. "I totally want to see it."

"Yes!" Wendy echoed, with an uncharacteristic degree of excitement.

What was wrong with them? They were way too chipper.

"Ladies." When they pushed through the heavy oak doors to the Cohen & Smith lobby, Jay rose from a sofa. He must have been waiting for them.

His eyes roamed over everyone as he greeted her friends, but then his intense gaze landed on Elise and stuck there. "Hi."

"Hi." Her heart stuttered. It had been four months, but he still had that effect on her.

"Oh, for Christ's sake," Wendy said. "Get a room."

"We just said hi!" Elise protested, but she knew what Wendy meant. Jay's intense look had not dimmed. It promised possession and protection and tenderness, and, amazingly, the doses of those things he delivered seemed to grow with each passing day.

"Let's see this magical rug," Gia said, "and you two can get on with it."

"We're going for dinner," Elise said to the girls as they followed Jay into his office. They'd booked tonight as a girls' night, and they were sticking to it. She would admit to being a little torn, though. Now that she was in close proximity to Jay, it was hard not to want him to throw her over his shoulder and cart her off to have his way with her. But she wouldn't admit to that publicly. Besides, Mr. Intense Look would wait up for her.

They filed into Jay's office. The old rug—the ripped one—was still there.

"I thought you returned it."

"Well, yeah, I didn't actually."

Huh? He'd just told her, via text not thirty minutes ago, that he *had* returned it.

Jay moved over to the rug, which wasn't in its usual place under the coffee table, anchoring the casual seating area in his office. It had been sort of awkwardly placed next to that area.

"Well, you can't leave it there. It looks terrible there."

"I got a new one. It's underneath it."

What? That was so *strange*. "You can't leave the new one there, either. You can't put any rug in that spot. It's squished in and not anchored with anything and looks totally random. Whichever rug you're using needs to go back under the seating area."

Gia coughed, and Jane made a point of clapping her on the back.

"Yeah, they're just out here temporarily to show you," Jay said, crouching down and snagging a corner of the old rug.

"You are so weird."

He shot her a grin, knelt, and started rolling the rug back.

"That color doesn't work in here." It was a dark red. Not a bad color inherently, just not for this office. "And I'm not sure a straight-up solid is what you want in here. A print would—"

Gia's coughing fit seemed to take a turn for the worse. A little alarmed, Elise turned and walked over to her, but Gia just shook her head and made an urgent pointing gesture back toward Jay and the stupid rugs.

She turned back. Okay, the rug did have some pattern in it. A white loopy—

She gasped. He wasn't kneeling in order to roll the rug back. He was on one knee gazing at her with undisguised love. And those loopy things were letters. The rug had words woven into it.

Will you marry me?

Jay had been pretty confident she would say yes. He'd put his odds at maybe 90 percent. They were moving fast, objectively speaking, but from the inside, it felt like they were moving at just the right speed.

But in that moment, with her standing there, postgasp, utterly silent as she stared at the rug, fear started to sink its claws into his gut. Maybe it *was* too soon. Or the rug thing, which had seemed like a cute inside joke when he thought it up, was actually really dumb and not even remotely worthy of her. He should have hired a freaking skywriter. He should have—

"Yes. Of course." She looked down at him with watery eyes. "Of course I'll marry you."

All his fears flitted away as she pulled him back to standing and threw herself into his arms. He could feel her shaking, so he held her tighter. Buried his face in her hair and marveled that she'd said yes. She was his. He was never going to let go.

He'd meant that last sentiment metaphorically, but when she eventually pulled back against him, he had a hard time lowering his arms and letting her step out of his embrace.

He was glad he had, though, because the look she gave him, so full of love and heat and promise, was not a sight he would have liked to miss.

He cleared his throat. "I didn't get you a ring. I figured you'd have opinions."

"Smart man," Wendy deadpanned.

The interjection reminded him—and her, judging from the way her eyebrows shot up—that they had an audience.

She turned, and her friends rushed her. He stood back and grinned at the group hug that transformed into a group squeal.

When it broke up, Elise kept one arm slung around Gia's waist. "*This* is why you're in town!"

"Yup. When Jay told us he was doing this, I knew I had to be here."

"Really, he didn't tell us," Jane said. "It was more like asking our permission."

"It totally was!" Wendy confirmed.

She looked at him, equal parts amused and incredulous. He shrugged. "It wasn't like I was going to ask your parents. And anyway, you all are kind of a package deal, right?"

He was teasing, but not really. The early weeks of his relationship with Elise had been insular, private. But he'd learned pretty quickly that these women were her soul sisters. And he was glad of it. Each was amazing in her own right, and as a unit, they provided Elise with an unshakable support network.

"We *are* a package deal." Elise went in for another group hug with the girls.

"Yeah," Gia said. "We already gave him the if-you-hurt-our-friend-we-will-rise-as-one-and-murder-you-in-your-sleep speech, so we're all good."

"And then we signed off on this rug idea," Jane said.

Elise's head popped up from this latest group hug. "The rug thing was great. It totally makes me think we could incorporate some cute rugs into the wedding itself—you know, because they're kind of our thing? Where did you get it?"

"Well, I thought I was going to have to get it custom woven, but it turns out proposal rugs are a thing."

He chuckled. He could see her perfectionist designer brain firing up. Then her eyes sparked, and she lifted her arms to the sky like a revivalist preacher. "Oh my God! I have the *best idea* for a wedding venue."

A peal of laughter from Gia drew his attention. She was pulling a bottle of champagne out of a giant handbag. To his amusement, it was followed by five stemless plastic flutes. Gia, he had come to learn, was known for her giant bags, but even for her, that was impressive. She passed the glasses around, popped the cork to cheers from the group, and started pouring.

When she was done, he followed her lead in lifting his glass.

"I say this with love," Gia said, winking at Elise, "but you are going to be *such* a bridezilla."

About the Author

Jenny Holiday is a *USA Today* bestselling and RITA®-nominated author whose works have been featured in the *New York Times*, *Entertainment Weekly*, and the *Washington Post* and by National Public Radio. She grew up in Minnesota, where her mom was a children's librarian, and started writing at age nine after her fourth-grade teacher gave her a notebook to fill with stories. When she's not working on her next book, she likes to hang out with her family, watch other people sing karaoke, and throw theme parties. A member of the House of Slytherin, Jenny lives in London, Ontario, Canada.

You can learn more at:

JennyHoliday.com
Twitter @JennyHoli
Reader group: facebook.com/groups/NorthernHeat
Facebook.com/JennyHolidayBooks
Instagram @HolyMolyJennyHoli

Want more charming small towns?
Fall in love with these Forever contemporary romances!

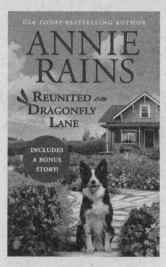

REUNITED ON DRAGONFLY LANE
by Annie Rains

Boutique owner Sophie Daniels certainly wasn't looking to adopt a rambunctious puppy with a broken leg. Yet somehow handsome veterinarian—and her high school sweetheart—Chase Lewis convinced her to take in Comet. But house calls from Chase soon force them to face the past and their unresolved feelings. Can Sophie open up her heart again to see that first love is even better the second time around? Includes the bonus story *A Wedding on Lavender Hill*!

DREAM A LITTLE DREAM
by Melinda Curtis

Darcy Jones Harper is thrilled to have finally shed her reputation as the girl from the wrong side of the tracks. The people of Sunshine Valley have to respect her now that she's the new town judge. But when the guy who broke her heart back in high school shows up in her courtroom, she realizes maybe things haven't changed so much after all...because her pulse still races at the sight of bad-boy bull rider Jason Petrie.

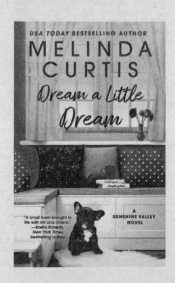

"Holiday is a consummate master of witty banter."
—ENTERTAINMENT WEEKLY

SANDCASTLE BEACH
by Jenny Holiday

What Maya Mehta really needs to save her beloved community theater is Matchmaker Bay's new business grant. She's got some serious competition, though: Benjamin Lawson, local bar owner, Jerk Extraordinaire, and Maya's annoyingly hot arch nemesis. Turns out there's a thin line between hate and irresistible desire, and Maya and Law are really good at crossing it. But when things heat up, will they allow their long-standing feud to get in the way of their growing feelings? Includes the bonus story *Once Upon a Bride*, for the first time in print!

A WEDDING ON LILAC LANE
by Hope Ramsay

After returning home from her country music career, Ella McMillan is shocked to find her mother is engaged. Worse, she asks Ella to plan the event with her fiancé's straitlaced son, Dr. Dylan Killough. While Ella wants to create the perfect day, Dylan is determined the two shouldn't get married at all. Somehow amid all their arguing, sparks start flying. And soon everyone in Magnolia Harbor is wondering if Dylan and Ella will be joining their parents in a trip down the aisle.

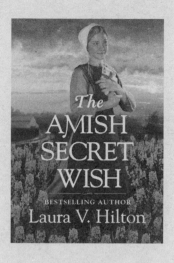

THE AMISH SECRET WISH
by Laura V. Hilton

Waitress Hallie Brunstetter has a secret: She writes a popular column for her local Amish paper under the pen name GHB. When Hallie receives a letter from a reader asking to become her pen pal, Hallie reluctantly agrees. She can't help but be drawn to the compassionate stranger, never expecting him to show up in Hidden Springs looking for GHB . . . nor for him to be quite so handsome in real life. But after losing her beau in a tragic accident, Hallie can't risk her heart—or her secrets—again.

HER AMISH WEDDING QUILT
by Winnie Griggs

When the man she thought she would wed chooses another woman, Greta Eicher pours her energy into crafting beautiful quilts at her shop and helping widower Noah Stoll care for his adorable young children. But when her feelings for Noah grow into something even deeper, will she be able to convince him to have enough faith to give love another chance?

Discover bonus content and more on
read-forever.com

ONE LUCKY DAY
(2-IN-1 EDITION)
by Jill Shalvis

Have double the fun with these two novels from the bestselling Lucky Harbor series! Can a rebel find a way to keep the peace with a straitlaced sheriff? Or will Chloe Traeger's past keep her from a love that lasts in *Head Over Heels*? When a just-for-fun fling with Ty Garrison, the mysterious new guy in town, becomes something more, will Mallory Quinn quit playing it safe—and play for keeps instead—in *Lucky in Love*?

FOREVER FRIENDS
by Sarah Mackenzie

With her daughter away at college, single mom Renee isn't sure who she is anymore. What she *is* sure of is that she shouldn't be crushing on her new boss, Dr. Dan Hanlon. But when Renee comes to the rescue of her neighbor Sadie, the two unexpectedly hatch a plan to open her dream bakery. As Renee finds friendship with Sadie and summons the courage to explore her attraction to Dr. Dan, is it possible Renee can have the life she's always imagined?

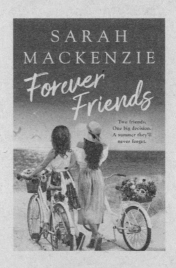